Operation Faust

Fridrikh Neznansky

CORGI BOOKS

OPERATION FAUST

A CORGI BOOK 0 552 13269 1

First publication in Great Britain

PRINTING HISTORY
Corgi edition published 1988

Copyright © Fridrikh Neznansky 1988
Translation copyright © Alan Myers 1988

This book is set in 10/11 pt Plantin
by Colset Private Limited, Singapore.

Corgi Books are published by Transworld Publishers Ltd.,
61–63 Uxbridge Road, Ealing, London W5 5SA, in Australia
by Transworld Publishers (Australia) Pty. Ltd., 15–23 Helles
Avenue, Moorebank, NSW 2170, and in New Zealand by
Transworld Publishers (N.Z.) Ltd., Cnr. Moselle and
Waipareira Avenues, Henderson, Auckland.

Reproduced, printed and bound in Great Britain by
Hazell Watson & Viney Limited
Member of BPCC plc
Aylesbury, Bucks, England

03562517

FS 3/89

terrorists . . . What? Oh yes, what was happening on the platform . . . Millions of people, tons of police, everybody watching the escalator – waiting for the General Secretary . . . I wasn't bothered, that is, I mean . . .'

'. . . No I don't remember any explosion. I saw what I saw, but I didn't hear anything. So what if I am a KGB captain? Aren't we people? (Almost weeping.) We can suffer from shock as well, you know, that's for sure . . .'

'. . . No you won't find the swine – I'll find them myself and throttle them! I won't forgive you my little lad, not for anything: I was taking my wee boy to the music school for his exam . . . and now . . . you're sods, the lot of you . . . driving the country to this . . . and let go my sleeve – without the wee boy gaol or grave is all the same to me . . .'

I'd been writing down the evidence of scores of people, my hands were shaking, there was a lump in my throat and my eyes were full. I felt like swearing and weeping the same as them and I'd got a lot more of that to live through. I was the one who'd got to investigate this horror.

Merkulov wasn't sitting in his usual armchair; he was perched sideways somehow on an ordinary chair by the other side of his desk, with his bony knees jammed against the polished wood. He was dialling continuously. I waved my arms about behind his back getting more and more annoyed: the metro bomb inquiry had been handed over to an investigator at the office, Joseph Grechannik. I'd been through so much in the last twenty-four hours, questioned nearly thirty witnesses and victims, considered various scenarios and mapped out my plan of investigation. And now they'd given the whole damned thing over to Grechannik. Merkulov remained oblivious to my whining, or so it seemed. I did try to study the chief investigator's facial expression, but he just kept on dialling, trying to get through to the dry-cleaners who had managed to lose his sheepskin-coat the previous winter. Eventually he did turn round and put a cheerful face on it:

'Well, no need for jealousy, Sasha, it's not the best job to have in our line.'

I was stung:

'Who's jealous?! It's annoying, that's all, Kostya.' (When we were alone I could use his first name.)

'Sorry, that's how it looked to me . . .'

He was right enough. Grechannik and I had taken a dislike to each other even at University, for no obvious reason. After graduating he had worked for a while with the CID. Whether or not it was because he thought police work beneath his intelligence, Parkhomenko, the recently-appointed Deputy City Prosecutor of Moscow had towed him over to us.

'Do you feel like talking your theories over with me?' enquired Merkulov tentatively.

I was tempted to be stubborn but knew I shouldn't give in to it. I lit a cigarette and started walking up and down behind Merkulov. I could tell from his slight head movements that he was observing me.

'Well now . . . the theoretical set-up . . . er . . . the investigative premise . . .' I managed to get out, 'before looking for the criminal you have to determine the reason for the crime. If you start from the subject – you've had it. I'm absolutely convinced that the women and children killed in the carriage were not the primary target of the terrorists. Several people on the platform died. The Gensec was expected. Everybody knew about that. That he was coming, I mean. I may be wrong, but it all looks like an assassination attempt to me.'

I hoped my speech sounded more convincing than I suddenly felt.

'Yes, Sasha, you know somebody once said that when there's a bomb attempt on the chief, it's usually the chauffeur who gets killed . . . Anything else?'

Anything else? My detective enthusiasm had evaporated along with my annoyance. Lack of confidence in my own words threatened to develop into total helplessness. Even Grechannik all of a sudden seemed more intelligent and likeable and I was quite prepared to hand over a couple more of my cases, if I could only be rid of Merkulov's calm, almost monotonous voice and this pacing about behind his back, seeing his ears follow my movements like radar.

'You see, Sasha,' began Merkulov, then suddenly shouted: 'I can't talk with you walking about behind my back!'

I obediently sat down facing him, ensconced in the chief investigator's armchair.

'The fact is, Sasha, the bomb business was given to Grechannik at my request. There was an argument upstairs about who should deal with it, the KGB or us. The decision was to work jointly: they take care of the operational side and we do the investigation.'

Merkulov fished out a cigarette, broke it in half and stuck one piece in his cigarette-holder. It was his way of cutting down on smoking. By my calculations he was smoking four times as much as he had before.

He started nagging the dry-cleaners about his coat again.

'Listen, Kostya, I'll find your coat tomorrow or get the money out of them. Politeness just gets on their nerves. You only get things done properly in our neck of the woods if they're scared of you.'

'Yes, I can see you won't get off my back, Comrade Turetsky, till I give you a full report on the Politburo meeting.'

He extracted the cigarette-end from the holder and poked the other half in immediately.

'The Republic Prosecutor Yemelyanov was summoned to a Politburo session to give his report on the metro bombing. The new General Secretary's brought in a new procedure: all emergencies are to be discussed by the Politburo. Well, Seryozha Yemelyanov, you know him, he's always keen on protecting his rear-end. What could he tell the high-ups if he hadn't been on the spot himself? So he dragged me along there with him . . . The people from the Moscow KGB directorate tried their damnedest to show it was an act of terrorism so they should handle it. Our new Gensec, however, permitted himself to disagree. That's just what he said: "Permit me to disagree with you." '

So saying, Merkulov had a try at imitating the round-faced Gensec with his own gaunt features. To my surprise, he brought it off brilliantly.

'The present day is a lot different from the 30s,' Merkulov went on in the same spirit, 'the people and the Party are one. Therefore the Soviet people cannot act against the government. Those capable of a crime like this are: one, foreign secret service agents, two, an escaped lunatic, and three, so-called dissidents. Professor Lunts has proved that they are mentally ill and we in the Politburo are in complete agreement with him. The Politburo has taken the decision to commence a comprehensive restructuring of the nation's economy (Merkulov stressed the first syllable of 'commence' mimicking the Gensec's southern accent). An economic struggle between two systems, socialism and capitalism, is in progress; from a political point of view we can't afford even a hint of political opposition in this country, let alone terrorist groups.'

So there it was, the new line. As if the Tbilisi explosion never happened: that time they planted a bomb in the Republic KGB building and getting on for thirty Gee-Bees got killed. And the plane that blew up in mid-air with the staff on board during the Caucasus – 85 manoeuvres – not forgetting the kidnapping of the minister's fiancée and the ransom demand for ten million roubles. They were all solved and each time there was a different group behind it, armed with automatic weapons and explosives.

'You know what, Sasha . . . come to think of it I've told you a thousand times,' Merkulov said suddenly, irritated, as if answering questions I hadn't asked. 'I've always regarded my job as solving crimes. So the lot of us, police, KGB . . . you and Grechannik, we've all got to find whoever killed those people in the metro. Looking at it objectively, they've committed a horrible thing. Subjectively – we've got to find out the motive. The top brass use soft words and say the right things to the politicians, not to us.'

There was a knock on the door and Grechannik came in without waiting for permission.

'Sorry to burst in, Konstantin Dmitrievich, but something interesting's turned up. A man's just rung Moscow CID and said: "Faust planted the bomb on the metro." '

Consternation.

12

'That's what he said . . . But they couldn't catch the end of the sentence; there was some extraneous noise and he was speaking in a whisper.'

'Did they get it on tape?'

'Of course, Konstantin Dmitrievich. All 02 calls are taped,' Grechannik stated rather less confidently, rounding his chubby lips at the '0'. He obviously noticed my ironic expression at this and added hurriedly: 'Of course it's practically impossible to identify anybody whispering . . .'

'When was this?'

'8.07 this morning, er . . . nearly three hours ago . . .'

'I trust the tape's on its way here with the voice of our Goethe-lover?'

'Not yet, but . . .'

'Well get on the line to Captain Griaznov, look alive, everything'll be all right,' Merkulov said encouragingly.

'Right away!' Grechannik's lips wriggled.

He left at a run to carry out Merkulov's commission.

'Everything'll be all right. Everything's wonderful . . .' repeated Merkulov mechanically, watching the door close behind Grechannik. I didn't notice any joyous notes in his voice.

I left off tormenting Merkulov with my 'Sasha-questions' (he'd given that name to my amazing curiosity in my trainee days nearly three years before). I had my work to do – 'my' crimes and 'my' criminals. At eleven some denizens of a hang-out run by a celebrated lady soloist were coming in for a confrontation; there was a big shot to be exposed as the financial backer of this 'salon' as well as for personal participation in orgies with young boys. After that I had to finish off a bill of indictment concerning a breach of safety standards in a block of flats in Matveyevskoye – half a house full of people had collapsed. At three I was expected by a lawyer at Butirka prison to be filled in on a case (under article 201 of the Criminal Code); a heavy-industry minister was accused of misappropriating large sums as well as bribery. So there. Joseph Alexandrovich Grechannik could keep Mephistopheles.

13

'Sasha,' Merkulov called after me softly as I went out. I turned. There was a hint of alarm in Merkulov's sky-blue eyes. 'What do you think of this "Faust" business, then?'

I decided not to give in, just for the hell of it.

'Our General Secretary is a hundred per cent right: we're surrounded by loonies.'

2

I was on my way to the car when I got the idea of walking to work. The June morning was glinting on Moscow River and there wasn't a soul on the embankment. It felt as if the entire city had gone off on holiday.

I strode along as far as the Frunzenskaya metro where the picture suddenly altered: hundreds of Muscovites and tourists began thronging the pavements and crossing the square, strolling, hurrying, idly gazing in shop windows, jostling round the newspaper-kiosks. And then I saw her.

Unfortunately I'm not the type to pester girls in the street, so I just walked behind her, anxious not to lose her in the crowd. What was I hoping for? That she would just turn round and . . . well, 'and'? She had something that made even the most striking talent scurrying round me seem faded and insignificant. Now she'd stopped in front of a shop-window and I could see her reflection – straight shoulders, fair hair uniquely framing a sun-tanned face. She turned sharply, looked me straight in the eyes and . . . walked on, indifferent. The situation was hopeless, that was clear enough. For a long time I kept track of her very tall erect figure and heavy mass of blond hair swaying in time with her walk. Then she turned suddenly into the metro entrance. The end.

I cut across Komsomol Prospect and made for the 'Romantic' to get a coffee. My appetite had vanished completely.

Something unusual could be sensed in the stuffy atmosphere of the Office. I stood for a moment in front of my door, turning the key with slow deliberation. There was a continu-

15

ous puzzling hum of noise from the criminal section; doors kept slamming. I sat down at my desk and called Moiseyev.

'Good morning. Turetsky here. Would you mind telling me what's going on in there?'

'I'll be there directly, Alexander Borisovich!'

'No need for that Semyon Semyonovich . . .' but Moiseyev had already hung up.

Criminalist Semyon Semyonovich Moiseyev edged in sideways through the half-opened door. He was in full fig – juridical counsellor's uniform smothered in medals. His face bore an expression of extreme embarrassment mixed with triumph. Only the worn cuffs of the dazzling white shirt betrayed the former Moiseyev.

'What's up – on the chief's carpet are you?'

'Wrong, citizen boss . . .'

'You're going to the doctor's? Wearing that lot's going to help you to queue-jump?'

'Sasha, don't force me to have recourse to censorious words . . .'

'Go on then, tell me. Don't be shy.'

'You're not much of a detective are you?'

'I admit that, not much. Well, what's it all about?'

'Now that's my little secret, Alexander Borisovich.' It occurred to me that Semyon Semyonovich was mumbling less than usual. 'Well all right, just joking, Sasha. You weren't here yesterday, you see, and we have some amusing news, as you might say. While you and Captain Griaznov were busy with your brothel, we got some girls sent over here . . . No, No!! I don't mean like that! They're trainees, and there's three of them! And two lads.' He winked conspiratorially, 'Follow me!'

A very slender, very pretty young girl with slant Japanese eyes was standing by the counter with the arms display. What was going on today – it was raining beautiful girls! At any rate Semyon Semyonovich's behaviour now seemed more comprehensible.

'Kim.' She held out a tiny palm.

16

'Kim's the first name, by the way,' fussed Moiseyev, clinking his medals. 'The full name is Kim Artiomovna Lagina.'

'And you're Turetsky, isn't that right?' Kim enquired, fluttering her lashes.

I bowed stupidly in agreement, adding:

'Or Sasha, if you prefer.'

'I prefer,' Kim smiled with her vivid mouth and started inspecting the arms display, looking at me out of the corner of her eye.

'But where's everybody got to?' Moiseyev was flustered.

'Somebody they called the prince invited them all to a meeting; they asked me to guard the fort here till you arrived. Who is this prince – the long thin one is he? Why "prince" – is it because he's so intellectual?'

Moiseyev and I burst out laughing – she was right enough about Merkulov.

'Right then, Semyon Semyonovich, what news have we got about the metro bomb?' I put on my serious expression, particularly as I was dying to hear about any developments and wounded pride prevented me asking Grechannik. Parkhomenko had seconded Moiseyev to assist Grechannik, because of his expertise in all forms of weaponry and explosive devices.

Moiseyev and I sat down opposite one another at the pointlessly long table, surrounded by portraits of celebrated criminal investigators. Moiseyev took out a plump notebook, terminally dog-eared and scrawled over with notes and sketches only he could understand. He began his account, oblivious to the exchange of glances between me and Kim.

'. . . This same Sviatov was found guilty of sabotage on the railways – he blew up a derelict carriage, past repair. Nobody was hurt. He was judged to be of unsound mind and put in the Stolbovaya hospital for the criminally insane. He escaped a year ago. On November 17th 1984 Sviatov placed explosives in the window of the cathedral in Armenian Lane, the empty one . . .'

A noisy company poured into the office led by the Deputy City Prosecutor Parkhomenko. Merkulov's head poked up right at the back. The very next second I ceased to hear anything. I hadn't gone deaf or anything, it was like listening to some alien language: she was among the newcomers, my unknown girl of the morning. Parkhomenko was saying something as the others got seated round the table but I was conscious only of a powerful beating inside my chest . . . She looked at me without the least interest, then raised her dark eyebrows . . .

'Alexander Borisovich, can you hear me?' I registered that Merkulov was addressing me; clearly not for the first time. 'Leonid Vasilievich has organised the schedule for the trainees and I am asking Semyon Semyonovich, in his capacity as head of trainees to supervise their work. Leonid Vasilievich and I will be sitting in with the Party municipal committee today. I'm asking you to behave yourselves in our absence. So far, I'm sorry to say, you've been making it a sort of open day . . .'

The higher-ups left the criminal office and Moiseyev started on Sviatov's history again from the very beginning. Parkhomenko's words seemed to be going round and round in my head: 'Svetlana Nikolayevna Belova . . . Svetlana Nikolayevna Belova . . . Svetlana . . .' I couldn't recall the names of the other trainees.

'. . . Yesterday Shura, sorry, Alexandra Ivanovna Romanova, chief of CID Department Two picked him up along with all his gear, dynamite, so forth. By the evening Sviatov had confessed that he'd placed the bomb in the metro carriage to spite the world.' Moiseyev paused before adding: 'Of course we still have to check that . . .'

'If he's confessed, what's there to check? Who's going to grass on himself if he didn't do it?' She spoke softly as if just casually putting in the odd word.

'You're forgetting presumption of innocence, Lana. A final-year student like you should always remember that. The burden of proof lies on the organs of justice.'

Grechannik wiggled his eyebrows as he uttered these sententious remarks; his whole appearance seemed to say to those present: 'This is just talk about presumption of innocence, actually there's a bit more than that between us.' Well, I might have been imagining things, but they were on first name terms at least. Then I spoke up, a bit louder than I'd meant to:

'He's a neurotic that's all! People like him confess to anything! Up to now he's never hurt a soul, just the opposite in fact: after the explosion in Armenian Lane, they handed the church over to the Patriarch, it had been a warehouse before . . . Why in hell's name should he want to massacre people?'

Moiseyev gave a little cough behind his hand to bring me to order. I was still wound-up, though:

'All right, all right. You have it your own way, but I've got work up to here. Who's on with me?' I picked up a paper from the table. 'Stepanyuk Nikolai!'

A young chap with a countryfied look about him despite a lively pair of blue eyes, got up from the table ready for action.

'Right, let's go, Nikolai, and do battle with the homos!'

As I went out I heard behind my back:

'Quite a character . . .'

Lana Belova said that.

By five I was back in the Prosecutor's Office where CID inspector, Captain Vyacheslav Griaznov was supposed to be waiting for me with additional reports from the agents about that brothel business.

As I was going in I bumped into our driver Seryozha who was coming downstairs at a rate of knots and nearly knocked me off my feet.

'Oh, er, Alexander Borisovich, it's you! I've just been . . . Semyon Semyonovich . . . well, that is . . . sent me on an errand . . . won't be a minute!'

It occurred to me that in spite of the warning 'open day' had moved up a gear. Without going into my office, I yanked at the handle of the criminal room. It was locked on the inside and Moiseyev let me in only after a complete voice identification.

It was a jolly company: Moiseyev, Grechannik, Griaznov, the four trainees and two birds from the typing pool had set the long table and furnished it with eatables from Lord knows where.

'Hooray! Turetsky's arrived!' Kim clapped her hands.

'Well now, has the inaccessible Turetsky come to join us or chase us out?' asked Lana Belova. I think she had been wearing a different dress that morning, but she'd taken her jacket off now. Instead of replying, I stared at her bare shoulders.

'What d'you mean! Of course he's come to join us!' Grechannik chirped rather too joyfully. I was thinking 'inaccessible, in what sense?' Aloud, I said:

'Did you send Seryozha for vodka?'

'Well now we didn't! Your detective intuition's let you down again! Seryozha's gone to fetch his guitar!' At this, Moiseyev opened up his fireproof safe to disclose an appropriate quantity of liquor.

'His *guitar*!?'

'Slava's going to give us a tear-jerker,' Semyon Semyonovich continued skittishly.

I looked at Griaznov. He signalled as much as to say: I've done the job you gave me and I'm not passing up a party! He threw a hefty corkscrew across the table:

'Get busy, Sashok, a little wine for the girls . . .'

. . . I was drunk after the first glass. I hadn't had a bite to eat since morning, since last night rather. Griaznov sang a bit of Visotsky before going on to the old-time romances. Kim unambiguously rubbed her knee against mine under the table. Moiseyev was making great efforts to get the third probationer drunk, a plump bespectacled girl with a turned-up nose. She shook off his arm from her shoulders every now and then, but went on listening intently. What he was saying was unmitigated tripe. I listened in and tried to catch the sense:

'. . . The brain capillaries are surrounded by atrocytes . . . Once alcohol gets into the blood, the capillaries start to dehydrate. The passage of liquid into the atrocytes gives rise to oedema, which in turn causes heightened pressure inside the skull . . . Since the capillaries supply the tissues with oxygen, their dehydration causes hypoxia.'

The fat girl threw off her suitor's persistent arm for the umpteenth time and said in a loud bass voice:

'Let's dance!'

Seryozha got the stereo working and the defiant voice of Gloria Gaynor blared out: 'I'll get by, no matter what.'

Meanwhile I was sitting opposite Lana and couldn't take my eyes off her. It seemed to me she wasn't drinking much, hardly smiled, though she did survey everybody slowly now and again. Grechannik had placed his hand on the back of her chair and was languidly sipping his wine, but I felt instinctively that he had little chance. Trying not to knock against the chair I went up to Lana and held out my hand. And at that moment I caught sight of a tiny green bow in her hair, almost on the nape of her neck. It drove me crazy.

Our dancing was fast and furious. We barely touched one another, transmitting energy through our tightly linked fingers. She had as much stamina as me and the dance was more like a struggle of equals in some strange form of sporting contest. The earth for us shrank to the space between the table and the material evidence cupboard, we were totally alone, at one with the music and the rhythm . . .

Our dancing was interrupted in the most imbecilic way. Semyon Semyonovich boldly got between us and suddenly began wailing:

Zoë, hup-hup,
She does it standing up!

'Semyon Semyonovich!' I shouted as I seized the criminalist under the armpits before he crumpled to the floor.

I led him into the photo laboratory and there under the red lamps he laid his head on the table, shaggy grey hair trailing in a dish of developing fluid. I located some liquid ammonia in the dispensary and forced him to sniff several times. He had to be got home in a hurry and I discreetly beckoned Seryozha through a crack in the door . . .

When I got back to the criminal office I couldn't grasp what had happened at first. Griaznov waved his arm vaguely:

'They've pushed off.'

21

'Who?'

But I already knew. Lana had gone off with Grechannik. While I'd been stowing Moiseyev in a car and explaining to Seryozha how to find the house in one of the side-streets near Neglinnaya, Lana had gone off with Grechannik.

I poured myself a glass of vodka and sat down next to Griaznov:

'Let's have a drink . . .'

'Haven't you had enough, Sashok?'

I only have a fuzzy recollection of what happened after that. Somehow or other I found myself in my own office, with Kim. She sat down on the edge of the desk and drew me to her.

'Now then, Turetsky . . .' she whispered, 'now, then Turetsky . . .'

My reason struggled with the promptings of the flesh and was a clear loser in an unequal contest. I kissed her hot lips and Kim began frantically unbuttoning her silk blouse. 'Now then, Turetsky!' I was trying to make objections to myself, something in my subconscious was saying no, no, not here . . . Kim placed my hand on her breast . . . Reason hung out the white flag and I thought triumphantly: 'And why not? Why the hell not?'

3

The dehydratation of the brain capillaries had reached critical. Hypoxia, occasioned by oedema of the atrocytes, was increasing with incredible rapidity. I drank down three litres of tap water and later stood over the toilet for a long time. Carried out in conjunction with a fifteen-minute shower, this operation had the desired result: I was perfectly prepared for a deep, refreshing sleep.

Twenty minutes remained before the start of the working day.

I couldn't find my car. Just couldn't recall where I'd left it two days before. Maybe it had been pinched. I sat down on a bench near the Timur shop and took out a cigarette, but I just couldn't put it in my mouth: I hadn't only drunk too much yesterday, I'd smoked too much as well. Where on earth was my car anyway? Not strictly mine, of course. My stepfather, who was a director of Moscow Sports Trading as well as a former Party worker – and a wheeler and dealer on the side – had got scared stiff at the clampdown on economic fraud. He decided to shuffle his honest pennies about a bit: the dacha was put in my mother's name, he put the Zhiguli he drove himself in the name of his daughter from his first marriage. I got his place in the queue for a Moskvich. He paid over the cash-price on condition that I got it fully insured and kept it that way. He trusted me to sell it to anyone he named at the first time of asking and hand the money over to him. He was taking very little risk, I wrote out an I.O.U. in my mother's name for the full cost of the car.

I tried not to think of what had happened the day before. It wasn't my conscience, I didn't look on myself as a crafty seducer. Or, incidentally, a corrupted minor. I just couldn't work out what to do, how to behave towards Kim. I could almost feel her caressing my neck; I even touched my head to get rid of the feeling. I was in a whirl. I loathed myself. Yesterday I had met a girl who was to be my destiny. She'd gone off with Grechannik. They'd just gone off. I started working up a furious jealousy. So what should I do, go up to Kim and say: 'Sorry, we shouldn't have done that. There's someone else.' The horrible thing was, it was true. But I couldn't have said it, even if it meant a firing squad. What a sod, spoiling everything I touched ... Just then I remembered where I'd left the car: it was outside the Horizon cinema.

According to the trainees' duty roster I was due to spend the morning with Svetlana Belova in Matveyevskoye getting into the supervisor's quarters there. The supervisor himself was already in jail and it was down to me to collect witnesses and conduct the seizure of documents according to the rules of criminal procedure. It wasn't all that important as far as the investigation was concerned (the accounts expert already had copies), but Parkhomenko insisted that the trainees were shown routine investigative techniques, in this case, so-called 'seizure'.

I was an hour late for work. I had to find Lana, but I was just too scared to open doors in case I met Kim ... I went straight into Parkhomenko's office.

'Leonid Vasilievich, excuse my lateness . . .'

'Oh, never mind that Alexander Borisovich. You put in too much overtime as it is . . .'

The mulish face of the deputy prosecutor took on a certain attractive quality. Why on earth was he so gracious all of a sudden? I realised why in a flash; through the half-open door of the common-room I saw Lana. She was sitting writing at a little desk piled up with folders. Parkhomenko intercepted my glance:

'To fill her time usefully, I told Svetlana Nikolayevna to

compile a statistical report of cleared-up cases . . .'

The dirty old man, I thought, (though Parkhomenko was only thirty-nine) fixes himself up with a dolly-bird next door and puts on a show for me as well. That's all I needed, the deputy prosecutor of Moscow as a rival . . . So then, our trip was to be put off indefinitely – that stupid list would take at least two days.

'In that case I'll get on, Leonid Vasilievich.'

'Yes indeed, comrade Turetsky, off you go. There's a big responsibility resting on us just now . . .'

Ah, to hell . . . Lana raised her green eyes from her work – they danced with mockery.

'. . . The Central Committee has given the Prosecutor's Office the task of coordinating the legal system of the entire country . . .' Parkhomenko was pressing on. 'Our job is to bring to light every crime, abuse, misdemeanour even. The main thing now therefore . . . our whole team therefore . . .'

Parkhomenko faltered over a word and I didn't fail to seize my chance.

'I'm off on the job, Leonid Vasilievich,' I said keenly and shot out of his office.

There was no point in just one of us going to the building-site. There was no point in working at all that day: the thing I wanted most of all was to sleep. I went off to see Merkulov.

'Konstantin Dmitrievich, I'm off now to Vernadsky Prospect (I'd just thought that up as I stood there), let's have your receipt and I'll call in at the cleaners about your sheepskin.

'Has something happened, Sasha?'

I trembled.

'Where?'

'I don't know – where?'

'Who to?'

'You.'

'What?'

'You look as if you'd just come out of jail.'

He fished about in his pocket for ages and finally produced a pink ticket. He held it out:

'Yes, you go over there and get a breath of air. Take a

sedalgin, that helps . . . And I've got another big favour to ask: when you don't want to answer questions – and that does happen with perfectly ordinary people – just say so: "Today I'm not answering questions." And then I won't ask any . . .'

Lord, why did I have to lie about Vernadsky Prospect? It would have been a sight easier just to say I couldn't work, I had a splitting headache, a hangover. Parkhomenko could have the wool pulled over his eyes, deserved it even. People like that didn't recognise nuance, intuition or doubt. Documents, signatures, phone-calls from the Central Committee – now they were facts.

'You've got some sedalgin?'

'No . . .'

He rummaged through his pocket again and pulled out a packet with some missing.

'Here, take two at once . . .'

'Thanks very much . . . Kostya, I'm sorry. I'm just not myself today . . .'

'Double coffee as well, in an hour's time, not now . . .'

Two hours later I returned and triumphantly placed in front of Merkulov a set of papers giving entitlement to 373 roubles from the till.

'Have they gone barmy or what?'

'It's not a lot, I know . . .'

'What d'you mean? I got it second-hand off a neighbour for three hundred!'

'Don't you worry about them: they'll have flogged your sheepskin to somebody else for six hundred.'

'But, that's really out of state revenue . . .'

'Konstantin Dmitrievich, if the state can't guarantee the protection of private property . . .'

'All right, all right. Don't overdo it . . . Thanks anyway . . . Ah yes, Sasha, Colonel Balakirev's just been over from the KGB. His section's dealing with the metro explosion from their end and they've come across this Faust in the course of operations. There's an underground organisation active in Yerevan. It's called NLPA – National Liberation

Party of Armenia. The leader's name is Faust Akopovich Gevorkyan. He's a circus performer apparently . . .'

Well that was just great. So they'd discovered him, so what? Faust . . . Armenians like calling their children after the classics: Hamlet, Isolda . . .

'So where's that "terrorist" Sviatov in all this? Didn't the KGB like his name? It would be interesting to know just what these operations were that led them to . . . what was it – NIPL?'

'Be serious, Sasha. Going by the Interior Ministry's information, it's the same group that organised the disorders during the November demonstration in Yerevan.'

'Yes, yes I know. They set fire to the rubbish urns. They pulled them in for disorderly conduct.'

'I can see you don't like this scenario.'

'No, why shouldn't I? A nice smooth scenario.'

I was trying to convince Merkulov, or rather myself that all this had nothing to do with me. My eyes kept seeing those dozens of charred bodies, though . . . There's no point in arguing with the KGB. They can cook a case up out of anything.

'Well what are you mumbling about? Still worrying about climbing the promotion ladder? Sasha, if we look at it objectively . . .'

'Whenever we can't do anything, we talk about "objectivity". Sorry I interrupted, Kostya.'

'No, no, it's all right . . .' Merkulov thought for a moment, then suddenly clapped his hands to his brow: 'Hey, listen, I completely forgot. In your office that tall one . . . Belova. She's waiting for you.'

I deliberately dawdled out of the office. Lana sat cross-legged reading *Socialist Legality*.

'I want you to do me a favour, Alexander. Could you look over that summary before I give it to the chief? There might be something not quite right . . .'

I could see straightaway it was all correct. What I didn't understand was how she'd managed to get it done so fast.

'Aren't you feeling well?' she enquired.

'No, no it's all right,' I responded with a certain lack of conviction and a glance at my reflection in the bookshelf glass.

'Let's go and have lunch,' I suggested, surprising myself, 'then we can go over to Matveyevskoye, if it won't be too late for you . . .'

'Oh I enjoy walking out late,' she said. I couldn't make out whether she was joking or not.

There weren't many people in the Warsaw. I had no appetite at all and I stared at the menu unable even to read the names of the dishes.

'You know, Alexander, all I want is ice-cream . . .'

Ice-cream, of course. I didn't even notice that she'd used my first name. We drank aromatic hot coffee and ate our ice-cream, exchanging meaningless phrases. But I did see actual interest in her green eyes, and barely perceptible wrinkles around them whenever she smiled. How old was she? Twenty-five, six? What did I know about her anyway? When she placed a sunburned hand on the snow-white table cloth, I spotted the thin pale mark on the ring finger – engagement ring?

All the doubts of the morning and hung-over aches and pains gave way to a wonderful feeling of lightness. If there were silences, there was no strain, if we talked I found, or so it seemed at any rate, just the right words and tone. I was totally content . . .

We didn't get to Matveyevskoye till nearly four. I hoped I could get this damned lift done in a couple of hours. It wasn't to be, though. The site-supervisor's office was located in a rickety rail-car standing dismally in the middle of the building-site. The workmen had finished the shift and there wasn't a soul about, except for the watchman. We had to foot it for about fifteen minutes through the dust to the nearest housing office, where I finally managed to round up two witnesses – a sozzled yard-sweeper woman and the house-manager himself.

When we got the rail-car open at last, using an axe on the

padlock I was horrified: there was about twenty times the quantity of documents I expected.

We were sorting out transport invoices, worksheets, quota-statements, bills, estimates and calculations till late in the evening. Lana quickly got the hang of things and went on raking through box after box without displaying the least sign of boredom or discontent.

'Now here's building directorate number thirteen. February delivery. Large–panel blocks from the Ochakov house-construction combine . . .'

She held out a sheaf of dog-eared papers. Instead of them I seized her wrist and didn't let go. And once again, like the dance the day before, I seemed to feel an answering excitement, though she freed her hand.

The sweeper elbowed the house-manager in the ribs as if to say, take a look at that, our investigator's on the ball . . .

I drove the car along the twisting 'stalin' road. The white buildings of the Kuntsevo hospital, former residence of the generalissimo, drowned in greenery on the left. To the right was the slope shading into soggy woodland by the River Setun. Lana's luxuriant hair flew in the wind and she raised both elbows high to keep it in check. My eyes glanced sideways involuntarily and I thought, how beautiful she was . . . Lana frowned slightly and pulled out a head scarf from her bag; this she wound oddly, across her forehead and back behind her head. It changed her face completely, making it coarse and rough-looking. I tugged the scarf by the corner, trying to loose her hair again. She grabbed hold of my hand and flung it from her with such unexpected force that I let go the wheel. The car slid sideways, bumped down the incline into a lilac bush and cut out.

'Are you crazy?' I yelled, gripping her shoulders.

Throwing her head back, she began to laugh. My hands slid down her chest and met between the shoulder-blades. She threw her powerful body towards me. We struggled, crushing one another in our embrace, searching for lips and refusing to give them. This was the prelude and we knew it, instinctively prolonging it, working ourselves up to that pitch of passion when you don't remember how it all happened, or how we found ourselves on the strawberry-fragrant grass, our clothes thrown God knows where.

She promised to come to me the following day and I thought of nothing else. I worked like one possessed and everything went my way. Even the paperwork was pure joy. Now and again I felt a stab of anxiety: suppose something happened, if I had a crash, say, or I was put on night duty . . . Or if she just didn't come . . . And I got stuck into work again with redoubled energy, urging on the time.

'Turetsky, you busy?'

I hadn't noticed the door open. Kim was standing there. So this was it. Now I had to make things cruelly clear.

'I have to have a talk with you, Turetsky . . .'

I felt irritated at her calling me by my surname.

'No, no, don't get the idea that I . . .' as she looked at me anxiously, I noticed how pale she was. God almighty, all I needed was her to fall in love with me! All the words I'd prepared to say to her flew out of my head. I went over and took her arm. It was trembling.

'Listen Kim, you've got to understand . . . We're mature people after all . . .' What sort of tripe was this? I halted, uncertain of what else to say.

'No, listen to me Turetsky . . .'

'Don't call me Turetsky please, I do have a first name.'

'All right Turetsky, I mean Sasha . . .'

'Turetsky to Leonid Vasilievich' announced the intercom and I tore off, treacherously pleased to have escaped further explanations.

'Sorry, Kim . . . We'll talk later.'

'Can I ring you at home, Tu . . . Sasha?'

I felt much happier about talking it over on the phone.

'Right, give me a ring, the number is . . .'

Lana arrived at my place on the dot of nine. By then I'd

scrubbed the whole flat out and fetched a mixed assortment of goodies over from the restaurant.

She came in and I forgot all about my preparations. In fact I ceased being aware of our surroundings at all. She brought with her all the scents of yesterday's strawberry meadow. I remembered that Kim was supposed to ring, so I reached out and disconnected the phone. And time and again we submerged ourselves in the depths of that ancient rhythm, unknown to anyone before us, of bodies intertwining . . .

I was awakened by a sound, something had jerked me out of sleep. It might have been a dream, because all around the silence was total, save for the occasional swish of tyres on wet asphalt. How long had I slept? Ten, twenty minutes?

'What's the time?' Lana whispered.

I put the light on and was astonished to see it was after two in the morning.

'I have to go . . .'

'Have to? Why?'

She laughed:

'I don't want this to turn into a kitchen romance.'

'Kitchen?'

'You know, washing up after the morning coffee, wandering in slippers round a messy room . . .'

'I'll see you home . . .'

She laughed again:

'It's ten minutes slow walk to where I live.'

She began dressing and I didn't hear her leave, as I fell at once into a profound satisfying sleep. I dreamed I was trying to remember something but just couldn't, I had an argument with somebody and was surprised at something else, but in the morning I'd forgotten the events of my dreams.

4

The powerful jets played over my face, shoulders and chest.
The pleasure of the morning shower was increased by the
knowledge that there was no hurry. It was seven in the morning and there were still two hours till my Moscow city duty
began. At last I turned off the tap. The telephone burst into
life.

'Turetsky! You don't half sleep! Sorry to wake you anyway.
Lieutenant-Colonel Yakovlev here.'

I swore almost aloud.

'What's up, Colonel?'

'We need help, Turetsky. You're the duty man today
according to the roster. There's been a murder in the October
quarter, and we've got nobody to send: the investigator you're
relieving is still messing about with another body in
Textilshiki. So get yourself ready, pal . . .'

'Okay, I'm on my way.'

'You don't have to: let me get your address right and my
laddies will pick you up . . .'

Morning Moscow was shrouded in mist and rain. The June
heat had turned overnight into almost autumnal drizzle. The
wipers could hardly cope with the water streaming down the
windscreen. I left a pool by the telephone from the shower, I
reflected, detached. I wasn't my own man anymore. I was the
leader of an operational-investigating team, assigned on June
14th 1985 to cover premeditated killings and other especially
serious crimes occurring over a twenty-four hour period
within the area of Greater Moscow. I looked over the people
riding with me in the police 'rafik'. Some were new to me,

32

others I'd seen often before on similar swoops, 'hot on the scent' . . . It was my twenty-first Moscow city duty.

Leninsky Prospect. A high-rise block, rammed down into Gagarin Square. At the bottom – a shop 'A Thousand and One Things'.

'. . . The father comes back from a trip this morning . . . both of them, mother and father are geologists . . . So he finds her – dead. The neighbours came running when they heard him shouting. Rang the station, we're not far, next to the Sputnik hotel . . .' the local police captain managed to tell me as we climbed the stairs to the fourth floor. 'There you are, comrade investigator, flat number 322, directly above the shop . . .'

Standard Moscow flat with standard Czech or Yugoslav furniture. Everything was upside-down: by the wardrobe lay a heap of underwear, clothes, scarves and headsquares, the floor round the writing-desk was littered with papers and exercise books, drawers had been pulled out and emptied; the coffee-table was covered in photographs with a tattered photo-album beside it on the floor; two suitcases had been pulled out from underneath the sofa and their contents pillaged; jewel-boxes had been overturned on the dressing-table, the valuables left lying there in piles . . . Through the open kitchen door, I could glimpse the shapeless, almost flat features of a female body, stretched out on the floor.

I touched nothing, merely walked quickly through the rooms. My mind involuntarily seized on the photo-album and the jewelry. But that was just instinct, you can never tell beforehand what fact will prove useful eventually.

'Okay then, boys, let's get to work,' I said in the routine voice.

The forensic pathologist had already bent over the body, picked up the lifeless wrist and at once released it. The criminalist clicked his camera several times, fixing the general position of the body and gestured me to expose the face. I got down on one knee and flicked back a lock of blue-black hair.

Before me, in a pool of blood, lay Kim.

* * *

33

'No, Turetsky, listen to me . . . I have to have a talk with you.'
Her voice haunted me, I saw her before me trembling, pale
and . . . alive. I did everything a duty investigator is supposed
to do at the scene of an incident. I instructed the team in how
to examine the place, carried out the external examination of
the body along with the pathologist, crawled about the floor
looking for traces of the criminal's footmarks, listened to the
tracker-dog handler's report. The dogs had picked up a scent
near the corpse and lost it in the street. 'I have to talk,
Turetsky' . . . I questioned the neighbours, sorted out the
material evidence . . .

I'd said to her 'You've got to understand,' and she'd interrupted me: 'No, Turetsky, listen . . .' but I hadn't let her
speak . . .

And now I wanted to take her lifeless hand and say: 'Forgive
me, Kim. Tell me what was it that happened to you? I swear,
Kim, I'll find him, me Turetsky the investigator, I'll find
him. Only it won't help you now.'

So I heard out the experts carefully and entered their words
into the examination report, but I kept feeling that I was
hearing her voice, that I was writing this tedious report in dry
legal language at her dictation.

'. . . Body of citizeness Lagina, 23, discovered on the
floor close by the door. The considerable quantity of blood
beneath the body suggests that the killing took place
here . . .

'Death was caused by a penetrating wound, delivered in
the region of the heart by a sharp cutting instrument. Judging by the shape of the wound (both angles acute) the murder weapon was a double-edged knife or dagger. The blow
was delivered with considerable force from behind . . .

. . . Changes in the body after death: fall in body tem-
perature, skin discolouration – indicate that death
occurred some 7–8 hours before examination, i.e. around
24.00 the previous night . . .'

Around midnight. Where was I when someone struck you

that fearful blow in the back? And you called me and I'd disconnected the phone, and for me everything was blotted out in the passion of love . . .

'. . . 14 (fourteen) traces of papillary patterns made by various parts of the human hand. These traces have been lifted off on special film and filed as material evidence. One of the fresh prints was found on the wooden frame of the dressing-table mirror in the parent's room, using an iodine vapour tube on finger-prints invisible to the naked eye . . . Between the mirror and the wooden supporting frame a black and white photograph was found, which had not been seen during the preliminary examination. The photograph shows citizeness Lagina and an unknown man of 22 or 3. Both are dressed in ski-suits against a background of a portico with a marble representation of a crouching lion, some part of an ancient, ruinous architectural ensemble. There is a date on the back "February 4 1985" written in longhand . . .'

The boy had a pleasant face. It was hard to imagine him killing anybody. Still who knew? Who had hidden the photo so carefully – and why? Kim herself? And the murderer had been looking for it – why should he do that if he wasn't on it? What had Kim wanted to tell me? And why me? Why not any other investigator? Who was she afraid of?

'. . . In the corridor, in the cat-tray, the impression of a man's shoe, size 43 was discovered. Using a chemical reagent – polyvinylchloride resin, the said impression has been fixed, lifted and filed as material evidence . . .
. . . The examination was conducted between eight a.m. and one p.m. by daylight and electrical illumination . . .'

Justice is truth in action. Now there was only one just course for me – to hunt down Kim's murderer.

But the inescapable obligations of a duty investigator hung on me like so much dead weight.

After the examination of the Lagin's flat our group moved on to the three stations area, to Komsomol Square where the body of 'Big Tamara' a well-known station prostitute had been found in the attic of the railwaymen's club, strangled with her own tights. At seven in the evening we were in the garage of the Council of Ministers, where one of the mechanics had been electrocuted. Finally we dealt with a suicide, the wife of the former trade minister; she couldn't take the disgrace of her husband's sacking for corruption.

After that, I slept for three hours on an uncomfortable sofa in the duty investigators' room. My sleep was like the oblivion of the seriously ill, oppressive and feverish.

In my sleep, I heard Merkulov come in early in the morning and talk to Griaznov in a barely audible whisper, discussing the results of the first inquiries, roughing-out theories and the initial plan of investigation into Kim's murder.

'Well now, Konstantin Dmitrievich, that print in the cat's tray most likely belongs to the murderer, that's exhibit number one. When we catch this sod, he won't wriggle out of it. The MVD labs say the guy wore American-made boots.'

Griaznov's ginger head jerked amusingly in time with his words.

'What about the fingerprints?'

'So far rubbish. Five belong to the victim herself, four to the father. Whose the rest are we don't know yet.'

'On the mirror?'

'Kim's right thumb.'

'Done anything with the photos?'

'They've started. So far they've been working with Lagin. They're all family or school or university group snaps, they'll have to get onto this skier.'

'Well, Turetsky can do that himself.'

'Turetsky himself' – means it's my investigation. Good, good, I thought and fell asleep again.

I was woken up properly at last by the loud voice of Colonel Romanova:

'Whassall this then, they've done for the little girl and you lot still snoozing?'

In the first place it was only me who was snoozing. And secondly, Shura had no idea how close she was to the truth when she said we'd done for Kim, but again it applied only to me.

'What're you shushing me for?! Your precious Turetsky's sitting up like a cucumber on a compost heap. Just take a look at his face – give him a swig of vodka and he's ready for action.'

You couldn't lose your temper with Alexandra Ivanovna. She spoke the same way to everybody, from the policeman on the beat to the Minister for Internal Affairs.

I was sitting up dishevelled, unshaven, hungry, knowing already that we, that is Merkulov, Griaznov, Romanova and I would very soon find the man who had murdered Kim. At that moment I was a hundred per cent certain of it.

'Are you thinking of hanging about much longer? Well, come on then, let's go along to my section. Turetsky, you get your fiz washed and get something in the buffet, the canteen isn't open on Saturdays – then on the double to me!'

I hungrily gulped down a glass of yogurt and a marzipan bun, then actually did run to Shura's section. Passing the vast waiting-room of the city internal affairs directorate I heard the nasty treble voice of the duty officer:

'Today, dear citizens, the management do not see callers. Come in on Monday.'

At first I thought it was some children standing next to the tall major. Then I saw that it was a boy and girl, small and very young-looking.

'Well, here's the investigator coming, he'll tell you the same . . .'

I looked at the girl – either I'd seen her before somewhere or she reminded me intensely of someone else . . .

'One moment, comrade Major. You young people, just why are you here? Wait, wait a second! Are you the Lagins' neighbours?'

'How did you . . .'

'Oh there's no trick, you've the face of your mother. Korabelnikova?'

37

I towed the youngsters up to the sixth floor to CID Department Two.

'Comrade investigator we've got a favour to ask – can you give your word you won't tell our parents we came?'

'I can't honestly promise you that. It depends why you're here . . .'

'No, no, you see my dad doesn't allow me to see Tolya here. Well, he thinks I'm still a little girl . . .'

'Liuda, let me tell him, you'll go all round the houses . . .'

We went into Department Two. I nodded to the duty personnel and took over an empty office, opposite Shura's palatial residence. I went on with the conversation we'd started in the lift.

'Listen, young people, I can see you've got something to tell me. Most probably something important. Take a seat.'

'It's just that Liuda and me were standing in the entrance passage the day before yesterday and . . . well that doesn't matter. Just standing. All of a sudden the outside door banged and we were scared it was her parents. Her father's a nasty, I mean strict. So we, er, hid . . .'

Come on, love, get on with it for heaven's sake. I get the picture, you were kissing in the hallway, scared you'd get a rocket from your parents; I thought this to myself and felt my knees shaking from excitement.

'You see we just don't want them to know, our parents that is.'

At this point I could hold out no longer and spoke out loud.

'I give you my word I won't tell anyone about your kissing. Now get on.'

Liuda spoke alone this time.

'Well, anyway, in they came and we were standing in the corner, there's a corner there completely dark, so when you come in the hallway and go up to the lift or up the stairs, you can't see anybody in the corner. I was hiding behind Tolya, peeping out from behind to see if it really was my parents. But it was two men and they rang the Lagins' bell.'

'How do you know it was their bell they rang?'

'There aren't any flats on the ground and first floors at our place, the shop – A Thousand and One Things, occupies all that. They went up two flights and then stopped. The Lagins' flat is opposite ours.'

Liuda Korabelnikova was now answering my questions crisply and directly. I was noting her evidence in large letters and fast.

'Do you remember the time?'

'Yes, exactly – when they came in it was quarter past twelve.'

'You what, looked at your watch?'

'Yes, when the flat door opened I looked at my watch straightaway. We stood another quarter of an hour. I have instructions to be home by twelve. My parents were out and I was frightened they'd be back any minute.'

'Can you describe what they looked like?'

'Sort of ordinary . . . I didn't get a good look at them, but . . . you ask me the questions.'

Well, done, Liudochka . . .

'Age?'

'One not so young, say, 26–28.'

How sad: to a seventeen-year-old girl, I'm an old man.

'The other was younger, say 22, maybe less.'

'Height?'

'The older one was tall. The young one medium.'

'Colour of hair?'

'Colour? You know it didn't have a colour. I mean, it's funny but they were . . . no, not bald, no, no not shaved . . . I mean yes, shaved but say about two weeks ago. And they were both grey . . . faces, hands – grey. I couldn't see their eyes. The older one had a round head. The younger was very handsome, I think . . . Wearing? Jeans, designer label. And leather jackets. I don't remember the colour, dark. They didn't have anything in their hands. Oh no, there was, yes, the younger one had an umbrella . . .'

'Umbrella?! It wasn't raining was it?'

'Yes, it had just come on to pour. An umbrella, you know, foreign with a leather case, folds up. I think it was black. Shoes? Don't know, can't remember. I believe one of them

39

had heavy shoes. No, they didn't say anything. Not to each other, or to whoever was in the flat. The door was opened straightaway and that was it.'

That was it. Umbrella . . . I asked a final question.

'Could you both recognise them if you saw them again?'

Tolya said nothing.

'The young one, yes. The older one I'm not sure,' said Liuda.

'Yes there was something else though,' said the boy impressively. 'They didn't ring the bell immediately, they stood for a bit, ten, fifteen seconds . . . Then they pressed the button. She opened the door at once or almost at once. You know there's usually a wait before somebody comes to the door.'

'Did she say anything. For example "ah, here you are" or "you've taken your time"?'

'No, she said nothing at all. Not even "hello" or "cheers". They went inside without speaking as well.'

So then, Turetsky, no emotions. You've got to construct a scenario, imagine what took place. Work out a plan of campaign. That is, work out how to test the theory. Job number one – the verbal portrait given by the young people.

In the presence of witnesses, organised by Griaznov, I showed young Korabelnikova all the Lagina photographs, including the 'skier'. The two leather-jacketed midnight visitors were not among them. She'd never seen the skier before.

Now it was Griaznov's turn to torment Liuda. He got some long pieces of cardboard out of his cupboard, and started on his wizardry:

He kept switching the strips with different foreheads, noses, mouths and spent a whole hour combining them. At length two photo-fit pictures were ready, containing the external features of the two unknown men. Now these monsters would be reproduced in the MVD labs and distributed to the various criminal investigation services. I'm a pessimist, actually. I don't have any faith in this miracle of technology: nine out of ten criminals we catch bear no resemblance to their synthetic portraits, issued in wads by police lab people.

At a brief operations conference in Romanova's office it was decided to use all detective resources in discovering what personal attachments the victim had and in tracking down the skier.

Clutching their photofits and copies of their skier photograph, the boys of Shura's section scattered all over Moscow.

Soon Merkulov and I were left alone.

'So, Sasha, the young lady wanted to tell you something, and you wouldn't listen. And now you're punishing yourself. Rightly so. Don't expect sympathy from me,' Merkulov broke three matches before managing to light his cigarette.

'I don't expect any, Kostya, I needn't have told you that after all . . .'

'Don't lie, I know very well you couldn't not have told me. The one thing I don't understand, Sasha, is – why didn't you listen to her?'

'I thought she was on about something else.'

'What something?'

I smoked a whole cigarette before replying. Merkulov waited.

'You see, she and I . . . well, anyway . . . there was a party here, I took a lot too much on board and . . . Kostya, honestly, it just sort of happened by itself . . .'

I knew I looked stupid, to say the least, but Merkulov had no thought of laughing. He was looking at me as if he'd never seen me before.

'You see, Kostya . . .'

'No I don't see. Still it's your affair, very much so.'

'She wanted to ring me at home but I wasn't there . . . I mean I was, but I'd disconnected it. But that's another story . . .' Like a drowning man, I was giving myself a final clout over the head with an oar.

'Telephone? Wait, wait a minute, Sasha,' Merkulov began dialling quickly. 'Lelya, Lelechka, did you tell me somebody had rung me the day before yesterday? No, no, two days ago when I was at the Architectural Institute celebrating Tanasevich's retirement . . . No, try and remember exactly

41

what she said. What do you mean, nothing? She did say my name, didn't she? Yes . . . yes.' Merkulov picked up a pen and prepared to write, 'Exactly that, she said comrade Merkulov? Ah, "can I speak to Merkulov" no comrade? . . . Yes, Lelya it's most important. Yes, yes. What time was this? About eleven or just after.' Merkulov wrote quickly.

That was Kim who phoned. She's got this habit of calling everybody by their surname . . . Did have . . .

'Sasha, she said: "I must speak to Merkulov on a personal matter, not as an investigator." You know, I'm sure whenever people say that, they really do want to talk to me as an investigator. You think it was her ringing?'

Merkulov was just asking for asking's sake. He knew it had been Kim as well as I did. He looked extremely upset, feeling he was involved in my grimy affairs.

'Why didn't she tell somebody else, that's what bothers me.'

'She didn't have time, Kostya. Apart from me, yours was the only name she knew. She probably rang me for a long time and got no answer, so she got your number from enquiries. She rang you after eleven and at quarter past twelve they arrived, the two in the leather jackets. She looked through the eye-hole and let them in. That means she knew at least one of them. She didn't expect danger. Otherwise she wouldn't have opened the door . . .'

'You realise what that means?'

'Yes, yes, yes. Those two were somehow linked with the danger she sensed or knew about, but she didn't suspect these two.'

'Bear in mind, they didn't even try to pretend it was a robbery, but they didn't leave behind a single letter or notebook. What did they want them for? Or was there something in them they didn't want known? That's what we've got to find out and pretty quick . . .'

I was driving slowly along Gogol Boulevard towards Kropotkinskaya. It was just here in a back-street behind the Filippov church that I lived for six years in a messy little room in an overcrowded flat with the minimum of mod cons. It seemed ages ago now, but really only a year had gone by since the moment the union committee chief summoned me and solemnly announced:

'You're receiving your due, Turetsky. You're getting a one-room flat on Frunze Embankment . . .'

My heart shrank at that: Rita had lived on Frunze Embankment once. Three years had passed since her death and only a bunch of keys which had once belonged to her, now lay on my bookshelf. That had been an eternity ago and now another woman had come into my life.

I hadn't even seen Lana for two days, as though I'd forgotten her even – Kim's death had torn me away from everyday existence, its worries, griefs and joys . . .

Stop! I jammed on the brakes so fiercely that I almost spun round at the cross-roads. I reversed on the square in some crazy fashion and tore off back towards Sivtsev Vrazhek, the residence of two great people, Julia and Oleg, both architects with an odd surname, Chipiga. I found Oleg in the usual place; he spent all his days off under his car, forever tinkering.

'Cheers, Sash,' he shouted, pulling his head out from under the bonnet. 'Hang on, won't be a minute.'

He disappeared once more, clanked about with his tools and went on in a depressed voice:

'We'll think up something in a minute . . . There's a bottle, Julie can rustle up something to eat.'

At last he emerged and wiped his hands on an old rag.

'Actually, Olezhka, I'm here on business . . .'

'That's fine, we'll discuss it over a little glass.'

'Yes, you see, I want you to dig in your reference books or whatever you call them, booklets.' I got out the skier picture. 'I'd like to find out what these ruins are.'

Oleg glanced at the snap and said:

'It's Tsaritsino, Catherine's palace, built by Bazhenov and Kazakov, geniuses both, but, alas, construction was frozen by the royal edict of crazy Catherine. Now a new "genius", Ilyusha Glazunov wants to restore some of it and organise a museum. That lion's head belongs to an amusing little house on the central island of the Tsaritsino Ponds.'

'How do you manage to know that, Oleg, off the top of your head?'

He laughed.

'If I asked you, for example, what's', he rolled his eyes upwards, 'er, yes, what's "essential defence", would you need to dig it out of a reference book? Come on then, let's have a drink.'

'I can't Oleg, I've got to go.'

'Oho, something serious, is it?'

'I've got to find that guy.'

Oleg glanced at his watch:

'It'll be dark in half an hour, what can you find?'

To be honest, I did want to have a sit and chat with my friends, and a stroll around the Tsaritsino Ponds at ten on a Saturday night was a pointless prospect. I put the snapshot back in my breast pocket and said:

'Okay, let's go.'

First off, I rang the Moscow CID and gave them Chipiga's number, where I could be reached during the evening in case of emergency.

'Turetsky,' the duty man was pleased. 'Some bird's been looking for you all day. She won't speak to anybody else. She says you're the only one who can sort it out.'

'The bird thinks along the right lines.'

'Don't get big-headed. Let's have your phone number.'

A minute later came the ring.

'Alexander Borisovich, this is Liuda Korabelnikova. I don't know if this will come in useful . . .'

'First of all, hello Liudochka. Secondly anything you say will be useful to me.'

'Oh, hello . . . you see, yesterday I pictured them to myself suddenly and remembered that the hefty man was holding a book, and the other one . . .'

'Hold it, Liuda. What sort of book – a notebook?'

'Oh, what I meant was a book, pretty thick. In a dark cover. Not a very new one I don't think . . .'

The murderer was a reading man. Goes out to do the business and takes an adventure book along. And I'm going to have to go over to the Lagins' again and carry out an extra search. They could have left the book behind in their flight. Or it might belong to Kim.

'Well that's all about the book . . . I've got another idea though . . . that is, I think that the young boy was er, a homosexual . . .'

'What?!'

'I know it's a stupid idea, but that's what I thought . . .'

'Liudochka *why* did you think that? Was there something about the way he walked? Or . . . or did the two of them behave that way?'

'No, no . . . I'm sorry Alexander Borisovich, I just don't know *why*. I just felt it instinctively . . .'

Things are going at some rate these days. I can't recognise one of those instinctively. Even in a crowd of homos at Sokolniki metro, where they usually meet, I can't tell who's who. Where did this young lady pick up her instincts?

'You know a lot of them, or what?'

'No, of course not! They say one of the hairdressers at a place on Leninsky Prospect . . . I know him pretty well, my mum has her hair done by him. Nobody else though.'

I gave the word to the CID and the extra information went along the chain to the identikit pictures of the wanted men.

I stayed the night at the Chipiga's and slept a profound and dreamless sleep. An insistent ray of morning sun lay across my face and I opened my eyes: little Katka's pink foot was hanging out of her bed through the wooden bars.

I quietly opened the fridge, poured myself a blackcurrant purée and ate a cold meat pasty. The tiny kitchen – you couldn't turn round in it – shone with cleanliness and mod cons: the Chipigas had recently done the place up themselves. Well, some people could lead a normal existence it seemed, have children and days off, go where they liked without leaving their phone number so they could be woken in the middle of the night, hauled off the dance-floor, or away from fishing or boiling pelmeni. Yes, I know it was my decision. Still I wasn't as resolutely sure as I had been three years ago that my choice had been the right one.

I recognised the Tsaritsino palace ruins at once, though everything looked different now it was summer. The black and white photo had been taken in winter. The watery expanse of the ponds, stippled with rain, separated me from the ruins.

'Hey, young and handsome, are you wanting a boat?'

A limping man with a matted beard slid out of a green kiosk.

'Thanks. Next time maybe. You wouldn't happen to know if there's a ski centre round here?'

'Are you off your nut, friend? In June – and you want skis?'

'No, no, I meant winter. I have to find one of the workpeople there.'

'A workpeople, that's us. I am, I mean. In summer it's boats and skis in winter.'

The lame man studied my I.D., warily comparing my photo with the original. He took his time over Kim and the skier as well.

'The Korean lass here we saw in the winter period. The lad as well. Up to something are they? The little girlie's from Moscow, I do believe. The young lad's from Biriulovo here that's for sure. Seen him a few times near here at the Biriulovo passenger station in railway uniform. By the way, they behaved themselves properly here. They did kiss though . . .'

Biriulovo station. Line section of railway police. Duty man listens carefully to me. Goes off into the Lenin room. Sound of dominos clattering in there. Fetches back a rosy-cheeked oldster of indeterminate age, wearing a vest and railwayman's cap.

'Matveyev,' asked the duty-man 'ever met this one in the ski-suit? The Moscow investigator wants to know.'

Matveyev held the photo at arms length.

'That's Dubov, the young one, Alexey, driver's mate out of our depot. Doesn't work there now, last year or the year before maybe, he got called up into the army. The old dad Nikolai lives in the railwaymen's settlement. Three Station Street, block 5, can't think of the flat number. Well they'll tell you there.'

Vast courtyard. Sheds with seats, tables for the domino-players, garages up against the five-storey blocks. People everywhere – on benches, windowsills, in the wide-open garages. I ask where the Dubovs' flat is. Everything goes quiet. In the Dubovs' flat I understand why. In a corner of the room, like an icon, hangs the portrait of Alexey Dubov in a mourning frame.

'He was killed, our little one, killed . . . Yesterday was the fortieth day since he died,' said the father.

'And just where was that?' I asked for some reason.

The father was silent. The reply came from the mother, whom I'd barely noticed, so small and withered was she:

'In your damned Afghanistan he died! Where else, I ask you? And they never even said where his grave was. They don't send their own precious sons, they keep them at home.'

She looked at me with hatred.

Getting a strong grip on myself, I managed to put the question:

'Forgive me, but this is important, do you know Kim Lagina? Your son was seeing her . . .' I showed them the photo.

The mother turned away from me, crying. Dubov shook his head:

'We don't know any of your whores.'

Roma Rozovsky was regarded as a bit of a dreamer by his colleagues. He, however, thought of himself as representing a new branch of science – criminal psychology, on the border-line between forensic medicine and the law. In his thesis, which he'd been working assiduously on for twenty years, he was trying to prove that only a specialist who was a medical man as well as a detective was in a position to work out the version of events at the outset of a fresh investigation. As if in confirmation of his own theory, Rozovsky had completed an evening course in the law faculty as well as his medical qualification. As far as I was concerned, these alleged dreams of the medical expert were the stimulus, if not the driving force, of the subsequent course of the investigation.

Apart from which, Rozovsky was a true enthusiast for the cause, nobody denied that, and I had no great difficulty in persuading him to carry out a medical examination on Kim's body, autopsy – Sunday, that was all.

By four it was all over and we were sitting in the morgue manager's office. Rozovsky balancing his fragile spectacles on the tip of his nose, said:

'Let's lift the curtain of secrecy on this affair. You first.'

No one enjoys an autopsy and the opening of Kim's body had so depressed me I could hardly force myself to speak:

'Two people in leather jackets went up to the door and rang. Kim was already in bed. Just as she was, in a short nightie, she ran to the door, looked through the eye-hole, saw only one person whom she clearly knew well, possibly intimately, seeing she didn't put a dressing-gown on, she just opened the door straightaway. We have information that Kim was afraid of somebody (I kept my voice wooden here) but the one she opened the door to was not a threat, or so she thought. Then she caught sight of the other one and rushed into the kitchen . . .'

'No she didn't, then, oh no she didn't!' Rozovsky shouted out, very pleased. 'Remember the way she was lying? The moment you found her, I mean. She was running, I grant you. But not into the kitchen! She was running for the front door! The murderer comes in, I don't know how many there were, and asks, insists, demands certain documents, photos or God knows what. And at some point my patient decides to make a run for it: she runs out of the lounge into the corridor and . . .' Rozovsky leapt up from his chair and ran towards the door. He froze, arms aloft . . . 'and she receives a terrible blow. A knife, or dagger if you like, penetrated under the left shoulder-blade and through the arch of the thoracic vertebra! It was thrown from a distance of not less than two metres. You know what speed a knife can reach thrown from that distance?

Ten or twelve metres a second! Our little girl here only weighs 45 kilos, no more, and the impact carried her into the kitchen. Well, I mean, why should she be running into the kitchen? She wasn't going to make them a cup of tea, was she?'

'Roma, that would make him a professional, this killer?'

'Exactly, Sasha, the very word. This person is a professional killer. Been trained to kill. Look for a hunter or a circus performer. Or maybe a soldier . . . ?'

5

Kim's schoolmates and girlfriends, students at the Law faculty, shop assistants in A Thousand and One Things, people living on the floors above ... one by one they came to Griaznov's office on Petrovka 38 where I'd been in residence since 8 a.m. seeing all the witnesses in the case. None of them were witnesses in the proper sense of the word, but under our law, anybody questioned by an investigator is a witness.

Griaznov twitted me, 'Sash, you're like our local dentist, ten minutes, tooth gone – next! The queue outside looks like a regional outpatients, half a mile long.'

I felt like a wind-up toy myself, with a set programme – question, answer, question, answer, sign ... I was in a hurry. I was waiting for the door to open and the next witness to say ... But they all said the same thing, sometimes even the words were the same, and there wasn't a sentence you could latch onto – 'hold it, that's what I wanted' ... So it went ... question, answer, sign ... An ordinary schoolgirl, ordinary student. She'd gone in for law only because she wasn't good at maths or physics, or singing or drawing. There was only one area where she was pretty good – sexual matters.

'Some bird – got through seven in a year,' Griaznov summed up.

'Eight,' I corrected inwardly, irritated.

Aloud I said, studying the table-edge intently:

'Give those seven the full works. I need to know all about them. I can't very well question suspects if I'm in the dark. Secondly, have a word with Lagina, Kim's mother, you know, softly, softly. She's supposed to be flying in from Irkutsk today. Mothers know their daughters better than fathers do: especially the intimate relationships. I'm off to the Prosecutor's Office. I'm going to lock myself in, so's nothing can distract me. I need to look through everything you've got together over the past few days and compile a report for the Procurator General – and a plan of investigation . . .'

And I didn't manage to do any of it; there was a big flap going on at the Moscow City Prosecutor's Office. The authorities were carrying out a routine departmental check. This time Criminalist Semyon Semyonovich Moiseyev had dropped in it. Somebody had grassed to Parkhomenko that Moiseyev had organised a rave-up in the criminal office.

The Deputy Prosecutor of Moscow, Parkhomenko was quivering with fear: what if the high-ups found out about the booze-up and connected that with the violent death of a trainee? The whole country was in the grip of an unprecedented anti-alcohol crusade. Party and government resolutions called for the punishment of any department heads who allowed drinking at the work-place.

'Alexander Borisovich, who was the organiser of that disgraceful booze-up on Tuesday?' Parkhomenko inquired as if he was on about who organised the Great Train Robbery, at the very least.

'It just happened . . . We . . .'

'Just happened? Well I'll tell you who was behind it: Semyon Semyonovich Moiseyev.'

'Never, Leonid Vasilievich. Comrade Moiseyev suffers with his liver. He's a teetotaller.'

No doubt the other participants in the 'orgy' were interrogated in the same spirit. One thing bothered me: would Parkhomenko ask anything about Kim? I just hoped nobody knew about my adventure.

'Apart from which, I've got work up to here, and diverting me from matters under the direction of the highest organs of the party contradicts party instructions on standards of discipline,' I added, demonstrating my prowess as a demagogue.

He moved his ears nervously and cleared his forehead of wrinkles.

'Why do you hate me so much, Turetsky?' asked the chief, upset.

'Now then, Leonid Vasilievich, you're not Romeo and I'm not Juliet! Why should I love you?'

Parkhomenko's eyes glinted coldly behind his spectacles:

'Get back to work then, comrade Turetsky . . .'

As a result of all this damned silliness everybody was advised to keep quiet about what had happened and Parkhomenko issued instructions that the trainees be transferred from Moiseyev's supervision to that of comrade Merkulov.

A mountain of documents lay on my desk. There was a great deal more material on the Kim Lagina case than I had expected, though a good deal less than was needed to pin the killer by the throat. I knew I'd got him and I wanted it to be me, by myself. I didn't think of them as two, for me they had melted into a single figure; I believed I should recognise him in the street . . .

Only God knew how mistaken I was.

For the moment I had the job of sorting out this mound of papers, get them bound in shiny board on a special machine, number the pages. . .

There were a few pieces of paper on Merkulov's questioning of the probationers on Friday. Svetlana Belova's bold handwriting: 'We studied in different groups, I didn't know her at all, just saw her at the general lectures . . . Yesterday I got home about three in the morning. If necessary that fact can be corroborated . . .' I felt a twinge of annoyance at the word 'fact'. Still, what should she have said – that on the night of the murder she was sleeping with the investigator in charge of the case? Anyway what was Merkulov doing putting questions like that – 'what were you doing on the day the crime was committed' – to trainees, as if they could be suspected of having anything to do with it. I would have to have a word with Lana all the same, now we knew what the killers looked like. She was intelligent, quick on the uptake, maybe she would remember something – a chance meeting in the cafeteria, the sports ground, the club . . .

All my efforts to get hold of Lana were fruitless: every time I glanced into Grechannik's office, where she was now firmly ensconced assisting Joseph in the metro bomb business, somebody was standing by her desk. She was wearing a dark-blue suit and white starched blouse. Her severe clothes only emphasised her extraordinary allure. I strongly suspected that Grechannik, and sometimes Parkhomenko himself, just thought up excuses to go over and talk to her or give her some pointless instructions. She would hear them out, all seriousness, but I detected a hint of irony in those green eyes. Lana knew the power of her attraction all right.

Eventually I got fed up with all this doggy flirtation and broke it up in the crudest possible way. I dialled Grechannik's number and barked:

'Probationer Belova to Investigator Turetsky's office.'

I don't think Grechannik even know who was phoning . . .

She stood in the doorway, tapping her pen against her palm. I don't know how long the silence would have lasted if Lana hadn't asked in her quiet, low voice:

'May I sit down?'

She smiled and I felt like kissing her then and there. Instead I had to question her, and she had to answer. So we fulfilled our obligations impeccably, both thinking of something else altogether, what had been and what would be between us, when this had all blown over, the unpleasantness and grief, and only happiness remained . . .

She was sitting in front of me, head slightly lowered, sketching something on a piece of paper. She would lift her eyes to listen to the next question, then glance down again at her fanciful doodling. Then I saw the little green bow, clinging by some miracle to her hair.

We were separated by the width of the table on which lay a hundred pages devoted to Kim's life and death: it was like the photo-element set up at airports to detect metal objects, not allowing us to cross the unseen barrier. An outstretched hand would trigger the alarm.

To get past the danger area, I asked:

'Well what's new on the explosion?'

Lana laid her pen to one side and I sensed, rather than heard, her sigh of relief.

'You were right: that chap Sviatov, the one who blew up the church, had nothing to do with the metro bomb. He made a slip, he's got an alibi – when the bomb was planted he was having tests in the cancer clinic all day . . . Still we managed to pick up another lead . . .'

That 'we' was spoken with unconcealed pride.

'A group of Armenians responsible for acts of terrorism has been identified. They tried to set off an explosion during a demonstration in Yerevan. Judging by the similarities, the metro bomb is their handiwork.'

'Have they admitted it?'

'No, not yet. But they will,' replied Lana confidently, 'we've got the assistance of an experienced KGB team.'

There was something oddly secretive about her eyes as if she was shutting herself away from me – 'we' 'the KGB' . . . Well it was just the fancy ideas of a young investigator. I'd been through it myself. Give it a year or so, it would all become a routine – the chase, the working with agents, GB operations – and goodbye to all that romantic enthusiasm for the investigating profession.

The phone started ringing. I took a look at my watch; five thirty P.M.

'Good day to you, comrade general!' I heard the typical Griaznov little joke and fell in with his banter.

'Greetings to you, colonel of the guards! How are things at the front?'

'All quiet on the second Turetsky: the enemy is advancing, and we as usual are up shit creek . . .'

I held the receiver tight against my ear – Captain Griaznov was capable of producing much stronger expressions, but probationer Belova was serenely engaged in studying the Napoleonic features of the new Gensec's portrait hanging on the wall above my head.

'Okay, Sash, to business. During the day via the Regional

CID I've picked up her sexual . . . partners. Listen, none of them fits the identikit. Five have got alibis, I'm still checking the other two but I think this line isn't going to lead anywhere. I've just finished questioning the girl's mother, she had nothing worth saying. Her daughter used to write to her about some soldier, saying it was "serious" with him. That's it. In a word, comrade general, no luck!'

Grechannik's well-tended features appeared in the doorway:

'I might have known you were here, Lana. Come on, I need you.'

She rose shaping her lips to say:

'I'll ring . . .' and walked to the door, swaying her narrow hips under her close-fitting navy-blue skirt.

'Grechannik's taken your dame away again?' said Griaznov on the other end of the line. 'Call yourself a black belt? Give him one in the groin and goodnight!'

An idea was spinning round in my head and the question came to my lips unconsciously:

'Listen Griaznov, have you looked at the mail?'

'What?' Griaznov didn't catch on. 'Hold it, hold it, Sash. What mail? The Lagins'? But I did what you told me – I took your instructions on re-directing mail to the local post office. If anything comes in addressed to the girl, they'll send it straight on to you.'

'I'm not talking about that, Slava. Today's Monday the 17th. The murder was on Friday. We checked the place on Saturday. But the post gets there before eight in the morning, get me?'

'I might add, comrade general, that people used to go down to the post office for their letters at one time but for the last hundred and fifty years it's been delivered, get me?'

'Don't be facetious,' I was losing my temper now, 'get back there straightaway and take a look in the Lagins' post-box, the parents won't have looked in there most likely, they've got other things on their plates.'

'Alexander Borisovich,' Griaznov had sobered up. 'In ten minutes I'm due to meet a person, "my person", you know?'

In operatives' talk that meant contact with an agent, Griaznov's personal agent: there was a secret directive that nobody could make contact except Griaznov. Not even the head of Moscow CID.

'Okay, I'll see to it myself,' I snapped shortly and replaced the receiver.

All of us had forgotten about the post-box, I thought, foot down hard on the accelerator. The killers were obviously after something among the papers. Kim had concealed the photo of the soldier who had fought in Afghanistan. It wasn't impossible that a letter could have arrived from him either on Saturday or today, Monday. God had I gone round the twist? A letter from Sergeant Dubov could only arrive from the next world.

Kim Lagina's mother, a tiny Korean woman with a face drained by her loss, silently offered the post-box key across the door-step and at once closed the door. I found no. 322 with difficulty among the vast metallic array under the meagre staircase light. The key wouldn't fit the hole. What the hell! My hands had turned black for some reason. I got out my lighter and saw . . . there were tongues of soot on the surface of the box. Somebody had already had a go at opening it and broken the lock; when his efforts had failed, he'd just stuck a match through the eye-hole and burned whatever was inside.

I went upstairs again to the Lagins' neighbours the Korabelnikovs.

'Oh, it's those punks, yobs playing up again. They dye their hair lemon-colour and smoke hash then they go daft: they think it's a game, setting fire to the post!' Korabelnikov was getting worked up. He had the look of an unofficial artist, unkempt and shaggy, not a lot different from the Muscovite punks he was criticising. 'Somebody started a fire here on Sunday. You could smell smoke all day . . .'

I rang the office from the Korabelnikovs' and was lucky enough to find Moiseyev still there – working off his alcoholic sins no doubt.

While he was on his way, I nipped over to the housing

office and got hold of two inebriated locksmiths.

Half an hour later, Semyon Semyonovich rolled up in the departmental car armed to the teeth with anti-crime technology and we set about examining the conflagration. As a preliminary we lit the stair-landing with a powerful electric lamp, taken from the criminalist's research-case.

One of the workmen forced the lock with his chisel . . .

The charred wad of paper with its fluttering grey fringes reminded me of my grandmother's Epiphany fortune-telling: she used to crumple up a few leaves from an exercise-book, place them on a porcelain saucer and strike a match: 'You see, Sashka, there's war on the way again;' with her finger she traced out the shape of the charred paper on the wall – 'you see, a warrior in a shako, he's got a spear in his hand . . .'

I would draw my knees up on the rough chair, back bent, staring intently at the outline, but I couldn't see any warrior or spear; it looked like the fantastic whale, the kindergarten teacher had been telling us about that day. But for some reason the shadows reminded me most of all of ancient ships . . .

Just as now I saw in the depths of the box a charred 'frigate' swayed by the wind, ready to disintegrate at the first touch – all that remained of the original letter.

We set up a locksmith cordon, conscripted to guard the front entrance and prevent the wind from dispersing our fragile hopes. The locksmiths were delighted to exercise their repressive function and allowed nobody in until Semyon Semyonovich had used a scoop and soft tweezers to transform the paper 'ship' to a box of cotton-wool covered by cigarette-paper.

He then rubbed celluloid platelets on his knee and their electrified surfaces picked up the tiny pieces which had fallen off; finally he retrieved from his suitcase a rubber bulb with a glass tube, rather like a child's enema, and drew the tiniest specks of ash into it.

He did all this with surprising speed and I shuddered at his every movement.

'Stay cool, Alexander Borisovich, the patient's still alive, the operation's a success,' Moiseyev summed up, closing the box. 'Now comes the final stage – bringing out the text of the burnt letter. For that we need glycerine. Let's get to a chemist.'

He paused, lost in his own thoughts, then made a suggestion:

'If you've no objection we'll do all that at my place. My boys have promised to lay on supper. It's a year to the day since Anna died . . .'

Moiseyev's wife, Anna Petrovna had been our manager before she died of cancer the previous summer, leaving Semyon Semyonovich with twin 16-year-olds, Misha and Grisha. Not only had I no objection to driving over to Moiseyev's, I most definitely had to go, certain as I was that he would decipher what had been destroyed by fire. Somewhere at the rim of my mind flickered a thought: Lana had promised to phone me. It vanished at once, as something of secondary importance. Moiseyev dismissed the duty Volga, and gently cuddling the box of dust to his chest like a new-born babe, got in beside me in the Moskvich.

While the twins were laying the table, Semyon Semyonovich was using an atomiser of glycerine solution on the burnt letter, against a sheet of glass. Before my eyes the damaged fragments began to soften, settle down and flatten out. The criminalist moved them into place with a spatula and covered them with a second sheet of glass.

'I hope, Alexander Borisovich, that the letter was written by a ball-point pen. That way we'll see something. I can't promise a lot, but something.'

Semyon Semyonovich led me into a store-room, his private criminal laboratory. He took about thirty photographs in infra-red light, illuminating the surface of the burnt sheets by a crafty arrangement of mirrors set at a variety of angles.

After that he immersed the film in the developing tank.

'We've got twenty minutes free, Sashok, till the film develops. Let's drink to Anna's memory . . .'

Semyon Semyonovich poured out vodka from a crystal decanter, making sure each glass was level.

'Anna actually bought this decanter for my birthday, the day before she found out about her illness. She loved beautiful things. That's her aristocratic ancestry coming out . . . Me, I'm one of the local Jewish poor-folk – she always used to grumble that I didn't give a hang what I ate and drank out of, or what we put up at the windows . . .'

He wiped his hand across his eyes. We drank in silence. Misha and Grisha flung themselves on the cold meat and salad they had prepared and after eating their fill, adjourned to the other room to watch the football on T.V.

We had another drink and that inner string, so taut when we were standing in front of the Lagins' post-box, began to relax.

Moiseyev went in to wash and dry the film. I wandered over to the window; I like looking out on Moscow on summer evenings hearing the noise of the streets. Where I live on Frunze Embankment it's pretty quiet of an evening, all you can see are the lights of Gorky Park, but you can't hear any noise – it's as if the Moscow river absorbs it all. Here it was the centre of town and the traffic would be continuous till nightfall. I wasn't thinking of that though. I was waiting, and afraid. I was afraid Semyon Semyonovich's messing about with the film would be a waste of time. I was afraid the burned letter would be a dead-end, anybody could have written it, on any subject. I was hoping. Hoping we'd crack it today. And that the secret would lead me to Kim's murder.

Moiseyev re-entered the room, limping on his wounded leg.

'Come on, Alexander Borisovich, I think we've got something.'

On the rickety table in the store-room stood a microscope, the film threaded under the lens.

'Be careful, Alexander Borisovich, it hasn't completely dried yet. It's all right, just sit on the chair and look in here.'

I peered into the microscope and saw absolutely nothing. Or rather I saw an amorphous yellow stain with prominent brown dots. I looked over at Moiseyev, bewildered.

'Get yourself sat comfortably and look straight down it!' repeated the criminalist.

I moved myself and the tottering chair close up against the little table and altered the focus of the instrument according to Moiseyev's instructions. At once the brown dots resolved into a 'P/YA'. I could hear my heart knocking. Post Office Military unit. Afghanistan. Or was it? Could it just be somebody working in a secret organisation, in Karaganda or somewhere? Or it could be a delayed letter from her parents on their geological expedition.

Moiseyev broke the spell by carefully winding on the next frame. For all my efforts I couldn't find even a hint of letter or figure.

'The frames are in logical order, Sasha. First, what was left of the envelope, then the paper inside.'

Yes, of course, envelope, paper, I thought, ash inside ash . . .

Frame after frame, millimetre after millimetre a good hour and a half we sweated over that microscope. I jotted down what I was able to decipher . . . 22 . . . K . . . Lag p/YA. That was all that was left of the envelope.

Then came the letter itself:

```
        ello   dea        stant K
This is      ate        iend      ey Du
         already              tragi    s
    Lekha's been killed        ying out       inter
  ty   in Afg            Go.      course post
Her    sta
```

My eyes had started watering and I could pick out nothing more. I was very tense by now. I had to have a break.

'Let's have a quick one, Semyon Semyonich, eh?'

Moiseyev dispensed the vodka.

'Now then, dear boy, drink up – to the success of lost causes!'

I chewed on a pickled gherkin while every possible combination of words I had half-read, swirled about my brain.

'Why not call them out loud, Alexander Borisich? Maybe I could be of some use!'

'Don't put yourself down, Semyon Semyonich, I'm an ignoramus compared to you.'

'Well then, let the old rat help.'

'Hello, dear, far-distant Kim,' I began. 'This is a mate of your friend Aleksey Dubov. Then comes something about a tragic event, probably, since we've got the word "Tragi".'

'I think – "you've already received the tragic news that Lekha's been killed." '

'. . . carrying out his international duty in Afghanistan!'

'There you are, we've got something already, Alexander Borisich. Next, not a clue, some star is it?'

'Hero's star? He got it posthumously, of course, the Hero's star. We're not just making this up are we Semyon Semyonich? Let's have a look what comes next.'

So it went, millimetre by millimetre, letter by letter . . .

```
     But Le          illed dushma
bullet          own      s. He to   me
he'd sent you          ents about the ba
       gs     in Afg              oldiers
     ions   , so that          fear  But Lekh
     and he  rgued              nder. Le
   he had a gi        nd in Mos
   ing law          ell     where he
ought
```

```
Dear K        lie      ekha shie          nder
             st from the bullets. They
   ves. And        oma              tab
   nd.              ing     inj        all
```

The next second I almost knocked the microscope on the floor as I clearly made out the word 'Faust'. I couldn't believe my eyes, I thought I'd got the D.T.s. I pulled the film back:

```
     lex      Faust, that is   committing a sta   cr  e.
Dear Kim! Take c          a's pap         I'll write
to you again soon and com
```

ad r s   The   uments sh   giv
   ghest author   and C u
      main   unk   nd.
                A Mo ov

'Now it really is a charade. Guessing-game.' Moiseyev tousled his hair disconsolately.

'What d'you mean, guessing game? But Lekha was killed by a dushman's bullet.'

'I don't think so, Alexander Borisovich. Between "Lekha" and "bullet" there's more than two letters. It's more like "But Lekha was *not* killed by a dushman's bullet but by his own friends . . ."'

'. . . by his own hands! Semyon Semyonovich!' I pleaded.
'Wait just a minute. Or rather, write down everything you can make out.'

I walked out into the corridor, lit a cigarette and sat down on an antediluvian trunk. What was this Faust all the time? Weren't there too many Fausts for one week? Or was it the same one, the one who blew up the metro and the one in this letter from Afghanistan? I dropped my ash straight on the floor. It was uncomfortable sitting on the sloping top of the trunk and the shouts of the football fans on the other side of the door made it hard to concentrate. I waited for Moiseyev to call me, but as I reached for my third cigarette, I began to doubt it. I opened the door of the store-room: Semyon Semyonich, his grizzled head on the table, was snuffling peacefully.

I picked up the sheet Moiseyev had been scribbling on.

'But Lekha wasn't killed by a dushman's bullet, he died by his own hands. He told me he'd sent you the documents(?) about the bad things going on in Afghanistan . . . soldiers . . . But Lekha wouldn't agree(?) and he argued with our commanding officer. Lekha said he had a girl-friend in Moscow, studying law . . . tell, where he ought(?) Dear Kim! It's all lies that Lekha shielded the commander with his chest from the bullets. They fought with knives. And . . . stabbed(?) your friend . . . Alexey Faust, that is committing a state crime. Dear Kim! Take care of Lekha's papers. I'll write to you again soon and come and see you even at your address. The documents should be given to our highest authorities and the Party. I remain your unknown friend. A Morozov Molokov? Mosolov?'

I put the film and notes in my case and woke Moiseyev.

I paced from corner to corner of my flat, without putting the light on. I didn't know what I was doing. I carried out a search of the premises according to all the rules and discovered almost half a bottle of cognac in the television cabinet. The fridge was empty, a single orange glowed in the white silence. I settled down in a comfortable armchair with the brandy and the orange. I drank straight from the bottle in huge gulps and greedily sank my teeth into the tart icy pulp. Total physical exhaustion had cleared my brain – now I could think, put two and two together . . .

An investigative hypothesis, as everyone knows, represents a *probable* explanation of the incident being investigated, the circumstances and all the facts individually considered. Naturally, the nature of a hypothesis as a *probable* judgment allows for the possibility that it might be mistaken. All sufficiently well-founded theories should be put forward and tested. In the end, none of them may turn out to be sound. Theoretical arguments over the classification of theory verification, with regard to their priority – sequence or simultaneity, boil down to one thing – one must intensively test the most dangerous hypothesis.

So then, first of all I could pick out a link: a man by the name Faust had placed a bomb in the metro, the letter to Kim mentions a certain Faust. Moiseyev gave him a name, 'Alexey'. Because there was a part of a word 'lex' in the letter. But that was a large question. It was just a guess. What if Kim knew about the metro explosion? Why didn't she tell anybody at the Prosecutor's Office about it? She was happy and carefree till the last day. What did she want to tell me and Merkulov? And what did the war in Afghanistan have to do with the metro explosion anyway? And how could the military censors overlook a letter like that – especially one that had to cross a frontier? The girl's murder was starting to look more and more weird.

I shuffled and re-shuffled the facts, concentrating on one group then another, each attempt confirming how little I actually knew. On the one hand, the description of the shaven-headed young men indicated newly-joined soldiers and Afghanistan. On the other was Rozovsky's statement that the dagger-blow was delivered by a professionally trained hand, and that didn't suggest rookies.

At all events, what I had to do was check in detail the most dangerous theory – metro explosion – Afghan soldiers – Kim's murder. That meant digging about in military circles, prod the Moscow and Moscow Region military commands, traipse about among military units and get in contact with the Judge Advocate's Office and the Ministry of Defence . . . In this country, the armed forces doesn't just mean the army. There are three types of forces: apart from the MOD itself, there are the internal forces of the Ministry of the Interior (MVD) and the frontier troops of the KGB . . . I had my work cut out all right. I really doubted whether I could cope with such a volume of field investigation, even if all Romanova's department were handed over to me tomorrow. I drained the last drops of Cognac down my throat and lay down in my clothes on the unmade sofa.

6

At 7 a.m. I drove up to Post Office no. 78. Despite a sleepless night and more than enough booze I felt fairly fresh. The office chief advanced her mighty chest and with a flutter of violet lashes twittered:

'Ah, comrade Turetsky, Alexander Borisovich, dear boy! How could we remember just one letter in particular? You know the enormous number of postal packages that pass through our hands!'

I gave way before the thrust of that low-cut bosom and flopped onto a chair. The postmistress sat down alongside enfolding me in a wave of pungent scent and sweat.

'You know, our Soviet post office carries ten thousand million letters a year, that's sixteen times more than in Tsarist Russia in 1913,' pursued the chief adding, with a surprisingly loud laugh, 'Do you know, they actually carried the post on horses in those days, horses with bells!'

'Please fetch the postman who delivers to the Thousand and One Things building,' I said.

She snapped her mouth shut, and sailed out into the corridor, wagging her backside in annoyance:

'Afanasyeva!' she yelled. 'The investigator here wants you! Afanasyeva! How many more times?'

A minute later I was questioning a young lass with naive blue eyes, in the postmistress' office.

'Tell me, Afanasyeva, can you recall who got letters on Saturday the 15th?'

'All of them, well some I can.' She answered calmly, wiping her palms on the lap of her skirt.

'I'm interested in the mail for flat number 322.'

'I thought as much. Yes, there was one letter for Kim Lagina.'

'What, you know her? Knew her I mean?'

'I knew Lagina. We were at school together.'

Well, what do you know. Fine staff we've got missing a witness like this!

'What sort of a letter was it – ordinary envelope or a triangular army one?'

'It was an ordinary letter, with a stamp on it, posted in Moscow.'

'How do you know that?'

'There was a post-mark on it "Moscow, Kazan Station".'

'Can you remember the return address?'

'No. But there was a post-box number and a signature. Not very clear though.'

'Surely you can't remember all that with the amount of mail you deliver every day?'

'Yes I can,' Afanasyeva responded, unembarrassed.

'Kim asked me to give any letters from her boy-friend, Dubov, in Afghanistan to her personally and not drop them in the post-box. But there haven't been any from him for a long time.'

'You know somebody set fire to the post box?'

'Yes. That often happens. Vandals.'

'You're sure this was just vandals?'

'Yes, I know who they are, 13-year-olds from the school I used to go to. They're after the stamps and if they can't get the lock open, they set fire to it. We've got a copy of the charge – the police caught them in the next entrance along on Sunday. Now the locks will have to be changed. The locksmiths should have done it yesterday but our chief here couldn't get through on the phone.'

'She didn't tell me anything about that.'

'She's a bit . . . casual.'

Lousy little sods, I thought, destroying evidence like that.

'You know what happened to Lagina?'

'Of course, the whole district knows about it.'

'Do you have any suspicions . . . Who might have done it?'
'No . . . it's not my job to suspect people.'

Conversations with Merkulov always give me aesthetic satisfaction. I'm not afraid to use the word – aesthetic. Our talk pours out lazily like a pint of beer in a bar. But the casualness is deceptive: we weigh our words, looking for exact definitions. Gradually the picture emerges . . .

The conversation we had that morning contained no pleasure for me, however. No picture emerged either.

Merkulov was standing by the window with his nose up against the glass, observing the wind channelling the raindrops into little streamlets and forcing them towards the frame. There was a storm getting up.

Every now and again Merkulov turned towards me and I could see the dark spot on the end of his nose – dust from the window-pane. The prince had aged a bit over the last year, the anxieties of being head of the Inquiry Section of the City Prosecutor's Office had speckled his ginger hair with grey and etched two deep furrows from nostrils to chin. Still, the chief's grey-blue eyes peered out at a restless world with their old mixture of curiosity and understanding. He interrupted me only occasionally, usually with some reproof like 'repeat that, leaving the theory out, just the facts,' or 'now say what you did next and leave your speculations for some other time.' Still I got my theories and speculation in, because otherwise we'd get nowhere and the facts contradicted themselves anyway. On my own with Kostya I felt the pressure of my guilt even more: if only I'd listened to what Kim had wanted to tell me . . .

'Have you eaten today?' Merkulov broke in unexpectedly and without waiting for an answer opened the door into the reception-room. 'Klava, fetch us some coffee and sandwiches from the cafeteria, half a dozen will do.'

'Oh dear, Konstantin Dmitrievich, what's that on your nose?' said the secretary, alarmed, and extracted a scented handkerchief and powder-compact from her handbag.

The little business with Merkulov's nose gave us a sort of

break and I did begin to feel amazingly hungry. Merkulov rummaged about in the desk-drawer, fished out a newspaper and outlined an article in the last column with his fingernail.

'Here, read this.'

The secretary brought in a tray of coffee and ham sandwiches. Merkulov took a sip of the hot coffee with a childishly protruding lip and proceeded to the door.

'I'm just off to see the chief for a minute, you have a read over your sandwich.' Outside there was thunder and lightning and rain was lashing the pavements. The room grew dark. I switched on a desk-lamp and sat down in Merkulov's armchair. The newspaper was the On Guard of the Moscow military district, and two months out of date. The article was headlined 'Paratroopers'. Chewing their ham and bread and drinking their unpleasant coffee, I began reading.

. . . The platoon is working on techniques of hand to hand fighting. But not on the mat in the gymnasium. Out on asphalt as rough as emery-paper, or under teeming rain, the lads 'stab' each other with bayonets, 'smash' one another with the butt-end of rifles or sappers' shovels, knives flash. While the troops are busy with their training, I feel one of the knives. It's honed like a razor . . .

'And you thought we were just play-acting,' grinned the battalion C.O. 'What has a boy in a para's beret got to beat first of all? Fear!'

Merkulov had given me the paper for a reason and I paid close attention to every word penned by the correspondent – who was he? – Savkin.

. . . Present special forces with their tank, artillery, engineer and other arms form part of the paratroop forces of the USSR Ministry of Defence. Dropping as tactical units, they are capable of independent action in seizing islands, military bases, ports and aerodromes.

Service in 'special force' battalions demands special training. Among those entrusted with the supervision and command of the young paratroops, there are no casual personnel just 'serving their time', unwilling to put their whole heart and strength into it. Take just one of the special force soldiers, Sergeant Alexey Dubov . . .

I automatically stuffed a whole sandwich into my mouth and drank off the dregs of Merkulov's coffee.

Sergeant Alexey Dubov is 23 years old. Life has tried him to the utmost more than once. He grew up in a railwayman's family in Biriulevo, near Moscow. Joined the para special forces. His section was dropped into Afghanistan. Once . . . Well, let him tell it.

'We were assisting the Afghan troops evacuating wounded from a village under dushman attack. I went into one of the houses and sensed I was being watched. I turned sharply: a hefty young guy came flying at me with a dagger. I managed to get the butt of my rifle up and divert the blow but the blade pierced my wrist. I hooked him off his feet, but as he fell he tried to stick his dagger in me. He didn't make it. My knife was quicker . . .'

'You can't remember how many fights you've had like that – one to one?'

'I certainly can. You don't forget that sort of thing. Twenty-two . . .'

I put the paper aside. Which one was the fateful one for you, the twenty-third? Twenty-seventh?

The storm had subsided. And, as in all good plays, Merkulov appeared in the doorway. He surveyed the empty cups and saucers with satisfaction. He got yet another newspaper out of his briefcase.

'Is this a political education class or what?'

'A criminal law class,' replied Merkulov as if to a backward pupil.

This time the headline read 'A Step into Immortality'. It was in Red Star.

... The platoon commanded by Vladimir Ivonin had instructions to dig in at a strong position along a gully in Kunar province. According to reports, a considerable dushman force was heading in that direction. The platoon commander ordered Sergeants Dubov and Morozov and Privates Halilov and Smirnov to go out on patrol and cover the platoon against sudden attack from the rear.

Just then a dushman machine-gun in the bushes opened up at point-blank range on the platoon-commander Lieutenant Ivonin. In a flash, Sergeant Dubov placed himself in the path of the stream of lead and shielded his commander with his own body . . .

I chucked the paper on the table.

For the first time in the three days following Kim's death, something more than endless plausible conjectures was occupying my mind. I still didn't know anything though. Merkulov used to call it 'thinking concretely about the future'.

If the letter-writer was Ivonin's platoon-sergeant Morozov, then we could lay our hands on an eye-witness of Dubov's death. If Moiseyev and I had correctly deciphered Morozov's letter to Kim, then her murder must be directly linked to her contact with Dubov. After all, she was in possession of certain documents sent by Dubov. As near as could be gauged, this Morozov knew what was in them too. The killers, no doubt, were looking for the papers in Kim's flat and found them . . . We had to find the army unit, or platoon rather, that Lieutenant Ivonin had commanded some months before. Those privates, Halilov and Smirnov too. We needed to know what had really happened to them in Afghanistan – it was all one knot, however bafflingly tied. But first of all we needed Sergeant A. Morozov . . .

'We did agree, Sasha, that we'd just take the separate facts and look at them from all sides, not try fitting them together till . . .'

Oh, great; I hadn't even noticed I was talking aloud and there was Merkulov standing meekly by while I conducted the meeting in the chief's chair.

'I still think "Faust" turning up in my case and Grechannik's can't be coincidence.' I pressed on regardless, 'We'll have to ask Joseph and that Gee Bee Balakirev to give us a hand in dealing with the military personnel. The Lubyankers will have more pull when it comes to approaching the military and sorting out any links with the murders. Say I'm right.'

'If you want the Gee Bees to take your case away from you, you're right . . . And don't put on your outraged look, you have to think concretely about the future. Yes, yes, I mean concretely, don't sniff. We won't go to the comrade Lubyankers. We'll go to the "Boyars".'

'Boyars' was the name we used for the Judge-Advocate General's Office: in the first place it was located in an ancient boyar's mansion on Kirov Street, formerly Butchers Way; secondly the various deputy provost-marshals and investigators were *de facto* subordinate to the military department and were far better off than us civilians in terms of pay and sundry privileges. The Judge Advocate's Office also had a strong hand in that it had a certain power over the KGB: if one of the state security personnel stepped out of line, the case would land on the Judge Advocate's desk.

'We'll make this the starting-point of the operation, code-name "Faust",' Merkulov went on.

'Is that your idea of a joke, Kostya?'

'What's wrong with it? Nice little name, like a detective novel. Anyway, apart from you and me, Turetsky and Merkulov, nobody should get to know about it, or the operation.'

He moved to the mirror, straightened himself up a bit, winked at himself and turned round singing:

'Don't be angry, deary,
Wipe away that tear!
Life is not so dreary
Sunny days are here!'

I burst out laughing:

'All right, you carry on singing and I'll give Griaznov something to do.'

'Make it quick, Sasha, it's got to be done before lunch. Give it to Klava to type and she can ask, say, Grechannik to sign it and pass it on to the Moscow CID.'

I gave Griaznov the picture and told him to ascertain the whereabouts of Sergeant Morozov and Privates Halilov and Smirnov. In under a quarter of an hour I was at Merkulov's disposal.

'Start her up, Konstantin Dmitrich?'

'Start her up, Alexander Borisich!' And when I was in the doorway, he called out after me:

'Sasha. We've got to be specially careful. We're conspirators.'

Honestly, I didn't know whether he was joking or not.

Merkulov and I sat alone in the vast hall of the Judge Advocate's Office. This audience was as much use to me as an umbrella to a fish. Sit and wait for the chief boyar to deign to notice you – all military and defence personnel came under the jurisdiction of the Judge Advocate. That was around fifteen million people by my reckoning. If it had been up to me, I'd have been off to Sheremetyevo like a shot and on a plane to Afghanistan. I'd have sorted it all out down there. But there was no going without high-level blessing, it was abroad after all.

'Kostya, how many men have we got in Afghanistan just now, do you think? I mean the "limited contingent"?'

Merkulov looked at me and burst out laughing.

'I don't recommend you to use that phrase with such obvious revulsion.'

'It's crazy, though, isn't it? What's limited about it? Every time I see that rubbish in the papers I feel they're trying to convince me that of course, these Afghans are worth sending five million against, but no, we'll just send a limited number of yours and ours to the next world . . .'

'That's just how it is, Sasha. Just how it is . . . Well, I think we've got something in the region of two hundred thousand engaged on a permanent footing. What with rotation of units, that means more than a million have been through the mincer. And not less than twenty thousand killed on our side. And a mint of money spent, not less than fifty thousand million roubles. But since the figures are, so to speak, unchecked, I would request you not to spread these things around.'

While announcing all this, Merkulov had been pensively studying the crystal chandelier below the plasterwork ceiling.

Colonel-General Artyom Grigorievich Gorny wasn't in the best of shape: gaunt yellow face, dark rings round the eyes. Bottles of water, pill-boxes and ampoules stood near him on a little table.

'How's life treating you, dear man?' Gorny rose heavily and came forward to meet us.

That was Merkulov's surprise number one: he knew the Judge Advocate General well.

'Sit down, won't you, young people, but don't smoke please, I can't stand tobacco-smoke . . . the lungs, you know.'

Merkulov introduced me and got onto the meat of the matter. Gorny paid close attention though he kept spraying his throat with an atomiser and swallowing mineral water.

'All right, Konstantin Dmitrievich,' Gorny breathed heavily, 'one good turn deserves another.'

He pressed a button and an adjutant appeared in the doorway.

'Send Bunin in.'

A minute later a tow-haired six-foot-six character entered the office, grinning from ear to ear.

'Major Ivan Alexeyevich Bunin, identical namesake of the famous Russian writer. With immediate effect, you are seconded to the Moscow Prosecutor's Office. You're just back off leave, so you haven't got too much on yet. I'm transferring you for two weeks only to start with, then we'll see. All clear, Ivan Alexeyevich?'

The famous namesake spoke in a surprisingly husky voice, either he had a cold or he'd cracked it somehow – or maybe he was born with it.

'Very good, comrade Colonel-General!'

'So let me wish you luck. You're free to go.'

So the Judge Advocate General brought the audience to an end and we went out into the corridor.

'Comrade Bunin, I'm leaving my investigator with you, allow me to bow out,' said Merkulov and actually did bow. I still had the feeling though that he hadn't taken a fancy to the complete namesake.

I waited till Merkulov had gone a decent distance before shouting after him:

'Konstantin Dmitrievich, just a minute!'

I caught up with him at the exit.

'Why's he parked this major on us? Is he going to keep an eye on me?'

'It's all right. Without him we won't get into a single military organisation. Gorny won't do the dirty on me.'

'Are you so sure of that? Just because you did him a favour?'

'That's got nothing to do with it . . .'

Bunin was making impatient beckoning signals. I'd been landed with an eager beaver as well . . .

'But?'

'I stopped a case against his brother. He'd got drunk and caused an uproar at the stadium and in the police station later on. They booted him round the head in there, and he called them fascists . . . He's a law-abiding gent by the way . . .'

'Listen, Sasha, you've got a flat, haven't you?' said Bunin, hoarsely confidential, as soon as we were alone together in his office.'

'Yes, I have. So . . .?'

'Self-contained?'

'Self-contained, one room . . .'

'Let's have the key, okay? There's this chick I've got to screw.'

I was taken aback, but said politely.

'Why ask, Ivan Alexeyevich? I'll let you have it sometime.'

'Sometime! It's now I mean! She's waiting for me now at Child's World. I'll let you have it back in two hours. You can sit here meantime.' He opened a cupboard and got out several old porno magazines. 'Here – enjoy yourself. Tomorrow's too late you see, she's going back to the unit with her husband.

While her man's seeing to things, we'll manage . . .'

He fussed round me, seeing I wasn't too pleased at his request. Actually I was thinking how I could best exploit the situation. Bunin undid his tunic, pulled up his shirt and began scratching his sunburned belly furiously.

'You know, on my last day of leave I burned myself here on the beach, God it doesn't half itch.'

'What happened about your voice?'

'Oh, that was cold beer. I'm a hard man, you know, but my throat's weak, sort of. One touch – and it's tonsillitis. Or I lose my voice. The vocal cords are weak. And I don't half love cold beer . . . Okay, can I have the key, or are you trying to get me off the subject?'

'Listen Vanya, there's no sense in me sitting here, right? I've got a job on. This is what I suggest, Vanya. I give you the keys and you phone where necessary and organise my inquiries. I'll go to special section for a permit and you go off to Child's World.'

Bunin stared at me transfixed for about ten seconds, then picked up the phone.

'Give us your particulars.'

'I need an access-permit to special forces – on the territory of the Soviet Union . . . and Afghanistan.'

He threw the receiver back down and squeaked:

'Listen, I don't really know what you're working on . . . fuckin' 'ell! Afghanistan!'

'Well go and see Gorny, he'll explain what I'm up to. And don't forget to tell him you're expected at Child's World.'

But that wasn't all yet. I knew I'd have a hard time on my own. I went for broke.

'The second permit application should be for Moscow CID Inspector Captain Griaznov, Vyacheslav Ivanovich . . .'

I do believe he was on the point of bursting into tears.

After picking up my order for the issue of a permit valid for Special Forces units, I sped off to Great Pirogovka to reach the Main Air Force Directorate before they closed for the day. There my first disappointment awaited me. A grizzled head at a window informed me that special forces had nothing to do with the airforce. I asked whose business they were in that case. The grizzled head screwed up its little eyes conspiratorially:

'Mine not to know, young man, that's a state secret. Inquire at the Ministry of Defence. I don't want to get myself involved in any unpleasantness on your account . . .'

So with nothing for my pains, I headed for Frunze Street and the Soviet Pentagon. Another let-down. The lady-sergeant gave out that special forces came under the navy first and land forces second. I got an address: the staff office for land forces was on Pirogovka next door to the Air Force Directorate I'd just bowled in from. The Navy Office was at Red Gates. I started up the car and set course back to Pirogovka. My motor was giving trouble: something to do with the ignition or the starter . . . 5.15 already. Military offices work till six.

At the land forces staff building I heard, at long last, something like articulate language. A very young-looking general whom I bumped into in the lobby coolly explained what the airforce official had called a state secret. It turned out that special force units had recently been placed directly under the State Intelligence Directorate of the USSR General Staff, that is military intelligence and its head, Marshal Nikolai Arkhipovich Agarkin. At breakneck pace I shot off towards Horoshevka. The duty lieutenant announced evenly that reception had closed and that General Agarkin did not receive visitors in any case. To see his deputy, General Rogov, it was necessary to make an appointment in advance. The lieutenant offered his services.

'I can put you on the list. You should see him in three weeks or so.'

This time the engine wouldn't start at all . . . I messed about with the throttle and loosened the spark-plugs. Sounded hollow, like a tank. I rang a mechanic I knew and tried to explain the problem as professionally as possible. He cursed like hell, what do they teach you at that university if you can't tell the throttle from the accelerator? That wasn't the end of it: I told him I would like the repair done on credit. The mechanic went quiet for some time. At length he said quietly:

'All right. I'll be over.'

He was busy on the engine two hours while I was dying of fatigue and hunger.

After my second cup of coffee and brandy I was ready to drop off then and there at the café table. I paid and staggered out to the car, pulled my keys out and sensed an unusual lightness ... well, bugger you Major Bunin! I'd completely forgotten I'd given him the key to my flat and which he was supposed to 'lob in' at the Prosecutor's office. I kept a spare key in the drawer of my desk at work, so I got behind the wheel and started up. I didn't know where to go. I laid my head on the wheel and saw Lana. She was walking along a corridor, which had no visible end, and the gold of her hair bounced to the rhythm of her walk. She walked slowly and I ran after her but couldn't overtake her whatever I did. Then she stopped and I almost ran into her. She inclined her head, concealed her face with her hands and began laughing loudly and unnaturally, then I realised she was crying, not laughing, and the little green bow had come loose, and I kept wanting to take her hands away from her face, but the green ribbon had stuck to my palms ... Finally she revealed her face and hugged my neck tightly. And I felt so great and happy that she was alive, because it wasn't Lana, it was Kim. 'I love you, Kim! I love you!' I shouted very loudly, but the locomotive whistle at Biriulevo goods station drowned my yelling ...

'Wake up, citizen, and let's have a look at your bits of paper ... Hooting your horn fit to wake all Moscow ... Good Lord, it's you, comrade investigator! I'm sorry I ... but the disturbance ...'

I gazed blearily at my former station copper.

'Are you ill at all? Or, pardon me, a bit drunk?'

'I'm okay, Vassili Ivanich, I'm not ill and I'm not drunk. Just tired. Thanks for waking me up.'

'How's life at your new place, comrade investigator?'

'The new place? It's . . . all right, I suppose.'

'You haven't forgotten the old flat? Half the old ladies have died off, there's a girl pianist in your little room now. D'you remember, frail little thing, the late Klavdia Petrovna's niece? Well, take care.'

The old patrolman went clumping off along Gogol Boulevard. I was practically sobbing with grief that Kim had been alive only as a dream. I was ready to love her for life, deeply and faithfully, if only she would come alive. God, my head was in a state again. Good job Vassili Ivanich had woken me up. Already said that, I believe. Oh yes; he'd reminded me of my old flat as well.

The door was opened by Irka, the niece of my former neighbour, recently gone to her rest.

'Shurik! I'm so glad you dropped in. Not Shurik though, I'll call you Sasha, okay? I'm in your old room on the bunk; you left a lot of stuff behind – I found some books, good ones too.'

'All right, Irka, we'll sort that out later. There's been a mess-up over my keys. Can I sleep here tonight?'

'Of course you can! Auntie Klava's room's still empty. I'll make up her bed . . . No, you can take my sofa, I'll go in there.'

'Really I don't mind at all, I can sleep in Auntie Klava's bed. My, you're all grown-up and beautiful – and smoking?'

'Yes, well, you know. Everybody at the conservatoire smokes. I just picked up the habit.'

We walked into my old room, as narrow as a ruler. There wasn't much room for Irka, half the space was taken up by a piano.

'I'll make your bed up in a minute. Let's have a cup of tea first, and we can split my calory loaf.'

'Keep the loaf, tea's fine.'

Irka dragged her down-at-heel shoes off into the kitchen. The skirt she was wearing was one I remembered from the old days.

'What d'you do for money, Irka?' I asked her when she appeared with a kettle in her hands.

'I get by,' Irka responded jauntily. 'There's my grant and

. . . I give lessons on the side. I go over to Lidochka twice a week, thanks for your concern.'

What Lidochka's this, I wondered.

'Your Konstantin Dmitrievich's very fond of her, like his own daughter. His wife's nice as well.'

I looked into Irina's feline eyes and thought what a swine I was. A year without lifting the phone just to ask how things were. True, I'd always suspected Irka was secretly in love with me. That was all over now, I thought.

'And how are things on the personal front?' I wasn't sure I'd phrased my question properly.

'Everything's fine as well,' Irka replied just as cheerfully and it was perfectly clear that there had been nothing fine in her life. Apart from music maybe.

7

Senior Investigator, Moscow Prosecutor's Office

Jurist, 2nd class
Comrade A. Turetsky

SPECIAL REPORT

I, Senior Inspector Moscow CID, Captain V. Griaznov,
in accordance with your written instructions, carried out a
number of investigative procedures with a view to estab-
lishing the whereabouts of witness Morozov, Albert
Ivanovich . . .

By law, specifically article 127 of the code of criminal procedure, an investigator is afforded wide authority with regard
to the organs of inquiry, i.e. the police, who carry out the
work of detecting criminals and vital witnesses. This fact calls
for cooperation on the part of the Prosecutor's investigator
and police. In practice this legal requirement often leads to
friction between our services. Perhaps I'm overestimating
myself, but I believe I did achieve cooperation with Department Two of Moscow CID headed by Shura Romanova. It
was a great slice of luck for me that I had the help of Captain
Vyacheslav Griaznov in my inquiries: in three years of working together we'd learned to understand one another almost
without words. Our profession is what is known as 'critical'
and investigators and operatives work in 'critical situations'.
A law degree and long service isn't enough. Something has to
come from God. Whatever that something was, Captain
Griaznov had it and to spare.

The circumstances of the case: according to information received at Directorate No 5, State Intelligence, Sergeant A. Morozov was seconded from the 40th Army, located in Afghanistan for a course at the Riazan advanced parachute training school, preparing officers for secret operations with USSR General Staff State Intelligence – 'Special Forces'.

Morozov arrived in Riazan, was enrolled on the course of instruction and resided in the school hostel. Yesterday, however, he disappeared: received a twelve-hour pass into town, but failed to return to his military unit. The Director of the Riazan School, Major-General Sliussar, A.E. took measures to apprehend Morozov, but so far without positive result, as I report.

Captain Griaznov

'No mistaking that signature.'

'So nobody can forge it,' he explained, 'I don't know how many times crooks have tried to sign my name to get their pals out of the cells – caught every time, piglets.'

'You do realise Slava, we need this Morozov like I don't know what.'

'I know, Sasha. Thinking over all the circumstances, I don't think he just went and vanished.'

I feverishly tried to imagine who could have known we were onto this Morozov: Merkulov for one, me two, Gorny three, Bunin? No, he had other concerns yesterday. Something wasn't right. Or was it coincidence?

'Here's a puzzle, Sashok, which is the most powerful service in the country? You'd say the KGB. Nuts. It's the GRU – State Intelligence. Sliussar was telling me something. He picked up a Hero's Star in Afghanistan . . .'

I found it hard to recognise Griaznov: either he'd got even paler or he'd lost weight. Whichever way it was, he looked younger. Then as I studied his sharp chin, I realised: he'd shaved his beard off. I automatically ran my fingers over my own chin. Griaznov chuckled:

'Hint taken, citizen chief. The beardlet had to be liquidated yesterday. Your fault, incidentally: a beard is a strong identifying mark, especially a ginger one. It's a moral loss though, with a beard I reminded Lucy of Visotsky, now I haven't got a dog's chance of getting my leg over my Marina Vlady. What a life . . . Sash, let's have a quick one, you've got some stuff I know.'

I poured some diluted spirit out of a confiscated ten-litre can. This can was part of the evidence in the vice-den case and had become an object of particular interest to the investigating section. Still, it was my responsibility in due course to get the ten litres to court. I had imposed a strict condition on anyone wishing to partake of the life-giving spring: one tot of spirit poured out, one tot of water poured back. Over a period of time the concentration of the liquid had reached the usual 40 degrees. We drank off a tot apiece without the usual bite to go with it. Griaznov proceeded:

'Anyway. From what this Sliussar was saying, the special forces can compare with the GB. They've got more tanks than the French and German armies put together.'

'And how many units are stationed in Moscow, do you know?'

'Not exactly, but I think six battalions – not less.'

Griaznov winked at me surprisingly and without asking permission, poured himself another measure out of the can.

'And now, Sashok. Lend me your ears. Here are facts worth pondering . . .'

Here, Griaznov pulled a book out of his 'diplomat' briefcase. I leapt off my chair and tore it from his hands.

'Come on, spill it, Slava!' I roared.

I already knew it was *the* book, rather tattered, that odd violet colour, thick. Some inner vision showed me Kim's murderer going up the stairs with this book under his arm.

Twirling his empty glass, the senior CID Inspector eventually spoke:

'I roped in my laddies, agents I mean, to help in finding the photofit villains. Up till now it's all been just hope and pray, useless. I've got one lad, Stasik, young man of culture, product of the Stroganov Institute. He doesn't want anything to do with riff-raff and so he's got himself the job of covering more select spots. On Sunday, Stasik was going round the city bars: he had breakfast in the National, lunch in the Actor and later on he was in the Zhiguli. He wasn't wasting his time, he kept asking the waiters, under-managers and commissionaires about any visitors resembling our photofits. Well, in the Zhiguli one waiter admitted seeing the 'phiz' of one of them, the hefty one. This 'phiz' was sitting with the poet-songwriter Derbenyev and Karasiev, the artist on Smena. They were sitting all neat and clean as if they'd just come from the bath-house, and putting away vodka and beer. Stasik, like a good professional, twigged what was going on and went to Karasiev's place on Taganka. He's got a house half in ruins over there . . .'

I didn't interrupt Griaznov by asking questions, I just twirled my pen and leafed through the Dumas novel *The Vicomte de Bragellone*. I automatically read and re-read the epigraph to the first chapter: 'In which it becomes evident that if one cannot do business with one, nothing prevents one doing business with another.' On the inside cover was a card-holder with an inked number in longhand, 12773/81. A library book. Title page torn out. I opened it at page seventeen where they usually put the library stamp. No stamp of any kind . . .

'Well, he's a well-known boozer, but Karasiev did remember something: yes, he'd met an athlete chap at the Sanduni baths; he said his name was 'Dima' and had a handshake like a pair of pliers. One thing led to another and all pals together they pressed on to the Zhiguli. They're known there, queuing's no problem. They sat for three hours or so and polished off a dozen Czech beers. They arranged to meet again in Sanduni next day. All Monday I mounted guard for that Dima in the bath-house, I boiled the poet and the artist alive, but he didn't turn up. I pumped Derbenyev and Karasiev as best I could, and I did get something. The poet remembered Dima had left a book in the bath-house and was all broken up because of it. Derbenyev thought he was a bit, you know, touched. He used to warn everybody that a new age was coming and only supermen would live on the earth. Or something like that. Later on, after he'd got a skinful, he said he was off to Afghanistan in two days time.'

'Afghanistan!'

'Afghanistan. So it looks as if it's all one gang, the special forces boys are throwing their weight about. Incidentally, I found the Vicomte in the bath-manager's floor-cloth locker. Go on, look through it. I've had a sniff all round it as well.'

'Hang on, Slava,' an idea was dawning, 'we should ask that artist, Karasiev, to draw a picture of Dima from memory.'

'If you're going to interrupt me with advice we'll never get to the end of this. It's not from memory, anyway – Karasiev has a habit of drawing, a little portrait of every new person he meets.'

Griaznov again dived into his 'diplomat' and drew out a squared sheet of paper: round head, hair just starting to grow all over, scar on the chin, eyes wide apart . . .

'We'll have to show this to Korabelnikova double-quick.'

'Already have. Positive identification.'

I felt my hands tremble and linked my fingers to keep steady.

'So there I was leafing through the book . . . You'd best have another, Sashok, you've gone all to pieces I can see . . . and in between the pages I found a piece of carbon paper. It was old, it didn't come off on your fingers. If you hold it up to the light you can make something out – figures, a few letters. I shot round to the labs and stood over them while they messed about with their apparatus. They've just got hold of it from West Germany, the latest thing . . .'

'Slava, to hell with the latest scientific advances, get on with it.'

'Conclusion: the carbon had been used for electric and gas bills. The letters read: Flat 3, Block 27 Dibenko Street. All right, put your eyes back in, Block 27 Dibenko Street in Moscow is a research institute, there's no flats or tenants there. Our Shura dug up a consultant with a list of every street in the country named after a civil war hero. We've sent out around thirty requests to the town councils where there's a

Dibenko Street. So now I'm just sitting and hoping.'

'Where's that list?'

Griaznov looked in his case for a third time. Twenty-eight towns: Leningrad, Krasnodar, Oriol, Karaganda . . .

'You realise it's impossible? You can't just sit and hope.'

'Have you heard about the lift murders?'

'What lifts?'

'Ordinary lifts. Some guy lies in wait for women on their own late at night by the lift, rapes them. He's killed ten. Staraya Square orders find him and no buts. Our whole department's on the job. You and your "impossible".'

I couldn't say anything to that. For Moscow CID, my case had low priority. I was lucky I still had Griaznov.

'Last information, Sashok: Moscow libraries don't have a *Vicomte de Bragellone* no 12773/81 missing.'

Moscow . . . And we've only got 400,000 libraries in the country.

'So there it is. We halt upon this spot, citizen chief. By the way, bear in mind that "Dima" isn't necessarily short for Dmitri. There's other names, such as Demyan, Dementy, Vadim, Nicodemus . . . well, hardly that of course . . .' Griaznov said sadly and began packing away his trophies.

'Hold it a minute, Slava. Just give us that list again. I can't very well fly to these twenty-eight towns but I can phone. You've got a spare copy haven't you?'

Griaznov stared in amazement as I tore the sheet into four equal parts, each containing seven towns.

'How much time have you got, an hour? Here, you can manage these. When did he say he was off to Afghanistan? Two days time? That means today. Maybe we can do it, eh? You go to Merkulov's office, he's got two phones . . .'

In the corridor, elbows on the window-sill stood Lana. I hadn't seen her for ages. The times we'd met before had begun to seem unreal to me, existing only in my imagination. I needed assurance that it had all really happened.

'Lana . . .'

She didn't even turn round.

'Wait for me, I won't be long.'

I guessed she said 'all right', I didn't hear; she nodded towards the window, as if this was all for the benefit of some passer-by and not me at all.

'She's a looker, the bitch, say what you like,' Griaznov hissed in my ear – 'a bit too cool, though.'

Cool . . . No, proud rather.

Merkulov listened to my brief resumé of Griaznov's report.

'All right.' He reached for the list. 'We'll split this, I'll ask Parkhomenko.'

'He'll spend his time telephoning you! I wanted to ask Grechannik, at least our cases are parallel.'

'Not Grechannik. Here's the phone, Viacheslav, get dialling. Leonid Vasilievich will be pleased to tear himself away from the paperwork and get in on the operations,' grinned Merkulov.

I knew why Merkulov had chosen Parkhomenko. He didn't want this to leak out. Parkhomenko was a pedantic, by-the-book man. Grechannik's office was an open one with loads of people passing through. Wait . . . Grechannik had given me my flat key after Bunin had left it with him. Bunin hadn't struck me as tight-lipped, he could easily have blurted out in conversation that Turetsky was looking for a Sergeant Morozov of special forces. So what? Grechannik send someone to Morozov? Why would he do that?

I kissed her cool lips and my head began to spin. Lana reached out for the lock and turned the key. Everything was back in place. We were in my office where it had all started – the party, Kim. 'Turetsky, I need to tell you something.'

Lana moved away, clearly sensing I was depressed.

'Will you come to me tonight? Only I don't know when I'll get away.'

For this woman I'd have sent the lot to hell. But not Kim's case.

'I'll wait. You can give me the flat key, I'll wait for you there.'

'I'm not sure it's very tidy in there . . .'

86

'Never mind that.'

I was in luck. Three towns out of the seven could be deleted straightaway. Dibenko Street had little private houses, no Block 27. In the fourth town, the street didn't have gas laid on so there couldn't have been a gas bill. I had switched the attack to Karaganda where the head of the identity card section was a total nitwit and refused to give information over the phone, when Parkhomenko came in. I told the passport-man where he could go. The deputy city prosecutor frowned as he placed a piece of paper covered in small neat handwriting on the desk and silently withdrew.

. . . Vikulov, Igor Trofimovich, born 1941, resided in Krasnodar: Dibenko Street, Block 27, Flat 3 from 1958 to 1984. Gas is laid on in the Block, gas and electricity bills are written out using carbon. At the end of last year moved to Moscow. Works at Ministry of Agricultural Machinery. Lives at address . . .

I dashed in to Parkhomenko:

'Thank you, Leonid Vasilievich!'

Parkhomenko was jotting something down with the phone jammed against his shoulder:

'Thank you, comrade, the Block doesn't have gas laid on . . . There you are Alexander Borisovich, so far the only positive result. And, so to speak, the higher the probability that it's your man . . .'

If the deputy prosecutor of Moscow had been content to remain an operative, he would have been invaluable. In the post he actually occupied he had reached his level of incompetence – a phenomenon so widespread that no one evinced any surprise that it should be so. He would sit there till his pension, hanging on to his status for dear life, contributing nothing.

The porter obligingly gave me the number of I.T. Vikulov's office and I whizzed up to the 17th floor in the speed-lift. The chief specialist turned out to be a fat jolly chap, not at all put out by my credentials; he admitted at once that he had 'nicked' the Vicomte the previous year from the sanatorium library in Kislovodsk. How the carbon had got between the pages of the book he did not know but he did use it for electricity and gas bills.

'And just where did you find him?'

'Who?'

'The Vicomte, of course!'

'That's just what I wanted to ask you Igor Trofimovich, how this book could have reached a certain Dima?'

Vikulov knew nobody called Dima and couldn't remember at all where the book had got to. Since he wasn't being charged with theft, he wasn't worried over losing it. Looking at Karasiev's sketch, Vikulov was delighted:

'Why that's Vovchik!'

Mother of mine, complications by the hour . . .

'Now I know what happened, comrade investigator! Or should I say citizen investigator?'

'Say what you like best. How do we find this . . . Vovchik?'

Vikulov rubbed his nose with his palm till it looked like a beetroot.

'The matter is a little delicate, but I gather you've got good reason to look for him. Have you got a car? Let's go. The VTO theatre in the side-street near Yermolov Street. You know it? Never mind, I'll show you. As Visotsky used to sing: 'Where's your black pistol? On Bolshoi Karetni. That's where it is.'

It took only six minutes of southern fast-talk to fill me in on the whole Vovchik-Dima story.

A week previously the object of his affections, who was an actress at the VTO theatre, a gay sociable sort of woman unfortunately (or fortunately) married, had landed at Vikulov's flat along with her girl-friend Lala, a fellow-actress. Lala had brought along an athletically-built young man – Vovchik. They'd sat about talking and drinking mulled wine made by Vovchik, and listening to Arkadi Severni and Julio Yglesias. The girl-friend and Vovchik left about eleven and in the morning it was discovered that something was missing: an antique-style silver cigarette-lighter and cigarette case, which he'd put on the writing-desk where, as he recalled, the edition of Dumas had been lying. The object of Vikulov's affection taxed Lala with this; what's the idea of bringing crooks into decent houses to rob friends of mine. Lala asked how she dare talk like that about her own acquaintances. They had a slanging-match.

'You're sure . . .' I attempted to break in.

'Sure, yes I'm sure, all the little things were lying together . . .'

'No, no, Igor Trofimovich, I mean, are you sure he was called Vovchik?'

'I'm sure about that as well. He had a bit of a bee in his bonnet and kept trying to prove that all the evils of mankind stemmed from the world population explosion, the weak had to be eliminated and only the fit should be left. He obviously counted himself in the second category. I told him the world had heard that theory fifty years ago. And not much good came out of that . . .'

'Well, I never knew policemen could be so handsome,' Lala reached out a limp hand.

'I'm an investigator, actually.'

'Oh, I see. Of course that changes everything,' Lala smiled ironically.

I wasn't in the mood for humour. The actress listened to me intently and shook her head:

'I swear to God I only met him that day. It was last Saturday. After rehearsal I dropped into a cafe . . . the cafe? The one in Hermitage Gardens, the open-air one. The two of them were sat there . . .'

'Two?!'

'I'm short-sighted you know, I don't feel like admitting that to good-looking young men. I prefer not to wear glasses. Vovchik had a youngster with him and I made eyes at him, you know, just out of habit. He didn't pay any attention to me though. There was something odd about him, you know. Could have been one of those, I'm not sure of that, naturally. Then the young one disappeared somewhere, just

89

vanished and Vovchik sat down at my table, brazen as you please . . .'

I showed Lala the identikit photo of the second murderer.

'You know, there is a resemblance. The hedgehog haircut, like Vovchik's, incidentally. I wouldn't stick my neck out though. The drawing's a bit fuzzy . . . still I'd know him if I saw him. At least I think I would . . . What was he wearing? Both of them had black leather jackets, that I do remember . . .'

The day after Kim's murder, the two villains sit opposite the Moscow CID building and drink coffee. These killers just had no sense of self-protection: instead of holding up somewhere and trembling with fear in case they were discovered, they stroll around Moscow, pick up women, spread Hitlerite ideas.

Lala could add nothing more to Vikulov's story. She hadn't asked Vovchik's second name. Hadn't met him again. No, he hadn't mentioned where he lived or what he did for a living. He'd escorted her home after the party. He didn't even try to kiss her. I put question after leading question but I got no answer worthy of the name.

Except right at the end:

'. . . Oh, yes! He said: "You know Lalechka, I'm like Cinderella – at exactly midnight I have to be at the gates!" I asked him: "Have you far to go, Volodya?" What's the matter, Alexander Borisovich?'

What an idiot! Of course, of course – Vovchik – Volodya – Vladimir – Dima!

'No, no, it's all right, go on. You asked: "Have you far to go, Volodya?" . . .'

'Yes, I said: "Have you far to go, Volodya? It's half past eleven already you know." "No," he says, "fifteen minutes on the bus. There's one due in five minutes." That was it!'

'Where do you live, Lala?'

'Baku Commissars Street, next to the South-West metro station.'

'Are you on the phone?'

I dialled 02, gave the day's password for information – 'Wings of the Soviets' – and got a reply inside thirty seconds: at 23.36 on Saturdays, bus no. 258 left South-West metro station; route from there to Advanced Officer Courses, USSR Ministry of Defence. Journey time, fifteen minutes.

I wanted very much to believe these people, the fat man Vikulov and the beautiful actress Lala Istomina, and I did believe them. I was certain they wouldn't run away as soon as the door closed behind me and ring up this Dima – Volodya. Still I didn't have the right to tempt providence, so I made a suggestion:

'I'm sorry, but you'll have to come with me to this course establishment.'

The chief specialist of the Ministry of Agricultural Machinery, was, I believe, simply glad of an adventure. The actress shrugged her shoulders and asked:

'It looks like this Cinderella stole something more important than a lighter?'

Things turned out differently from what I had expected. I thought I'd turn up at this military establishment, the stamping-ground of Colonel-General Dragunsky and sort of quietly, like an experienced operative, make a few inquiries about this Dima-Volodya. After I'd called in Romanova's boys, softly, softly, no yelling, no resistance I'd arrest the bastard on suspicion of the murder of Kim Lagina, he'd sing all right, I'd make it so rough for him he'd break in ten seconds – without stool-pigeons or cell interrogations; the devils in hell would be sick to look at him.

At the camp I was met, not by General Dragunsky, but by the duty sergeant. He called the duty captain. He installed my companions in the Lenin room with newspapers to read and took me to the unit duty officers HQ. The colonel removed his cap, scratched his bald-patch and began riffling through some thick journals: no computers were in sight. All he did was check my story, frowning and removing his glasses as he did so:

'Vladimir, you say? This one here in the picture? Ye-e-s, you've given us a bit of a job. We get hundreds of officers come here. If you had his second name now or his unit, that would be different.'

'If I knew his unit and second name, I would hardly have come to you, comrade Colonel.'

He nodded understandingly and made some phone calls to the hostel commandants.

They entered the HQ one after another. They examined the caricaturist's picture. At length one of them, a rather dandified subaltern, spoke:

'Comrade Colonel, but this is Lieutenant Ivonin, or Senior Lieutenant as he is now, Hero of the Soviet Union. He lived with me in barrack 15; he came to Moscow from Afghanistan to have the star conferred on him in the Kremlin. You've heard of the seven heroes, of course. Andrey Andreyevich Gromyko awarded them all stars for actions in Afghanistan. They were all with us, except for Dubov, naturally. He was awarded his posthumously . . .'

My heart stood still:

'Where is he now? This Senior Lieutenant Ivonin – is he in hostel or has he gone to town?'

'Why should he be in the hostel? Or the centre? He went back to Afghanistan this morning.'

I opened the door and decided I was in the wrong flat; it was a bit too clean and tidied up differently somehow. My Mam sometimes gives the place a clean: scrubs the pans and washes out the fridge. This wasn't Mam's handiwork obviously, she wasn't too good at making a place tidy and my stepfather usually had to gather up skirts and bras around their flat and never complained because he knew Mam had no conception of 'everything in its proper place'. I took after Mam in every way: I used to leave my shoes in the bathroom, my ties draped on a hook on the kitchen door and my returned laundry on my writing desk. So, all this had found its proper place as if by magic and under the kitchen sink lay a well-washed out rag (my old running shorts).

And I could hear the shower. Good heavens above, surely Lana hadn't done all this?! I took a cautious glance into the bathroom – behind the transparent plastic curtain, in the cone of water, stood Lana in a towel-turban with her arms raised as in an eastern prayer. I stood stock-still at the astonishing beauty of her naked body. She wasn't in the least embarrassed and said in an everyday tone:

'Why did you say the place was untidy? I think it's tidier than it ever was . . .'

Then I understood the secret of the magical transformation of my living quarters: it was Bunin's service-wife who'd done the blitz.

'Why are you laughing?'

'Oh, just . . . glad you're here,' I lied. I mean I was glad about that, but I was laughing about something else. I was imagining Bunin's fat bird, who was so efficient and let herself go on the housework as well.

Lana was still in her attitude of prayer, eyes closed, tanned to a dark bronze, at once powerful and graceful. I turned off the shower-tap and without opening her eyes she placed her hands on my shoulders . . .

8

I got to work disgracefully early – even the duty policeman was astonished. I'd wasted my time too, Merkulov having got me up with his early call, had not yet arrived. I didn't go up to my office; I decided to wait for my chief under the lime tree in the street and have a smoke in the fresh air. Just then a fabulous limousine, the sort only the very top men use, ministers – some – and Politburo members – rolled up to the entrance and Merkulov clambered awkwardly out. The dark glass of the rear window crept down and the square head of Judge Advocate General Gorny emerged:

'Good morning, colleague. You must excuse me for detaining Konstantin Dmitrievich. Terrible snarl-up at Paveletsky Station. Even we couldn't get through.'

'It's quite all right, Artyom Grigoryevich,' I said condescendingly at which he waved his hand and the black monster pulled away from our residence.

'I had to waste an evening at Gorny's dacha last night', said Merkulov without waiting for my leading question. 'He made use of me, pouring his heart out over some intrigue against him. That works both ways, I got him to sanction the arrest of this . . . shitty hero . . . Ivonin. Now it's your turn: go over to Horoshevka straightaway to the Main Intelligence Directorate, General Rogov. Bunin will meet you at the entrance at nine.

I squeezed my chariot in by the newspaper kiosk next to the 'No Parking' sign. I slapped a Traffic Police sticker on the windscreen and put a striped policeman's truncheon on the back window ledge – preventive measures against traffic-wardens. To avoid being swept up in the crowd, I stood about ten yards away from the door of a modern glass and concrete building, an 'aquarium' as the jargon of military reconnaissance has it. There was no sign of Bunin as yet, so I fell to studying the crowds surging in from all sides. Calm, well-fed, well-shaven faces. Self-satisfied even. Senior officers and junior generals for the most part. Now and again there were one or two pretty girls and expensive-looking women, secretaries and translators no doubt.

'Sorry, old man,' croaked Bunin from behind me, 'over at our place in Ochakovo it's pure hell. There's engineering works on the line, they've got the sleepers up. And at home we're all over the place. Son's got flu, father-in-law's on a bender and they've let my mother-in-law out of Stolbovaya mental clinic without warning us.'

Bunin smiled and I decided he was joking, telling me some funny story in his own way. But his smile was sort of pitiful, totally unsuited to his large round face and his whole bulky figure. I also noticed his uniform was crumpled, collar grimy, boots scuffed. Clearly he wasn't running away from the good life when he chased other women. He swapped his vast briefcase to his other arm and we shook hands.

We weren't held up for long in the State Intelligence reception area, my pass had been ordered. The duty captain threw me a steely glance and returned my ID somewhat grudgingly: he was really keen to capture just one spy at the approaches to GRU.

Through the door with the name-plate 'Rogov A.S.' I glimpsed the colonel-general's broad back standing in front of an open safe. He placed a thick folder in the depths of the massive steel box, spun the combination disc and turned towards us. He was a powerful man, completely bald, and had a black patch over his left eye (could he have lost it fighting the dushman?). I already knew that Rogov, who was one of the deputies to Marshal Agarkin, the head of State Intelligence, had charge of Directorate 5 which included special forces.

'I hear you're thinking of a trip to Afghanistan, boys, not afraid are you? Our lads out there aren't playing with the

Muslimkins you know, those barmy asiatics, dushman, crazy Mojahedin shoot very precisely I may say, every one a sniper – filthy bastards.'

Bunin was standing to attention: he was in the presence of top brass after all. I was thinking to myself that it wasn't only Afghans who could use guns and knives; aloud I said, just as if it was one of my office workmates:

'In times like this, comrade Rogov, one doesn't know where it's safest, Afghanistan or dear old Moscow. You've heard about the lift murders, perhaps?'

'No, no,' Rogov livened up at this, even laughing a bit in his kindly rather unsteady way. 'It's like living in a barracks here, we don't even know what's going on round the corner – in the Botkin Hospital or the Hippodrome.'

We sat down and the conversation started. Not a bad conversation at all. Normal, male talk. Every so often Rogov would narrow his one eye and say frankly that Afghanistan was a boiling cauldron with the lid tight shut. Whichever way you tried, the result would be the same, steam would escape. Marshal Agarkin had thought up the idea of shock party detachments and had concentrated all the special forces units scattered among the various arms: air force, navy, land forces, and formed out of them a special tactical complex directly linked to the Central Committee and the Politburo with command centered in State Intelligence. The Seventeenth special task-force regiment was operating in Afghanistan at the moment. Their job was to wipe out the counter-revolutionary insurgent movement. This way the lads were being given the chance to prove themselves in the field. This regiment was made up of professional sportsmen – even the commander, Major-General Seri, was an honoured master of sport. And now I'm going to order the special section to arrange a trip for you according to all the rules of military science: permits, enclosures, travel-warrants, etc.'

Travel warrants and enclosures were handy things to have, naturally, but after all we'd come on a different matter entirely. We needed Rogov's sanction for the arrest of Senior Lieutenant Ivonin. I already possessed the authorisation of

Deputy City Prosecutor Parkhomenko and from Judge Advocate General Gorny, but they had no validity in Afghan territory. Only the top executive ranks could sanction the arrest of special forces personnel. And Rogov had just explained in words of one syllable why they had been given that authority.

'Comrade Colonel-General,' I said 'I hope Artyom Grigoryevich put you in the picture as regards the main point of our business? We are going to Afghanistan in order to arrest a dangerous criminal, a murderer. We need your sanction to apprehend Senior Lieutenant Vladimir Ivonin.'

'Ivonin?!' Rogov's cheek twitched like a stroke-victim. He stared at me with his eye and in his look there was something I hadn't been able to catch earlier. 'Sanction? Sanction, did you say, prosecutor's arsehole? Who do you want to arrest, pipsqueak? A Hero of the Soviet Union? Our pride and joy? You want to put a crack Party soldier in jail?'

What a transformation! I had guessed that Rogov up to now had been making himself out to be the kindly countryman, but this . . . Actually these military types don't really scare me, I just can't stand martinets ever since I did my two years national service in Ulan-Ude.

'They're asking me, your sanction please!' Rogov was not letting up.

Bunin was wiping rivulets of sweat from his brow with his grubby handkerchief. As for me, I responded as coolly as I could:

'You can talk like that when you're having dinner with your brother-in-law, General. Here please do try to be a little more correct. I do have an official position, I may say.'

'What do you mean, brother-in-law . . .' began Rogov, but at that moment one of the phones began winking red.

Rogov picked up the receiver and I saw how he stiffened under his uniform, as if coming to attention. He said virtually nothing except 'Yes' and 'Very well, sir' but for some reason I gained the distinct impression that this phone call had a direct bearing on our visit. The general carefully replaced the receiver, and the simple military man of peasant stock was once more before us. Now, however, I knew that kindly unsteady laugh for what it was. He even looked rather sheepishly at us and made an effort at conciliation.

'Sorry about all that, lost my wool for a minute. I can't stick it when they arrest a serviceman, ever since the war.'

Rogov lifted the receiver again and asked some Colonel Nezhni to make out documents for our visit to the 40th Army, 17th Special Forces Division, commanded by Major-General Seri. He then drew out of his desk a warrant to arrest.

Merkulov used his long fingers to line up the edges of the folders which lay neatly piled on his desk. While fiddling with this, he rapidly shifted his cigarette from one end of his mouth to the other. I'd never seen mannerisms like this from him before.

'. . . So the plane leaves late tonight, lands in Tashkent at two and we're in Kabul early in the morning,' I concluded my report buoyantly, as if I was set for a holiday cruise on the 'Odessa' instead of a flight into a war-zone. 'Don't worry yourself, Kostya, we've got three on our side anyway. Griaznov's worth a regiment on his own.'

Merkulov stopped tormenting the folders, stubbed out his cigarette and spoke, seemingly without reference to my report:

'There's a smell of naked violence in the air. The time of old Gensecs dying off is over, and frankly I don't know if that's a good thing or not. There might be more high-grade sausage or fashionable shoes in the shops. That's always a good thing. Everybody realises that. That's simple. And obvious. As for the increasing militarisation of our society, that's not obvious to most people. Shock Party Detachments – they would be!' Merkulov snapped his plastic ballpoint and flung the pieces into the waste-bin. 'That's not in line with a few nods towards democracy in our society – calls for openness and publication of investigative journalism in the press. There's something fishy . . .'

'Kostya, I've brought you the Kim dossier, lock it up in

your safe. I'll take the necessary copies to Afghanistan.' I waggled the tightly-stuffed briefcase.

Merkulov thrust the folders into the fireproof safe, came over to me and even attempted to kiss me on the ear.

'Well, come back soon . . . and don't go looking for trouble. You've got your whole life ahead of you . . .'

9

The embarkation hubbub ceased at once as the indicator displayed: 'Fasten seat-belts. No smoking.' The faces of the passengers took on an expression of docility, even drowsiness. It was as if all their anxieties, failures and achievements were left behind. The aircraft began to gather speed for its long hours of flight. I glanced at Griaznov – his pale, freckled face was tense.

'Don't you get scared? I mean, just flying through the air.'

'There are moments,' I admitted.

'Well, I just start talking tripe. You'll see. I'll be shaking with fear for the whole seven hours.'

'You're not putting it on are you?' I had my doubts, knowing Slava's desperate courage on a number of risky operations.

'No, no, honestly, I'm scared. Remember Zhenka Zhukov? You couldn't imagine a braver man, but if he had to fly he used to shake in his shoes!'

He lay back in his seat, half-closed his eyes and then sat up again:

'By the way, how did I forget? – Zhenka's actually in Kabul, he's building mosques. He came back on holiday a while back, telling the tale about all the horrors going on . . .'

There was no forgetting Evgeni Zhukov! His daring and resourcefulness were legends in Moscow CID. Prince Merkulov was still distraught over what happened to Evgeni Zhukov, a story which had gone down in the private chronicles of the CID as the saga of Police Captain Zhukov.

Two years since, towards the end of a spring day, two

respectable Moscow citizens had emerged from the Yar restaurant and were crossing the street when they saw some rough types swearing and dragging a struggling girl into an underpass. Furious at the indifference of the public, the respectable citizens rushed to her aid and achieved overwhelming success: one of them twisted the arm of the ruffian wearing the hat, and the other began walloping the hooligan in the raincoat with his 'diplomat' briefcase. The hooligan, however, in some unexplained way, managed to get possession of the briefcase. The worthy citizen attempted to regain possession of his property, with the result that the handle came off. In even more mysterious fashion, the whole group found themselves at the police station.

The investigation of this incident, begun and ended on that same spring evening by the police personnel of Moscow's Leningradsky district, amended in some particulars the version put forward by one of the respectable citizens, by name Zhukov. It was established that on the 24th of May 1984 at 8.30 in the evening, two civilian police auxiliaries were assisting old bolshevik and honoured pensioner Paulina Vasilievna Voronina down the underpass on Leningrad Prospect. At that point, two distinctly unsober citizens crossing the street, in gross violation of traffic regulations, from the direction of the Sovietskaya Hotel (the detained men persisted in calling it the 'Yar', though since the New Economic Politics times the name had not corresponded to reality) hurled themselves on the auxiliaries. One of them, who later turned out to be a citizen Bakin with no visible means of support, twisted the arm of bolshevik Voronina behind her back, but on receiving a kick from the pointed toe of a female shoe in the groin region, fell down on the central reservation of the road. The second, Evgeni Zhukov himself, Senior Investigator of the Moscow CID, began hitting his friend Bakin lying on the road with a briefcase of the 'diplomat' type, brown in colour. The auxiliaries took the briefcase away from him just before the arrival of the police. Citizen Zhukov, however, breaking free of the police, ran over to a by-stander, knocked his hat off and began to pull a black holdall belonging to the said by-stander from his grasp, as a consequence inflicting damage to the personal property of Professor Y.A. Sidorov of the Moscow Food Institute, to wit by ripping off the handles of his holdall. The briefcase belonging to citizen Zhukov, containing the dossier on a classified investigation was lost . . .

The result of this distressing affair was the dismissal of Captain Zhukov from the police force. For two months he looked for work, beginning his day by weight-lifting and running round the Young Pioneers Stadium, so as to keep himself fit. His work-seeking efforts proved fruitless. Zhukov's reference preceded him everywhere: 'Unsuitable for work in a responsible capacity owing to his tendency towards alcohol.' He looked like settling in as legal consultant to the mysteriously-named 'South Western Region Restaurant Car Office' but resigned after two months, being unable to stomach the open thieving engaged in by everyone in the office, without exception, from dish-washer to manager. Still, every morning he would lift his weights and run. On his birthday, September 1st, he bought a cake and a bottle of vodka with his last tenner. When he got home he found his wife had left him. He drank the bottle on his own and didn't do any running next day. Instead he dug out his long-forgotten technical college certificate and got himself onto some construction project out in the sticks somewhere . . .

That Zhukov was building a mosque in Kabul was news to me.

'What was he on about, Slava?' I asked for the sake of it, without any particular interest, but as I did I thought: 'Pity I didn't know Zhukov was in Afghanistan. Should have got his address.'

'He got himself into some scrape. Our lads were tangling with the Afghans and there were knives out, Zhenka got into trouble over that . . .'

'The Mojahedin?'

'What Mojahedin? No, the Afghan government troops. Our specials had been drinking some filthy stuff or injecting themselves with it . . .'

Griaznov stopped and I saw his sky-blue eyes cloud over.

He fished out a cigarette and took a long time striking his match before croaking at length:

'Strike me dead if I lie . . . bugger me . . . they called it . . . "Faust".'

'Slava,' I said as quietly as I could, but as I could see everybody looking round at me, I realised I was shouting. 'Repeat what you just said!'

'Cross my heart, Zhenka said they were using, or had prescribed even, this "Faust" an elixir of courage or something . . . No, no, I'm not making it up, honestly! Or am I just impressionable, Sashok?'

'What d'you mean, Slava?'

'Oh just . . . all these Fausts everywhere . . . Maybe I dreamed it.'

'Slava, Slava!' I shook Griaznov by the sleeve of his natty new civilian suit. 'Look, remember and get it right! This turns the whole case upside down!'

'If nobody's fighting why all the noise?'

Bunin's shape loomed before us with a bottle of cognac in his hand.

'I could hardly wait to get the straps off. Got glasses?'

Griaznov and I put down a double each from our plastic cups. The fragrant liquid pleasantly scorched our innards as I pressed as hard as I could on Griaznov's sandal: he musn't mention this 'Faust' with Bunin around.

Griaznov bent his ear to my muttering and from time to time cursed himself in remorse.

'What a stupid swine I am, drunk my brain away . . . what a sodding cop . . . Yes, I should have jumped when I heard your Faust mentioned. And what did I do? Sashok, first thing is to find Zhenka in Kabul . . . You know Zhenka lived there for seven years when he was a boy: his father was first secretary at the embassy there. Farsi is his second language. That's why he was in charge of training the Afghan police when they were with us at the Police Academy on Leningrad Prospect. The MVD's agent set-up in Afghanistan is far more reliable than the KGB's. That's down to Paputin, the deputy Interior Minister, may he rest in peace.'

Bunin regarded us jealously from the opposite end of the row of seats.

As I dozed, I kept trying over and over again to restore a fuller version of the burned letter from Sergeant Morozov:

'. . . But Lekha wasn't killed by a dushman bullet, but by his own hands. He told me he had sent you documents about the . . . in Afghanistan . . .'

Then came the words 'oldies', 'ions', 'so that . . . fear'. Maybe 'to our soldiers so that we (they) would have no fear. But Lekha didn't want this (was against) and he quarrelled with our commander. Lekha said that he had a good friend in Moscow studying law and she would tell the story where she ought. Dear Kim! It's all lies about Lekha shielding the commander with his chest from the bullets. They fought with knives and the commander stabbed your friend. They're giving us injections. They're called . . .'

Why of course! Elixir Faust! Semyon Semyonovich thought that Alexey Faust didn't mean anything. It was just that Morozov didn't know how to spell 'elixir', we had just the letters 'lex'. 'They're called elixir Faust, that is they're committing a state crime . . .'

The aircraft had crossed the mountain ranges and begun its descent into the rocky bowl that was the Valley of Kabul. Only now did I begin to sense an alien land – I glimpsed it as soon as the aircraft pierced the cloud strata and nosed out into sun-drenched space. Everything was yellow: dirty-yellow river, yellow rocks, yellow air, and everywhere naked earth, scoured bald and yellow-black with signs of recent conflagrations.

'Where on earth have we come to, eh, Sash?' Griaznov was staring out of the port, bewildered.

The plane was circling over the aerodrome once, twice, three times . . . Now everybody was staring downwards where a fuel tanker was a torch of yellow flame in the middle of the landing-field, surrounded by half-naked people busy with sand-spraying equipment.

'That's the Afghans rolling a burning barrel down from the mountains again . . .'

'It's our own side, the government troops, I'll bet!'

This conversation going on behind us was between two soldiers returning from leave – a swarthy corporal with eastern eyes and a blond sergeant-major.

'Are you off your head Kunaz? Look out Seri doesn't show you who's on our side if you don't keep your mouth shut.'

These were specials then: General Rogov had told us that Seri commanded 17th Regiment, Special Forces.

Eventually the aircraft put down and we went out into the scorching air. Underfoot, the earth was cracked and fissured, the sky overhead wasn't blue, though the sun was blazing and there wasn't a cloud in the sky. It was brassy-yellow and a thin film of brass-dust lay on everything: soldiers' faces, on the fuselage of the helicopter in which we had to fly to the 40th Army.

'Ever fired an automatic weapon?'

A darkly-tanned major, hair bleached by the sun, had come to meet us at the airport and knew the situation.

'Of course,' I replied quickly 'about seven years ago. Why?'

'All right,' sighed the major. 'Comrade Bunin gets the AKS. You hang onto the grenade.'

I tried to stuff the grenade into my jeans pocket but it wouldn't go. Instead I put it in the briefcase with the Kim dossier.

'Be careful with that. It's in case of emergency. Hold it by the pin and chuck it right in the middle of them.'

He glanced at my face and waved his arm inviting me to look around: craters, signs of firing . . .

As soon as we landed, Griaznov had whispered quickly in my ear:

'I'll drop out, Sashok, on the quiet, don't make waves, I'll find you . . .'

This he accordingly did and I never even noticed when it happened. Bunin was in charge of the parade, talking now with one officer, now with another. He didn't notice Griaznov's disappearance either and when he did it was too late to make waves: we were standing in the Judge Advocate's Office.

The Judge Advocate of the 40th Army, boyishly thin, laid before me the classified dossier on Vladimir Ivonin.

In Soviet criminal procedure, there are two sorts of inquiry: collecting evidence, and the basic type of inquiry, namely preliminary investigation. The former precedes the latter in complex cases and in minor crimes is carried out entirely by the police. The personal particulars of those responsible for such work in the military units in Afghanistan were kept in the 40th army Judge Advocate's safe. Among them was the dossier of the legal representative of the 17th Independent Regiment, Special Forces, V. Ivonin.

Quite a different face looked out at me from the photograph than I had imagined from the CID indentikit picture and Karasiev's sketch. Smarmed-down hair instead of prickles, low forehead, predatory nose, thin lips. Old Lombroso would have been pleased with a mug like that; every mark was there indicating obdurate inborn criminal tendencies. I read through the details. Father – well-known poet. Mother singing teacher. They were divorced when Vladimir was ten. His mother went to work in the haberdashery department of a big store and two years later married the transport manager of the store. School teachers' reports: literature – literacy poor, good memory, mathematics – ability in the exact sciences, rude and overbearing, P.E. – physical development poor, no interest in sport displayed.

He left school early and went into the Leningrad Suvorov Military College. His tutor-officer had noted in the record that Ivonin had done well in his military subjects, and distinguished himself as a sportsman. Rude and arrogant towards his peers, polite towards his tutors. He had no relations with his mother and step-father, spent his free time with the family of his uncle, his father's brother, who ran the regional club in Repino, Leningrad province. He was visited in 1978 by his mother, who had filed for divorce against his step-father on account of his alcoholism. In 1979 he enrolled in the Kirov Special Forces Higher Command College and after graduating was posted, at his own request, to the limited contingent of Soviet forces on the territory of the Democratic Republic of Afghanistan. In 1983 he became a member of the CPSU (Communist Party of the Soviet Union). Reference from the commander of 17th Independent Regiment General Seri: 'Ivonin is a fine soldier. I can recommend him as an investigator in carrying out any inquiries into military crimes in the regiment entrusted to me!'

I read through Ivonin's dossier several times weighing up the discrepancies in the various opinions. Discrepancies at first glance that is. This Ivonin was no real puzzle. All the marks of so-called social schizophrenia fairly stood out. Stepfather makes fun of physically weak stepson – mother goes into the retail business for the money. Thieves, naturally. Otherwise you don't last a year: either you go yourself or you're pushed out, the crooks look after their own. Got away from his family, ran away, clearly, and he thinks he's got rid of the burden of the past. He doesn't know yet that he can never be what he once wanted to be. He wanted to pitch into his drunken step-father when the garage manager beat up his mother. But he was too weak. Now he was strong and . . . could kill a woman himself. That was the end product. It wasn't my idea, all this; there are hundreds of examples like that in Professor M.B. Singal's classified dissertation. That's its name in forensic psychiatry – Singal's syndrome.

The Judge Advocate of the 40th Army nodded understandingly.

'In my time I've seen men you'd pick as cosmonauts. Then after he's gunned down half his company, the experts say: totally psychotic, has been since his childhood!'

'Maybe he couldn't get out of it?' Bunin uttered suddenly. 'A servicemen has to carry out orders.'

I looked at Bunin as if he were an idiot.

'What order, Vanya? What commander would have had to give an order like that – kill Kim? Eh?'

Bunin stared stubbornly at the desk.

I began to feel very depressed, as if I were at a funeral. I'd flown to a foreign country at the back of beyond to arrest

Kim's murderer. And now I'd got the feeling I was investigating a matter I knew precious little about and which was diverting me from the real task. And Griaznov had gone missing. I hoped nothing untoward had happened. With one little pistol on my side I wasn't going to ask for trouble . . .

Now Bunin was trying to catch my eye, but I just stared dully into space.

'Sasha, give us a ciggy.'

I snapped out of my trance:

'You don't smoke do you, Ivan?'

'I'm just feeling a little bit nervous that's all . . .'

Bunin's voice was starting to go again.

'This is how the matter stands, comrade Turetsky.' The Judge Advocate looked at me, his eyes serious. 'At four today, Zaitsev has invited the staff officers to the bunker. There's going to be a little meeting. Or rather a meeting of activists to honour the heroes of Afghanistan. Ivonin, who got the Hero's Gold Star, is bound to be there. I'm invited. I can take you and the major along with me. I'll ring the staff now and ask permission. Are you on?'

'Yes,' I replied. 'We're on.'

We were sitting in the rather cramped office of the Judge Advocate of the 40th Army. One p.m. local time. Blazing hot outside. In the office as well. I looked out of the window: huddled clay alleys and a long modern block – a light building of seven storeys; nearby, some greenery . . .

'That's the Central Military Hospital,' explained the judge advocate intercepting my glance. 'Apparently there's nothing like it now in the whole Middle East, never mind Afghanistan.'

'How we're going to arrest this Ivonin, I can't figure out. It's a sort of vicious circle,' I said.

We were travelling in an army *gazik* through hell. Battered taxis hurtled towards us, decrepit buses lumbered along, garlanded with paper flowers and the Judge Advocate as he swallowed yellow dust, gave a staccato explanation.

'The other side of the square there, Dar-Ul-Amman quarter,

that's where the Soviet embassy is. In a fortress . . . the muslims have learned to fight a bit over these last years. Against the Americans and us. They fire rockets into the centre. They fire them at the Afghan government offices but we get it as well . . .'

He hawked and spat several times out of the window and I felt my own mouth full of sand, gritting between my teeth.

'. . . In June the terrorists organised six explosions. On the 13th they threw a grenade at an army patrol, five of our men in pieces. On the 14th a car loaded with explosive blew up near the army HQ. They were trying to get Zaitsev the O.C. He was lucky, he was at Shindal base at the time . . . A day or two ago, they shot a helicopter down with the army correspondent, Savkin, on board. Killed of course.'

We cut across the business section of the city in the direction of the motorway. Narrow alleyways, blocked by stalls and hawkers. What didn't they have – I tried to get a look whenever we halted: the latest model Japanese radios, bolts of Indian cloth, Chinese umbrellas . . . have to get Lana one of those . . . although how was I going to explain where I got it? No one at the Prosecutor's Office, including her, knew about my trip to Kabul, apart from Merkulov and Parkhomenko, that is . . . Great heaps of raisins, dried âpricots, roasted nuts . . .

Correspondent Savkin . . . Savkin. It was his piece about Dubov that Merkulov and I had read! I'd wanted to talk to him, question him about his meetings with Dubov, Morozov, Ivonin . . .

'In Kabul itself every morning they find the bodies of Afghan officials and HAD people – that's the Afghan KGB. Well, bugger them, our people are getting it, that's the trouble. Yesterday two of our generals were killed right in the centre of Kabul.'

The rows of traders' stalls ended as unexpectedly as they had appeared. We turned onto a concrete highway. The major-general took his cap off and rubbed his hand over the sweaty back of his neck.

'We've got plenty to worry about. Low morale in the rank's

our disease and bad food, especially hepatitis and stomach complaints.'

'Plenty of drug-addicts as well I suppose.' This was Bunin's contribution.

'Disaster,' said the judge advocate. 'It's the only word for it. And because of it, murders, rapes . . . both sexes, knife-fights. Murders. Hostility between our own people. That's the awful thing. There's friction between the regular troops and the Intelligence, KGB and MVD specials. Riflemen won't go into battle with paratroopers from the specials: they'll shoot us in the back, they say. There's not enough staff to sort everything out – just green youngsters. Gorny keeps the experienced law-men himself, he doesn't send them out here. And it's got to be sorted out or where shall we be? Especially if the special forces get dragged into some sort of emergency situation. It doesn't take much for them to start complaining, and not just anywhere either, they've got a direct line to Moscow. They've got a friend at court up there: Marshal Agarkin won't hear a word against them, he sticks up for them. You might as well talk to the wall . . . That's how things are . . .'

A steel door led off to one side. Down concrete steps. Down deeper and deeper. We came into a narrow tunnel, dimly lit by ceiling-lights. A turn, then another. Our steps echoed in complete darkness. The subterranean way was barred by a hatchway. It admitted us and slammed to behind us. Try and get out of here without a guide. We entered a lift. Then down again.

I tried to count the levels as they flashed by, but I lost track.

At last the lift nestled softly into its concrete bed and was still. The steel doors parted. The major said something into a microphone and yet another door opened wide to reveal the Army Command Centre. It was a large room, with subdued lighting. Polished wooden furniture, carpets, colour television. A group of young officers in blue parade uniforms bearing the Hero's Star of the Soviet Union were smoking near a vast ash-tray supported by a mighty bronze pedestal.

110

And then I saw . . . several Ivonins. About five. Or even six. They all had round heads with short hedgehog-cuts and eyes set wide apart. All had smiles fixed on their faces, revealing no teeth. And they were all grey.

Liuda Korabelnikova had said: 'They had no colour. They were grey.'

Just then the bright ceiling lights came on and the riddle was solved: under dim lighting conditions, strong sun-tan looked liked grey . . .

Kim's murderers had looked grey because the landing in the block had been lit by just a single fly-spotted bulb.

Their commander's called Grey (Seri) as well, I thought idly as I caught sight of the real Ivonin.

'You are arrested on suspicion of murdering Kim Lagina on the night of June 13th – 14th.' That's what I was supposed to say as regards the subject of my investigation. But I just couldn't get that out. Ivonin stood in the group of his lookalikes and stared me straight in the eye. Then he turned his gaze on Bunin, said something to the officers, pulled a steel comb out of his breast pocket to tidy his non-existent hair-do, and headed over towards us. The other five followed him.

'Blast, I left the AKS in the *gazik*,' I heard Bunin say. He swore and added. 'Otherwise I could let them have it . . .'

I looked at Bunin and felt considerable doubt whether he could let anybody have it: his large face was completely white and sweat was streaming down its pasty surface. I suppose I looked pretty pathetic too in my cowboy-shirt and jeans, carrying my enormous briefcase.

'Well, how's the weather up in Moscow? It's nice here. Nice and warm. I hear you want a word with me? My name's Ivonin. So what have you got there, out with it, don't be afraid.'

He was looking at us with incredible coolness as if to say: 'What's the matter, boys, looking so down in the mouth?' No, this was no game, somebody had got word to him about our mission, but he didn't give a damn.

'Citizen Ivonin, we need to have a very serious talk with you. You will have to accompany us to the Judge Advocate's Office in Kabul for questioning, since you are suspected of committing a serious crime,' Bunin rapped out, suddenly finding a normal human voice.

Good lad, Bunin. I clicked the lock on my briefcase and pulled out the order for Ivonin's arrest. He meanwhile was gazing in astonishment at his silent 'brothers' and the smile on his lips grew even wider.

'You've got something mixed-up there, comrade Major. We'll talk to you in this room. And why shouldn't we talk?'

Ivonin laughed without opening his mouth making snorting noises down his nose.

He was a devil. A real live devil, and I'd let him murder Kim . . .

'I would ask you all, comrades, to pass through into the hall. You, comrade Ivonin and you comrade medal-winners are invited onto the praesidium,' came the stentorian voice of a stout colonel, and there was nothing for it but to ascend the escalator, surrounded as we were by Ivonin's group, up to the next floor where the corpulent army commander, General Zaitsev sat in presidential dignity in the centre of the hall.

Ivonin and the officers passed on ahead of us turning round and winking at us, as if we were all the best of friends. Bunin and I stood about foolishly until the fat colonel invited us to take our places.

Zaitsev looked keenly round the assembled group:

'Comrade generals and officers, we have no time for speechifying. Everybody has work to do. So we will conduct our assembly efficiently and without pointless chatter: seven special forces men have been awarded the honoured appellation – Hero of the Soviet Union! Six of them are present in this hall. One of our comrades has gained his honour posthumously. I am referring to Guards Sergeant Dubov . . .'

Zaitsev put aside the list he had been glancing at when going through the list of medal-winners, and rubbed his triple chin with pudgy fingers:

'I ask all present to honour by one minute's silence the

memory of comrade Dubov, Hero of the Soviet Union, who died the death of the valorous.'

Where the devil was Griaznov? Our situation was hopeless, that much was clear: Bunin and I would get no support in this crowd. I felt that if Slava Griaznov had been with us, he would have found a way out. How, I'd no idea. Without the captain, I had no hands, it was as simple as that.

When everyone had re-seated themselves, the commander went on:

'Developing marxism–leninism in new historical circumstances, the Politburo has adopted the tactic of spreading communist ideas in other countries. The concept of "international duty" has been created. At the request of a government, a people's rising or a communist party, a "limited contingent" of Soviet forces would be sent into the territory of a given country, in the present instance Afghanistan. In the future, Soviet limited contingents . . .'

However I was not fated to hear what they might do in the future, because I saw the fat colonel on door duty waving his arm. I shot off my chair.

'You're wanted on the phone, comrade Turetsky!'

He led me into the staff duty officers room.

'Sashok, everything's okay here. I just couldn't find you,' Griaznov was shouting hysterically but I could hardly hear him. 'Zhenka's here, and the boots as well!'

'What boots, Slava?'

'American! The ones that left that impression in the cat-tray! Where do you want Zhenka and me to go? The transport round here's bloody awful, bear in mind. We're in the Kabul Police Directorate just now. Should we wait for you here?'

'Slava haul yourselves over here straightaway. I don't care how. Camels if you like!'

'What? I didn't catch that. Caramels?'

'You're the caramel, Griaznov! Just move yourself over here, right? Grab a taxi and come!'

There was half a minute of crackling in the receiver before the high-pitched cut-off signal came.

I went back to the door of the assembly hall in quite a

different frame of mind. I peeped through the crack – Ivonin was standing on the dais. I listened:

'They burned us in locomotive boilers, buried us alive up to the neck, filled our mouths with lead and tin . . . "Recant!" they bellowed. But from those burning throats came only three words: "Long live Communism!"'. Ivonin was reciting Mayakovsky.

I closed the door to firmly, went along a corridor and found myself in a cafeteria. Bunin and the judge-advocate were sitting at one of the tables drinking vodka.

'Where did you get to? I ran out after you but you'd disappeared, so we decided . . .' Bunin clicked his fingernails against the bottles. 'Sit yourself down, Sashulya. Get a glassful down your neck, you'll feel better. Do you know where we are?'

'In the bunker, Vanya. In the command bunker.'

'Ha! And do you know exactly what this underground fortress is? Do you know that here in this shaft there's strategic rockets? If Zaitsev gives the order, the ops team launch them at the Nato bases. It's a launch-pad for a nuclear strike . . .'

'Griaznov's going to be here in a minute with a . . . CID inspector.' I decided to give Zhukov back his former rank. There was no need for Bunin to know the sad details of Zhukov's career.

'Great! We'll need another bottle!'

'Vanya, we've got a job on, arresting a dangerous criminal . . .'

Bunin stared at me in alarm.

'What d'you mean, job? Wake up man! Who's going to let you arrest him? Let him go to hell, that Ivonin! D'you want me to be slung out of the service on his account?'

The waiter brought some *zakuski*. I drank another half-glass and had a bit of herring.

'All right, I'll do it myself . . .'

'Alexander Borisovich,' said the Judge Advocate, very serious. 'I'm also of the opinion that the present situation doesn't lend itself . . .'

'I know it doesn't lend itself,' I interrupted the General not very politely, realising I still didn't know his name. 'I'm sorry, what's your name?'

'Slavomir Vasilievich.'

'Right then Slavomir Vasilievich, please bear with me, I've got my own scores to settle with this one. I don't give a damn about the situation.'

To myself I thought: 'I hope the lads get here sharpish.'

'The only thing I can do to assist would be to invite Ivonin to talk to you one to one. After all, he's not just an officer in the specials he's my enquiry agent too. I'll tell him his help is needed. He has to obey an order from me. Do you want me to do that?'

'Slavomir Vasilievich, it's a trap, you know. Breaking the rules. Why do you want to risk it?'

'Let's just say it's because I'm in sympathy with you personally . . . By the way, this is an excellent Georgian wine "Akhasheni", harsh, marvellous bouquet. Would you like some?'

I understood perfectly that personal sympathy had nothing to do with it. Most likely it was professional solidarity. I refused the wine and accepted the help.

'. . . On the night of 13th–14th June of this year, you, citizen Ivonin, Vladimir Alexeyevich, born 1959, Russian, no previous convictions, serving the Soviet Army . . .'

My voice echoed around the concrete walls of the bunker and returned to me in distorted fashion, while Ivonin sat in a comfortable revolving chair apparently oblivious to my words. He did rock to and fro, however, in time to my words. This rocking irritated me. Questioning is a two-sided affair: the investigator puts pressure on the suspect and vice versa.

'. . . a dagger thrust to the vital organs of the body was the cause of death in the case of Lagina, Kim Artyomovna, who died at the scene of the crime from wounds sustained . . .'

The small pale eyes looked at me with open insolence and a hint of derision. He wasn't taking me seriously as an investigator. Don't get bogged down in minor matters, Merkulov would have said at this point, just drive calmly on, keeping to the main line. But I'm not Merkulov, and this turn of affairs irritated me.

'. . . In brief, you, Vladimir Alexeyevich, are accused of premeditated murder in aggravated circumstances as defined in article 102 of the criminal code. Do you admit your guilt?'

'What is all this you're trying to say? What have I got to do with it?' Ivonin asked, amazed, and continued to rock to and fro.

'Where were you on the night of the 13th–14th Thursday to Friday?'

'Well I just don't remember.'

'Try.'

'I don't believe I will.'

I rummaged in the briefcase for copies of the witnesses' depositions – Istomina, the actress, the engineer Vikulov and the commandant of the officers' hostel. I patiently read them all out. Ivonin was undismayed.

'You're all mixed-up, comrade investigator. I don't know anybody and don't want to know.'

Rocking.

'Who was the other person with you on the day of Kim Lagina's murder?'

He stopped his rocking abruptly. Silence. Then he began again, this time observing me with a certain wariness.

'The day after the murder of Lagina, you were with him at the cafe in the Hermitage gardens. Who is he? A serviceman? One of the special forces?'

I was making some sort of mistake obviously; Ivonin was making snorting noises with his mouth closed, his little eyes darting about in high glee. I cleared away the forms into my briefcase and my hand encountered a rounded knobby metal surface . . .

'Listen you,' Ivonin laughed, '– off to your precious capital, while you're still in one piece. Otherwise I'll give the word to the boys and they'll rip your head off, you streak of piss! *I'm* talking, you hear?'

Calmly, oh so calmly, I began to utter words almost without considering their meaning:

'The investigation as touches you, Vladimir Alexeyevich, is only just beginning . . .' (from me to Ivonin was about four yards, I reckoned) '. . . and we shall have plenty of time yet for conversation I trust . . .' (the door into the corridor was about a yard to my left, peripheral vision told me it was not shut). 'I will just say one thing: you're young, your life's ahead of you . . .' (pretending to fiddle in my briefcase for papers) '. . . I have a warrant here for your arrest and transportation . . .' (the walls here were impenetrable, I'd blow him to bits after I shot into the corridor . . . I'd say he attacked me) '. . . And if the tribunal hands down the maximum sentence' (I just had to pull the pin and lob the grenade into the corner where Ivonin was sitting.)

I didn't have time to do it however because the door of our capsule – compartment was flung open and Army Commander Zaitsev stood on the threshold.

'I beg your pardon, but I need Senior Lieutenant Ivonin urgently . . . What's the matter, comrade investigator?'

I made no reply, actually I didn't even hear what the commander said. I registered his question only after several minutes had passed and I was sitting with Bunin once more in the cafeteria. Somebody was playing the *bayan* in a passionate version 'The Slav Girls' Farewell' as I silently poured another tot and little by little recovered myself.

'Vanya I nearly killed a man just now.'

'Don't talk daft, T'retský,' Bunin was beginning to drop vowels, sign of a high level of inebriation. 'Let's dr'nk.'

'Vanya, I wanted to kill Ivonin. If I hadn't been interrupted I'd have done for him.'

'Stop making things up, y'can't do f'r 'im. Y'd have to throw a gr'nade at 'im.'

'That's what I . . .' I opened the briefcase a little. Bunin stuck his nose in and was instantly sober.

'Sashok, I've found out something. They're all for one here. They won't give Ivonin up to us. We'll have to try something different. We'll have to ring up old man Gorny. He's got a head on him, he's a cunning devil. He'll make . . .'

'Alexander Borisovich,' I heard the quiet voice of the judge advocate, 'it would be best if we quietly disappeared from here. There's an emergency situation not far from Kabul – an armed clash between our own troops. They've sent Ivonin's squad to quell things . . .'

The major-general stated all this as he stood next to me, looking intently round the hall.

'They say eighty people have been killed . . .'

The command adjutant moved past our table, obviously listening in to our conversation.

'Let's carry on the conversation at the office. They're keeping an eye on us here. Get up and walk to the lift, then the *gazik*. Quickly, but no fuss.'

'Look, they're standing by the doors, and over there. Don't lag behind the general, Sash. They won't touch us while he's here.' Bunin had lost his voice again.

'You're seeing double, Vanya,' I said encouragingly but picked up my pace just the same.

I'd been trying to get to sleep for two hours, but Bunin's mighty snores were rocking the whole provost-officers hostel, never mind our own little room. I'd run out of cigarettes and was smoking 'Partagas' Havana cigars, a present from the judge advocate. They tickled my throat. The namesake of the great writer wouldn't fit into his bed and I saw his great extremities lying across the pillow of the spare one. I yelled in his ear as hard as I could.

'Vanya!'

He was instantly awake.

'What – has Griaznov arrived?'

'Nobody's arrived. You're snoring like an engine and your feet are across somebody else's bed.'

'Well, hell . . . This bed's not designed for the likes of me. The snoring, yes, I forgot to warn you, sorry: just hiss at me, like that and I'll give over . . .'

10

I woke with a desperate thirst. My mouth had dried up completely and my tongue rustled like an autumn leaf. Somebody was crying outside the window, heart-breaking sobs. I lifted my head from the pillow but stygian darkness lay all around. I listened intently and it suddenly occurred to me that it was Bunin. Was he dreaming or what? I was just about to wake him up when I caught his quiet croaking voice against the ceaseless weeping:

'Now, don't take it to heart so, Mansur, we'll think of something. We'll wake Sasha and there's another lad due to turn up. He's just got lost off somewhere . . .'

'You'll never . . . lay a finger . . . on him. General Seri's behind him . . .' snivelled the invisible one.

I felt for the table-lamp switch.

'Well, you sleep like a pig in straw, Sashok. We've got some rough business on here. This is Military Investigator Mansur Mansurov. Something awful's happened to his kid brother.'

I glanced at my watch. Five past one in the morning: I'd slept about three hours. Bunin was sitting on his bed in his underwear alongside a youthful lieutenant. The latter pulled a hand-towel from the bed-head, blew his nose and coughed for some time. Calmer now, he spoke in an apologetic tone:

'You'll have to forgive me, please. You've got your own business to attend to, don't get all worked up over other peoples worries, Ivan . . . I'm still going to get this Ivonin, I swear by Allah . . .'

'Just hold on with the curses, Mansur. Let's tell Turetsky,

119

I mean Sashka all the details . . . Listen, have you got anything to drink here? My insides are burning.'

'The water's very bad in Kabul, don't drink from the tap or you'll get dysentery or some other filthy thing. I'll fetch you some Narzan from the fridge.'

'Well, it's all happening here,' said Bunin, when Lieutenant Mansur Mansurov had gone out into the corridor, 'while you were sleeping like a log, he was crying all over me . . .'

My insides were burning as much as Bunin's. I could think of nothing else but a glass of Narzan from the fridge. Unsticking my mouth with some difficulty, I rattled:

'What's happened to him?'

'Not him, his brother. Ivonin's squad, the specials I mean, wiped out the population of Keral village. By mistake. The specials had been ordered into another village where the menfolk had gone over to the partisans. The Keral men had been press-ganged into the government army.'

'Hang on, Vanya. You mean to say our people murdered the whole population? Mistake or not – what's the difference?'

Bunin knit his brow as if I'd asked him an impossible question.

'That's the whole point . . . The special forces exist for these punitive operations. Soldiers of other formations don't make war on the peaceful population. The spooks take their revenge later on our boys and they don't distinguish between the specials and the rest.'

'What blasted spooks are these?'

'That's what the boys call the dushman.'

Bunin had certainly familiarised himself with the situation while I had been asleep.

'What's Lieutenant Mansurov got to do with it?'

'It's like this. The garrison soldiers ran amuck over the lousy food. The specials get different rations. It's like a Kremlin sanatorium for them, they eat their heads off. One kid just went and lost his wool. It happened in the canteen. He told the specials what he thought of them. He said they got a jar of caviar for every corpse. A specials officer started to tick him off. The youngster called the specials officer a sod, and a cut-throat. At that the officer shot him point-blank with his pistol. The garrison lads grappled with the specials, hand to hand at first. Then it came to a shooting-match. The garrison troops, or what was left of them barricaded themselves in the blocks. Then they called in Ivonin. He knows his "international duty" all right: he brought up an artillery piece and blew the barracks to bits.'

'And Mansur's brother was inside?'

'Of course!'

'Dead?'

'That's why he's on his way over there now. Maybe his brother's only badly wounded . . .'

Mansurov was standing in the doorway with two beaded glasses. He'd managed to tidy himself up: all his buttons were done up, his glossy black hair was impeccably parted. He was strikingly handsome, he could have been on the cover of Ogonyok, with the caption 'Where the action is – Afghanistan'. He held out the bottles – his hands were tapered, only the nails were bitten away.

'It's night-time now. You can't get to Baglan, it's different when you're in a helicopter. I've got to avenge my brother in any case. I don't want to involve you. I can use a knife as well as any special.'

'Steady on, where are you going to find Ivonin?' Bunin tried to cool Mansur's hot eastern blood. 'You'll get yourself killed for nothing.'

'I'll go on foot, I'll find the dog,' the lieutenant was implacable.

'He's really going,' Bunin turned to me, at a loss.

I could see for myself that Mansurov was still wound-up.

'Comrade Mansurov, we'll go with you. I've got a score to settle with Ivonin as well.'

'I know. Ivan told me he'd knifed your girl. I'll settle it for all of us. You needn't risk yourself.'

Bunin, however, was already pulling his trousers on:

'I'll lay on a helicopter . . . I've got an idea. I saw an old mate of mine, a pilot, he's from Rostov, same as me – and he's on duty tonight.'

'You're not from Rostov, are you?' I was surprised.

'That's not the point, Sashok. If I have to, I can be a Rostovian, you'll see.'

I sat on a bench near the officers' hostel gazing up at the bright stars in the velvet sky. If the aim of the Afghan sun was to boil the infidel's brain and turn it into a shapeless pudding, the Afghan night, with its scents of riotous blossom floating in dense aromatic waves, was quite a different matter. The moon's dim radiance silvered the mountain tops. Silence. The Afghan sky was like an Afghan carpet: a dense, rich, dark-silver vault with tens of thousands of starry clusters. They say it takes several women two years work to produce a medium-sized Afghan carpet.

I shuddered as two figures materialised by the bench.

'What's the time?' asked one of them.

'Half one,' I answered moving my wrist under the street-lamp.

I wanted to ask these lads whether they were helicopter pilots and had seen a tall major, but I never got the chance. A fearful blow knocked me off the bench onto the ground . . .

The first thing I saw was my own knees – my chin was practically touching them. I tried to flex my lips, but they were taped over; I tried to unpeel it but my hands were secured behind my back. A severe bump drove my chin against my knees: I was in a lorry. I turned my head with difficulty. Boys in camouflaged overalls and berets were sitting along the benches. They were caressing the barrels of their AKS and talking quietly among themselves. I was flattened against the side as the truck halted. Clatter of army boots, a word of command, 'Form up!'

I was picked up under the arms and dragged out . . .

'Come to, have you, Turetsky?' asked a man's voice.

The man was barefoot, and wore shorts and a vest with the crest of the Dynamo sports club on it. He was half turned away from me, looking straight into my eyes as he directed a bright table lamp in my direction.

I said nothing. The man nodded his grizzled head with the hedgehog cut and the soldiers rushed to take the gag from my mouth.

'Wh-o-o a-are y.you?' I asked.

'My name isn't important. I command a unit . . .'

'What unit?' I asked, stuttering slightly. I found moving my lips painful. 'Government or dushman?'

'Soviet. A Soviet unit . . . Stop playing the fool now . . .'

He paced about the room as if he was in front of some gymnastic apparatus.

His face was deeply wrinkled, but his arms and hands, bursting with strength, proclaimed him a professional sportsman. Gymnast or acrobat.

'All right,' said the sportsman, 'untie his arms . . . Sit down!'

I subsided on the chair I was offered.

'It's as simple as pie. We need to have a frank talk. We've carried you off so you can decide either . . . or. Either we deal with you and no one the wiser, or we agree to cooperate . . .'

'You've made a mistake, comrade Seri! My friends are going to twig the specials have kidnapped me.'

'Oho! You've sussed me out have you? Listen, I've taken a fancy to you! How about a drink?'

'Okay.'

Seri took a sweating bottle of Moskovskaya out of a fridge fitted inside a metal cupboard, along with a plate of sausage and cheese sandwiches, a jar of gherkins and a bottle of Borzhomi mineral water. He put the whole lot on a table and poured the vodka into mugs.

'Drink up.'

Then he poured out the mineral water.

'You know,' he went on after getting his breath back, 'I can smell out any spy just by the way he drinks vodka. A foreigner doesn't wash it down with water. Not like us, Russians.'

I grinned.

Seri looked intently at me. His eyes were odd, somehow. Watery, filled with tears almost.

'Why do you laugh?'

'I never expected to be drinking vodka in Afghanistan in circumstances like this. They won't half laugh when I tell them about it in Moscow . . .'

'I don't think you'll be doing that somehow. Mind you, if we find common ground, you really will be able to tell them in Moscow about . . . General Seri's hospitality.'

'And if we don't agree?'

'In that case . . . your little bones will rot here on Afghanistan soil . . .'

'Just don't try to scare me!'

'I'm not. I'm just telling you the truth.' Seri sighed, then smiled. 'Now to business. Tell me, why did you come here to Afghanistan?'

'You know very well – to place under arrest and transport to prison in Moscow one of your subordinates.'

'Who?'

'You know perfectly well. I came for Ivonin.'

'I see! Ivonin!' He scowled, nostrils flaring and forehead deeply furrowed. 'And what on earth's he done?'

'I'm conducting the inquiry into the murder of a female employee of the Moscow City Prosecutor's Office.' I had decided to upgrade the importance of my investigation. 'The case is under the control of the Central Committee of the Party and I have the minimum of time to clear it up.'

'Go on.'

'I am in possession of proof that it was Ivonin who killed the woman when he was in Moscow receiving his decoration. He delivered the fatal blow. By law I am required to produce him for witness identification, confrontation . . .'

'Couldn't you be mistaken? You know it's happened before – somebody gets executed then it turns out somebody else did the murder.'

'There's no mistake.'

'Have you got sanction for his arrest?'

'Yes, I have.'

'Where is it?'

'In my briefcase.'

He marched off with his springy step over to the cupboard,

got hold of my shabby briefcase and held it out to me . . .

Seri smoked as he scanned the signatures of Merkulov, Gorny and Rogov.

'What article is that, number 90?' enquired Seri.

I replied as if I were doing my oral exams again:

'An investigator is empowered to detain a suspect for ten days. If he has assembled sufficient evidence in that time, he brings a charge and the suspect remains in prison until the trial.'

'And if he doesn't get the evidence?' Seri asked quickly.

'If he doesn't, the investigator is obliged to release him and no buts.'

'So that's it!' The general was delighted. 'If I've understood you correctly, you intend to arrest one of the finest officers in the special forces! A knight *sans peur et sans reproche* so to speak. And your proof – nothing at all.'

'Did I say I had insufficient proof? You asked and I explained the law . . .'

'Witnesses, confrontations! It's unheard of! A witness can swear to any rubbish! Well, I'll just tell my lads and they'll swear they've never set eyes on any Turetsky in the unit. Well lads, will you swear?'

The soldiers began to laugh.

Seri glanced at his watch and hurried on.

'All right, leave that. Tell me something else: what percentage clear-up of murder cases do you have in Moscow?'

I didn't see any catch. I just couldn't get what he was driving at.

'On average in Moscow the figure's eighty per cent – eighty-five of premeditated cases . . .'

'Out of ten guilty, two are walking about free . . . That's good.'

'What's good about it? Committed a murder and walking the streets. Drinking beer . . .'

'What's good is that you're going to include Ivonin in that twenty per cent,' said Seri harshly, 'otherwise you don't get out of here!' He fixed me with his tearful eyes.

'You're what, trying to scare me?'

'No. Change your allegiance.'

'But that's against the rules. Prosecutor's Office personnel are not allowed to work for other services. Even the KGB . . .'

Seri came up to me. He took my chin in his powerful fingers and forced my head back, saying slowly and clearly:

'For the KGB, no. For the Party, yes. The special forces serve only the Party. And only the central organs at that. So this isn't a switch of allegiance my dear boy, it's something else.'

'You'll never get away with it,' I parried. 'There's a logical link missing. It's not enough to do a deal with me. You'd have to fix it with five other people! And they're not all here, they're in Moscow . . .'

'That's not your worry. They'll be fixed in Moscow without us. My job is to do a deal with you, Turetsky. Those are my orders!'

'Whose orders?' I asked.

He didn't answer. He went over to the cupboard again and drew out a packet:

'Now listen carefully! I'm about to thank you for finding a way of closing the Ivonin case. I'll give you money. A lot. There's ten thousand here. And you will take it in front of witnesses. And you'll give me a receipt stating that in exchange, Investigator Turetsky binds himself to drop Ivonin Vladimir from the case. And so forth, you know how these things are done . . .'

He came right up to me and opened the packet: a thick wad of hundreds. He placed it neatly on my knee.

I threw it on the floor:

'I don't take bribes. And . . . I don't play games like this.'

Seri sat in his chair, impassive. But his fingers were trembling.

'Without agreement, I'm sorry. I haven't the right to let you out of here. Even though I like you . . .'

The general turned to his men.

'Take him to the cell!'

And to me:

'I shall wait two hours, Turetsky. Just two hours. Either – or!'

I revolved in my head the whole course of the conversation with Seri, as I sat in a solitary confinement cell with a heavily barred window. Actually I could sign any piece of paper Seri wanted. I could get out of that. Merkulov would believe that I had no option and I would have saved my life just like that. He would find the right move as well and get in touch with the people at the very top through Yemelyanov. I could just deceive the general, good God, sprawling on the plank-bed, I was amazed I hadn't done so. Still, all was not lost. Seri had given me time to consider. It would all look very natural: I'd weighed everything up and decided that to die for nothing at my age was pointless. Keep your Ivonin, what's he to me?

. . . But I was caught: I knew, had known from the very beginning that I'd never compromise whatever happened. 'I have to have a talk with you, Turetsky . . .' She took me by the arm. Her hands were like ice . . . And a sea of blood, and in the midst, like an island, Kim's lifeless body. 'I swear I'll find him Kim! I, the investigator, will find your murderer . . .' They say scientists have made a discovery recently: the brain receptors, so-called, programmed by the central nervous system, make selective use of medicines. My organism's receptors had selected only one acceptable train of thought – I had to render Ivonin harmless and my receptors couldn't allow me to conclude any deals, even if it cost me my life.

Still if I have to be really honest, I couldn't believe they would finish me off. Ivonin was devoid of any sense of self-preservation, that was clear. General Seri, though, was an intelligent man. He realised he would have to account for the disappearance of an investigator from the Moscow Prosecutor's Office.

Someone entered the cell; an escort, I thought, come to take me to Seri, the two hours was up.

'Stalen has ordered me to ask for your decision.'

Before me stood Ivonin. This time he was in shirt-sleeves,

without the Hero's star. I felt oddly that he was different from that time in the bunker. More normal, maybe.

'What Stalen is this?'

'Seri, Stalen Josifovich.'

Now I understood. This Seri's first name was Stalen, Stalin – Lenin, two leaders in one name, a trifle too much, perhaps.

'You can tell him: no papers, no deals . . .'

I turned to the wall without getting up.

'Hey, investigator! What's this. Turetsky, we need to have a little talk!'

I felt a twinge of anxiety at these normally-spoken words. A new kind of fear, as if a hyena had begun to use a human voice . . .

'Why talk? Specially here, in these surroundings.'

'There won't be another time, you hear, Turetsky! I want to talk now.'

He wasn't demanding or threatening, although he had all the advantages and could easily have stuck his Finnish knife in me as he had Kim. Or shot me between the eyes. He was looking at me the way a little boy looks at his older pal when he wants to tell him about his doings and ask his advice on how to keep it from his parents.

'I don't quite understand, what do you want to talk to me about?'

'This case. That little girl, what's her name, Kim, I killed her. That's right! You're right, I tell you, you solved it.'

'Well, well.' This was a turn-up for the book. I hadn't expected this. 'And why did you kill her?'

Ivonin sat down on the planking, offered me a packet of Salem and a lighter.

'The charter.'

'What d'you mean, charter?'

I lit up and my mouth filled with the taste of mint. There were initials on the lighter: I V, Ivonin Vladimir? No, of course not, Igor Vikulov! It was that silver-ornamented cigarette-lighter belonging to the engineer.

'That's how it is in my profession,' sighed Ivonin, 'I'm a serviceman, I carry out my orders, the charter rather than orders. That's our bible. "The charter of the Afghan Brotherhood" it's called. I remember what it says by heart, I have an excellent memory: to prepare selected young people to fight to the death not only for today and tomorrow, but the day after . . . In the first place must be the reformation of society, to get rid of dragging ballast in our own environment; then comes the extension and re-shaping of living space, there also a policy of getting rid of the dross among the population must be followed . . . In order to ensure the moral purity of the people, the worst examples must be destroyed, and a stratified caste system introduced . . . Total extermination of the alien principle guarantees the achievement of a noble end . . . There is no more base occupation than that of "thinker", and no more noble thing than to be a soldier. The intellectual is the slave of dead reason, whereas the soldier is a lord of life . . . The destiny of a man is related to his strength and his breeding. And so that the people shall not become degenerate, not become slaves and robots, we must resurrect and maintain for ever the healthful cult which leads to the true immortality, the cult of the soldier who has passed through fire and sword in Afghanistan. For this purpose our "Afghan Brotherhood" is instituted . . .'

I was stunned by this lunacy.

'But we've had all this! We've had it before! The whole of Europe is under our feet. We are a race of conquerors! Away with Jews, gypsies, Slavs and the rest!'

'No,' he responded calmly. 'There's been nothing like it before. Our brotherhood has resolved: to eliminate the worst part of the population so that the better part can flourish.'

'Just how many are you thinking of eliminating?' I asked, feeling cold.

'We'll destroy seventy per cent. Maybe even eighty. Why keep a rabble? The rabble has accomplished its mission: it's grown so much you can't turn round on this earth of ours! Overpopulation! The best ideas are vulgarised by the stupidity of the rabble. They produce governments worthy of themselves. And they propose reforms: indeed, but you can't let yourself be led by the masses, that's unworthy of a government. And if the governments are unworthy then they have to be destroyed also.'

'Destroyed how? Cut them up with knives?'

'Why knives?' Ivonin was affronted. 'That wouldn't be rational, it's ... unhuman. Bacteria, radiation, chemical means.'

'I don't understand how you intend going about all this. A mere bunch of soldiers. What are the guiding principles?'

'Class principles. Collect up the riff-raff and rat-a-tat-tat, that's them done. Example? Here's one. Listen. One fine day Stalin gives the order: get ready.'

'What Stalin? You mean Stalen – Stalen Seri?'

'No. A new Stalin will arise. Everything must be as it was before. Do you know how many atomic reactors we have? Fifty-one. Put explosives under five of them and boom! ... The explosion itself won't kill many, couple of thousand or so. But the radiation ... millions.'

'Which stations are first on your list?'

'First one Chernobyl, near Kiev. Dubno, near Moscow, that's number two. Leningrad, Sverdlovsk. They're actually the easiest to blow up ... We've had a good rehearsal. We blew the Moscow metro and the atom reactor in Volgodonsk. You know about the metro yourself, I expect. Only those in the know have heard about Volgodonsk – and those already in paradise. You can check.'

I listened without interrupting. I had trouble taking in the words of this madman.

'What had the girl Kim to do with it? How was she in the way of your brotherhood?'

A repulsive little smile played across his face, the old, old smile:

'She most certainly was in the way. Judge for yourself, Turetsky. You're an investigator. Dubov sent documents about our brotherhood to her. Secret plans. He betrayed us. He got what was coming to him. The little bitch wanted to broadcast the news.'

I couldn't bear to listen to him talking about Kim. I lit

another cigarette and returned the packet and lighter to him. He flipped them up on this broad fat-cat palm and put them away in his pocket.

'Nothing's going to come of all this, you know. You're planning to destroy the population, yet you steal cigarette-lighters. You'd cut each others' throats for a jar of black caviare.'

I thought he was going to strike me, but he burst out laughing instead, like he had in the canteen – snorting, with his mouth closed.

'What about that partner of yours, the one with you when you killed Kim? Who is he? A soldier? Is he here in Afghanistan or is he in Moscow?'

He stopped snorting and stared for a long time at the breast pocket of my checked shirt, as if he were aiming at the heart.

'That you will never find out . . .'

'Why not?'

'Because, Turetsky, death has come for you. In five minutes, Ensign Tsegoyev will arrive and slice you into pieces . . . and throw them to the Afghans. Not ours, the dushman. Your mother will be informed that her sonny boy died the death of the valorous . . . Maybe you'll get a posthumous star. Like Dubov . . .'

Again I was on my way somewhere, not in a lorry this time, it was a *gazik* driven by Ivonin with Tsegoyev – a squat unshaven fellow – squashed up against me and breathing foully all over me.

'Just a lil' bit longer, friend!' and he showed me a row of sparse yellow teeth which presumably indicated a smile.

I'd seen that ugly mug somewhere quite recently. And those evil, brutish little eyes. I kept trying to remember as if my life and salvation depended on it.

I peered into his face and saw his eyes, caught by the rays of the rising sun turn from dark grey to translucent green.

And then I remembered: he had been one of Zaitsev's body-guards, standing behind the general when he had come into the interview-room and taken Ivonin from me.

131

'We'll shortly be at Nightingale Grove,' advised Tsegoyev. Observing that this information meant nothing to me, he added: 'It's a pretty wild place, bullets flying ever'where like courting nightingales . . .'

As illustration, I saw the burned-out skeleton of a bus, heeled crazily into a ditch and brown patches of blood on the asphalt. I kept peering into the scrubland: if only the dushman would attack, damn and blast it . . .

Now with every yard the rise in the terrain became steeper. The road, as resilient as rubber, got extremely bumpy as it wound round the very edge of the galley, hugging the overhanging rocks. Silence hung in the clear mountain air. I wished the silence would be shattered by the sound of rescue. I considered again: if they really did finish me off, the killers would not be punished, Kim's murder would go unavenged. For that to happen I had to complete my work, my professional duty. But I knew miracles don't happen in this world and my situation was hopeless . . .

Tsegoyev and Ivonin hauled me out of the *gazik* and led me into the thickets. We walked for quite some time.

'Here,' said Ivonin.

I leaned up against a cypress and laid my head back. A raspberry-red dawn lit the tree-tops. The sky was filled with light clouds like those at home, in Moscow. Somebody was breathing next to me, shuddering, sobbing. It was me. My God, was I really weeping?

'Take his gag off, let him have a breather before he dies,' said Ivonin.

'Can't do that, he'll make a noise, we'll take it off later. Y' can never breathe enough before you die,' said Tsegoyev.

He began brandishing a huge, fantastically huge fist and I guessed a knuckle-duster was clamped in it. This was the end.

And – I did my chop, as I had done once on the mat at the Field Sports Palace, during the Moscow Judo Championships. That was when, for the first and last time I became middleweight champion of the capital, winning against the invincible Rodionov. I did my *pièce de résistance* too. This was a terrible blow my trainer had spent a great deal of time on with me. My left foot struck Tsegoyev on the hand holding the knuckle-duster while the right went into his belly. The force of the blow, multiplied by its unexpectedness, was conclusive and Tsegoyev dropped to the ground like a stone, his mouth reaching for air. I flung myself on Ivonin with my hands tied behind my back and my mouth taped over: fury gave me strength. I landed a powerful butt with my head on Ivonin's chin. He reeled under my attack and found himself on the ground. I drove my foot into him. Ivonin was sharp, though, he wasn't a special for nothing. As he fell, he parried my kick and got his own blow in, in the solar plexus. I doubled over but didn't fall and again hurled myself at Ivonin. My attack was so desperate and bold, that he leapt back, giving me a sharp but not very powerful blow on the cheek-bone. I took aim: now I would leap as I had on the Sports Palace mat, do a twist in the air and deliver a strike so powerful, he wouldn't get up anymore. His spine would be broken . . .

I was on the point of taking-off when someone hit me in the back. I went flying, my body actually hung in the air. A stunning smash from a knuckle-duster . . . It was Tsegoyev, he'd come to, the swine . . .

I was lying face down, shattered. Severe pain in the ears and nose. Tsegoyev was above me, booting my ribs and stomach as I rolled over and over among the grass, tree roots and thorns. As I groaned, he kicked and kicked my curled-up body with his steel toe-caps. I could hear my own sobbing – my ears weren't taped after all – and they picked up my sobs as they were forced out through my nostrils. I couldn't get air into my exhausted lungs, I couldn't breathe . . .

Tsegoyev, the executioner, was ripping my clothes to pieces. My shirt had split, buttons flying.

'I'll cut the bastard in pieces,' roared Tsegoyev, and I saw the dagger in his hand. I tried to turn away, but the knuckle-duster had done its work I'd lost my coordination and my attempts at evasion were slow and clumsy.

'Finish him!' yelled Ivonin. 'Quick! Somebody might come!'

'No-o-o,' my last sob.

A dagger thrust . . . I just managed to roll over on my side and the blade whistled past my ear, a millimetre from my skin.

'Get back, Tsegoyev,' shouted Ivonin. 'I'll do it myself!'

Ivonin stood over me. Three paces from me. I could see his face contorted with hate, the face of a psychopath.

'It's all over, you've had your time law-man.' He hissed and aimed his pistol.

He fired. Once, twice, three times. I could hear the shots, one after another . . .

I fell away into another and better world. In this world I wasn't killed, I was victorious . . . Ivonin flew at me, falling as he did so, twitching oddly and screaming:

'I – I! You-u!'

Then he was crawling onto me. Pinning me and crushing me to the ground which smelt of mould, then crawling on. He disappeared and I was free. Because Tsegoyev wasn't there either. Or rather he was there but had fallen down a yard from me. I even thought there's been something like an earthquake. My hands were bound together as before, my mouth as well, but my feet, my feet were free. So I got up on my tottering legs and saw some Afghans, dushman, running towards me . . .

I leaned my back against a cypress. I was in the next world, and in that next world my friend Griaznov was running towards me. It didn't matter that he looked like a dushman – some sort of striped gown and turban. My head spun and my head was fairly splitting with pain. I realised then that I was not dead. You don't get headaches in the next world. My eyes filmed over and I saw nothing. I could hardly breathe and my eyes were smarting, but I heard Griaznov's familiar voice:

'We'll make it, Shurik, never fear!'

My sight was returning. I saw that it really was Griaznov. My ginger-nut Griaznov . . .

'Let's get ourselves out of here, brothers, time for hugging and kissing later,' he said, and we got out of there, especially as I found the going easier as my arms were free and I could make sounds, not yet articulate though; only my head wasn't in its proper place, literally, it was bobbing about in the air on a level with somebody's delicate, almost elegant hands, which were engaged in cleaning a blood-stained knife. Then I saw the hands shoving the knife into the top of an officer's boot. I couldn't recall his name, but I knew that it was that Uzbek officer from the Judge Advocate's Office. It dawned on me then that I wasn't walking, Bunin was carrying me across his shoulder. I protested most strongly, but he kept tight hold of my legs with his bucket-like hands and paid no attention to my moaning.

I kept turning my head from side to side, with considerable difficulty. Our little detachment was moving along a narrow path across a depression towards a village. Bunin's back rose and fell with his heavy breathing.

'Ivan Alexeyevich, put Sashok down and let him have a try himself,' I heard a very familiar voice say. When Bunin had carefully placed me on my feet I saw that it was Zhenya Zhukov, in a similar Afghan turban to Griaznov's. I strode out manfully with the rest, but I noticed that our group had slowed its pace. I felt no pain but nausea kept rising in my throat and the houses leapt before my eyes. All around stood square blank dwellings with narrow embrasures, reminding me of a stage set for a play about Afghanistan. The village was a ghost one seemingly. Somebody was talking quickly in an unfamiliar language – we were accompanied by two genuine Afghans with automatic weapons.

'What did he say?' asked Griaznov.

'The village has been destroyed, but nobody knows who did it,' Zhukov translated.

The body of a young Afghan sprawled by the road-side. I shuddered: it could have been me lying like that, gazing unwinking up into the yellow-blue heavens.

A few more steps and the tops of snow-capped mountains came into view round a turning, towering over a sun-baked valley with a few ancient habitations scattered about its floor. Near a stream stood an MI-24 helicopter.

The silence was so tangible you could pick it up and carry it.

'We'll halt here. When we've recovered ourselves a bit, we'll fly out. Sashka's in shock, mind. Main thing, don't let him sleep. Keep him on the go, you hear, Sashok – sing, yell, swear, just don't sleep!'

I listened dully to Griaznov, then looked at Bunin just as dully: he was pulling faces in an effort to make me laugh. I observed the black-bearded Afghans whispering with Zhukov, but my brain – that all-powerful governor of the body – had more or less atrophied, all it did was register surrounding circumstances, it could not analyse. I didn't feel like singing, yelling or swearing. More than anything in the world I wanted to sleep . . .

'Well, it's not turned out so well, boys. We should have taken them alive. We started the operation all right, but we couldn't finish,' Griaznov was clearly peeved about this.

'You know where you can go. If I hadn't put a hole in that Tsegoyev, he'd have carved Shurka into little bits,' croaked Bunin (his voice had gone completely) and blew his nose in a dirty hanky.

'Allah saw that I could not have acted differently! Ivonin killed my brother! I take the responsibility, comrades. I'll go before a tribunal.'

'There's not going to be any tribunal. Nobody's going to find out what happened here. Translate Zhenya, for these . . .'

The Afghans listened to Zhukov and made some odd hand movements, they might have been praying or then again . . .

'It's all right,' said Zhukov.

Griaznov explained, this time addressing himself to me:

'At one there's a plane flying out of Kabul, special flight. The Judge Advocate's despatching a group of smugglers on it. We'll be on the plane, I've fixed it. We've got to get out of here otherwise its curtains – We're going in the helicopter to fetch friend Zhukov's bits and pieces, he's got no reason to hang around here either . . . You needn't translate that Zhenya.'

Somebody picked me up under the armpits and sat me down in the helicopter cabin.

'Hey, pal, have you got a plastic bag? Our boy here's not

feeling too bright,' Griaznov inquired of the pilot, who nodded and passed the bag over.

I burned my tongue on the hot tea and my chattering teeth broke a chip off the edge of my china cup. I was terribly afraid, I felt like crying from fear. I held my tears back but every now and again they rolled out from under my lids and dropped into the black tea – plip, plop . . .

'Never mind, Sashok, all this messing about's nearly over. When the lads have had a rest, we'll get you to the doctor and then it's goodbye Turdistan. There, you're smiling already.'

Zhukov was looking into my face with his deep, deep blue eyes. It occurred to me that he hadn't changed at all in the two years I hadn't seen him, apart from being burnt black by the sun. That and the strip in his light brown hair which had been bleached white by that same sun.

'Don't you want any tea?'

'Tea . . .' Zhukov consulted his watch. 'You think it's too early for vodka?'

'Have you got any?'

'Spirits. A woman doctor I know keeps me supplied. Want some?'

'Okay, Zhenya. I'll fall apart otherwise.'

'I love that, Sashok! Falling apart! You could just say that you had one foot in the next world,' he spat for luck.

We drank pure spirit and nibbled some shaggy-skinned fruit I'd never seen before and I began to feel pain throughout my whole body: my back ached, I felt a dragging under the diaphragm and my head was humming. I felt a powerful urge to sleep . . .

'No, no Sashok. Sleep not allowed. Let's talk about something.'

I tried with all my might to lift my eyelids and recall what it was I wanted to talk to Zhukov about. Wasn't it most important what I wanted to know?

'Slavka was telling me the mess-up over Faust you'd got yourselves into. Well, this is the situation . . .'

Of course, Faust!

'. . . I've got a lady-friend, she's a doctor at the Central Hospital. She told me they'd got a secret department, where they put any of our soldiers suffering from hallucinatory disorders. Do you know what that means?'

'Somewhat.'

'Same here. And these disorders are the result of injections of a preparation called,' (Zhukov got a piece of paper from his pocket) 'phenol-alkaloid-ultra-stabilising. Get it? No? Phenol, call it F, alkaloid A, Ultra U, stabilising St. FAUST. I'm not sure that's its official abbreviation, but it works as a sort of elixir of youth, like Doctor Faust had in Goethe's book. All these experiments are top-secret. Slavka and I thought up a plan of how to get into the secret area – you can't get in by day, the doctors get there at eight a.m. There's one doctor on at night. And guards a-plenty, of course. They've got to be tricked somehow.'

'Zhenya, I can't quite visualise this. Maybe I could have a word myself with this er, lady-friend?'

Zhukov looked at his watch.

'She'll be at the hospital in half an hour. If you can learn Farsi in that time you can certainly have a chat.'

'She's what . . . Afghan?'

'Well.'

A mess-up right enough.

'I have to go with you to the hospital in any case, she can have a look at your nut. And backbone. The rest we can forget . . . Yes, he gave you a biff all right . . .' Zhukov removed my striped gown and looked my body over. 'There's not one spot left untouched.'

'To hell with the bruises,' I told Zhukov, and thought, 'I'm not dead anyway.'

'Zhenya I can't fly with you to Moscow.'

'Your brain's not working obviously, we're flying with you, not you with us. You've got to be evacuated from here, urgent.'

'I haven't completed my inquiries in Afghanistan. I was supposed to locate Dubov's platoon-members and find out how he was killed. I've got the names – Smirnov, Halilov. I

138

can't leave without talking to them. Through them I can get on to Kim's other murderer. He exists you know, Zhenya! He's even more important than Ivonin. Kim knew him you see, she opened the door for him. Ivonin wasn't lying – the day of the murder was the first day he'd seen Kim.'

'Very impressive. But if you don't get out of here straightaway, I can't see anybody rescuing you from General Seri's boys. As for Smirnov and Halilov, Slavka and I have already dug up a list of Ivonin's platoon: since Dubov was killed, three have been posted away on courses, seven others killed . . . To be more specific – as of today – nine . . . The rest are hospitalised.'

'Wounded?'

'Well, that's the mess-up. All our wounded are taken to Central Hospital, they never keep them in field hospitals for longer than twenty-four hours. None of Ivonin's platoon appears on the list of wounded, though. Anait suspects they're in the secret department.'

'Who's Anait?'

'That's her. My . . . acquaintance.'

From his denim jacket Zhukov pulled out a piece of paper, folded in four and handed it to me. It was written on a form belonging to the Chief Medical Authority of the USSR Ministry of Defence:

> To: Head of Kabul City
>   Central Hospital (Afghanistan)
>   Comrade Valoyat Habibi
>   Major-General Medical Corps.
> Respected comrade Habibi!

Comrade Klochkov, Victor Petrovich, major of Medical Corps, a microbiologist of the Central Medical Authority USSR MOD and comrade Osipov, Boris Ilyich, Candidate of Medical Science, chief psychiatrist of the Tashkent department of the Central Institute of Advanced Research, are being sent to study the culture of the virus strain merobius.

I suggest that you furnish the above-mentioned comrades with all necessary materials (histories of infected persons being treated in section AB of your hospital) as well as contact with patients mentioned on the attached list. Since the action of the virus merobius, the carrier of which is the asiatic merobi-mosquito, has turned out to be molecular-active to a significantly higher degree than we assumed, it is requested that you afford comrades Klochkov and Osipov all possible assistance with a minimum of delay.

> Head of Central Medical Authority
> of the USSR MOD, Colonel-General
> of Medical Corps . . .

'Who are they – comrades Klochkov and Osipov?' I asked Zhukov, as I strained to read between the lines and make some sense of it all.

'I think the microbiologist is you, and the psychiatrist is – me. Relax, Sash, apart from the genuine names of generals, all the rest is pseudo-scientific rubbish Slavka and I made up yesterday. I'm afraid we just have no time. There's two hours left before the doctors turn up. We didn't know you'd get yourself into a mess did we? We should have gone at night.'

'Zhenya, we'll go to the hospital right away, understand, right away . . . God, how can I, looking like this?'

Zhukov stared intently at me then struck the table with his fist:

'All right.'

He went into the other room from whence issued the cacophonous snoring of Bunin and Griaznov, and returned with a suit on a hanger in one hand and a package in the other.

'My Anait could only pinch one army doctor's uniform from the Quartermaster, so I'll have to wear civvies.'

'Hold it, Zhenya. How'm I going to be a microbiologist? I don't know a single technical term and I've got a black eye.'

'We'll disguise the bruise. As far as terminology goes, I'm

not too strong either. You'll just have to make noises like a microbiologist. The dietician Klopova's the one on duty, she's the wife of the chief surgeon there. She knows as much about microbiology as you do. And less about psychiatry than I do.'

'Listen, that mosquito, what was it again? Merobi – does it really exist?'

'Quite possibly,' answered Zhukov coolly, pulling on his blue shirt. 'Incidentally, one condition: first, Anait examines your boko, and backbone. She's coming specially at half six.'

'Zhenya, there's no time for that.'

'Okay, I'm taking my new pants off then . . .'

'All right. Ten minutes – agreed.'

'Get your uniform on then. I'll go and get the motorbike out of the garage.'

I very much wanted to appear brave in front of this stunningly beautiful woman and I made tremendous efforts not to flinch at the gentle touch of her fingers on my cuts and bruises. My stoicism had no effect on Anait however: she was looking at Zhenya Zhukov over my shoulder, or rather, they were looking at each other, as if they were alone in the office what's more. Her eyes were so blue I just couldn't understand how a woman called Anait Seddik could possess them.

She said something to Zhukov and he translated:

'You should have an x-ray. Two head injuries and a blow on a vertebra, that's bad. And she's asking you not to pretend, because you're confusing the clinical picture.'

Anait started to laugh and I began to smell a rat.

'You know Russian?'

'Yes of course I do. I'm a graduate of the First Medical Institute in Moscow. I've got a terrible accent though . . .'

I shook my fist at Zhukov.

'And sometimes I can't find just the right words.'

'Couldn't we do without the x-ray?'

'No. That's out.'

Oho. A character.

'It'll be soon. Ten minutes. Or should I say "quick"?'

'Are you a surgeon?' I was intrigued for some reason.

'Neurosurgeon. I did my practice at the Burdenko Institute.'

At these words, she and Zhukov exchanged such a meaningful glance that I guessed it was there that they met. Zhukov had spent about three months in that institute on some case two and a half years ago. I also guessed that Zhenya's flight to Afghanistan was not in the main prompted by his knowledge of Farsi.

'You'll have to wait two or three minutes,' said Anait, as she did about ten photographs using various pieces of x-ray equipment; then she led me into a tiny cubicle.

Somebody was singing to a guitar. I thought: 'The boys can't sleep', and partly-opened the door to listen. The tune was somehow familiar, but it was the first time I'd heard the words.

> The wind disperses smoke above Kabul.
> That girl now walks the street with someone else,
> That girl who promised once that she would wait.
> The melting snow has now erased the name . . .
>
> The mother weeps, the father stands, a shade
> So many of them, unreturning hearts,
> So many who had scarce begun their lives,
> Now coming home in coffins made of zinc . . .

'You can get dressed now,' came the voice of Anait. 'Anything the matter?'

'N-no . . . Can I look and see who's singing?'

'Do you like it? They sing very nicely, mostly sad songs.'

Anait opened the door into the ward: mere boys were sitting there on the beds, looking as wounded should, some with arms bandaged, some with heads.

'Hi,' I said, over-loudly.

Anait regarded me with astonishment. I couldn't very well explain to her that I just had to see those boys. It had seemed to me that it was dead men singing.

'No concussion, vertebra undamaged, no damage to cranial bones . . .'

142

Anait indicated the grey-white blotches on the illuminated screen.

'. . . But you'll have to avoid . . . stress, shock for six months, even a year, because the intracranial haematomae . . .'

I wasn't paying too much attention to all this and openly looked at my watch. One thing was clear, I had to guarantee myself a peaceful existence at least for the next six months. That was one thing I couldn't promise.

Klopova, the duty doctor, waved her plump hands about and said languidly:

'Well, tell me all about it, how are things in Moscow? It's so provincial here, you know, so provincial . . .'

I suspected that Madame Klopova had maybe passed through Moscow now and again, but I nodded sympathetically and spoke firmly:

'Comrade Klopova, we're very short of time, since the activisation of the merobius is assuming threatening proportions. We'll be delighted to swap reminiscences when our work is finished.'

'Yes, yes, comrades, of course. Follow me.'

'We are requesting comrade Seddik to accompany us,' added Zhukov, 'we shall need her assistance, not only as a doctor, but as interpreter.'

'Yes, I understand.'

What she understood would be hard to say. Fortunately for us, Madame Klopova was as dumb as they come.

The subaltern on duty saluted me and stood to attention as if I were his senior in rank. I deliberately held my white coat in my hand, so the duty-man could see my major's epaulettes. He studded the 'letter from the Ministry' with care, and I anxiously expected him to ask us to show our papers. Surprisingly, the subaltern smiled broadly and with a glance at our faces, unerringly addressed Zhukov:

'So you're from Tashkent as well! I'm from Hospital Street, where do you live, comrade Osipov?'

I stopped breathing. But only for a second, because Zhukov was cheerfully clapping the officer on the shoulder:

'Right in the middle! On Twelve Poplars Street.'

'That's next to me! And here I've been in Turdistan three years now . . . well, what am I doing holding my friends up? Follow me, I'll show you everything. Only the documents etcetera are in comrade Habibi's safe, you'll have to wait for him . . . He'll be here soon.'

'Where's comrade Habibi's office?'

'Ground floor. The safe with the case histories is behind the door,' the officer announced cheerily.

Too good to be true, as the English say in similar circumstances. Truly when one is far from home a fellow townsman is a welcome sight.

The door bore the sign 'AB Department'. A soldier in an Afghan military uniform lazily opened the door at a sign from the officer. A lengthy corridor. A table by the window. Seated there, a slip of a nursing sister. The subaltern adopted a bossy tone towards her – showing off his authority in front of his townsmen:

'Olya, let's have a list of sick personnel.'

'Everybody?!' asked Olya, alarmed.

'Are there so many?' I inquired.

'Around two hundred . . .'

Well, well.

'Yes, of course, everybody.'

Zhukov and I looked through the lists, and at once I saw it: Smirnov. There was another Smirnov on the next page. And another one. Quite inappropriately I recalled the children's poem: 'In this world there's a lot of Smirnovs, just a few less than Ivanovs'.

'We'll start with Ward No. 4,' said Zhukov. 'Everyone may consider themselves free to leave, with the exception of Doctor . . . I'm sorry, I've forgotten your name . . .'

'Seddik,' Anait replied, her voice barely audible.

* * *

There were two people in Ward 4. The bed-heads bore cards with names and a short anamnesis in Latin. But I knew without the name-plate that one of them was Halilov. He was making flying gestures with his hands and on seeing us, laughed and stuck his head under the blanket. Anait took down the cards.

'Both are seriously affected. Consciousness unstable. Amnesia.'

'Can you get him back to reality by some means?'

'It's very dangerous. I could give him an injection to . . .what did you say? . . . get him back to reality but only for five minutes.'

'Please, Anait.'

With an abrupt movement, Anait flung the blanket aside and raised Halilov's slack arm. The boy gave no reaction to the needle but his face gradually took on a normal appearance, however – he was frightened.

'Hello, Bulat. I'm a doctor. I want to help you. All of you. You must tell me what happened to Dubov, Alexey Dubov. You remember him?'

'Alyosha, Alyosha, I remember, I do. He died, so he did.'

Bulat Halilov keened thinly, and howled in between times. Zhukov left the ward as soundlessly as a shadow, clutching his lists of soldiers.

'How did he die, Bulat?'

'A knife.'

'Who stabbed him with the knife?'

'The commander.'

'What was his name?'

'His name was Lieutenant Ivonin.'

'Why did the lieutenant do this, Bulat?'

'Alyosha swore at him a lot. He was very angry at the commander.'

'Why was he angry?'

Halilov began to howl thinly again.

'Why did Alyosha swear at the commander, Bulat?'

'Alyosha didn't want to have the injection. Alyosha didn't want us to have injections.'

'Who gave you the injections?'

'I don't know the name. Bad doctor. Said, "You will be brave".'

'Russian doctor or Afghan?'

'Russian doctor, bad.'

'Who else saw the commander kill Alyosha, Bulat?'

'Sergeant saw. Nobody know he saw.'

'What is the sergeant's name?'

'Morozov. He wrote a letter to Moscow. Alyosha had girl. Very pretties girl. Morozov wrote letter to him. Was big fighting. Nobody saw. I saw. Morozov saw. Sergeant Morozov said: "We don't talk, Bulat. They will kill us".'

Halilov paused for a moment, then suddenly began singing in Tartar.

'Bulat, hold on, don't sing. Smirnov was with you as well. Private Smirnov?'

The expression of alarm disappeared from Halilov's face. He wagged his arms about again as if trying to take off.

'That's all there is, Sasha,' said Anait.

I had the photofit picture of the second murderer in my hand, Griaznov's copy, as mine had been left in the briefcase with General Seri. I hadn't had time to show it to Halilov. Now I needed the Smirnovs.

Vitali Smirnov was in Ward 2. Fortunately for me (and the rest of the Smirnovs in the hospital) he turned out to be the Smirnov from Ivonin's squad. However, he knew nothing of the circumstances of Sergeant Alexey Dubov's death. That is, he knew only the official version. No, he'd never seen anybody resembling the photo-fit. Who did the injections? Doctor Zinaida Pavlovna. Anait added quietly that the surname was Golovko. Did he know why she did the injections? Yes, so that nobody would be afraid.

I felt I couldn't stay any longer in section AB, my heart was lacerated with pity for these boys. We left the department and I glanced into all the wards where the 'ordinary' wounded were. I showed the photo-fit. No, nobody had ever seen that young man . . .

'Sasha, Anait, we're clearing out of here!' I heard Zhukov's penetrating whisper. 'Habibi's arrived.'

'What does "clearing out" mean?' asked Anait anxiously.

Zhukov said something quickly in Farsi and hugged her. We walked along a corridor leading to the exit on the opposite site of the building, with Zhukov turning round all the time. We reached the staircase and here Zhukov halted and stood motionless for several seconds looking back towards the end of the corridor where the tiny figure of Doctor Anait Seddik could just be seen.

'We're letting her in for it, Zhenya.'

'No, the story's been rehearsed. She'll cope. Come on, down to the cellar, there's a way out there into one of the side streets.'

I had difficulty in pulling the heavy steel door towards me and it was Zhenya who closed it tightly behind us . . . and swore savagely. I didn't at once realise that we'd gone through the wrong door. It wasn't the cellar, it was the boiler-room, and we couldn't open the door from inside. We were trapped.

Around us everything was hissing and whistling in the pitch darkness. The only thing I know about boilers comes from a lecture on anti-aircraft defence – boilers have a tendency to explode.

'Have you got a lighter?' asked Zhukov. 'I left mine in my jeans.'

I found my lighter and we felt our way slowly round our damp and stuffy prison. It must have been 130° Fahrenheit in there.

'There has to be a ventilation hatch, dammit!' shouted Zhukov.

Well he ought to know, he was a builder.

'Zhenya, we can't breathe here, lets get our clothes off,' I suggested, whining.

'Aha! There she is! See the grille?'

I couldn't see a thing except the lighter flame. Nor could I look up at the ceiling where Zhukov was indicating, because my head was spinning and I could barely suppress the nausea rising in my throat. Zhukov, with some swearing, was clambering along the narrow little metal ladder of one of the boilers and shouted down:

'Strip off, Sashok, underpants only. I've found a little hole! We'll be out of here in a minute.'

I turned my head upwards. Zhukov was standing on the top of a boiler with an enormous grille-cover in his hands. I could see the sky, a tiny square of sky. An extremely tiny square. And the grille-cover began to spin slowly then faster and faster . . .

I came to as a stream of cold water struck me in the face.

'Phew-w, Sashok. You had me really worried there, old pal. See, I've found a water hose. The lighter-fuel's finished, we'll have to get sorted out in the dark. You sit there, like me, hold onto the pipe, I'll just get the ladder set-up . . . Idiots, there's no light switch inside the boiler-house, it's on the outside . . .'

A dim illumination penetrated the place from the ventilation hatch all the same. I dragged my clothes off and was left in my shorts. The water in the pipe was icy and I was soaked from head to foot. Zhukov meanwhile was tying together belts, trousers, and gowns with deft and rapid movements.

'I reckon seven yards will do it. Can you get up on the boiler? I'll try and crawl out through the hatch and let this lot down on you. You tie my attaché case with this vest, it'll go through the hatch, I've measured. Don't forget the case, its got the films of . . . well the Faust thing. The hospital chief's safe wasn't too hard to get into . . . turn that hose on me, Sashok.'

I guided myself by Zhukov's silhouette in the hatchway. As he rose it looked as if he was contradicting human physical limitations. He was moving away from me very slowly, so slowly indeed that he seemed to be moving on the spot – elbows, back, knees . . . elbows, back, knees . . . I tensed with his every movement and I felt a spasm under the diaphragm. I tried not to look up, since there was nothing I could do to help Zhenya. I just waited. I sat in a pool of water and waited. I waited a good hour probably. When I eventually did raise my head, I saw again that far-off square of sky at the end of the empty hatchway. Then I heard a quiet whistle and the improvised ladder was lowered onto the boiler. I secured Zhenya's attaché case to it and looped a strong military belt under my armpits . . .

We rolled into the courtyard of Zhukov's block on the motor-bike and saw Bunin and Griaznov sitting on a bench in the shade of the building. They were dressed and combed ready for the journey home. Their faces were very sad. On seeing us, however, our comrades ceased to be sad, quite the reverse in fact – they started to crease themselves laughing.

'What's up, cadets?' Zhukov was irritated. 'Men have, you might say, torn themselves from the shaggy paws of death, and here's you cackling like children at a circus!'

'Just turn round, my son!' sobbed Bunin, slapping us on the bare shoulders.

'Simple-hearted savages! Just what I need. What's so damned funny?' This was exasperating.

'You are, pals, just take a look at each other! What do you look like?' Griaznov was killing himself.

Zhukov and I stared at each other: naked, just drawers on, filthy, carrying armfuls of wet rags, complete with gleaming metal motor-cycle helmets and Zhukov's elegant little attaché case. All four of us fell about.

'Can you imagine . . . the capital . . . of the Democra . . . Democratic Republic . . . of Afghanistan . . .' Zhukov couldn't get over it, 'and not one police . . . dog . . . after the Russian "shuravi"!'

'In Moscow the first traffic cop would have wondered which mental home you'd escaped from,' chuckled Griaznov.

'Pity Doctor Seddik couldn't see you now, Zhenya,' I said. 'She's missing a lot.'

'That's enough of that, why don't you tell them how you sat in that puddle squealing: "Mama, I want to go home"!' Zhenka got his own back. 'Incidentally I'm famished. Sashka and I'll have a shower while you lads empty out the fridge, it's all got to go, who knows when I'll be back . . .'

He slung the remains of his suit, the major's uniform and the hospital gowns into a dustbin.

When I emerged from the shower an enormous egg fry-up courtesy of Bunin and Co. was standing on the table; Griaznov had concocted a salad out of scores of vegetables. Zhukov was yelling incoherently down the phone.

'. . . Tell the trust manager I've had to fly out urgently to HQ to get hold of funds, about two weeks. Got it, Arkady Abramovich? Don't forget to sign the quota sheets for next month otherwise people won't get paid! And send a car, say half an hour. Got that Arkady Abramovich? All of it, you old prick.'

The last sentence of course, was said after he replaced the receiver.

11

'Citizen passengers,' said the sergeant-stewardess walking between the rows of seats, 'our aircraft is on a special flight to Moscow. One stop – Tashkent. You are requested to fasten your seat-belts and refrain totally from smoking.'

'No need for them to strap in,' Bunin prodded me in the ribs, 'they're tied up already . . . to their escorts.'

I took a look and saw it was true. Every passenger was chained to an escorting soldier. Bunin grinned as he explained:

'Its the Judge Advocate's Office, they've got a big case on – around 30 million involved. These chaps are wheeler-dealers, big noises in the frontier admin, customs and so forth, along with various Afghan dealers, they've been transporting heroin and Japanese cameras and suchlike, inside zinc coffins, like corpses. The documents were made out in the name of officers and generals who'd been killed. From the Moscow end, into Afghanistan I mean, they sent gold, diamonds, antiques, all supposed to be packaged goods, medicines, magazines . . . get the idea? See that fat one there in the front row? That's Rajanov, former Minister of Justice in Tadjikistan and First Secretary of our embassy here after that. What he got up to would make your hair curl. He bribed the customs men. Gold was sent in from various countries in his name. He passed it over to Afghan businessmen and they in turn to the Mojahedin. During customs inspection at Sheremetyevo, a suspicious-looking parcel from Saudi Arabia was found addressed to him. They found twenty-three kilos of gold in there, you'll never guess – one million roubles! Now do you realise, Sasha the class of people we're travelling with!'

Actually I didn't take all that much in. I was more interested in the whereabouts of the hygiene-bag. I eventually found it in the seat-pocket right under my nose.

'Not feeling well?' asked Bunin.

'Not yet,' I answered, without much confidence.

In front of us Griaznov and Zhukov were sitting, writing on the tip-up eating tables. Griaznov was, anyway. Zhukov was lying back in his seat, eyes closed, dictating to him quietly.

'What are you doing there?' I inquired.

'You just go to sleep. You'll find out anon.' Griaznov winked at me.

'Listen Sash,' Bunin dug me in the ribs again. 'The Judge Advocate let me in on something else. It seems he's investigating the illegal use of narcotic substances. They've invented some new sort of drug.'

'Who's "they"?'

'Hell knows. The doctors I expect. They tried the stuff out on officers. It costs plenty – each injection costs about six thousand roubles, so they can't afford luxury like that for the troops. Once you get the injection, you feel no fear and you're ready to carry out any order. The main ingredient is a stabiliser – that's what cost the money. This stabiliser balances up the action of the narcotics and there are no harmful aftereffects. The only reaction is a disturbance in visual focus, reverse astigmatism so-called.'

I knew what Bunin was on about. Faust. 'They' had been trying it out on troops as well, in a simplified form. Without the stabiliser. And now those soldiers, 250 men, were sprawled around the Central Hospital. With irreversible brain damage. The officers, Ivonin and co., had contracted the astigmatism, their eyes darted about from side to side.

'Vanya, this adds up to a terrible crime. Why the hell didn't the Judge Advocate report it to the higher-ups?'

'They had no proof. They've not got much now. Slavomir Vasilievich passed on the material for Gorny and I rang him this morning, while you and Zhukov were climbing up your boilers. Tomorrow morning I'm going to him with a report

... You can't keep your eyes open, Sashok, why not have a snooze?'

'Vanya . . . I want to thank you.'

'Whatever for?'

'You saved me . . .'

'What a weirdo! What would you have done in my place then?'

'Then . . . you'd be . . . thanking me . . .'

I fell into a long dreamless sleep and only opened my eyes when we were landing at Tashkent. We four were alone in the cabin – they'd taken the criminals off the plane and through the port I could see a black maria driving up alongside. Griaznov was sitting next to me now, while Bunin snored away in front, lolling on Zhenka's shoulder.

'Had a little snooze? Enjoy yourself, read a detective story.' Here Griaznov held out some sheets of paper covered in Slava's familiar handwriting.

Top Secret
One copy only
Not to be filed

To: Head of Inquiry Section
Moscow Public Prosecutor's Office
Senior Juridical Counsellor
K. D. Merkulov

Senior Investigator, Moscow
Public Prosecutor's Office,
A. B. Turetsky

Special Report

I, Militia Captain Griaznov, V.I., Senior Inspector Moscow CID, City Executive Committee, assisted by E. I. Zhukov, former Senior Inspector, Moscow CID, at present acting head of Building Assembly Directorate No. 1, Special Construction Trust No 4 in the territory of the Democratic Republic of Afghanistan, have been engaged in field-agent operations to discover the persons who murdered Kim Lagina, and in addition witnesses who may be in possession of valuable evidence concerning the circumstances of the above-mentioned crime.

As a result of operations the following has been established:

Evgeni Zhukov has retained important contacts within the police service in Kabul. Several of his 'sources' have risen to positions of prominence in the government of Babrak Karmal (General Said Haleg, for example, has become first deputy minister for state security – HAD), while others have joined the partisans and become leaders of the resistance (for instance, one of the highest-ranking Afghan policemen – Golam Niraki at present heads the Kabul city partisan movement). Naturally, both sides have a ramified network of agents throughout Afghanistan. At my request, Zhukov entered into contact with Generals Said Haleg and Golam Niraki and obtained valuable information as well as affording me the opportunity for active operations.

Using Zhukov's agent network, I was able to penetrate the special forces barracks and take from V. Ivonin's locker a pair of boots of American manufacture, which he was wearing during the murder of Kim Lagina. (Since a print of this boot was found at the scene of the crime, I have added it to the file of material evidence.)

General Haleg is a personal friend of General Seri, Special Forces. They spend their free time together in the city's open spaces, visit restaurants as well as underworld haunts. This acquaintance with Seri gives Haleg valuable information which he has shared with Zhukov. In particular, there was discussion of the re-organisation of the bodyguard system for members of the Politburo Central Committee. The point is that the head of Special Forces, Marshal Agarkin, has persuaded the General Secretary of the Central Committee of the CPSU of the unreliability of his personal bodyguard, consisting as it does of KGB personnel who have been supplying the GB leadership with information concerning the private lives of previous General Secretaries of the Party. Two months ago a new bodyguard service was formed, made up of special forces officers who had been trained in Afghanistan. At present, the head of the General Secretary's bodyguard is special forces Major Edward Troyan, formerly commanding the battalion in which V. Ivonin served. Troyan and Ivonin are close friends and Troyan has been agitating for Ivonin's secondment to the Gensec's bodyguard.

I also report that with the aid of Golam Niraki and his partisans we succeeded in saving Investigator Turetsky from death. (He had been abducted by the specials and thrown into prison. During an attempt on the part of the criminals to kill Turetsky, who had declined to acommodate General Seri in dropping the investigation of Ivonin, we were compelled to liquidate Vladimir Ivonin and his accomplice Tsegoyev.)

Since the further presence of our investigation group in Afghanistan was hazardous to the lives of its members the decision was taken to cease work in the DRA and return to Moscow.

I request that this report be destroyed after familiarisation with contents.

June 23 1985   Senior Inspector Moscow CID
                             Militia Captain V. Griaznov

'I wonder if this Troyan was bitten as well?'

'I imagine we'll find that out in Moscow, when we develop the films.' Griaznov indicated with his thumb where Zhukov's case lay on the hand-baggage rack. 'Ooh! Another air-pocket. I hate those things, Sashok. Do your ears pop? We've still got two hours' flying left, I wish we were down, Godammit.'

'D'you fancy a drink? I slept through dinner incidentally.'

'Hard liquor is forbidden on board aircraft,' came Zhukov's hoarse baritone, with poorly disguised regret.

'We could have a couple of bottles of Riesling.' Bunin had come alive, as if he hadn't just been snoring like a bear in its den.

With the assistance of the sergeant-stewardess, we organised a picnic aboard the airliner. We tipped back the seats and improvised a table. We got three bottles of Riesling (acting on Bunin's valuable suggestion) and the sergeant fetched four portions of chicken and some shortcake.

As we plunged into air-pockets and dived through thick banks of cloud, we worked out a plan of further investigation. An hour later, two circumstances had become clear: firstly, we needed another one, no, two bottles of Riesling and secondly, our aircraft was going to land at a military field near Kalinin, owing to severe thunderstorms in the Moscow area. Certain adjustments had to be made in our plan of operations, as we only arrived in Moscow at ten in the evening after three-hours lolling about on the electric, which terminated at Leningradsky station and from where I phoned Merkulov. After hearing my brief report, occasionally interrupted by hiccups (caused by the air-pockets, or as Zhyukov suggested, the acid wine), Merkulov advised everybody to have a good rest and appear at the Prosecutor's Office by 12 the next day.

So it was, that without putting on the light and wearing only my socks, I crossed the room to my armchair, pressing the tape-recorder button on the way. I was home. How long since I was here? A month, a year? Don't get soppy, Turetsky. Only two days. Dust levels normal on polished elbow-rests. Two Days?! My hand fell on the telephone. Ring Mam? Say I'm alive? She didn't even know I'd been anywhere. The receiver trembled gently under my palm – a ring. Before answering I remembered: no need to yell into the membraned opening like in Kabul, just pick up the receiver and say calmly:

'Hello . . .'

And I heard a low throaty voice:

'You're back . . .'

'It's so good you're here . . . No, so good that I'm here,' I was prattling some nonsense as I embraced Lana's cool body, 'I though I'd never . . . you'd never . . . that we'd never see each other again . . .'

I wanted very much to tell her about my Kabul adventures, wanted her to feel sorry for me the way a soldier's wife feels about her wounded husband. Griaznov had said she was indifferent and I thought no, she's proud. Could she be both together? No, I'd no idea what she was. I only knew how strong and demanding her hands were, I knew she was the most beautiful woman in the world, I'd never had anyone like her and never would . . .

I lit a cigarette. Lana leaned up on her elbow:

'Now I know why you didn't put the light on.'

She was looking at my cheek, where a huge red blotch stood out in glory.

'That decoration was worth it for the information I'm laying before Merkulov tomorrow.'

'Tomorrow's Sunday.'

'That's all right . . . We're meeting in the Office tomorrow at twelve. You know we were looking into the circumstances of Kim's murder.'

I felt her body tense.

'You found the killers?'

No, she wasn't detached, I could see her eyes glistening in the darkness, two emeralds.

'We found one.'

'How many were there?'

'It's a long story . . .'

'I understand. Secret.'

I grinned. She was right, more or less.

Lana lay back on the pillow and closed her eyes. She was far away from me again, like before, that day when I had first seen her in the street: she'd ducked into the metro and disappeared for ever . . . It was with something like fear that I waited for her to say as she always did: 'I'm going'.

She looked at her watch and slid out from under my arm.

'I'm going.'

I closed my eyes and saw myself high above yellow earth. The door had barely closed behind Lana when, as I fell asleep, I heard the sounds of the national anthem as I had that other time. Midnight exactly . . . If you believe the Pythagoreans, everything in life is repeated and you can't remember when it was you know for certain, sense it, feel it – exactly how it was, but you can't remember – when the devil it was: yesterday? A year ago? In some former existence? She'd said exactly that: 'I'm going', closed the door soundlessly, and as I dozed off I heard the far-off melody of that boring anthem . . .

. . . In the boiler-room it was damp and stifling. Bunin and I were scrambling along a hot, wet ladder. The ladder ended and we hung in the air; one more minute and we would plunge into a huge blazing crater. Then the telephone rang. I wanted to shout at Bunin to tell him not to pick up the receiver, there was no telephone here – and woke up. I put the light on. Twenty past twelve. The phone was silent. Had I just imagined it? I got up and went into the kitchen for a fresh packet of cigarettes. Somebody was standing outside the hall doorway, shifting from foot to foot. I grabbed my little souvenir axe and ripped open the door. Standing there was Irka Frolovskaya. Her face made asking 'Is anything the matter' superfluous, there clearly was.

'Sasha, somebody's got into your car. I rang you from the kiosk but I got no answer. I'm sorry to burst in on you, but . . .'

'Did you ring the door-bell?'

'Yes, almost five minutes ago.'

Irka and I rushed downstairs. After twelve, the lift in our block doesn't work going down. Just as I was, shorts and bare feet, I raced out onto Frunze Embankment. My Moskvich was standing near the flats on its own.

'They've run off, obviously,' gasped Irka. 'They stuck one of those metal things with holes in through the window, between the glass and the door. I was off to the telephone by the Timur shop. I rang and rang . . .'

'Yes, I know, my phone was disconnected.'

I opened the car door and inspected the interior. Everything was in place, radio, West German secret lock, gloves and technical passport in their compartment. I lifted the bonnet, all seemed in order.

'They wanted to steal it, I expect,' said Ira, tentatively. 'Don't think I just made it up.'

'Of course not, Irka, I don't think anything of that sort. What were you doing out here at this time any way?'

'Oh I was just passing. Just passing . . .'

There was something fishy about this. If Irka had been walking along the street, how had somebody dared to break into a car?

'Or rather, I was walking along and decided to sit down for a bit on a bench in the gardens.'

'Irka, you are making it up now. Twelve o'clock at night and you suddenly decide to sit on a bench well out of your way. Do people always sit on benches at midnight outside other people's houses when nothing's the matter?'

Irina laughed, though not very naturally. I became aware that I was standing half-naked in the middle of the street with a small axe in my hand.

'Right, let's go up to my place, Irka and you can tell me all about it, okay?'

Irina couldn't utter a word and it looked to me as if she'd been crying. A vague idea flashed across my brain and I took Ira firmly by the hand.

'Come on, let's go, I'm shivering.'

I pushed her into the lift almost by force and when we were seated on my hastily-tidied sofa, and the aroma was rising from two cups of coffee made by Irina, I began the interrogation, sympathetically of course, though I was aware how cruel I was being.

'You often sit like that near my house?'

'No, not often . . .'

'How long have you been doing it?'

'Oh, a long time . . .'

'How long do you mean to go on doing it?'

'I don't know . . . Till it's over.'

'What's over?'

Irina dragged on her cigarette and calmly sipped her coffee.

'If it bothers you, I won't do it again. If this hadn't happened, you'd never have known about it.'

'Ira, Irisha . . . I'm not the only fish in the sea.'

'Yes you are. At any rate for now – you are.'

159

Well this was a situation and no mistake – reluctantly I felt an extraordinary warmth from Ira's words. She placed her cup on the magazine table, took another drag and spoke at length letting it all out – as if for one last time.

'For you there'll never be anyone who's the only fish. For her either. She's cold. And she doesn't need you. You wouldn't follow each other to the end of the world. I hate her. I don't have the right, I know, she didn't take my place. Rita was . . . something else. She loved you. All the rest . . . everything before Rita and after . . . Passing the time. I didn't want you even to guess about me. It'll pass. I'm just . . . just waiting for it to pass.'

'Ira, honestly, I never thought of anything like that.'

'And if you had, it wouldn't have changed anything.'

'Irina . . .'

'Don't try to console me, please, or I'll hate you as well, or . . . cry, and that would be awful . . . Well, I'm off!'

'Don't go, Irina. D'you want to hear about Afghanistan?'

I told her everything from the very beginning about Kim, the burned letter, the special forces, the Faust elixir and the Kabul hospital. It didn't seem to me that I was contravening the regulation stating that an investigator must be vigilant, keep professional matters secret and not talk at large concerning preliminary investigation data or other evidence of a confidential nature.

Irina listened, chin resting on fist, as the room grew cool and I had to close the window. The stars were invisible, the short June night was coming to an end.

'I'll tell you what Irka, why not lie down and have a sleep. I'll put some sofa cushions on the floor and get a couple of hours myself. I'll see you home in the morning.'

Irka protested feebly but I pulled the cushions out from behind her back and made my bed on the floor.

She was asleep in five minutes, curled up like a croissant on the wide divan.

I felt as if I'd only just dropped off when the door-bell rang, but it was already half past eight.

'Who's there?'

'It's me, Bunin.'

I opened the door and Bunin burst in. Irka looked about her in confusion, hands clutching her head. She was dishevelled, with an odd-looking red triangle on her cheek from lying awkwardly. Bunin stared at her.

'My, you've got good taste!'

Irka and I laughed as I asked him:

'To what do I owe the honour?'

'Owe the honour! Your telephone's not working! Merkulov couldn't get through to you.'

I picked up the receiver and heard a steady humming sound.

'It is working, dammit! Where did you get . . .'

'No time to explain what you've got working and what not . . .'

With these words Bunin threw a teasing glance at Irka.

'Merkulov wants us both urgently at the Office.'

'Us? What about the others?'

'He didn't say and I didn't ask. He said everything had changed and he wanted us at nine.'

'I'll phone him now.'

'Where? He's already left the house. Get yourself ready and I'll go for a walk.' Bunin set off for the door, wafting a kiss to Irka.

'Hang on, Vanya. Here's the car keys, warm up the engine. I won't be a second.'

'What a funny man,' laughed Irina, when the door closed behind Bunin.

I looked at her and sensed a subconscious thought: 'I don't want to get over it.'' But I had no time to think of anything else as an explosive blast of tremendous power echoed from the street into the flat. Irina and I ran to the window. Where my Moskvich had stood, huge yellow-blue flames were raging.

12

The investigation of the circumstances surrounding the blowing up of the Moskvich car MTT 24–75, the death of Legal Service Major Bunin, assistant to the Judge Advocate General and the attempted murder of Senior Investigator Turetsky of the Moscow City Prosecutor's Office, had been going on for over five hours. The firemen had doused what was left of the car in some special compound; all witnesses in the area, including citizens Frolovskaya and Turetsky, had been questioned and evidence taken. Personnel from the local police stations had gone heading off in all directions. A CID investigation team had checked over the scene of the incident. What was left of Vanya Bunin had been taken off to the nearest morgue, that of Medical Institute no. 2. Investigators from the different departments, Prosecutor's Office, police, KGB and experts of various professions had given their opinions. I entertained no hopes, however, of any eventual solution to the crime.

It was in a dream-like state that I accepted what was taking place in my little flat, now invaded by dozens of officers of all ranks from every conceivable service. I didn't even attempt to close the doors as people jostled in the corridor and on the landing. They all talked among themselves, nodded in my direction and gave advice.

As in a dream I listened to the investigator from the Judge Advocate's Office – they were in charge here – of course he was sorry about his colleague Bunin, but the main thing now was to find his murderers; for that, a great deal depended on the nice girl, that is Irina Frolovskaya. She should compile a

162

word-portrait of the terrorists who had tampered with comrade Turetsky's car. This black-browed pretty-boy for some reason read Irina a long lecture on the process of making-up a suspect's portrait. I couldn't understand why the hell he had to show off his erudition just at this moment by lengthy explanations that the term 'photo-fit' had been invented by Pierre Chabot a police commissaire in Lille, whereas 'identikit' was the suggestion of Hugh Macdonald, an assistant sheriff from Los Angeles.

I suspected he was simply trying to chat Irka up, but I felt a strong desire to beat his head in when he started on me with a nasty expression on his face and even nastier questions – how did I get an eight thousand rouble car on a basic salary of 200 a month, why had I handed over my keys to comrade Bunin just like that while I stayed alone with citizeness Frolovskaya and never went near my own car. Still I didn't do anything silly because at 2.30 exactly the lanky figure of Merkulov appeared. He spoke to the investigator and the KGB personnel and the whole lot bowled out of the flat. Merkulov looked at Irina and me, led us out to the duty Volga, and whispered to the driver, who thereupon drove all three of us through the Moscow streets and out onto the motorway towards the suburb of Udelnoye.

The little terrace of Merkulov's *dacha*, bathed in bright sunshine, a summer lunch with *okroshka* (which we barely touched), the noise of volleyball and voices on the beach at Malakhov Pond and many another inevitable accompaniment of a suburban Sunday, all this made the world unbearable for me since it no longer contained Ivan Bunin. We walked along the beach, wandered through the sparsely-wooded copse, sat on the terrace again, drank tea with strawberry jam made by Lelya Merkulova that morning, and we talked about nothing at all – the projected clean-out of the pond, the different kinds of summer honey-mushroom, the high price of fruit, how well 13-year-old Lidochka was getting on with the piano and Irina Frolovskaya's considerable role in her success. We tacitly kept off the events of that terrible morning until a cool night fell on the suburb of Udelnoye. Then Merkulov and I went to the shore of the lake where we all sat down on a bench, still warm from the heat of the day.

All around was still, the watery depths glimmered with stars . . . Then I returned to the world where Bunin was still alive, losing his voice because of cold beer, womaniser and slob, Bunin, the friend who had saved me from death.

Merkulov listened to my tale in silence. I turned my head from time to time to check if he was still there and saw his pallid profile and lips pushed out, trumpet-fashion, chewing on a grass stalk. I left absolutely nothing out, I had no trouble in remembering what came next. It was like watching 'Thirty Hours in Afghanistan' in the cinema and recounting it to Merkulov who couldn't see the screen.

Merkulov interrupted me just once in my narration, when I was talking about the documents given to Bunin by the Judge Advocate.

'You've got this information?'

'Everything went up with . . . with the car. But we've still got Zhukov's films.'

The only thing I kept quiet about was my meeting with Svetlana Belova, since it hadn't the slightest connection with all this.

Merkulov went on without a pause:

'A short piece has been published in *Pravda* saying that a particularly dangerous recidivist Gevorkyan F. A. is deeply implicated in the murder of seven and the wounding of thirty-seven Muscovites unfortunate enough to be travelling in the metro carriage where he had planted a bomb. The inquiries had been completed quickly and the case transferred to the USSR Supreme Court. Before an indictment can be confirmed, as you are aware, the prosecutor is obliged to check the grounds for accusation. I was that prosecutor. Doubts as to the basis of the accusation occurred to me as soon as I ascertained that, on the day of the explosion, Gervorkyan was in Yerevan. The first thing I did was to interrogate the accused. 'The only thing I'm guilty of is leaving my two children as orphans. I know I'll be shot for a crime I did not commit', that's what he said to me and I believed it. There are statements from upwards of a hundred witnesses, testifying to Gevorkyan's innocence.'

Merkulov looked unblinking up into the ultramarine heavens, as if reading his text from there.

'. . . In 1978, when he was a student at the polytechnic institute, he founded the National United Party of Armenia – NUPA, which aimed at securing greater independence for Armenia within the framework of the Soviet federation, using peaceful constitutional methods. He got four years for that. According to the majority of statements he was opposed to terror, in particular he condemned the action of his comrades in setting fire to the stand-portrait of Lenin in the centre of Yerevan. After his release, Gevorkyan did not alter his views and tried to renounce his Soviet citizenship, by reason of his negative attitude towards the Soviet regime. He wasn't allowed to continue his studies, so he started work in a circus, as a labourer at first, then as part of a juggling act . . . Getting damp out here, Sasha. If you don't mind, let's get back to the house. Our womenfolk will be getting lonely. Incidentally I've got a decent cognac . . .'

Once again we were sitting on the terrace, where Irka, Lelya and Lidochka were playing *durak*. Merkulov retrieved a bottle of KV cognac from somewhere and poured some out into china mugs.

'If the women want to join us, they can help themselves. Children must be off to bed, it's one o'clock.'

The 'child' protested a little but went off to bed nonetheless, making mysterious signs to Irka as she did so.

Now Merkulov spoke, staring into his mug of brandy and inspecting the contents closely. Doubtless he was concentrating his thoughts.

'The day of the metro explosion, there were two other bombs discovered which hadn't gone off, one inside a rubbish urn in the GUM store, and the other in another urn in Red Square. Gevorkyan's guilt was beyond question. In the first place there were prints of the middle finger of Grevorkyan's left hand on the inside of the glass of the Glory alarm-clock used in the metro carriage bomb. Also prints of the last two fingers of his left hand on the Victory and ZIM clocks used with the explosives in the urns. Secondly, a sheet of paper was recovered from his flat which had drawings of electrical circuits for home-made explosive devices with annotations in the Armenian language, written by Gevorkyan, according to handwriting experts. I asked Semyon Semyonovich Moiseyev to check the experts' conclusions. As I expected the "incontrovertible" evidence was falsified: the Armenian writing had been traced, though the details of the hand did coincide. The glass of the Glory alarm-clock in the metro bomb was smashed and the finger-prints couldn't be identified. As for the bombs found in the urns, the fingerprints were not made by fingers, they had been photographed from dactyloscope charts of Gervorkyan already in existence . . . Lelya, Lelya! Another cigarette! That's the third one at least.'

Merkulov had put on a distressed expression before splashing more cognac into our mugs.

'You can drink, as long as you don't smoke. She doesn't smoke my Whiffs, but if somebody turns up with a packet of Capital – or even worse Apollo-Union, she'll always grab one,' complained Merkulov.

'It's my fault, Konstantin Dimitrievich, this is the second packet today I'm finishing,' Irina came to Lelya's support.

'Well, better get off to bed, ladies. Everybody's got to be up early tomorrow.'

'I promised I would sleep in Lida's room. Is that all right?' asked Irka.

Merkulov waved an indifferent hand and we were left alone.

'Let's get on. I questioned three witnesses chosen at random from those sentenced for belonging to NUPA. They'd been sent in to Moscow by the KGB from the 'Forest' camps in Mordovia and testified that while in camp, Gevorkyan had spoken to them of his intention to carry out terrorist acts after his release. They confessed to me that they had given their testimony under pressure from KGB investigators and . . . our own Grechannik, who had promised to "arrange" a pardon. One witness, Babayan, I found particularly interesting: his testimony was just a little bit too comprehensive *and* he added to it on many occasions. He was in love with Gevorkyan's sister, but she'd been forbidden to marry him. Babayan was a card-sharper who had been a member of NUPA but was kicked out for persistent lying. His testimony is in the file: he'd seen a clock in Gevorkyan's flat, one of three – a Glory alarm-clock, and Victory and ZIM wristwatches. Gevorkyan was certain that Babayan was a KGB agent. You remember of course that anonymous phone call to Moscow CID at 8.07 am. that day?'

'Of course I do. Grechannik came in, with a mouth like a Cupid's bow: "The bombkin on the metro was planted by Faust".'

'Don't make things up. He said "bomb" not "bombkin". So then, the CID labs managed to decode the garbled part of the sentence: "The bomb on the metro was planted by Faust Gevorkyan, the leader of the national-liberation party of Armenia" . . . don't be too quick with the disappointed face, Sasha . . . The scientific boys also managed to establish the fact that the sound which had obscured the last words of the message was the sound of a pneumatic drill breaking up asphalt. It wasn't too hard to find out, as you realise, that near Block 53 on Peace Prospect, where Babayan lived for a time in flat no. 6, there is a telephone box and there were road-works at the time. The drillers started work at precisely eight o'clock on the day after the explosion. The foreman explained that it takes seven or eight minutes to warm up the generator. I showed the foreman Babayan's photo: had he seen him that morning? There wasn't much hope of that, naturally, but the foreman actually did recognise him as the man of eastern nationality who had sworn at the workmen from the telephone box . . . I know just what you're thinking Sasha: "I knew from the very beginning that it was all a Gee-Bee frame-up". But the point is that I found out (it's a long story) that Babayan was an agent of State Intelligence, not the KGB. His codename is "Serzhik". Conclusions please, Sasha, in three sentences.'

'I can do it in one if I'm allowed to use commas.'

Merkulov smiled:

'Aha! If you're angry that means you're feeling all right. Well?'

'The bomb blast in the metro was organised by people from the special forces. It was used as a pretext by the KGB to discredit the dissident movement in the eyes of the Soviet people as well as world opinion, to prove that the dissidents and any other liberation movement inevitably degenerate from problems of human rights to terror directed against the population at large. It was with this aim and at the prompting of State Intelligence and the KGB that this case against Gevorkyan was cooked up.'

Merkulov evinced no reaction to my brilliant summary and continued:

'Now the epilogue. Along with the City Prosecutor Skaredov, I went along to the Republic Prosecutor Yemelyanov and all three of us announced ourselves to the Procurator-General, Rekunkov. He got in touch with Chebrikov, the chief of the KGB and received the reply: "My people have proved that Gevorkyan is an enemy of our system. They have put forward incontrovertible evidence that the explosion is the work of a hostile organisation. *Pravda* has already carried the news and the Politburo has been informed . . . Prove me another case and I'll set Gevorkyan free." A member of the Politburo said that to a member of the Central Committee, you get the subordination?'

We smoked in silence for a long time.

'Do you think we can give him that proved case?'

'I'm glad to be able to give a definite answer to that Sasha: I don't know . . .'

Merkulov rose and took the two overflowing ashtrays from the table.

'That's enough for today. Let's go and lie down.'

'Sorry, Kostya. One last question: why did you change the time of the meeting this morning?'

'What do you mean?'

He paused above the waste-bin and cigarette-ash trickled onto the floor.

'Who told you I changed the time? I was expecting you at twelve.'

'You didn't phone Bunin because my telephone wasn't working?'

It was just inertia that made me ask, since I already knew what had happened. They'd decided to rub out both Bunin and me. It wasn't just an attempt on me, we were both supposed to be blown to pieces before we could pass on the information we had collected in Afghanistan.

'Who else knew we were supposed to meet at twelve, Kostya?'

'Nobody. You rang from the station and I decided twelve o'clock would be best . . .'

'But you see Bunin said: "Everything's changed and Merkulov wants us at nine" . . . Were they just guessing?'

'Don't think so. It was all planned earlier. They knew you couldn't check, they knew I intended working on Sunday and had to be at the Prosecutor's Office by nine, Parkhomenko and I had discussed it on Friday.'

'So there's someone in the Office who's in touch with them?'

Merkulov finally shook out the ashtrays into the bin, washed them out and said again:

'Enough for today. Let's go and lie down.' And added: 'We'll go and see Gorny in the morning.'

13

Next morning at ten, Merkulov and I got out of the official Volga in the courtyard of the principal building of the Judge Advocate General's Office. The road-washing vehicle had just passed and the wet asphalt shone like polished boots. There was a smell of limes from the rows of trees on Kirov Street.

'From the City Office?' the duty lieutenant saluted. 'Has the news got that far? Bad news travels fast.'

We didn't understand his rapid words and passed through into the lobby where we stood stupefied. In the corner stood a portrait of Artyom Grigorievich Gorny, swathed in mourning ribbons and the dates 1912–1985.

We couldn't understand it:

He couldn't have died? When and how?

The lively old cloakroom-attendant explained all:

'Yesterday it was, at his *dacha*. Right in front of his deputy Popkov. 'Spect he'll take over from Artyom Grigorievich now. Thirty years we've worked with him in this 'ere building. Fancy sitting in that armchair all that time. Only he could do that, God rest his soul, he was a clever man – a statesman!'

We went up to the first floor and Merkulov announced our arrival to an aide. Literally within seconds we were being received by First Deputy Judge Advocate General, Legal Service Lieutenant General Popkov. Tears stood in his eyes, obscured as they were by the smoked lenses of his spectacles.

'I'm glad you dropped by, comrades. Artyom Grigorievich was wondering about you as it happened . . . It's a misfortune, such a misfortune for us all. He's irreplaceable, just irreplaceable. I'm being absolutely sincere about that . . .'

'Ye-es,' drawled Merkulov, at a loss. He seated himself in an armchair, 'Artyom Grigorievich was a strong, courageous and intelligent man . . .'

Popkov shook his head:

'You see how things are, comrade Merkulov. Yesterday there was a car-bomb that killed one of Artyom Grigorievich's aides – Bunin, anyway you know all that better than I do. Our duty officer informed Artyom Grigorievich about it. He spends his days off at his *dacha* in Barvikha. The duty man told me that he'd been very excited at the news and asked for me to be found. I was at my flat in Moscow and bowled round to Barvikha. Artyom Grigorievich had been unwell since morning and when I got there, he said there were to be important talks about events in Afghanistan. He was waiting for important documents from the 40th Army Judge Advocate Bodak and that these documents had gone up in the fire with Bunin. Artyom Grigorievich was in a bad way, I could see that. He had severe asthma and he was swallowing medicines. I suggested he called a doctor from the Kremlin Hospital for a home visit but he said he had more important matters on hand: he was waiting for a connection to Kabul and then he'd talk it all over with me. But the talk with Bodak never took place: the assistant on duty there said that on the way to work, his boss's car had blown up on a mine placed by the dushman bandits. The news seemed to paralyse Artyom Grigorievich – he couldn't breathe, he had a convulsion and died in my arms . . .'

'Excuse me, comrade general, but what were the first names of comrade Bodak?' I interrupted, I wouldn't like to believe that splendid man who treated me to 'Akhasheni' fragrant wine in Afghanistan had been killed.

Popkov rummaged about in his papers and said dryly:

'Slavomir Vasilievich.'

Then he raised his head from the desk and his face resumed its tearful expression. I no longer believed these marks of suffering, however. He wasn't concerned about the death of the skinny little General Bodak, 40th Army Judge Advocate.

And he needn't pretend to be so cut up about his chief, Gorny – he was likely pleased to be taking his place, had no doubt waited ten years at least for something like this . . . I glanced sideways at Merkulov as if he might read my seditious ideas but saw Kostya's cold gaze fixed directly on Popkov. I guessed that he shared my suspicions.

'Now there's all this funeral business as well,' complained Popkov tearfully, as he saw us to the door. 'The Judge Advocate General's Office would have liked to bury Artyom Grigorievich in Red Square by the Kremlin wall. Ministry Council say his services are insufficient, your chief's rank is appropriate to burial in the Novodevichy Monastery . . . Well, we wanted to put Bunin in Novodevichy but the Moscow City council won't wear it: the major rates only the Vagankovskoye – and only just that. Any arguing and you won't get that, you'll have to take the body to Vostryakovo or Nikolskoye . . .'

It was hot in the car and I took off my jacket and placed it on my knees.

'Good idea,' said Merkulov, who was sitting next to me on the back seat of the Volga, and followed suit.

We were bowling along from Kirov Street to Trubnaya along the boulevards. Moscow was living its own peculiar summer life, indifferent to tragedies taking place before its very eyes. Merkulov and I were quiet for a long time, wrapped in our own thoughts. Merkulov was the first to regain the gift of speech.

'We'll drop in at Petrovka, and I'll tell Romanova to issue you with a pistol. Double quick, without the usual red tape . . .'

'Why?' My protest was genuine. 'Now there's nothing . . . lethal threatening me.'

'You sure?'

'Absolutely. From the moment when I told you everything about Afghanistan, I've lost all value for them. You're more in need of weapons and bodyguards than I am, Kostya. Yes you are. I'm not joking. Since yesterday, not only are you the

172

carrier of information dangerous to *them*, but you're somebody with executive powers. You can put away whoever you
like and mix with the big-wigs at the highest level. And that's
dangerous to *them*.'

'Who are "them"? Well for heaven's sake, let's make the
pronoun concrete. Who's playing against us? Or rather, who
should be we directing operations against? Against the KGB?
State intelligence? The Special Forces? Or is it the "Afghan
Brotherhood" that crazy Ivonin told you about?' Merkulov
fished out a Whiff and took a drag. While I'd been away, he'd
gone back to his normal way of smoking and stopped snap-
ping his cigarettes in half. 'We have to define the subject
and . . .'

'. . . begin to think concretely about the future.' I waved
my arms and contrived to knock Merkulov's cigarette out of
his hand. He neatly caught it as it fell and stuck it back in his
mouth as if nothing had happened.

'I know you're hooked on that phrase, Sasha,' said
Merkulov coolly, rubbing his singed palm, 'what concrete
suggestions have you actually got?'

'I don't care who we direct our effort against, we should be
belting along to Staraya Square and shouting at the tops of our
voices that terrorists from the Special Forces blew up that
carriage on the metro, killing several totally innocent people
and that tomorrow they're going to destroy fifty atomic reactors and the planet along with them! This isn't NUPA – its
serious! And here's us toddling along to Petrovka 38 to arm
ourselves with one eight-round pistol. What the devil's happened to the heuristic thinking you keep harping on about to
your investigators?'

'I don't see any contradiction between the heuristic
approach and that of trial and error in the given concrete
situation. So far I see one thing: the members of the notorious
"Afghan Brotherhood" committed the bomb outrage on the
metro, they certainly murdered Kim Lagina, abducted Investigator Turetsky and attempted to kill him. It was probably
they (note – probably) who killed Major Bunin and Bodak.
You realise, the special forces are government troops, like the

frontier troops are. The "Afghan Brotherhood" is an illegal terrorist organisation against which we must concentrate all our resources now. If the specials are carrying out some government instruction you and I can't interfere in that process with our *investigative activities*. Its exactly the same as proving at the level of one Kolkhoz that a market economy is more efficient than a planned one. We need to be able to approach the proper higher organs as experts with questions like that. If we can prove that the "Afghan Brotherhood" committed all these crimes we will save an innocent man from death . . .'

I said nothing. It was hard not to agree with Merkulov. And I felt embarrassed about my stupid escapades.

'You know, Kostya, I didn't like that Popkov one little bit,' I said to change the subject.

'I wasn't exactly enchanted and I didn't believe in his prickish, excuse me, crying. But you and I are now on our way to a government establishment by name Petrovka 38, to see an ageing lady, whom I do have trust in, boundless, one might say . . .'

Near the office of Police Colonel Romanova, head of Department 2 of Moscow CID, was a small niche of a room with a low table, armchairs and standard lamp. Sunk deep in one of these chairs was Zhenya Zhukov with the look of a poor relation who had been ordered to wait in the hall. On seeing us, he leapt out of his chair and he and Merkulov began hugging and clapping each other on the shoulder, as men are supposed to after long separation.

'How could they have got Vanya then . . .' said Zhukov, turning to me. 'Another fine mess . . .'

'What are you sitting here for like a bump on a log?'

'Well I . . . the old woman's in a bad mood. Griaznov's in the lab – the photos are going to be ready soon, the ones I took in the hospital. The quality's not too good, I've only got an amateur camera. Shura wouldn't let me in there. She can't forget how I let her down over the business . . . well . . . when they threw me out. As if I'd done it to her deliberately . . .'

'If you had, Evgeni, I'd have killed you on the spot.'

Colonel Romanova stood in her office doorway, wearing something indescribable made of metal and plastic on her head. I didn't at once notice even that Shura had changed her grey police uniform for an elegant silver dress with a deep decolleté permitting a view of her majestic bosom.

'Well come on into the office . . . You as well, come on Zhukov!'

'Alexandra Ivanovna, I'm helping a citizen here to fill in an application [there really was a dishevelled grey-haired person sitting in the ante-room writing something], two men with moustaches and caps sold him a Volvo, and took the money – twenty thousand – but forgot to hand over the car. They were last seen making off with it . . .'

'Okay, okay. When you've finished with the comrade knock three times and come in.' Romanova indicated a sign on the door, 'In conference'. 'I get these moustaches and caps twenty times a day. Its all so obvious, like a headless nail all these gullible victims run onto,' said Romanova as she slid her head under the electric dryer.

We exchanged astonished glances: the office of the head of CID Department 2 had been transformed into a beauty salon, where two exotic-looking dolly-birds, beautician and manicurist no doubt, scurried about flaunting their bottoms, finely moulded in leather trousers, to the newcomers. In command of this 'operations conference' was a man strongly resembling a young Gregory Peck.

'Alexandra Ivanovna, you'll never have a decent hair-do if you don't dry it properly, please don't let things interrupt the process.'

'Don't keep on Vsevolod, I'm sitting down,' the police colonel said obediently and at once started complaining loudly to Merkulov, drowning out the noise of the drier:

'Work up to here, murders and robberies and now a delegation of American lawyers led by Professor Hazard has just rolled up and our chief Kotov has got his orders: look after them in due form and lay on a dinner, everybody to have their wives with them like they do in the West. And where are we going to get them from? Some are at their *dachas*, others can't get time off from their bosses. So Kotov issues the command: "Shura, you're going to be my wife!" What sort of wife would I make? I've never been out of uniform for a year. I've forgotten what a permanent-wave is. I'm like a cow on an ice-rink in my high heels. Thats why I'm in a bitch of a temper. Zhukov got the sharp edge of my tongue, well, anyway . . . What made me really mad that time, what I can't forget, is that he hit that food institute professor – Sidorov, the next day, when he was sober.'

'That was because he called the police station chief "rubbish", Alexandra Ivanovna,' said Zhukov as he entered the office.

'They call us that ten times a day, do we clout them all?'

'They're just riff-raff, this was a professor after all . . .'

Merkulov and I had a good laugh over Zhukov's cast-iron logic while Gregory Peck was putting the finishing touches to Shura's hair.

'Shura . . .' said Merkulov in amazement, 'why, you're the queen of the ball! No one would think you were, well I won't say the number!'

'Go on, Konstantin, go on, otherwise they'll think I'm sixty.'

Shura took a contented look at herself in the mirror.

'Yes, you really are a magician Vsevolod. There's still an hour till dinner, you've made it in nice time. Griaznov fixed this "magic" as a home visit, CID visit rather, they're only too keen, things are a bit tight in the black economy, am I right, Vsevolod?'

I wanted to compliment Shura as well. She really didn't look forty-eight. Or even forty. But I had scarcely opened my mouth before Romanova let fly:

'And what are you doing gadding about the streets? It's not enough to have your skull bashed in is it? D'you want to get shot? You should have bought him a pair of dark glasses Konstantin, that bruise makes his pretty face look a mess.'

'Well, why we came to see you, Shura . . .'

'Hold it, Konstantin, let's see the miracle-workers out, then we'll talk shop . . .'

Merkulov rubbed his cheeks with his palms as if to keep out the frost, though it must have been nearly ninety in that office. He spoke:

'Lay on a Makarov could you, comrade Romanova, for Senior Investigator Turetsky, follow all the rules of police bureaucracy, only quickly.'

'I already realised that, Konstantin. See – I'm holding the receiver and dialling the number . . . Is that Mikhailov? Romanova here . . . Get hold of a decent Makarov will you, one that shoots straight . . . What're you mucking me about for if you're not Mikhailov? Well, put him on quick then . . .'

While Romanova was giving Mikhailov his orders, a radiant Griaznov entered with a sheaf of photographs, not quite dry, and laid them on Shura's able.

'They've come out pretty well,' said Zhukov carelessly and sighed with relief.

'What d'you mean, "pretty well"?' said Griaznov sharply.

'No need to shout, Vyacheslav, can't you see I'm on the telephone,' Romanova intervened and continued sparring with Mikhailov as she ran her eyes over the pictures.

Griaznov went on in a whisper:

'Your film, Zhenya, you can't take your eyes off it, it's the goods. How you took pictures like that in the time you had, I just can't understand. Stirlitz behind enemy lines isn't in it!'

'Our lab boys are pretty experienced and their equipment – top class.'

Merkulov studied the photographs long and hard. We didn't distract him, though Shura did glance at her watch now and again. Finally he rubbed his cheeks again, blew his nose, smoothed his hair, lit up a cigarette and only then did he begin to speak, slowly:

'I would ask you, Alexandra Ivanovna, to get your operations team together and show them this list. For the most part the names are of soldiers who have lost their minds as a result of being injected with stimulants and have been under treatment ever since . . . more precisely they're waiting for death in Kabul Central Hospital. We can't help them now, sad to say. The ones following are of officers who received the so-called stabiliser. The majority of them are continuing to serve in Afghanistan. But there are others who have been posted to Moscow, the GDR, Hungary and elsewhere. Apart from those, there are men who've been demobilised and are scattered about in various towns and villages. We're most interested in them. Further on there are the people sent on courses, to academies and higher military colleges. These people are also to be thoroughly investigated . . . Third, I have an idea. From what I understood of Alexander Borisovich's report, and the materials I've already looked through, these people from the "Afghan Brotherhood" are psychologically deranged. People like that have powerful fantasies, by which I mean they commit rather unusual crimes. As you know, there is a criminal world where people commit routine crimes, and a criminal anti-world where extraordinary crimes are commited. Its about that anti-world that I wish to talk to your operatives and point them towards these unusual, as I would say, mad, criminal acts . . .'

Shura broke in:

'Kostya, let's have a good look at that list again. You know I've got an eye like a hawk, got a feeling I'd seen one of those names somewhere, just as it flicked past.'

Romanova took the lists and pictures again, her basilisk eyes filled with excitement; soon her hand reached out for the intercom:

'Pogorelov, come in please. No buts. Step on it.'

The stout Major Pogorelov, an old acquaintance of ours, came in. He greeted Merkulov and me, winked at Zhukov, and said, puffing somewhat:

'Stifling in here, just like before a thunderstorm . . .'

Romanova shuffled the photographs like cards.

'Valentin, does the name Gudinas mean anything to you?'

Pogorelov looked at her, frowning and rubbing his hand through the few hairs on the back of his head.

'If it's the Gudinas who ran amuck in the Tretyakov

Gallery, it does mean something. What was he called now, Yurgenas? Yurgenas Gudinas?' ·

Romanova opened out the photos and looked hard at the 'G' names:

'Gurdinas Yurgenas, 27 years of age . . .'

'Served in Afghanistan? It's him then,' replied Pogorelov without a pause, he knew his job better than anyone.

'I told you, didn't I: eye like a hawk.' Shura smiled contentedly.

'Alexandra Ivanovna – my beloved wife, it's time we were off!' The portly figure of Kotov, head of Moscow CID loomed in the doorway. 'Intelligence sources report that the Americans are languishing in the Budapest. Come along, come along!'

'Boys, I'll be back soon. Then we'll start operations. In the meantime, Pogorelov can tell you about that business from . . . the anti-world. Valentin's a dab hand at stories like that.'

'What about a few beers – it's mightly hot,' suggested Pogorelov when the doors had closed behind the management.

'With great pleasure,' said Merkulov unexpectedly in support, 'nip off to the cafeteria Sasha, and get a few pies while you're at it.'

He felt in his pocket for money.

'My treat! I've got currency haven't I?' announced Zhukov, 'We've got . . . you've still got – well, red caviare shall we say?'

'Get away – living it up again!' Griaznov shook his head but made little protest.

In fifteen minutes the office of the head of CID Department 2 underwent its second transformation of the day, this time into a pub. Crunching a smoked eel, Pogorelov began his tale.

'Just like people, works of art have their own lives, and go through exciting times and dramas. In January 1913 in the Tretyakov Gallery . . .'

'Valentin, have you gone barmy? Who the hell wants to hear about 1913,' interrupted Griaznov.

'You needn't listen, Slava, if you don't want to,' countered the police-major peaceably; wiping the beer-froth from his lips, he went on in the same spirit.

'Well now. In January 1913, a madman called Balashov drew a knife in the Tretyakov Gallery and rushed at Repin's picture "Ivan the Terrible and his son Ivan". And seventy-two years later, it happened again.'

'At 12.30 on May 13th a child was shouting out in the Repin room, "Oh, look, look! That man's killing the Tsar!" The policeman on duty raced out from behind an exhibition stand on hearing the shouting and saw the disfigured master-piece: across Ivan the Terrible's hips ran a gaping wound, while some strong-smelling lumpy mass of stuff was bubbling across the face. A man with burns on his face was bent over unnaturally in front of the picture. He was wearing a leather jacket. His right hand was pressing a jar against his chest, the left hand held a knife. The police sergeant got the better of him after a short struggle. The burned man kept shouting: "I've killed General Seri"!'

'He was right. After all, Seri does look like the Repin tsar,' I thought, 'he'll be exactly like him when he's an old man, if . . . he lasts that long.'

'. . . Well, briefly this is what we found out. A month before the incident, Gudinas had come back from Afghanistan. He'd got burned out there in a personnel-carrier and they'd fitted him out with a metal splint from wrist to elbow. He'd been living with his auntie in Moscow, no registration, working for the Aviation Institute exams. Inquiries were made at the Vilnius city military board where his papers had arrived from the Ministry of Defence. It turned out that Yurgenas Gudinas had been a senior lieutenant in the special forces, a first-class officer, it seemed. He had the reputation of being well-read, hobby was collecting side-arms and . . . he wrote poetry as well.

'. . . The findings of the psychiatric examination were: Asteno-hypochondric syndrome, brought on by deep traumas possibly at seeing people tortured . . . Experiences of this nature lead to the destruction of moral and spiritual values in a given personality and give rise to vicious emotions and urges. Scenes of torture are especially dangerous for youths and young men . . . At present the patient is suffering from a chronic mental illness in the form of schizophrenia which deprives him of the capacity to evaluate his own actions.' Pogorelov concluded his narrative.

'Have you still got the working papers on the case?'

'I'll fetch them now, Konstanin Dmitrievich.'

Without waiting for Romanova's return, Merkulov began a micro-conference with our tiny complement. Pogorelov, just as if he was playing a game of forfeits, dug his plump hand into a leather bag and drew out a number of objects of various shapes, dimensions and applications.

'Do we need this?' he queried uncertainly, looking at a jar of acid. 'And this?' He cautiously placed a 'Fox' hunting-knife on the edge of the table.

'Have we got specialists' reports on that knife?' asked Zhukov.

Pogorelov's reply was precise, as if it had been written out.

'Stereoscopic analysis of the blade revealed fragments of oil paint and canvas adhering to it. Nothing else. No human blood on this 'Fox'. Here's a second copy of the findings – twenty-five pages plus sixteen photographs.'

Then he began to make a pile of the pieces of paper and Merkulov carefully scrutinised each one before handing it on to us.

'Here's the pictures of the damage to the canvas. The specialists have restored it so it looks as if nothing had happened to it, by the way.'

But Merkulov and I were looking at the pieces of paper. We at once put on one side a note – a sheet torn from a writing-pad: 'Brother, we have to meet, ring 319-85-58 evening. Anatoli'.

'Has he got any brothers?' I asked Pogorelov.

'No, he's the only son.'

Pogorelov didn't quite realise why we were looking at each other so significantly. Was 'Brother' linked to the 'Afghan Brotherhood'?

'Get working on this telephone,' Merkulov handed the note to Griaznov, who left the office.

'This paper's a bit odd as well, something written in Lithuanian, it's nobody's name though. That telephone number – 225-23-44 – it's a Moscow number, a government office, what's more.'

Pogorelov pulled out his last forfeit – an exercise book in a grey cover.

'As far as I can see, it's his diary, look – dates on some pages. In Lithuanian.'

'Sasha, you deal with this. Get hold of some Lithuanian and hurry . . . And I think we'll take all Valentin's stuff along. Write out a requisition.'

Griaznov returned.

'The telephone belongs to Anatoli Andreyevich Tumanov, living on Chertanovskaya Street, Block 118 Section 3, flat 102. I've handed it over to the regional squad. We'll soon learn all there is to know about our dear "brother".'

Zhukov picked up the lists and checked the letter T. There were no Tumanovs.

'So then,' Merkulov announced, summing up his inspection, 'we'll find out this ex-special's contacts with his former comrades in arms. All telephone numbers to be checked out, I mean it, we might just get a lead. Well, Vyacheslav?'

'Can do, can do. If they're Moscow numbers it's simple.'

Merkulov, Griaznov and I looked through dozens of folders holding case-summaries – information on crime throughout the country. We were looking for criminals whose trademark resembled the young lad in the leather jacket, the one who used to go out with Ivonin on 'dodgy jobs'. We didn't find anything. Then we turned our attention to any specially daring crimes committed over the last month. In Marusino village in White Russia, a group of terrorists had kidnapped a policeman and two women and demanded ransom. In Leningrad, two boys with short hair-cuts had murdered a cashier. A bomb had gone off near Severodvinsk harbour.

After all this I went off to the armoury to pick up my nice new Makarov in its shoulder-holster. Merkulov meanwhile was tapping out his orders for the police with ten questions for Romanova's group to get answers to in the ensuing days . . .

The girl in the cafeteria scraped out for me the remnants of a semi-edible dish with a semi-censorable name – 'fried oar-fish'. After the invasion of the Prosecutor's mob there was nothing left in our cafeteria by four. I was washing the stuff down with some stewed fruit when Merkulov's secretary burst in:

'Turetsky, Konstantin Dmitrievich is looking for you!'

'Aye, aye,' I responded but stayed where I was, he could wait. I began to fish bits of black plum out of the fruit mush with my fork . . .

'Griaznov's looking all over for you,' said Merkulov without raising his eyes from his papers. 'A cashier was murdered an hour ago and a large sum of money stolen. According to witnesses, the villains were short-haired youths in black jackets. One resembles Kim's murderer.'

I dialled Griaznov's number.

'On your bike, there's a job on!' said Slava, business-like.

'Well firstly, I've got no wheels. My car's gone to the great scrap-yard in the sky. And second, what happened? Just give me a clue.'

'Well firstly a *rafik*'s already on its way for you. And second, I've already told Merkulov. Details on the spot. Out!'

Merkulov tore himself away from his papers to give me a smile. His face was pale and his eyes red.

PHONED TELEGRAM

To: Head of Moscow CID, City Internal Affairs Directorate, Moscow City Executive Committee, Police Colonel comrade Kotov V.N.

We report that today at 17 hours 30 minutes near Moscow City Savings bank no. 1558/149 adjacent to Preobrazhen-skaya metro station, three persons unknown carried out an assault on cashier Garusov and driver Shmelev. Garusov and Shmelev attempted to resist and drew weapons. The criminals opened fire, killing Garusov and severely wounding Shmelev. Snatching the cashier's bag which contained bank notes totalling 234,500 roubles, the three persons unknown vanished from the scene of the crime in the same Volga car which had brought the cashier to the bank.

Inquiries as to witnesses have produced the following persons: citizeness Rom, I.B. saw two men approaching the vehicle, citizen Mokhov A.B. heard shots from the balcony of his flat, citizen Filchenko O.A. heard one of the attackers shout the word "Knave" to another. The driver Shmelev has given detailed descriptions of the three robbers. He told duty policeman Agapov F.I., that all three were dressed in black jackets and had short hair. The first was 27–9 years of age, the second 25–7, and the third 22–3 . . . The scene of the crime examination was carried out by the CID investigation squad. The body of the murdered cashier has been taken to the morgue at City Hospital no. 1 and the wounded driver has been taken by ambulance to the Sklifosovsky Institute . . . A joint task-force Moscow CID and Kuibishev regional CID has been formed with senior Moscow CID inspector, Major Pogorelov, V.I. in charge.

Head of CID, Kuibishev, Regional Directorate of Internal Affairs Police Colonel Chernov, I.I.

I finished reading the telegram, flicked my lighter, lit a cigarette and blew into the long tongue of flame:

'Where's Pogorelov now – at the scene of the crime?'

Griaznov took a light from mine.

'I think not. He's a great bloodhound, big and fat though he is. Valentin's probably picked up the trail already and he's off and running. Pogorelov's catching them up and we've got to catch *him* up. Right, away to the car. Once we're in I'll tell you something interesting . . .'

'Sir, was it you who were interested in citizen Anatoli Andreyevich Tumanov?' Griaznov asked me in the car.

'Who's that?'

Griaznov leaned over from the front seat.

'You've got a memory like our lass, Sashok! She doesn't remember who she screwed yesterday. I'm talking about the number you and Merkulov got hold of in the Gudinas bag. Remember? That's the one. Interesting type actually. He's an Afghan war invalid, both legs gone. He gets about on his artificial limbs well enough though. A retired major, chest full of medals, open house for officers coming back from Afghanistan. He's the closest friend of dear comrade Seri. When he's in Moscow he drops in on Tumanov. Get the picture?'

I got it. This legless hero was straight out of the tragic tale of the 'Afghan Brotherhood'.

'Anything interesting from the local force?'

'Nothing special. They got their information from the cop on the beat after all. The only thing he's worried about is not drinking himself to death or making a row and getting ticked off by the neighbours. Good lord, he's not a dissident – he doesn't have a KGB section tailing him everywhere . . .'

'So, we have to do the job ourselves.'

'Your pardon, comrade investigator, we are just simple country-boys, we never thought of that! I'm already working that vein, Sasha . . .'

'We pulled in to the scene of the incident, just to broaden our minds a bit. There were masses of people about. When witnesses were needed of course you couldn't get them for love nor money, and now this circus. Well, fair enough, there was plenty of cause for talk. The things we heard: it's the Black Cat gang at work. Gangsters, grandsons carrying on the family business, it's the Americans trying to stir up panic, it's the Chinese, or lunatics from Stolbovaya, on the run three days . . .'

A yobbish-looking little lad ran over to Griaznov and stood on tiptoe to whisper something in his ear, then minced away adjusting his street-wise cap.

'An agent of yours?'

'Nah, its Colonel Chernov,' grinned Griaznov. 'He tells me Pogorelov's got something new . . . When these creeps were getting into their car, near here on Poteshnaya Street, they dropped a receipt for a speeding fine. The Moskvich belongs to the Gypsy Theatre in Moscow, and the driver's name's Biryukov, Igor Biryukov.'

We drove back to Petrovka. Ballistics was what interested us now; cartridge and bullet can tell you a lot sometimes.

'Old pal, I'm returning the loan,' said Griaznov to an expert, no longer young, who possessed a purple nose.

'Just in time, Slavochka.' The expert took the tenner, overjoyed.

'Old pal, any results in our case? I mean the recent one, the cashier on Preobrazhenskaya?'

The expert rubbed the nose and gave a cheery laugh.

'You're a right comic you are, Slavochka! It must be the clients you knock about with, proper jokers. Ballistics doesn't come across in ten minutes like a three-station whore. You realise when it happened? A couple of hours back. No time at all. How long have I had to test the bullets? Pogorelov gave them to me twenty minutes ago, no more . . . Come back tomorrow, Slavochka then we'll be in business . . .'

'Think I don't know you? You've tested them. Come on, spill it or I won't take you out for a beer to the Railwaymen's Club anymore.'

'It's against the rules normally,' said Kozlov looking around to see if the bosses were about. 'I did have a look, of course. They fired two pistols: one's a Walther, foreign thing, the other's one of ours, a TK, experimental model, the same type they used on the cashier in Leningrad. I've already rung them up in Leningrad and they're getting the bullets to me tomorrow, then I can tell you exactly. That's the lot just now, Slavochka.'

We sat in Griaznov's office to wait for Pogorelov who was out scouring the town for Igor Biryukov. Zhenya Zhukov rang to say he had also been on the hunt for the second half of the day round various departments and even at ministerial level to get the goods for his office in Kabul. Now he'd had an out of the way notion – a three-way brainstorming session. We started working out a plan of operation, taking it in turns at the receiver to feed in constructive suggestions to convert thought into action.

At this point the CID duty officer's mate looked in.

'Griaznov, give over gassing. Nobody can get through to you. I've got a lad on the line from the Riazan directorate. He wants to talk to you, urgent . . .'

14

The body of Albert Morozov, student at the Riazan Airborne
Forces College was lying in a shallow ditch, part-hidden by a
spreading fir-tree. The operatives from the Riazan provincial
directorate were waiting patiently for our arrival before com-
mencing the examination. Catching sight of Griaznov, the
leader of the group – an inspector – yelled on his drivers.

'Hey, boys, get those lights on!'

The headlamps of three cars lit up the clearing and the
inspector waved a hand, time to begin the examination.
The Riazan group, the inspector, the forensic pathologist
and the criminalist headed for the body.

Morozov was lying on his side, his right hand clawing into
the ground. It was a large peasant's hand. Why peasant's? I
checked myself. Was that a judgement based on knowledge? I
was still being influenced by his letter to Kim, the countrified
sentences. I felt rather odd and out of place not taking part in
the examination, just observing from a distance. The grass
seemed blue in the headlights, the violet branches of the firs
faintly swaying. It was all like a kind of stage performance
with me as spectator.

'I've been digging around for witnesses here. I dropped in
at the village shop and chatted to the little boys, and the
OAPs. There's lots of pensioners around here, their *dachas*
are only the summer kind though.' This was one of the local
detectives talking. We were sitting together on a fallen tree,
while Griaznov who had attached himself to the investigating
team, was crawling around on the grass with a flashlight.
'There's one old chap, Varava's his name, said he thought

he'd seen this lad with some bird, not a local girl, he'd not seen her before, green headsquare. The day he disappeared that was . . .'

I took down Varava's address in my notebook. There was no need to ask this detective questions, he was an old hand and knew what he was up to.

'. . . I've got my eye on another one of the students as well. He was Morozov's room-mate and he went off home to visit his family that very day. I checked on that – he got on the train at seven in the evening while Morozov was still alive. He's due back tomorrow.'

I noted down the student's name as I heard Griaznov's voice:

'Comrade criminalists, I've found the bullet! That's it shining over there, under the police *gazik*!'

I could see from the detective's face that he hadn't finished, so I stayed where I was.

'Yes. There's a couple of twin boys here always up to mischief, well that's all right – in our business it's even better – them sticking their noses everywhere they shouldn't. This evening, well yesterday now, when they found the body I mean, well tongues started wagging . . . These twins now, they were supposed to have seen this bird, with other young men though. She was supposed to have had a green headsquare on, this "stranger auntie". Well for ten-year-old boys anybody over sixteen's an "uncle" or an "auntie" . . . well anyway, take a little note of that . . . that's about the lot . . .'

A small middle-aged woman – the forensic pathologist – came up with the first results: a penetrating bullet wound through the temple area of the skull fired from short range – hair singed, skin scorched around the wound, death occurred around seven days previously.

I joined my Riazan colleague and carefully – yard by yard – examined the barely perceptible trail where the corpse had been dragged. It led to another clearing, rather more open, where an empty bottle of Cahors wine and two paper cups lay scattered.

'Who found him?' I asked the investigator while he was waiting for the plaster-of-paris mould of the killer's footprint.

'A pensioner out walking his dog. The dog pulled a jacket out from under a bush and Morozov's papers were in the pocket. He brought it to the police station, and they had your inquiry on file there. We came out here and found him in the ditch, got on the phone to you – it being your case like. Then we waited about four hours. Why we waited I've no idea . . .'

I felt a pang of sympathy for my Riazan brother in arms – I quite understood his annoyance. It was obvious now that they could have done the examination without us. From long-distance you always think they'll muck it up.

'. . . There'll be another examination tomorrow anyway in daylight. If you want to stay the night, come over to my place, I've got a spare attic and three beds as it happens.'

Around four in the morning the investigating team began packing up their bits and pieces.

'Slava,' I addressed Griaznov, 'you can go home if you like. I'll get back on the train tomorrow. I've got one or two things to check here. Okay?'

'No way, your excellency. If I leave you alone, you'll be kidnapped I shouldn't wonder. I heard the investigator offering a little attic for the night, anyway our driver's tired.'

'I'm all right, Vyacheslav Ivanovich, I've had about three hours' sleep while you were crawling about there, still I don't fancy driving now, to be honest . . .'

Griaznov took on the job of the twins and the pensioner Varava. I talked with Albert Morozov's room-mate in the paratroops' hostel. I put the same questions to him over and over and he answered just as patiently. Then together we examined the locker and cupboard and shook up the bedclothes. Then I put my questions to the course-director, the girl on the switchboard, the instructors, the college principal and his political, then Morozov's room-mate again. I was still listening to the answers when Griaznov came back and we went down to the bus-station together, then the shop, then the club. On the way back to Moscow we exchanged questions and the answers we'd got, trying to form a picture of student Morozov's grim misfortune.

Around one o'clock on Tuesday, June 18th Morozov was called to the telephone. It was a woman, young, and judging by the accent, a Muscovite. Where she was ringing from was difficult to say, connections with many cities, including Moscow, were automatic. The course-director replied that Morozov was studying, but the woman kept insisting that he be brought to the phone, saying it was a very urgent matter. Morozov was brought out of a lesson on electronics; he was very much agitated after the phone call and immediately asked the course-director for permission to go into town saying that he had to meet a certain person at five o'clock. The matter wasn't merely personal, but he couldn't say anything further at the moment. Morozov hadn't been long at the college but had made a good impression, his references from Aghanistan were excellent and his fellow-students thought well of him. The course-director bore this in mind and allowed him special leave.

Morozov had told his room-mate that a girl was coming from Moscow at five o'clock to see him and that she was the girl-friend of his pal who'd been killed. At twenty to five he went out and came back at about half-past five, very worked-up and started looking for papers of some sort. To the question, 'anything wrong', he just waved his hand and went on searching. He then said that another girl had come but he had to find a certain letter. He'd put it away somewhere and there was a very important phone number in it. Around six he went out and that was the last time they met.

The pensioner, Varava, confirmed his testimony that Morozov was apparently standing at the bus-stop a few minutes past seven close by the block where Varava lived, accompanied by a girl in a bright green head-scarf, dark glasses and trousers. He didn't glimpse her face, but she seemed a well set-up girl. Morozov had been carrying a newspaper with a bottle wrapped in it, while the girl had a white bag and two packages.

The girl assistant in the village shop near the bus stop, reported in rather grovelling fashion, that the young man in the blue-striped suit had bought a bottle of Cahors, sausage

191

and other items in her shop on Tuesday, the eighteenth. She remembered that because it was already seven o'clock and sale of alcoholic liquor was illegal, but he'd explained that a girl from Moscow was visiting him and asked her to sell him some Cahors at least.

The number six bus driver recalled that a couple – the young man about twenty-three in a dark jacket and the girl in dark glasses and a green head-scarf had asked to be put down at a request stop near the settlement club. That would be about six miles out of Riazan (and two hundred yards from where the corpse had been found).

The club personnel hadn't noticed any girl in a green head-square, or a young man in a blue jacket, but they had seen two young men in black jackets near a red Moskvich car with a Moscow registration MOG or MOE.

The twins had spotted a 'stranger-auntie' in a green head-square and dark glasses, at half past four not far from the club. She'd got out of a red Moskvich along with two 'uncles' carrying 'motorcycle' jackets.

'They did for the boy all the same, the bastards,' said Griaznov after a lengthy silence. 'So your Halilov didn't know it all. These Afghan Brothers knew that Morozov had the facts about Dubov and . . . Faust.'

'So why didn't they rub him out straightaway, Slava? Ivonin was one of those who signed his posting to the college. That means he didn't suspect him.'

'Yes, Sashok, what's it all worth, eh? Here's a young man living his life in a Taiga village, parents give him a foreign name – he's going to be special, he is. And now – what?'

Griaznov went on gloomily philosophising while I put facts together.

On Sunday, June 17th, Moiseyev and I had opened the Lagins' post-box. We'd sat in his flat till late at night and Merkulov had given me the paper to read next morning. Before setting off for the Judge Advocate General's Office, I'd given Griaznov's order to Klavdia, Merkulov's secretary, to type out.

'Slava, can you remember when you got my instructions to find Halilov, Smirnov and Morozov? The exact time I mean?'

'The packet arrived by special delivery straight after lunch, a few minutes after two. I'm not complaining of a poor memory yet, citizen chief. Sealing wax, stamped "top secret", all nice and official.'

Morozov had been rung up around one, before Griaznov knew the names of the wanted men.

'Why do you say "from me"? The instruction, under article 127 of the Code of Criminal Procedure was signed by Grechannik.'

Grechannik! That's right, Merkulov and I were in a hurry and he'd said – let Klavdia re-type the rough copy and give it to Grechannik to sign. Grechannik was in charge of the metro bomb case along with the KGB, they were busy cooking the evidence, 'Serzhik' the State Intelligence agent was at their beck and call and the special forces were under State Intelligence ... I was certain – virtually certain – that it was Grechannik.

Joseph Grechannik was looking very worried as he spoke on the phone. I observed the play of his pudgy lips and his arching eyebrows. I believe he was trying to get hold of some sort of medicine. At least it sounded like medicine. When he finally put down the receiver he started explaining to me that some amazing stuff had been developed in the GDR, but it was absolutely (the middle 'o' very rounded) impossible to obtain. It was marvellous and could be used night or day, the scent was incomparable . . .

'What are you talking about, Joseph?!'

'What do you mean? Lotion (both "o"s rounded). It strengthens the roots and retards balding. Much better than brilliantine or "Golden Cockerel".'

I couldn't deny that, but I found it hard to agree all the same, since I'd done without these necessities all my conscious life.

Grechannik got on my nerves so much with his lotion that I took the bull by the horns:

'Listen, Joseph, last Tuesday you signed a certain paper, at Merkulov's request, addressed to Moscow CID. His secretary, Klava, gave it to you . . .'

Grechannik's face lengthened suddenly as he hissed:

'I'm fed up with you, Turetsky. What are you after? You write it, you sign it. You're always trying to drag me into some risky business and then sicking your mistakes onto somebody else . . .'

'Hey, Joseph! What mistakes? What are you talking about?'

He hadn't read that paper! He really hadn't!

'What are you nagging me about then?'

'Just calm down, you . . . golden cockerel.'

I headed for the door.

'Stupid!' came after me.

I was already closing the door, but at this I stuck my head in his office again and said threateningly:

'I wouldn't be so sure about that, sitting where you are . . .'

'No harm in checking,' I thought and headed towards Merkulov's office.

Klava was sitting at her desk, applying bright blue mascara after she'd finished her lashes, she fished out another box from her bag and started dabbing silver dust on her eyelids. Then she left her mirror on the edge of the desk and caught sight of me.

'Oh, Alexander Borisovich . . .'

'That's beautiful. Really suits you. Why don't you do that all the time?'

'Konstantin Dmitrievich won't be in today. I have a feeling he doesn't like it when I doll myself up. He gets in a bad mood, and starts picking on me for the least little thing.'

'Well you know, I don't use make-up at all but he picks on me pretty often. So I think its just coincidence. By the way I wonder if you remember a certain thing. Between you and me, of course.'

I tried to put on a mysterious expression, that must have some effect on bosses' secretaries, I reckoned.

'Last Tuesday I asked you to type out a short message to CID and get Joseph Alexeyevich to sign it. Try to remember the exact time Grechannik signed it. Can you do that?'

'Have I done something wrong?'

'Klavochka, you're perfection itself. I just need to know the time that's all.'

'Let's see . . . You and Konstantin Dmitrievich left and I went along to Joseph Alexeyevich . . . he'd gone out to lunch . . . Then he came back . . . I couldn't get a word in . . . Oh, Alexander Borisovich, I'll tell you exactly. Right: look: 13 hours 50 minutes, the courier took the post for Petrovka 38 and I just caught Joseph Alexeyevich, he didn't even read it . . .'

I breathed a little easier despite the heat. Although I can't stand Grechannik, I was glad that this time at least my suspicions were groundless. I didn't care for the coincidence though, Albert Morozov gets rung up by some woman (obviously calling herself Kim Lagina) immediately after I'd given Klavdia my instructions to type? I would have to ask her if anybody had read the paper apart from her. But by the time this dawned on me I was already sitting in the metro on my way to Major Valentin Pogorelov who was on his second day of inquiries into Igor Biryukov, driver of the red Moskvich and possible accessory in the murders of Kim and Sergeant Morozov.

Pogorelov was sitting in his office dying of the heat, 'villa amenities' notwithstanding, a humming ventilator and a gallon of Kvass, half empty. The major's shirt lay across a chair, while the major himself sat in a vest of indeterminate shade wiggling the toes of his bare feet. All of which did not prevent him concentratedly tapping on his typewriter with his index finger at machine-gun speed.

'Hi, Valentin!'

'Hi, like some kvass?' he enquired without interrupting the rapid rattle.

'I'll say!'

He pulled a sheet out of the machine and poured me a glass.

'Phew . . . doing the paper-work. Worked with my feet for days, now my hands have got it to do. I can't think about the case at all . . .' Pogorelov reinforced his amiable humour with a succulent oath. 'You know, all this red tape and paper makes the hair on my neck stand on end, like a wolf! I'm like an invalid.'

As if in confirmation of his words he began wiggling his toes.

'The trouble is, my feet sweat and there's nothing I can do, I have to wear socks because of that bastard. He can be a thief and a murderer, but I can't just be myself.'

He was sitting in the pose of Rodin's thinker holding his boot in his hand. He put it decisively on one side and started pulling on his shirt.

'You glance through that just now,' he nodded towards the desk.

I picked up the closely-typed sheet and sat down in a corner of the office. Before settling down to read, I had a word of advice for the major:

'Don't put your socks on. Stick your feet in your boots and sit like that.'

'Good idea,' said Pogorelov, perfectly serious and rang the remand centre.

SITUATION REPORT

In order to uncover an especially dangerous crime, as indicated in article 77 of the RSFSR Criminal Code (banditry) certain measures have been taken by my brigade as a result of which one of the three members of the gang responsible for the attack on cashier Garusov, namely Igor Biryukov, 23 years, has been apprehended . . .

Biographical details . . . upbringing normal . . . Served 18 months in Afghanistan, and the last six months in the quartermaster's department of the USSR MOD. After demobilisation he got a job under the quota system at Triokhgorka, then he worked for a car-fleet. At present he is employed as a driver by the Roman gypsy theatre. Lives in flats vacated by actors on tour . . . No previous convictions . . .

The escort led a tall good-looking blond man into the office.

Short hair-cut, pale eyes, sunburned ... I was comparing him in my mind's eye with the picture I had already formed of Kim's second murderer. Very like, that was for sure. He didn't look like a homosexual, though. Normal looking lad ...

Pogorelov started putting his questions and it quickly became clear that Biryukov had no intention of answering.

I went on reading Pogorelov's report. I paused from time to time but all I heard was; 'I don't know ... never been there ... I never took anything ... never went anywhere ...'

... Biryukov was arrested late at night in the flat of theatre director I. I. Ivanov whose driver he was. He did not resist arrest, but was reticent on questioning, he denies involvement in the attack on the cashier. A search of his living quarters produced nothing, however in the boot of the Moskvich car 412 MOG 33–34 a man's leather sports jacket was discovered with, in one pocket, an unbroken wad of banknotes of the value of ten thousand roubles in hundred rouble denominations. In the garage of the Gypsy theatre, in the inspection pit, a Walther 9 mm pistol, with two clips of ammunition was found wrapped up in a tennis shirt ...

'The gypsies planted that lot! Ours, the theatre people!'
'Why should actors plant money on you? Got plenty to spare have they?'
'I don't know.' A shrug of the shoulders.

... Biryukov was brought in for identification by witnesses to Garusov's murder. Witness Rom stated that one of the two men who had approached the Volga was Biryukov. Witness Filchenko recognised Biryukov and explained that one of the criminals had addressed Biryukov as 'Knave' ...

Pogorelov was doing his very best to catch Biryukov out in a lie, but the prisoner had no intention of breaking. He behaved exactly like Ivonin: 'I don't think so', 'I just can't remember', 'You've got it all wrong'. No this was the wrong approach. You couldn't talk to him like a human being. In any case his admissions were of no use to me. Several people had identified him, his prints were on the Walther, in other words it was certainly possible to prove Biryukov's involvement in the three crimes, but to do it meant time and a lot of painstaking labour. What Merkulov and I needed was a *proved* case indicating the existence of a terrorist organisation *now*, while there was still time to save Gevorkyan from being shot for planting the metro bomb.

This Biryukov was the only thread we had to hang on to.

I made a slight sign to Pogorelov from my corner and the major, white ankles flashing, left the office.

I sat down in Pogorelov's chair and prepared myself for the show. A one-man show for a one-man audience who had to be drawn into the play, to make him believe that I was on his side, that I belonged to Seri and Ivonin's gang, that I was the same as he, Igor Biryukov, called 'Knave'. I didn't yet know what I would have to say, but somehow I had to convert myself into my opposite: the detective had to become the criminal.

I didn't look at Biryukov. I concentrated on recalling the rubbish Ivonin had come out with as he prepared to make an end of me, so I began speaking very slowly and quietly, repeating every phrase several times:

'The intellectual is a slave of dead reason, the soldier is a lord of life . . . The intellectual is the slave of dead reason, the soldier is a lord of life . . . the cult of the soldier must be resurrected as the only path to real immortality . . . the cult of the soldier must be resurrected . . .'

The main thing was not to stop, just like this monotonously, upping the tempo slightly, a touch louder . . .

'The cult of the soldier, who has passed through fire and sword in Afghanistan must be resurrected . . .'

I sensed rather than saw that Knave's face had twitched. A tiny bit faster, just a tiny bit louder . . .

'We have to exterminate the rabble. We will carry out the order. Stalin will come and give the order: get ready . . .'

Now I was staring Biryukov straight in the eyes grinding

out all that tripe about purging the population of its dross, the reformation of living space and hell knows what else. He couldn't take in what was happening. He was flustered by all this. I was thinking of just one thing, how to keep going at the same rate. I started all over again, this time bawling.

'We shall carry out the precepts of the charter. You and I brother, yes, we are brothers! No one will overcome our Afghan Brotherhood! We will round up the rabble and rat-a-tat-tat – all gone! Away with mean-minded thinkers!'

Biryukov was looking at me as if hypnotised. His eyes had widened and were focused unblinkingly at one point.

'We will blow up this world, smash it to pieces, just like we detonated the bomb on the Moscow metro. We will kill them the way we killed that traitor, the student from Riazan! A pistol to the head and he's gone! A knife in the back – agh! And that girl Kim, she's gone. She was against our brotherhood and we shall kill all who are against the Afghan Brotherhood! We shall kill and rob! We need money! Money for our revolution! We are the lords of life, we shall conquer!'

Biryukov wrapped his arms round his head and began rocking it from side to side, his chin was quivering feverishly and droplets of sweat stood out on his forehead. The comedy was almost over.

'You as well, Knave, you're rabble as well!' I began in a heart-rending scream. 'You'll get it in the temple – bang! – that's you gone. Who needs you? Stalin? You're not a knave, you're only a six, if that! They won't even waste a bullet on you. A bottle across your skull and that's your lot!'

Knave let out a fearful howl and fell head first across the desk. Pogorelov burst in at the door along with one of his men, pistol at the ready. I waved a hand at them just about ready to keel over myself.

If Merkulov had witnessed my performance, those would have been the last minutes of my career in the City Prosecutor's Office. The concept of 'moral choice' did not exist for him. He carried the inadmissability of moral compromise in everyday life totally and completely into the practical sphere of criminal justice and spoke out against any tactical manoeuvres which exploited the baser emotions of the subject under interrogation. What I had just done was immoral and illegal, but I had had no other choice, because I knew that if we found the real criminals and could demonstrate their guilt, we would save Gevorkyan. But that wasn't the main thing: Kim's second murderer still walked the earth and finding him justified the means.

Pogorelov switched on the tape recorder and listened to Knave without interrupting. Only twice, as he was changing the cassette, did he try to stop Biryukov, but in vain. He addressed himself only to me, his 'brother'. I listened to him and subtly guided his testimony – eliciting a symphony of nightmare by using leading questions. Right now I had to drag information out of this madman concerning the Afghan Brotherhood and the Morozov case. Information about the other two murders I was leaving for dessert – to comrade Pogorelov . . .

'I didn't kill that cashier in Leningrad. I was the look-out man.'

'Brother, listen, who's the chief soldier in our brotherhood?' I was getting him onto the point that mattered.

'Chief? Brother? Soldier? Well Caesar's the chief. I volunteered for the tempering three times instead of him. That's . . . you get body-blows . . . beaten with birch-rods, they're the best teacher, the "tempering" . . .'

'Who is this Caesar? What's his surname?'

'Caesar's called Caesar. His surname's Kurkin, Valeri Kurkin, he was my first commander in the specials . . . over there . . . in Afghanistan. It was Caesar who inducted me into the brotherhood, he was the leader of our threesome. He drank the first glass of champagne with me – with my blood in it. We swore then that we'd always be together. Together we would achieve victory . . . over the . . . over the thinkers and the rabble.'

'Knave! Who transferred you to Moscow . . . from Afghanistan? You were working in the quartermasters Department of the Ministry of Defence just before you were demobbed.'

'Caesar did it. First of all they sent him to the academy. Then

200

he got me to Moscow as well. It wasn't easy, but he's my brother. He loves me!'

Naturally I felt inclined to tell Biryukov that his 'brother' Valeri Kurkin was probably as much a dummy as he was. No doubt also in favour of wiping out eighty per cent of the population. Any reply at this stage however could spoil the whole case. I asked:

'What academy is Caesar at just now?'

'Dzerzhinsky. Not the military engineering one, the special one – for intelligence and special duties . . .'

'In fact he was there, Caesar, when you had to deal with the traitor, Morozov – in Riazan?' I said, inwardly tensing.

'Aha, yes. He wasted that fool student. He wanted to betray our brotherhood. Caesar said so – he wanted to tell people about our charter. You can't do that – it's secret, our charter.'

'What about the girl? Who was the girl who went with you to Riazan?'

'The one in the green head-scarf?'

'That's her.'

'Don't know. Caesar had nothing to do with her. Only our chief.'

'Who is he, the chief?'

'You know very well we operate in threes. The chief is Malyuta Skuratov, next Caesar, then me, Knave . . .'

'And you know nothing about that girl? Who is she? Where from? What's her name and where does she live?'

'Na-a . . . I don't know. I'm not supposed to, I keep to the charter. Then I'll be a chief, in another threesome.'

'Well what do you know about Malyuta Skuratov? Who is he?'

'Don't know anything.'

'They gave you injections . . . in Afghanistan?'

'Against cowardice? To be brave? Yes! When I was a civilian I was a coward, yes I was. I was afraid of blood and cried when the lads on our farm tormented a cat or a dog. You can't be like that in Afghanistan. Only brave people there. That's why we had the injections.'

'What happened after that – were you brave?'

'Need you ask! Of course we were!'

He was smiling slightly, like Ivonin.

'I was training all the time. Passed all the tests. To get to be a "noble and honourable soldier" in the brotherhood, you have to crawl 36 yards in 25 seconds, hit the bull in pistol shooting, hit the dummy's heart in knife-throwing . . .'

'Were you in the metro when the bomb was planted in the carriage?' I asked, nervously scratching my chin.

Biryukov shook his head and whimpered:

'Caesar was there . . . but they didn't take me. They had explosives experts . . .'

'How do you know it was your work then, if you weren't actually there?' I asked, looking up from the pad I was using to note down the main points of Biryukov's testimony.

'We were told . . .'

Biryukov dried up here, clearly unwilling to talk about the meetings of the brotherhood.

'Tell me, brother, where did you all meet? I mean the Afghan Brotherhood.'

'Don't known exactly . . . catacombs somewhere, underground. I used to get out at "Moscow River" and Caesar would be waiting for me. He put me in a car, blindfolded me and drove me off somewhere. We've got to do that while we're a secret group. Later on, when we've won, we'll come out in the open. Now we're a conspiracy. We sat in the dark in the catacombs, so we couldn't see each other.'

'What did they tell you in the catacombs? When Stalin would give you the most important order?'

'They said it would be soon! Maybe even this month!'

'What was the order? What had you to do? I mean concretely?'

'Concretely? I don't know. I know we're going to kill rabble and thinkers! Make a revolution! Concretely, Stalin's order will be announced the day before our revolution!'

I stared hard at Biryukov and yelled:

'Brother! Look me in the eyes!'

'I will!'

'Answer! Answer! Honestly, absolutely honestly as befits a

202

soldier. When will Stalin give the order to the Afghan Brotherhood? Answer!'

'I don't know! I don't know!'

'You lie!'

'No! I don't know. The balloon goes up and our time will come. Our hour will come! I don't know any more.'

'Good. Relax. I believe you. Tell me; who did you give the cashier's bag to, with the money?'

'I don't know his code-name. After Preobrazhenskaya we switched to my Moskvich – we abandoned their Volga. Then the brothers and I drove to "Warsaw" metro and Malyuta took the case away to some guy. We'd transferred the money to a suitcase and threw the cashier's bag away. I never saw the guy's face, I swear. This guy took the case over to a Zaporozhets . . .'

'What sort of guy? Characteristics? – No lying!'

'He had a funny walk, like he was drunk. I don't remember anything else.'

'Why did you think he was drunk?'

'He was rocking from side to side, but balanced somehow. Very strange . . .'

'Last question.' I tensed myself and stared into those dilated pupils. 'Who killed Kim?'

'Kim?! I don't know any nickname like that, I didn't kill him! I don't know!'

'You were in the Thousand and One Things block with Ivonin on the night of June 13–14th. One of you stabbed a girl called Kim.'

'I don't know Ivonin! I've never been in that block!'

'Remember; where were you and what were you doing on that Thursday night, the 13th June?'

'I don't know! I can't stand it! I don't remember!'

'Relax brother. It was ten days ago, you can remember!'

'I was in Leningrad! We got there on the night of the 12th. On the 13th we attacked the cashier, and jumped on the night "Arrow" to Moscow.'

'So, Knave,' said I, peaceably. 'Let's have lunch now – you'll get something to eat. After that you'll tell comrade Pogorelov everything in detail, repeat in detail.'

'What'll happen to me? Will I be shot?'

I answered seriously:

'If you were really the six in all three cases and the blood of the cashiers and their drivers is not on your hands. If you didn't kill Morozov, as you say, then you won't die. You'll live!'

'Are you speaking the truth, brother?'

'I am,' I replied firmly, adding: 'but first, Knave, you must tell everything to Major Pogorelov and sign your statement. Got that?'

He gave another of his forced smiles:

'Got it.'

'Good lad!' said Pogorelov.

I couldn't make out who that was addressed to, Biryukov or me . . .

I felt like a cigarette and I needed to think, but instead I went along to Romanova to ask her to get her people, the whole directorate if need be, onto the job of hunting down the other two members of Knave's troika: Caesar and Malyuta Skuratov. They had to be found immediately, literally within the hour.

Romanova heard me out attentively, without her usual jokes. She took notes along to the CID chief Kotov.

'Turetsky!' came a loud summons from the duty officer's messenger. 'Some bigwig at the MOD wants you on the phone. He says Deputy City Prosecutor Parkhomenko told him you were here. Shall I switch him through here or not?'

'Put him through,' I said not knowing who it was looking for me, probably someone from the Judge Advocate's Office about Bunin's death.

'Turetsky here.'

'Comrade Turetsky! Good job I found you. This is Rogov. Remember me?'

'I haven't forgotten,' I responded, as coldly as I could.

'It's like this, I have to see you urgently. It's an important matter: we're preparing a report for the Politburo about the activities of our section in Afghanistan. It's been six months you see since these sections were formed and the party leadership wants to know whether the initiative was justified.'

'What's it to do with me then?'

'Quite a lot actually. The top men have got to know about your trip to Kabul. Then the attack on you . . . The death of Comrade Bunin . . . the sudden death of Judge Advocate General Gorny here, the accident to his assistant down there . . . Anyway, your opinion would be most valuable, most valuable to us and the Central Committee. If you like I'll come over to you. Or you can come here if you've no objection, I'll send a car for you. Shall I do that?'

'Why?' I asked, provoking.

'What d'you mean, "why"?' Rogov was taken aback. 'I said your opinion as a pair of fresh eyes in Afghanistan was very important, didn't I?'

'Who for?'

'I told you – for the Central Committee of the CPSU and us at State Intelligence!'

'I haven't the time, I'm on a job,' I was standing firm. 'I'm investigating a high level matter. Also important to the Central Committee of the CPSU, I might add.'

'Alexander Borisovich, I realise you're not in the mood and so forth. As soon as you get a free minute phone me and we'll fix a meeting. Bear in mind the meeting's not just important to me. You as well. *Au revoir*, Alexander Borisovich.'

I heard him hang up.

I went down to the ground floor and headed for the canteen. The coppers have one of the best canteens in Moscow. The police watch over the restaurant and canteen trust strictly, ensuring that the capital's trade network thieves on an even basis, no overdoing things. So this was how the crooks showed their gratitude – by supplying the police with excellent produce.

When I came back to the office I listened to Shura Romanova's account of how the Captain Kurkin we were looking for had disappeared in a fog of secrecy and mystery, at which our armed services are past masters. They had said in the hostel that Kurkin was at a lecture, while the course-director intimated conspiratorially that the previous night an order had come down from above and the entire S-34 group of which Kurkin was a member was sent off to Alabino lock stock and barrel; there was a military aerodrome there. Where the group had gone after that, nobody at the Dzerzhinsky Academy had any idea: military secret.

'A weird business,' said Romanova and started coughing as she ended her tale. Shura had picked up a cold somewhere – in this heat.

Learning that Knave had been arrested, somebody power-ful had smuggled Caesar away and broken the contact. No doubt because Knave knew all about this Caesar – Kurkin. But he knew nothing about the next link in the chain – or about Malyuta Skuratov and whoever stood behind him.

The real Malyuta Skuratov, the head of Ivan the Terrible's bodyguard, had been the right-hand man of the Tsar himself . . . If one followed that logic, the logic of the anti-world (Kostya Merkulov had pictured that well), it meant Skuratov stood at the very top of the hierarchy in the Afghan Brother-hood . . . Wait . . . What had that mad guy Gudinas said? He said when he was aiming his knife at the heart of Repin's Ivan the Terrible, 'I've killed General Seri!' . . . Hold it again . . . that means 'Ivan the Terrible' is General Seri, he was at the head of the entire criminal organisation. And Malyuta Skuratov was obviously Seri's henchman . . . he had to pro-tect Caesar whatever happened – God forbid he should break in CID custody! That would put the lid on the lot of them, Ivan the Terrible first and foremost, General Seri that is . . . But Seri wasn't just the head man of the Afghan Brotherhood, he was a big wheel in Special Forces, the shock detachments of State Intelligence and the Central Committee of the CPSU as well. That meant all this was known to Colonel-General Rogov, one of the commanders of that legion, the man who was trying to wangle a meeting with me. So then, if I was to find a way out of the labyrinth I would have to make that contact. It might be the thing I needed most of all now . . .

I dialled Rogov's number.

'Turetsky here. You can send a car for me; I'll make sure I've got a free hour. I'll come out in twenty minutes, main entrance of the directorate.'

'That's more like it,' replied General Rogov satisfied.

Rogov looked me up and down as he sipped cognac and talked. He talked about contemporary atomic weapons and moral-psychological overload, the mounting stress on Soviet military personnel, especially those on special duties, the Special Forces . . .

'Without false modesty I may say that I was the first to raise the point that a man's behaviour – and a soldier's – is not regulated merely by his consciousness but by the unconscious sphere of his psyche – primarily by the instinct of self-preservation. These negative manifestations of the human psyche can become critical in the conditions of modern war. And then it's the end of our socialist . . . conquests you understand me? The end!'

Rogov poured mineral water into a crystal goblet and adjusted his black eye-patch.

'There are three approaches to psychological preparation for future conflict. The first is to develop the system of counter-propaganda, the struggle against information broadcast by emigre organisations and hostile "voices". Second is making use of information on the behaviour of people in circumstances approximating modern warfare: earthquakes, atomic power station accidents, the atomic bombs on Hiroshima and Nagasaki and the Afghan war . . . The third approach is the training of Special Forces units. I'll tell you a little secret – in an atomic war, the most important strategic operations will fall on the Special Forces. Operating in far-flung areas, in total isolation, not knowing whether anything living has survived anywhere, under conditions of extreme hazard, these units need a totally reliable complement of personnel. And there's not much point in trying to set definite criteria for selection into these units, there are no supermen on this earth . . . For that reason we were compelled to resort to extreme measures – the elixir of youth, mentioned by Goethe in his "Faust" . . . We started using injections, invented in our laboratories. That was our salvation, the Faust injections . . . The drug gave our specials an unthinking bravery, extinguished the fear a normal man would feel . . . Still you don't need telling, a medal has two sides . . . While we were testing the substance during the Afghan campaign we encountered negative effects as well – excessive cruelty, cynicism, tendencies towards criminal behaviour when soldiers returned to civilian life. I've been asked to explain to you that the substance isn't an end in itself – it's of immense national importance. Information about Faust mustn't be allowed to leak out to our own people or to public opinion abroad. That would be a major political mistake! You ask what's expected of you. Just one thing – drop out of the case, if you can't find a satisfactory way of closing it. As you see, we're not asking the impossible. We understand your limits as a human being . . .'

'Who's this "we"?'

'We are the Defence Council of the USSR, the highest level of Soviet authority,' said General Rogov and grinned.

I ignored the general's exaggeration, as I was not about to teach him that for the moment the highest organ of state authority under our constitution was the USSR Supreme Soviet. I was worried about something else: any hopes I had entertained of getting some information out of this audience had burst like a soap-bubble. I was furious with myself for my cocky naivety – some help-mate I'd found myself – the head of Special Forces! I shouldn't have come. I didn't want his explanations, excusing the murderers of Kim, Vanya Bunin or Dubov and Morozov whom I hadn't known. He had the gall to ask me to forgive the murderers of the little boy mangled by the bomb in the metro.

'Look general, how about if you yourself had to answer for allowing criminal acts to be perpetrated?'

'Are you trying to threaten me?' grinned Rogov.

'No. I'm not trying. I *am* threatening you. I think Marshal Agarkin will find it interesting that his deputy is covering up the bloody acts of a terrorist organisation called the Afghan Brotherhood and that, in the medical directorate entrusted to him, powerful narcotics are being used illegally, drugs which cause irreversible brain damage, even death.'

Rogov again transformed himself into the simple country-man, folded his arms across his belly and began twiddling his thumbs. Once-twice-three times one way, one-two-three back again. I had nothing more to talk to him about and began putting my papers away. Then he went on, softly, very softly:

'It would also be somewhat interesting for Marshal Agarkin to learn . . .'

He let fall the words so quietly I could hardly hear him. I even thought he'd said nothing at all, it was just my papers rustling . . .

'It would also be somewhat interesting for Marshall Agarkin to learn that Investigator Turetsky is sleeping with his wife . . .'

And he began rolling about chuckling in what I would even call a servile manner.

For the merest fraction of a second, my hand froze in the air and my heart leapt to my throat. What had he just said? It was absurd, incoherent, nonsensical rambling. 'Turetsky is sleeping with his wife.' Me? Whose wife? '. . . Somewhat interesting for Marshal Agarkin.' Agarkin's wife?! But I didn't even know her!

'What's this, blackmail?'

'You can discuss that . . . heh, heh . . . with your lady, heh-heh . . .'

I retained enough self-possession to leave Rogov's office unhurriedly and, as it seemed to me, of my own accord.

I was walking down Horoshevka without any clear idea where I was going, towards the centre, or in the opposite direction. When I found myself standing at the crossroads on Begovaya Street, I made two discoveries. First: I was going in the right direction after all. Second: Svetlana Belova was the wife of Marshal Agarkin. All my being rebelled against the sec-ond – no, it couldn't be! I even said it out loud: 'Of course it isn't her!' I ran energetically down the escalator at Begovaya metro, repeating in time to my steps: 'Of course she isn't, of course she isn't.' . . . I tried persuading, convincing myself, but I felt with all my skin that she was. I got into a packed carriage, changed at Barricades onto the circle line. There weren't so many people now, and I sat till Gorky Park calming my spirits: well what if she was the marshal's wife? So much the worse for him if she preferred me. He was the deceived husband and I the happy lover. But it was only words, I certainly didn't feel happy. There was nothing for it, I had to know the truth. Should I go round all the registry offices in Moscow? What if they hadn't registered the marriage – but Rogov wouldn't have said 'wife' in that case. What if they'd been married outside Moscow? The GDR for example, where the marshal had spent so much time lately?

That one-eyed sod had suggested talking it over with Lana. No, he said 'with your lady'. Maybe it wasn't her after all? . . . What if I just asked her straight out: 'Are you married to Marshal Agarkin?' Suppose she said yes? I'd have to tell her she was in danger. The marshal might shoot her, he had just the face for it. An executioner's face. I'd completely forgotten how recently it was that I'd liked his determined features a lot . . . But if she said no, what sort of an idiot would I look?

I changed again onto the Arbat-Pokrovskaya line. Why on earth was I going home? It was still only three in the afternoon, I had piles of work to get through and here I was homeward-bound. The nasal voice came over the loudspeakers . . .'This train is for University station, next station Frunzenskaya.' Then came the moment of decision.

I was using my service status for private purpose, let my old work-mates think what they liked – the young ones too for that matter. Even if nobody got to hear of it, it was still a low thing to do. But I was now going to the university law faculty to say . . . How would I put it? . . . Well we've got various people doing their practice at the Prosecutor's Office . . . The personnel department have ordered, no, asked me to make up a detailed report about all of them . . . What about? Well what difference did it make, a detailed report, that was a good one

. . . 'This train terminates here, all change. University station. This train terminates here . . .'

I needn't have bothered: in law faculty reception sat Golka Malakhova, a former fellow-student now a post-graduate and secretary to the dean. She was a good sort, apart from being as dumb as they come. One thing had brought us together: Golka (as our whole year knew) had lived with my friend Borya Nemirovsky, now resident in New York with his own photo-studio. So we had something to talk about. After which I could have just said – let me have the personal details of the 5th year, Belova. Still I took Nikolai Stepanyuk's file first and even made a few notes. Then I glanced at my notebook and asked casually:

'Belova, Svetlana Nikolayevna.'

'Belova, Belova . . . where's she got to? Aha, I've still got her under "A".'

'Why "A"?'

'Belova's her married name.'

Married name! That means it's not her!

'Her maiden name's Aralova.'

Lana's face, and her almost boyish hair-do looked out at me from the small photograph. A familiar face, familiar from a long time back . . . I turned the pages slowly . . . Father, RSFSR Minister of Municipal Economy, mother housewife . . . National silver medallist in track athletics . . . Second place in the pentathlon USSR – USA match . . . Svetlana Aralova!

'What's the matter, Turetsky?'

'Eh?'

'What on earth have you come across? Your face has gone all frozen.'

'I never knew Aralova was a student in our faculty.'

'Take a look there – she came to us from the Institute of International Relations. Third year. There was some kind of shady story, she dropped out for a whole year. See, academic leave certificate. I don't really remember now, they said she had some kind of illness. Or something like that.'

'Is she still married to this . . . Belov?'

'Seems so . . . She's sort of dead to the world you know. No friends. Given up sport. And she was such a big name!'

So that was that. Svetlana Aralova 'always second'. The one who came first was Anna Chudnova, six foot two, a horse of a woman – the Japanese had banned her from competing in Tokyo, obviously a hermaphrodite. Anyway to hell with Chudnova . . . Extract from Belova's exam report – straight 'excellents' and one 'failed' – in P.E. Address, Sadovsky Lane, Block 5, Flat 8. And phone number. Remember it just in case . . . Application in Lana's handwriting: 'I request permission to change my surname, having registered my marriage with citizen Yu. M. Belov . . .' Yuri probably. Or just conceivably Yuli. 'New address, telephone . . .' Remember them too.

I stood in the empty entrance hall of the university apathetically examining the photograph board for a long time before entering a phone booth and dialling the last number in the file.

'Allo-o . . .'

The voice was indolent, a sort of sleek voice. Must have belonged to a woman in a long silk dressing gown, with a cream mask on her face. I peered through the glass, nobody about. Using an assumed voice I squeaked:

'Svetlana Nikolayevna, please.'

A brief pause, then the same voice came again pronouncing each syllable:

'Svet-la-na Ni-ko-la-yev-na does-n't live in this flat any more!'

Hung up.

There was no sense in ringing again, the lady in the dressing gown was clearly in no mood for conversation. I cleared my throat, a lengthy process, and wandered slowly down to the metro.

Maybe Rogov had meant somebody else. I mentally ran the rule over my friends. There was no girl of my intimate acquaintance who could possibly have been a marshal's wife. Wait, there was one adventure I'd had at the seaside in Riga, a beautiful blonde around thirty-five. They'd called her 'the general's wife'. Had Agarkin still been a general then? Standing in the station hall, I once more dialled a number from my notebook, the one that belonged to the blonde Victoria:

'Is that Marshal Agarkin's flat?'

A sleepy male voice:

'Wha-a-t?!'

I took a shower and started on the paper. I read it from the top left-hand corner of page one to the bottom right-hand corner of the last page and didn't take in a single word. I tried to play chess with myself but two moves was my limit. I kept on thinking: 'I've got to know for certain'. I was alarmed, thinking I'd forgotten the Belovs' phone number. No. I hadn't. It was 291-4358. But was it Yuri or Yuli? I'd ask: 'Is that the Belov apartment, can I speak to Yuli?' The lady in the dressing-gown would tell this lisping friend scornfully . . . But all these preparations went for nothing as a chirpy boy's voice resounded in the receiver:

'Belov's flat!'

Damn, here goes . . . I lisped:

'Greetings!'

'Well, hi!'

'Can I speak to Yuli?'

'He hasn't been to see us today.'

'Are your parents at home?' (I dropped the idiocy.)

'Na-a. They've gone to the theatre.'

'Is your brother living with Svetka?'

'Na-a. Yurka and her are divorced. He married Natashka.'

'Which Natashka?'

'What d'you mean "which"? The daughter of Mikhail Sergeyevich.'

'What about Svetka?'

'How do I know?'

Daughter of a minister, sports star, beautiful, strong woman, thrown over by her husband for the sake of some Mikhail Sergeyevich's daughter. Student at the MIIR, then a year out for illness and a switch to the law faculty. Gave up sport. Instead of trips abroad she'd be sitting in some regional prosecutor's office or legal advice centre, maybe worse, a notary office.

But what if she really was married to Agarkin? The whole picture would change radically. Maybe she left this Belov and he married Mikhail Sergeyevich's daughter on the rebound. There was something in this whole story that made me uneasy and inclined me to expect disaster.

I looked through my notebook. Dozens of names, unhelpful in the circumstances . . . Ah, what about this . . . Mishka Golikov, a judo expert from the Institute of International Relations! Some years previously we used to go together to the Sports Club Nanka. Now he was a post-graduate at the MIIR and we kept in touch mainly by telephone.

'Svetka Aralova? I should think so – she really was a star, first magnitude – or second rather – Yes, I knew her, not closely you understand, she was out of reach, the elite. Daughter of a minister after all, even a pipsqueak RSFSR Minister of Municipal Economy, anyway he got the push later on . . . Incidentally I was on the same course as her future husband Yurka Belov, he was a careerist all right, there's a whole story attached to that . . . Something happened, she got ill or something, don't know exactly, it was serious – a nervous thing. Her father got the boot and Yurka practically wept: he'd married a minister's daughter thinking his career was guaranteed . . . he left Svetka for guess who?! The daughter of our new Gensec!·. . .'

'He and Svetka are divorced. He married Natashka . . . What d'you mean "which"? . . . the daughter of Mikhail Sergeyevich.' And I'd thought, just some old Mikhail Sergeyevich . . .

'. . . Yurka told me confidentially that Svetka wanted to kill him, but afterwards, instead of that,' Mishka began to laugh, 'she went and married Marshal Agarkin . . .'

Now I knew what it was that had given me no peace and had made me sense impending disaster. It was suspicion . . .

15 ·

Merkulov's secretary Klava was in a bad mood. She adjusted the sheet of paper in her typewriter with unnecessary force and in answer to my 'Good Morning,' barked, 'Good for some,' before bashing the keys. I couldn't have cared less about her mood or anything in the world. Except, I had to prove – to myself – that Lana had nothing to do with it. I had to get rid of my suspicions.

'Klavochka, I'm asking you to recall once more if anybody apart from you read the instructions I wrote for Griaznov . . .'

'You do keep on, Alexander Borisovich! I've told you, I gave it to Joseph Alexeyevich . . .'

'Klava,' I interrupted, 'do try and remember who could have read that paper. Just casually maybe. Maybe somebody was in your room or you popped out and left the door open . . .'

'No, I didn't go out, what are you . . .'

Klava stopped, seeing my expression.

'Well if you must know . . . It was like this: Parkhomenko, that is Leonid Vasilievich, as soon as you'd gone out with Konstantin Dmitrievich . . .'

'Go on, Klava!'

'. . . brought me a report to type for the city party committee. He said everyone was waiting for it . . . and you said yours was very urgent . . . So . . . I asked the student to type it . . .'

'Which student?'

'Belova . . . She's always in here with me, when Konstantin Dmitrievich is out. She was sitting here then. She

215

typed it and went out straightaway. She said she had a bad headache.'

Semyon Semyonovich sat alone in his office, sorting out his card-index. He usually did that when he was in low spirits, saying it was like patience, it calmed the nerves.

'What's new in the world of criminal statistics Semyon Semyonovich?'

Moiseyev took off his glasses, blinking.

'That's not what you're after is it, Alexander Borisovich, eh? Have you got any questions worth an answer? Make it quick, I'm retiring soon . . .'

That meant Parkhomenko had been talking to him about retiring. Parkhomenko was a fool if he didn't realise that Moiseyev, experienced and industrious Moiseyev, could give any novice cards and spades.

'Semyon Semyonovich why don't you complain to the city prosecutor? Or the Procurator-General even? Merkulov would always back you up.'

'You mean me complain with my . . . paragraph five?* Let's forget it Alexander Borisovich, it's not a topic for discussion.'

I thought I would have a word with Merkulov and said:

'Semyon Semyonovich, please be good enough to accompany me . . . to the toilet . . .'

Moiseyev displayed no surprise at my ludicrous request and pushed his chair away.

Having ensured we were alone among the urinals, I said:

'I urgently need photographs of our four students. Must be all four. Think up any excuse for taking them for the display-board or something . . .'

'No boards, Alexander Borisovich, and no excuses. I've got a photograph, more than one of all five of our students. I took them on the first day of their practice; you weren't present, I remember . . . and that little girl Kim was still alive . . .

*Paragraph 5 in a Soviet Passport gives details of nationality: in this case Jewish.

Come with me and I'll give you them and please don't warn me that this is just between you and me . . .'

Merkulov was going through a case with a young female investigator. She was seated next to him with her short uniform skirt hoisted high as she told the tale of her investigation.

'Excuse me, Konstantin Dmitrievich,' said I, 'I've just had a call from the City Committee people asking us to go over there, urgently. It's that control business . . . you know.'

The investigator glanced at me with distaste:

'We're busy, Turetsky.'

Merkulov, however, hastily deferred the case:

'Nelly Fiodorovna, you must excuse me. We'll have to go through your case another time.'

The investigator picked up her file and with a toss of the curls at her temples turned a hundred and eighty degrees.

When the door had closed behind her, Merkulov asked, barely audible:

'What's happened?'

I bent down to his ear:

'Operation Faust is moving into its closing phase.'

Aloud, for the benefit of listeners, if there were any, I said gruffly:

'Excuse me, but you asked me to keep you a place at the barber's. They've just rung me – it's our turn.'

Merkulov rubbed his ginger-stubbled cheeks:

'Yes indeed, I haven't shaved today . . .'

We left the office and went down Novo-Kuznetskaya towards the metro. Moscow was summery in tender foliage and the clear cloudless sky seemed to guarantee the permanence of life.

While we were walking towards the barbers, I gave Kostya a situation report and told him about yesterday's visit to Rogov at State Intelligence. I only left one thing out – any discussion of Marshal Agarkin's wife.

'Sit down here in the chair,' said the barber Lifshits to Merkulov, 'and I'll just go out for a minute and have a look at my car – and take off the windscreen-wipers otherwise you know how it is: two shakes and half your car's gone.'

That suited us. While Lifshits was out (he was a one-man outfit despite being honoured by the red banner of merit standing in the corner) Kostya and I went briefly over the Lagina case as it now appeared.

'What are we going to do, Kostya? To fight or not to fight?' I asked as the chairman of the conference. We were alone in the barber's shop.

Merkulov butted his head forward:

'Fight of course!'

'In that case I propose a plan: seize one of the links, hold on tight and pull out the entire chain. I propose to designate the 'objective' and start work on it, agent's work.'

'Do we have an objective then?'

'We do.'

'Who?'

'Tumanov,' I said. 'Remember Biryukov's testimony? You read it and heard the tape. He said they transferred the cashier's money to a suitcase and gave it to a strange person who drove up to the Warsaw Prospect in a Zaporozhets. Knave saw this guy from the back: he took the case from Malyuta Skuratov and carried it to his car. And he walked in an odd way, swaying from side to side as if he was drunk . . . I give drunks thirty kopeks towards drying-out expenses, but I don't know any drunks you'd entrust with quarter of a million . . . Know what I think? He was walking with artificial limbs. Looks as if he was drunk. There's other evidence as well. Tumanov lives near the Warsaw metro, and he drives a Zaporozhets, the car they dish out to invalids . . .'

'So what do you suggest?' asked Merkulov seriously. 'You want my authorisation for search and arrest?'

'I thought I would at first but decided that was the wrong way to go about it. You shouldn't frighten your pike, you have to take it on bait, a lure. This is how I see it. We'll have to tap his phone. And put a tail on him. Then we'll have to stick Zhukov onto him somehow. He's the best bet: he's from Afghanistan and hasn't been in Moscow for ages.'

218

'Alexander Borisovich, private detection in this country is not countenanced by the law,' said Merkulov and lay back in the barber's chair. The unnecessary emphasis he gave his words clearly showed that he regretted this legal flaw. 'I'll have to have a think,' he added.

'What's there to think about, Kostya? The public prosecutor doesn't have to sanction it, you don't have the responsibility.'

'Sasha, I'm speaking about keeping the law, not about responsibility.'

'According to the constitution we have no agents either, but all police detection makes use of a wide network of agents.'

'Yes, but that needs the authorisation of the chief of the police authority.'

'You needn't worry, for all her 'flu Shura can manage to squeeze an OK out of the chief of Moscow CID, you know that . . .'

Lifshits arrived at this point and proceeded to apply white foam to Merkulov's cheeks. Merkulov closed his eyes.

I sat patiently on a spare chair and observed the barber's movements above Merkulov's face. As soon as he opened his eyes, I asked abruptly:

'Well, have you thought?'

Merkulov gave one of his low throaty laughs:

'All right, your programme is accepted in full. No amendments.'

I dropped my two kopek coin into the coin-box and dialled Romanova's number.

'Merkulov gave the go-ahead . . . Set the operation going according to all the rules and regulations. That's not an order. It's a request, from Konstantin and me.'

'Got it. Don't worry, Sasha. It'll all be done as in the best houses in Lòndon,' said Romanova in her calm, decisive voice, then sniffed: her 'flu wasn't getting any better.

I replaced the receiver. I don't know how it is in the best houses in Lòndon but in our best houses – on Petrovka and

Lubyanka – they know how to listen in to people's phone-calls and snap people's secret meetings with hidden cameras . . .

I was sitting in Griaznov–Pogorelov's office having a smoke. I was calm as I inhaled deeply and watched the glow of the cigarette-end. Griaznov was trying his magic on some listening-printing device.

'Let's have a listen to what our tracker division had taped. First tape: telephone call on 225-2344. Ring a bell?'

'Yes. It's the same number we got from Gudinas.'

'By the way it's not in the directories, Sashok.'

'KGB? Or State Intelligence?'

'Listen here, as our mother-chief is wont to say.'

Griaznov switched on the tape.

Tumanov: Twenty-six and six. Good day Edward Nikitich!
Reply: Six and twenty-six, you mean. What's the matter?
Tumanov: I have to see you urgently. About the filling for the festival pie.
Reply: The festival's a long way off. Plenty of time.
Tumanov: I've got bad news.
Reply: All right. The old place in an hour.

Griaznov pressed the stop button.

'Twenty-six and six, what's that – an extension?

'I don't think so, Sashok. Pass-word, apparently. The reply is the reverse – six and twenty-six, you mean.'

'Today is the twenty-sixth, the sixth month, June.'

'Rather too primitive.'

'You know, sometimes what happens in life is really ordinary and really is what it seems to be . . . What're you laughing at? You think it's only you and Prince Merkulov who can make with the philosophy? . . . All right, let's listen some more. Our boys toddled after Tumanov. He got in his invalid Zaporozhets and led them – guess where? To Ilin Gates, right opposite the Central Committee building. Tumanov sat down on a bench near the monument to the heroes of Plevna. Fed the pigeons. Then a young man in a light suit came and sat down and started reading the paper. The CID boys naturally managed to get a couple of shots of him before he covered his face up.

Griaznov pressed the button again.

> Unknown: I warned you, Tamburlaine: ring only at the agreed time.
>
> Tumanov: Here birdies, cheep-cheep. Knave's been picked up, Malyuta . . . What if he said something?
>
> Malyuta: Well, what does he know? We've lifted Caesar. The catacombs have been abandoned. No traces . . .
>
> Tumanov: I feel uneasy.
>
> Malyuta: You called me over that?
>
> Tumanov: We have to hurry. Not enough filling. More dough needed. No people. Or transport.
>
> Malyuta: I'll see about it tomorrow.
>
> Tumanov: Better today.
>
> Malyuta: Today's out . . . Are you reading the papers?
>
> Tumanov: Cheep-cheep-cheep. I hate these pigeons. They've shat over all my windowsills . . . Yes, I read them. The football mainly.
>
> Malyuta: You know who's come to town?
>
> Tumanov: A-ha. Muhamed Nangar – yes? Big man now. He started with me when I was in charge of his HAD section. Not a bad operative, talks too much.
>
> Malyuta: So do you, Tamburlaine; so there's a reception at the Afghan embassy. I'll get busy tomorrow. I'll ring you.

Griaznov rewound the spool and asked:

'Can you guess where this Malyuta Skuratov went after that?'

'To the Party Central Committee building on Staraya Square!'

'Spot on. We copied the photo quickly – he's the chief of the Gensec's personal guard, Lieutenant-Colonel State Intelligence, Troyan. Edward Nikitovich in person. So we're fixing Zhenka to get acquainted with him today, it's already organised. Zhenka's at home among the Afghans – his friends from Kabul are going to be there as well. So we're getting to work on Troyan right away. Tumanov's small fry now, just means to an end. You and I'll be insurance for Zhenka outside. He's got to show he's on Troyan's side and wangle himself into helping with the transport.'

'Shall we try the pass-word, twenty-six and six? Or is it just on the phone?'

'Have you got any other suggestions?'

'Wait. Find out what they mean by their festival pie.'

'That's what he'll find out today.'

'What if he fails? Suppose Troyan puts cyanide in his champagne?'

Griaznov put his question again.

'Got any other suggestions? What if their festival's tomorrow – what then? We've missed out over those catacombs. What do you think they took out of there? Explosives probably. The pie-filling's explosives. They need money – that's for sure. That's why they went out mugging cashiers. Somebody's buying dynamite by the kilogram from military dumps. The KGB is going over one arsenal now: there's a 150,000 rouble deficit. Twelve thousand rounds five hundred hand grenades, a ton and a half of explosives, five small-calibre rocket-launchers even – they've all gone somewhere . . . They're trying to connect it to the metro explosion and the Armenian terrorists. I've seen Grechannik's documents . . . what're you looking at your watch for? Kiss your lover's meeting good-bye, you won't get home till late.'

'When's Zhukov arriving?'

'Seven. The embassy reception's at eight.'

'I've got an hour then. I have to go over to your remand cells and see Knave, Biryukov.'

'Don't be long. We've got to get our signal system working. Two of our people have got to go to the embassy with Zhenka. You've got to be kept informed.'

'What signals?'

'What an uneducated chap you are, comrade general. See, for example, if I smooth my thatch down like that,' Griaznov drew a hand across his ginger locks, 'it means: follow me. And if I do it this way it means call off the hounds.'

'Okay. I won't be long.'

'Hello, Knave.'

'They're going to shoot me anyway. They told me in the cell, it makes no difference.'

'That's not true, Knave. I'm telling you, you're going to live.'

He was going to live . . . Like Halilov, the three Smirnovs and the other two hundred soldiers in the Central Hospital in Kabul. Biryukov had been given the injection without the stabiliser. He was still in possession of his mind but soon it would begin to slide away, irreversible degradation of the personality would set in . . .

'Just look at these photos. Do you recognise anybody?'

Knave tensed himself to look, then slumped.

'That girl was with us in the car when we went to Riazan. Then she got on a bus and came back in an hour, hour and a half with Morozov. Caesar and Malyuta Skuratov followed them. Half an hour later we went into the forest. Caesar killed the student there. She looks more beautiful in the photo though, she was wearing a head-square and you couldn't see her hair. She told everybody what to do. Even Malyuta did as she said. Her voice was so quiet . . . and menacing.'

Within our investigative organs, KGB, MVD and the Prosecutor's Office, there are special secret services, so called staff inspectorates. Their job is to investigate misdemeanours and crimes committed by the investigative organs themselves. Now I'd decided to form such a service myself. It would consist of one person – me. The task of the newly-appointed inspectorate would be to expose the misdemeanours and crimes committed by law-faculty student Svetlana Nikolayevna Aralova-Belova, Marshal of the Soviet Union Agarkin's wife, my lover . . .

More than anything in the world I wanted to finish the investigation with the formula 'case closed owing to absence of criminality in activities of suspect'. I knew that could never be

223

and I would have to take upon myself yet another role – a judge pronouncing sentence. My head began to sing with pain at this thought. Everything went dark and as I walked down the corridor every step echoed in my head like the strokes of a hammer on an anvil . . .

A piercing cry turning into a shriek rang out from behind the door of Griaznov–Pogorelov's office. I opened the door and stepped in, carrying my grotesquely heavy head with considerable difficulty. I hadn't the right to be ill, it had to pass, I kept persuading myself, trying to focus my attention on Griaznov.

'But you have no right to detain the man. I don't give a damn for the judge's decision! You're ruining a case of national importance. I'm now passing the receiver to Moscow Prosecutor's Office Investigator Turetsky. He'll explain everything properly!'

Griaznov put his hand over the mouthpiece.

'It's the Cheryomushki region bailiff, Koshelyova. They've arrested Zhukov over there for non-payment of alimony.

'Wha-a-t?'

My headache ceased for a second, but resumed, though at somewhat lower intensity. I knew this Koshelyova, a butter-mountain with the face of a farm-labourer – it was useless arguing with her: she was stupid and obstinate 'in the performance of her duty'. How many of her kind did we have, hundreds, thousands . . .

'Hello, comrade Koshelyova. Could you explain what's happened?'

'Hello, if you're being serious. What's happened comes under article 122 of the RSFSR criminal code, wilful neglect on a parent's part in paying for support of minors, in accordance with a court order. Penalty up to one year in prison or three years in exile,' Koshelyova rattled off. 'I summoned your citizen of national importance today pursuant to an application by his former spouse to wit, that he had disappeared for over a year, had not put in an appearance at his permanent address and had not paid her money towards the support of their daughter Emma, twelve-years-old. Your national figure, instead of admitting his guilt and repenting, started yelling like a mad thing in the presence of the public that he'd paid everything. He also used bad language in the presence of the same public . . . Don't interrupt me, two can play at that game. He's had plenty to say here . . . It's a good thing the police and the court are in the same building. The police next door have put him in the remand cell and that's where he is now.'

'Comrade Koshelyova, I'm going to phone the RSFSR Minister of Justice . . .'

'Make it the USSR! Phone who you like. Until we see the money we're not letting him go.'

'What money?!'

'What are you getting all worried about? D'you think I'm screwing a bribe out of you? Ha-ha-ha! One thousand one hundred and fourteen roubles seventy-three kopeks. I have a writ of execution here. Once he pays the money, we'll let him out straightaway.'

'A thousand?! How the devil can he pay if he's locked in a cell?'

'That's his affair. He should have thought of that before.'

'Comrade Kosheloyova, I'm bringing the money over right away.'

'Like I said, once the money's here he gets let out. Get here before eight and you can have your priceless, wilful non-payer of alimony . . .'

Griaznov and I stared at each other for several seconds, at a loss.

'Where are you reckoning to lay your hands on that sort of money in ninety minutes, Sasha?'

'Hell knows . . . What are you sniggering at?'

'Oh, I can't help it, your face . . . just too miserable.'

'You realise I've got no friends with money like that.'

'Well I could find some from my clients but they don't keep money at home. It's all in bank accounts for safe deposits. Even then they're scared the police force will deprive them of their ill-gotten gains . . . And time is of the essence.'

'Can you fix me up with a car? I've got an idea . . .'

Irka Frolovskaya had told me once that she'd found my old books on the bunk-bed. They had belonged to my late father and his father before him. A certain antiquarian bookseller on Old Arbat had assured me they were worth an enormous sum. His shop was two minutes walk from my old flat. I had to get there . . .

I spent about five minutes hopelessly pressing the bell: no one at home. This was a quite unexpected setback: in my previous living quarters there were always three or four wives crowding around the kitchen. I went out into the street and walked round the block outside. At one time I'd slid out of the little corridor window of my flat onto the roof of the next building when I had to get out without being noticed. It was the other way round this time. Doing it in broad daylight however was fraught with awkward possibilities. I might be picked up for simple breaking and entering. This thought held me up for exactly five seconds. I went up the 'black' staircase to the top storey then out onto the roof; trying not to slip on the sloping surface I got as far as the wall of my building. The flimsy skylight gave easily under my palm . . .

Irka hadn't changed the lock of her room and I knew how to open it without a key, using a spoon-handle I found in the kitchen sink among a pile of dirty dishes. Kicking off my trainers, I reached up, pushing off from the piano and sprang onto the bunk. I saw at once the pile of Father's books, neatly parcelled by Irina. A piece of paper stuck out from under the string, with 'Sasha's books' written on it. I pulled the bundle out from under a pile of old sheet-music, slapped it, raising a cloud of dust and . . . saw Irina. She stood looking up at me, quite unsurprised at my odd location. Her cat's eyes were smiling and sparkling. Suddenly I lost all desire to go to the bookseller, back up Zhukov at the Afghan embassy or do anything at all, bar one thing: I wanted to stay in that room with Auntie Klava's old piano, just sit on the narrow sofa and look into Irina's eyes. I threw the books to the floor and

226

flopped down less than graceful myself, uneasily aware that my socks were far from fresh.

'I'm sorry, Irina for breaking in . . .'

'With a spoon!' She burst out laughing.

I took her hand and drew her to me.

'Shasha . . .'

'Not Sasha – idiot, I've been an idiot all this time.'

I kissed her docile, inexperienced lips, hugging her light body to me as hard as I could. I had never, never once, experienced such despairing happiness as now, standing in my socks in the ramshackle room I'd inhabited for six years and where Irina now lived, Irina who had loved me meekly all her life.

'You . . . have to go . . . Sasha,' she said, barely audible, hugging my neck. 'I don't . . . want . . . you to go . . . but you have to . . . I know . . .'

'You see, we need money. It's all a stupid mix-up, a vital case depends on it.'

'Faust? You said the operation was called "Faust".'

'Merkulov called it that. Actually there's no operation Faust,' I said lacing-up my shoes. 'Come with me to the bookshop, if you've got time.'

Irina always had time for me.

'You know what Faust means in German?' asked Irina, skipping lightly down the staircase. 'It just means a fist. It's a feminine noun in German as well. I always got the declension wrong in school, you know. I'd got used to thinking it was a man – Goethe's Faust, I mean. I couldn't help it. Actually I thought it was funny, calling a man by a feminine name.'

'Yes, well this book'll fetch 700,' said the bookseller, putting Garn's *Constructivists* on one side, 'it's the 1922 Kharkov edition, the real thing. Now these books of Mister Kruchonikh on the imaginists, they'll make a hundred each easily . . . Wood engravings, *Alkonst* Petrograd 1921 . . . Poems by Kusikov . . . Yes, treasure-trove here. If you sold them privately of course, you'd get more. I couldn't give you more than seventeen hundred for the lot. Come back on Monday and I'll have the money ready.'

'What – Monday?! I need it urgently, today, this minute!'

'I'm fond of you, Alexander, but I can't do it today, the takings have gone with the cashiers, there's no money in the shop.'

Total failure . . . Better if Griaznov had gone round his 'clients'; so, we hadn't worked out the signals and total failure here . . .

'What about privately?' I heard Irina's voice.

'How d'you mean, privately, beautiful fairy. I'm a state employee and your young man could . . . like they did our director one time.'

'You can buy them off me. The young man won't know anything about that. He's never been here.'

I saw a flicker of greed in the bookseller's eyes and added oil to the flames.

'And the fairy will come down to 1500.'

'I don't know, honestly, if I can find as much as that . . .'

'Yes you can, yes you can . . . Have a really good look and take your time,' said the fairy reassuringly.

'What a mess-up that was,' said Zhukov. 'They'd got everything in a twist, they'd taken the money off me but they didn't put it through the bailiff. My old woman was only too pleased to get her hands on the money using the duplicate sheet and drop me in it as well . . . Well, nuts to her. I rang Anait today, she'd been checking on what my HAD friends had been saying. Seri really has disappeared from Kabul. He's in Pakistan in charge of some amazing operation – he's acting as hit-man against some Pakistani big-shot . . .'

I switched the siren on in the police Volga and stamped on the pedal, breaking all speed restrictions in the centre of Moscow – lucky for me police regulations allowed that.

16

'You've got nothing to worry about, Zhenya!' Romanova was saying, as she equipped Zhukov for the 'Afghan operation'. 'The boys from division have peppered you with microphones, one in every pocket, Slava and Sasha will be sitting outside in a T.V. van. They'll listen in and tape everything that happens within a yard of you. The chief of Special Section no. 1 in your ministry will introduce you to Troyan: we've checked – he knows Troyan from Afghanistan, he's been there quite a few times on various bits of business. I've arranged it all with him. After that I'm relying completely on your operational nous. Main thing – take your time . . .'

Romanova really had organised the operation 'as in the best houses in London'. After we drove up to the Afghan embassy, Zhenya peeled off from us and attached himself to the delegation of his own ministry, this, the Ministry of Special Restoration and Construction, was rebuilding shattered Kabul and so occupied first place on the ambassador's invitation list. Griaznov and I meanwhile edged ourselves in among a group from the surveillance section of Moscow Internal Affairs Directorate. So as to lull the vigilance of the KGB – they were working inside the embassy as well as outside – the chief of the surveillance section explained that a special brigade of the Directorate, trained for anti-terrorist duties, would be on duty near the embassy. Its job would be to eliminate any 'excesses' which might take place in the district. He added that this 'trained brigade' wouldn't simply do its stint and go home – no, the boys would keep watch, relieving one another not only until such time as our Gensec left, but also while our honoured guest was here – the Gensec of the Peoples Democratic Party of Afghanistan.

Such warm concern about the two Gensecs got the upper echelons of the KGB into quite a state. A highly-placed Gee-Bee general, obviously responsible for security at the Afghan embassy stuck his bird-like head into our van:

'Good lads, you CID lot! Thanks for backing us up!'

The Afghan operation, surprisingly, went like clockwork. A few minutes after eight, a dozen limousines drew up at the embassy: our Gensec and his retinue had arrived. The reception hubbub went on for about an hour before the Gensecs withdrew to talk tête-à-tête. During these few minutes, to judge by the noises coming over the air-waves, Troyan's old Afghan acquaintance came over to him, a retired Gee-Bee general, now the chief of Special Section no. 1 in the Construction Ministry. After introducing Zhukov to Troyan, the chief complained of his weak bladder and withdrew for a moment – could happen to anyone, specially a retired Gee-Bee general . . .

We could hear Zhenya Zhukov's voice loud and clear:

'Good evening Malyuta! Twenty-six and six!'

'What's the matter? Who are you?'

'You've forgotten the password.'

Long silence. Or perhaps it just seemed so to us.

'Six and twenty-six.'

'You mean . . . no cause for alarm. My name is Zhukov, you heard that from the previous speaker.'

Their voices dissolved in the noise and swam up again about two minutes later.

'He ordered me to assist with the transport . . . You've got problems. I know. And I've got the solution. Tomorrow I'm getting a convoy of lorries at ZIL.'

'Right . . .'

'I can let a couple go. For a while. Say something Malyuta. Well?'

'I have to go. No time to talk here. Let's meet tomorrow. I'm getting off early tomorrow. The boss is going to his *dacha*. We can meet at seven in the Manège. There's a Glazunov exhibition on. Lots of people about, makes it easier. We'll meet in the lobby at nineteen hundred hours.'

Zhukov left the embassy with his 'own' people – the chief of Special Section no. 1 and two other members of the board. After saying goodbye to his colleagues and a quick glance around to see if there was a tail on him, he slipped into our T.V. van . . .

Late that evening the three of us were sitting in our monitoring centre on wheels munching some rather nice egg and rice pastries. Griaznov's latest flame was the production manageress of some kind of catering concern, and kept him supplied with these things in endless quantities, in exchange for 'love'. We were having a bite to eat after sharing a bottle of Grain vodka which Griaznov had paid over the odds for from one of the 'flatfeet' of the surveillance section.

Zhukov was analysing his conversation with Troyan:

'You know boys, I had the feeling he didn't believe me . . . Or rather, made out he believed me, but smelled a rat. Bet your life he's going to test my story. Probably phone Kabul to check what I said. Make inquiries among his 'brothers', my people in the trust – and in the ministry . . . anyway he'll sniff something out . . .'

'Hold it, dad, don't panic,' Griaznov interrupted, 'maybe you just imagined he was on to you?'

'No, I didn't imagine it . . .'

'So what then, cancel the operation? I mean getting Zhenka into the gang?' I said, glancing briefly at Zhukov.

'You know it makes no difference, Sasha.' Zhukov said, finishing off a pastry, 'whether he believed me or not . . . I haven't left a trail and there's nothing to compromise me, either in Kabul or Moscow – I wouldn't be working for the cops: on the contrary, since I was kicked out of the CID, I've been looking for revenge. I could easily have been accepted into the brotherhood by some 'primary organisation'. I expect they've modelled their structure on the Communist Party . . . And Malyuta won't find out if I am a brother till Seri returns to Kabul.'

'When's he due back?' asked Griaznov.

'Not before Friday, they said.'

'So we've still got twenty-four hours. More . . .'

'Anything might happen. What if Seri comes back all of a sudden? Or rings Moscow from somewhere? This is a dangerous business, Zhenya,' I concluded. 'They could pick you up, drive you out of town and waste you . . .'

'What's safe in this life? It's dangerous sleeping with a bird you don't know,' laughed Zhukov.

Griaznov poured out the last drops into the paper cups:

'Cut the cackle! Time to get the show on the road . . . And stay alive. That depends on whether Troyan connects Zhukov's appearance on the horizon with Knave's arrest. That's the question!'

He looked at Zhukov and asked:

'Well then, Evgeni Ivanovich, shall we risk it like in the good old days, never beat, eh?'

Evgeni Ivanovich nodded his curls decisively then throwing back his head, sunk the rest of the vodka in one go.

I spoke to Griaznov:

'Slava, keep up the good work on Troyan tomorrow. Keep it up till we send Zhenya into the enemy camp. Okay?'

Griaznov silently inclined his head.

'Irisha, are you in bed yet? Just ringing for the sake of it.'

'Were you in time?'

'What for?'

'The money.'

'Yes, yes, I was. What are you doing on Saturday?'

'Lelya, Lidochka Merkulova and I are going to the festival at Luzhniki Stadium. After that, free . . .'

'Ring me when you're clear.'

'Don't disconnect the phone then,' laughed Irka '– say hello to Faust . . .'

'Don't disconnect the phone then' . . . Vanya had come in that morning – 'Your telephone's not working.' Somebody had phoned Bunin and told him Turetsky's phone wasn't working. But I'd plugged it in hadn't I, the previous night when Irka ran in . . . When Lana came, I'd pulled the plug out of the socket. I always did that when Lana was with me. *They* hadn't known that I'd plugged it back in again. But they did know I'd pulled it out! I'd said to Lana then – 'We're due to meet at the Prosecutor's Office at twelve.' It was her then . . . again it was her . . . Had she really wanted to murder me along with Vanya Bunin? Perhaps she didn't know that *they* wanted to wipe us out? Just carrying out *their* orders: had she said we were due at the Prosecutor's Office at twelve and that was all? I really did want to believe that version, but I couldn't: I was sure she'd planned the thing *with* them, she was the only one who knew the telephone wasn't working, or thought she did.

Irka was funny . . . 'Say hello to Faust.' Faust is fist in German. Feminine gender. We're used to thinking of Faust as a man . . . We're used to think . . . Liuda Korabelnikova: 'I think he was a homosexual' . . . Lala Istomina: 'Could have been one of those' . . . What if he wasn't a queer at all and not . . . a man! 'We're used to thinking of Faust as a man' . . . We were talking – the second killer. They confirmed – two young men in black jackets rang the Lagins' bell . . . One of them had an umbrella in his hand. 'It wasn't raining then was it?' Liuda Korabelnikova: 'Yes, it had just come on to pour.' I had looked at my watch – Lana had asked the time. It was just after two. I'd heard the rain starting to rustle among the leaves and the car brakes at the crossing had started squealing on the wet asphalt. Maybe it had started raining earlier on Leninsky Prospect?

I never expected the meteorological service to work within such fine limits.

'Precipitation in the Greater Moscow region was observed everywhere on the night of June 13th–14th 1985 from 23.50 to 00.25, then from 7 o'clock in the morning – incessant rain for . . .'

'You're sure that around two in the morning or just after there was no rain on Frunze Embankment?

'I repeat: in the interval between 00.25 and seven a.m. no precipitation was recorded in the Moscow region . . .'

Maybe they had made a mistake anyway, I thought, hoping

233

against hope, and felt a clinging tentacle of fear coil about my heart . . .

I doused the light and sat motionless in my armchair, eyes closed. I must remember. I must remember everything as it was . . . I didn't want to, I was afraid to recall what would be intolerable to live with. But I had to do it: 'Kim, I'll find him' . . . I must remember . . .

. . . I had been woken up by a puzzling sound and thought I'd dreamed it, because it had been a very familiar sound which would have been totally out of place. Lana was by my side and rain was falling outside the window. Lana had whispered: 'What's the time?' I'd thought it was around twelve, and that I hadn't been asleep long. When I put the light on I was surprised; by the clock on the wall it was past two.

Now I knew what the sound had been – tack-tack-tack. A finger turning the hands of a clock . . . She'd been preparing herself an alibi: 'I got back home around three in the morning. If necessary that fact can be corroborated'. Then she'd got dressed, I went to sleep again and didn't hear her go out. I dreamed I was arguing with somebody but though I knew it was a dream I couldn't wake up.

On the day I came back from Kabul, she had left me and I'd heard the sound of the midnight national anthem through the wall of the flat next door. I had striven to remember when it had happened before – Lana went out, and the anthem played. Now I knew that it had been on the night of Kim's murder.

I put the light on and took out the photo-fit picture of the second killer. I picked up my yellow flowmaster and with an unpractised hand drew a woman's hair-do, a generous forelock to the eyebrows, ears covered, long almost shoulder-length braids . . .'We're used to thinking it's a man'. I found a green pencil, greened in the eyes just a fraction and placed a small green bow at the base of the neck . . .

17

In the morning Merkulov came in to see me.

'Sasha, yesterday, when you weren't here, they fetched in the translation of that Lithuanian diary. I glanced through it, but it makes no kind of sense to me. A madman's thoughts are a bit tedious for a normal mind. Anyway, read it yourself you might see something in it, I'm off. Today it's 'Landowner's Morning', millions of people with complaints.

He squeezed my shoulder with his powerful fingers and left. I had made no effort to stop him and report to the chiefs what my 'staff inspectorate' efforts had led to in the matter of Aralova – Belova – Agarkina. My head was full of thoughts which could well have occurred to Ivonin or Gudinas: I wanted to wipe half the humanity round me off the face of the earth. And I didn't want Merkulov to say: 'Sasha, you have all the signs of paranoia.'

I put the diary aside, I wouldn't have taken it in anyway since it was written in Lithuanian. I undid the grey tape round the folder which held the sheets and the translation. The longer I scanned it, the more obvious it became – it wasn't a diary in the proper sense of the word, it was the deranged monologue of a deranged person.

'. . . The world awaits a new New Flood, mighty, feral, a hundred times more purging than the first! The New Flood will come soon – a matter of days! We, the new centurions of the New Flood, we will bring it about! We are not only brothers, we are sons of the New Flood, the New Era! We will ignite the torch and the fire will swallow up the old world. For what are we raising our new palace? The old building is imperfect – it is overrun with rats, snakes and ants. There is no sense in living in such chaos of want, enmity and betrayal . . . We are brothers, we are heroes, we are individuals, we . . . will root out slavery in one day, one hour, one second . . . On earth slavery has seeped into the pores, sweat and blood of humanity, it permits evil to be done a hundred times faster, it leaves no time for reflections: either you carry out the order or you go to hell! And after the revolution when we have destroyed the rabble and the thinkers, we will speak the truth to those who remain: obscurantism has gone, we are victorious, the world is beautiful!'

Then there was a kind of poem:

> Amid mountains of rubbish, tares of slavery,
> There we shall ignite our torch of death.
> And the great outcast gave this bowl
> His name, dishonoured through the ages.
> Tremble, obscurantist curs,
> Even if we perish, brothers in brotherhood,
> Our genius will save the world!

There were thirty pages of text written in the same spirit . . .

Still, I wasn't in agreement with Merkulov that it was gibberish. I was able to detect a certain sequence of ideas. The madness had its own logic. Merkulov was a long way from madness, but that morning I was near the edge.

This Gudinas knew something: couldn't not know, he wasn't a private soldier in this brotherhood. Consequently he might know the method of destruction awaiting mankind . . . He hadn't written that mystic stuff for nothing: 'We are brothers, we are heroes, we are individuals, we . . . will root out slavery in one day, one hour, one second . . .' I thought he must mean an explosion, an explosion of titanic power . . . Well, that was no discovery, that's what the explosives were for and that's why transport was so necessary to Tamburlaine and Malyuta . . . The question was – where and when did they intend to set off this explosion?

The diary did not supply an answer to that. Still I read the ramblings to the very end and was about to analyse it more closely when Griaznov appeared in the office.

Slava always starts a conversation with a question, either its because he's used to the interrogation manner or because he's trying to get across some of his own imagination – of which he has an excess.

This time he began thoughtfully:

'Tell me, Sashok, do you remember what you had for breakfast today? Don't look at me like that. The majority of human beings can't remember what they had for breakfast or dinner the day before. But I'll remember that breakfast as long as I live . . . Who d'you think I had breakfast with?'

'Lay off.'

'I had breakfast today in the Prague cafe. They gave me schnitzel à la minister, and my lady had a lovely cheese omelette. Then cakes: a napoleon and an eclair, then turkish coffee.'

'Griaznov, are you out of your mind?'

'Not yet.'

'A really gripping conversation, I . . .'

'My fellow-diner wore a white jacket with lace trimmings and a black skirt. And she was beautiful, just beautiful. All eyes were on her. But I would like just one person to be attracted to her. Because, it turns out, she loves him.'

'Slava. No more puzzles.'

Griaznov smiled sceptically and gave me a photographic recognition form. Clipped to the blue police form were the photographs of three young men.

'What's this?'

'You can read.'

'I, Frolovskaya Irina Genrikhovna, recognise among the photographs shown to me, the man, shown in photograph 2. It was he who approached a Moskvich car belonging to citizen Turetsky A.B., late on June 23rd 1985 the night before the explosion in which Ivan Bunin was killed . . .'

'And who is it?'

'Caesar. More precisely Captain Kurkin, student at the Dzerzhinsky Academy. The same man the specials sent off on some imaginary hush-hush operation,' replied Griaznov evenly. 'I can see you're not in the mood.'

'No, Slava, I'm not. But I am listening and concentrating.'

Giving me a second to digest the news Griaznov proffered me yet another document. This was an information report on Troyan.

It stated that, 'Troyan, Edward Nikitovich, 32, born in Moscow, formerly lived at Sadovsky Lane, Block 5, Flat 8. Graduated Moscow Suvorov Military College, then with distinction the F.E. Dzerzhinsky Academy (training personnel for State Intelligence). On graduation, worked abroad but was expelled from Paris along with a group of Soviet diplomats. Carried out international duty on the staff of 17th Independent Regiment Special Forces: reached rank of major, commanded a company, subsequently a battalion. Awarded title of Hero of the Soviet Union for carrying out secret operation of vital national importance. Transferred to Moscow, attached to State Intelligence; carries out functions as head of bodyguard of General Secretary of the Central Committee CPSU. At present resides at Kutuzov Prospect, Block 36, Wing 2, Flat 39 . . .'

'Sashok, what's happened to you?' asked Griaznov seeing me unable to tear my eyes from the paper.

'No, it's all right . . . The address seems to ring a bell . . .'

'On Kutuzov? That's a massive twelve-storey pink-brick . . .'

'No, this one – Sadovsky Lane.'

'That's off Gorky Street, the Culinary shop's on the corner, Bolshoi Theatre house on the other, there used to be an eye hospital there, then they moved it further down the lane . . .'

But I wasn't listening to Griaznov, I'd just that moment remembered: at that address, Sadovsky Lane, Block 5, Flat 8, Svetlana Belova maiden name Aralova had lived.

'Where are you off to?'

'Slava, I have to pursue some inquiries.'

Griaznov looked at me strangely, as if he'd seen a spider on my forehead, and said coldly:

'Don't forget, we're going on with the Troyan operation today.'

* * *

The house at number five Sadovsky Lane no longer existed. That is, the house was there but it was occupied by an embassy of one of the friendly powers. I walked all round the quarter, along Three Ponds Lane, Annunciation Lane, and strolled into the courtyard of the eye hospital, but I saw no housing office. I lit a cigarette and dropped the empty packet on the lawn. A distinguished-looking old man came darting out from somewhere, picked up the packet in silence and carried it to a rubbish bin in the depths of the courtyard.

'I'm sorry!' I shouted after him.

The old man came back looked at me from under his glasses and said peaceably:

'Other people don't even apologise. You know near the beach at Riga there used to be no rubbish urns at all in the streets. But the cleanliness was – amazing. Now they've hung yellow bins on every lamp-post and they throw rubbish everywhere.'

The old man looked like Chekov – neat little beard, pince-nez, linen jacket.

'Are you looking for somebody or just out walking?'

'Oh, I was given an address, but it must be wrong, there's an embassy there.'

'The embassy's been here about five years. There was a dwelling-house there before. I lived exactly fifty years in flat 7 myself. With a break of eight years actually.'

'Thirty-seven to forty-five?'

'You're wrong. Forty-six to fifty-four. Well, why are we standing, there's a bench over there, I paint it myself every year. I live opposite now. Allow me to introduce myself – Polonsky, Semyon Yakovlevich, special pensioner, president of the society for preserving greenery in this micro-region, in times gone by – playwright. I wrote for the people's theatre. Whom do I have the honour of addressing?'

'Turetsky, Sasha, lawyer.'

'Well, then, my dear Sasha, I can give you information about all the residents of this house.'

'I'm looking for a classmate ... Yuri Vasiliev,' I lied fluently, 'he lived in flat no. 8.'

'Vasilievs . . . in no. 8 . . . No Sasha. There's been no Vasilievs in this house since 1935 . . . Academician Tiomkin lived here fifteen years, after he died and his family moved to Cheryomushki, there was an extraordinary woman lived here . . . Troyan, Nina Tarasovna . . .'

'Not *the* Troyan – the Heroine? Famous sniper in the war?'

'No. She was a sniper . . . but a special kind . . . You'll never guess, my friend, don't try. I'm now going to tell you an astonishing story about a remarkable and unique woman . . . I'm sorry. You do have time? I certainly have, a great deal and yet not very much. You're probably in a hurry? Young people, always on the go . . .'

Polonsky was one of those who like to exercise their tongues and remember times past – now it was no longer dangerous . . . A man's need to confess never leaves him, the confessional complex is the chronic disease of our OAPs. Especially those on special pensions, whether local, republican or national status. They've got plenty to remember and tell their grandchildren. It's a pity though that we of the younger generation are not too keen on the reminiscences of our grandfathers . . . In me, however, Semyon Yakovlevich Polonsky had found a grateful listener, although I didn't then suppose his memories of the Troyan family were necessary to my inquiries.

'Semyon Yakovlevich, I'm not in a hurry, do go on . . .'

'What does love mean for a man? Short sprints from a soft bed to a softer one? And for a woman? To conquer, attract, seduce – to turn a wild horse into a docile pack-mule! You follow my train of thought, Sasha? I mean everything is based on primitive instinct, whether it's a man or a woman: catch, tame, master. You follow me? Not yield yourself on the altar of love, as it was with us older generation, brought up in a sentimental spirit, but *take*! Not sacrifice yourself – sacrifice others! This grim truth about modern man – I mean the new generation of men – was grasped by an inexperienced girl from the beautiful Ukrainian town of Dnepropetrovsk. I was born there, incidentally . . . She was a most exquisite creation. I have to confess, I rather fell for her myself, even tried to charm her with the Moscow theatre world . . . But of course, she wasn't interested in me . . . She wanted to seize hold of life. Nina Troyan came from Dnepropetrovsk to conquer Moscow. She was a natural blonde with amazing dark-blue eyes, deep as wells. She worked as a stewardess on an airliner which soared aloft bearing the valuable bodies of our leaders . . . She was seduced, she told me, by a government pilot. He actually introduced her to Nikita Sergeyevich . . . I can see you thinking: which Nikita Sergeyevich? He can't mean Kruschev? I'm telling you – the very same! Nikita the maize-fanatic, Tsar Nikita, First Secretary, Prime Minister, so forth . . . He was so enchanted by the beautiful young stewardess that he was prepared to leave his old Nina Petrovna . . . For however long it was, Tsar Nikita picked up with Nina Troyan; she got a room opposite me, in Flat 8, and . . . had a baby Tsarevich, a lovely little lad, they called him Edward. Why Nikita Sergeyevich liked that name I don't know . . .'

As I listened to this wild tale I couldn't make up my mind whether the amateur-theatre man was telling the truth. Was it just the imagination of a professional story-teller?

Polonsky raised the spectacles on his nose:

'I can see doubts in your face, you probably think the old man's making it up eh?'

'To be honest, it is a strange story.'

I felt for my cigarettes and realised I'd smoked the last.

'I see you're out of cigarettes. I've got some "Prima" if you've no objection?' He pulled out an unopened packet.

'Actually I don't smoke but I carry cigarettes and matches just in case.'

'Thanks, Semyon Yakovlevich . . . So Nina Troyan just had one child by Nikita Sergeyevich?'

'Just the one, Edward Nikitovich Troyan. He keeps his mother's name. He's in the army now. After his father died somebody upstairs decided that Edik should be a military man. Nina Tarasovna had a daughter as well – Svetlana. Nikita Sergeyevich had an aide called Aralov, rather obscure dull chap. Anyway Nikita Sergeyevich insisted that he married

Nina Troyan. At first this was just for show but later, as is often the way, fiction turned into fact . . . They became husband and wife. Aralov was made a republican minister and they moved from here to the Soviet Ministry building . . .'

'Do you ever see her, Nina Troyan?'

'Sometimes, not often. Usually when she's in trouble. Then she rings me, pours out her worries and complains about life. Like it was recently when they dismissed her husband from his job as minister. Not just him, incidentally. New broom sweeping clean . . . It's interesting to talk with you, comrade jurist, let me have your phone number. We could have another chat . . .'

'Of course, Semyon Yakovlevich, that goes without saying. With pleasure.'

'Splendid!' said Polonsky, much pleased. He jotted down my home telephone number and having said goodbye, minced away down the path leading to the connecting court.

So, Svetlana was Troyan's sister. Troyan, a byproduct of the disgraced head of government. Svetlana was the daughter of a disgraced minister, abandoned by her husband for the new Gensec's daughter. My friend from MIIR had said: 'She wanted to kill Belov, but married Marshal Agarkin instead.' No, not instead. It was to revenge herself on her husband and his new family at the same time. An alliance of revenge and lust for power. Agarkin was in supreme charge. 'Stalin' – that was him for a certainty. Troyan was the instrument, Svetlana the inspiration and accomplice. Despite all these collisions of human destinies now revealed to me, I was untouched. *Let them devour each other*, let them struggle for power or the throne that was slipping away from them – I wasn't gloating over the fatal secret of Troyan – Belova – Agarkin. What was it to me who sat on the very top? Nothing would change for me. Or my mother. Or Merkulov, or Irina. My duty to the service, however, meant I was obliged to expose crimes committed out of festering pride, blind vanity, arbitrary power – and so I would back up Zhenya Zhukov when he met Troyan at the Manège that evening. Meanwhile there was a full stop left to put at the end of my 'inquiry'. With this in mind, I walked to Pushkin Square where I consulted a phone book for the number of the lady who had held European and world records . . .

Anna Chudnova's flat was cluttered with prizes and festooned with pennants and medals. Anna herself made coffee in the kitchen grousing in a bass voice:

'This coffee-grinder's a hundred and fifty years old. Time to throw it out, still it's a pity. Look at that handle – antique! Grab hold and turn it, I'll get the water on.'

I took the antediluvian machine and sat down in the armchair again. With Anna around, you feel yourself inadequate. She was six inches taller than me.

We'd only met ten minutes before, but we were already good pals. Anna was one of the boys so to speak.

'Sugar? Good. Milk? Without. That's good as well, seeing as I haven't got any. I can't cook at all, you know. Who for? I want to adopt a child from the children's home, I'd knit bonnets for it, I can do that, and porridge . . . What am I going on about, rubbish, you're here on business . . .'

Chudnova didn't have a pretty face, it had red blotches, without make-up. Her eyes were kind and sad though. She hadn't succumbed to stardom, obviously.

'Yes, now about Svetka Aralova. A beauty of course. Figure – top class. The guys on the beach used to drool. Cold though. Lifeless almost I'd say. And jealous. She hated me, I know. Her green eyes stare at you, quiet voice, seems just to let words fall. A girlfriend of mine used to say: 'Anka, she'll poison you, believe me'. What was I to do, then? Apart from sport, what was there in life for me? Who'd marry a lump like me? There I go again . . . So after the Olympics in Moscow in 1980 when she didn't just lose to me but didn't even get a medal, she developed stress problems and some sort of nervous illness. She spent a few months in hospital and we used to go and see her, but she didn't seem to welcome our visits all that much. She'd developed psoriasis over the whole of her body, especially the head. They did cure her – she was in the Kremlin ward after all, her father was still a minister. They prescribed constant quartz-lamp treatment, she'd have a tan all year round . . . Then she got married and I heard no more about her . . .'

'Which hospital was she in exactly?'

'Oh . . . I'll remember in a minute . . . Yes, of course, the Botkin, the Kremlin wing.'

The department head took a long look at my ID. She would have been perfectly within her rights in turning down my request, since it wasn't an official inquiry from the Prosecutor's Office. After that she studied my face at length, wrote something on a piece of paper and summoned a secretary.

'You can look at the medical history of Aralova's illness, but I can only issue a diagnosis certificate, an extract from the case history, with a written inquiry from the investigative organs.'

The secretary fetched the medical history and I leafed through it from beginning to end. There was an abundance of Latin.

'You couldn't tell me in your own words what . . .' – I searched for the words – 'citizen Aralova was suffering from?'

'A very severe form of ring-worm,' said the doctor. 'It led to virtual total baldness . . . I remember her, she was very upset and didn't want people to visit her. She livened up if it was her brother, but otherwise she said very little . . . She had a trying nature, nasty even. Yes, well, it's an unpleasant disease for a girl so young and beautiful. A tragedy, I'd call it. I ordered a wig for her myself from a hairdresser I know . . . before she left hospital.'

The trolleybus dragged along like a hearse, halting at a red light every minute. It was so stuffy in there that sweat fell from me like rain. I felt nauseated and the ache in my head had returned. I tried not to think of my conversation with the doctor but it kept coming back of its own accord. The nausea intensified.

244

18

Romanova spoke away from the telephone to Griaznov:

'You're sure you don't need back-up tonight?'

'Yes, otherwise it'll be ruined. Zhenka's going clean. I've taken every microphone off him including the one up his backside. He's going on the trolley, Turetsky and me by car.'

'Has he got a gun? Maybe you should have left him that, laddies . . .' Romanova was on edge and was using an uncharacteristically calm tone of voice. 'So what if they searched him? The worst they can do is take it off him.'

'Alexandra Ivanovna, he mustn't have a single suspicious object on him and you want to foist a gun on him.'

'I'm worried that's why . . . Vasya, your driver's a new boy. I'll be sitting here with Pogorelov till the all-clear . . .'

We got stuck at the crossroads by the Moscow Hotel, one minute to seven and we still had to cross Manège Square. At last the road was open and we hugged the pavement on the Herzen Street side. I immediately caught sight of Zhukov's lonely figure under the round city clock. Two minutes past seven. Zhukov glanced at the clock above his head and made for the lobby.

'Sasha you stay with Vasya and get the walkie-talkie.'

Griaznov slid out of the Volga and his red head was soon bobbing about near the queue which wound like a snake round the corner of the Manège. It was already five past. Just then, defying all traffic regulations a posh Audi rolled up to the very door. A tall soldier got out and we heard Griaznov's

245

voice: 'Stand by.' Vasya let in the clutch and Griaznov's tenor came through again: 'Stand back. They've got a tail of their own here.' I kept my eyes on Troyan. He went up the steps of the Manège and a sporty-looking youth in a yellow T-shirt standing near the duty policeman indicated the door with a nod. Two minutes later, both of them, Zhukov and Troyan, came out of the lobby. I was certain Zhenya had spotted Griaznov though he hadn't once looked in his direction. Troyan opened the car door for Zhukov, got in beside him and the Audi moved forward before turning left along the Alexandrov Garden. 'Attention! Following cherry-coloured Zhiguli on Herzen Street. After it!' I lost Griaznov, all I saw was the Zhiguli darting out of Herzen Street. Vasya did a U-turn on Manège Square, shielded by a trolley-bus and Griaznov burst into the car as he ran.

'Don't lose the Zhiguli,' he yelled at Vasya, before saying calmly to me. 'They've gone to fill their faces. Zhenka doesn't know where.'

We went round Revolution Square and once again returned to Manège Square, still tailing the cherry-coloured Zhiguli at a respectful distance. The Audi was a long way ahead.

'Well done, Vasya. He's come to us from the traffic police, Sashok. Shura knew what she was doing assigning him to us today. He sure knows how to tail. Am I right, Vasya?'

And Vasili replied with dignity:

'Sure.'

The Zhiguli led us to the Comecon building, where the empty Audi was already standing. We waited as the Zhiguli spun on its tail and drove off elsewhere before nudging the Volga into an inconspicuous space and settling down to wait. Vasya ran off into a shop and fetched two bottles of milk and a baton of bread.

'I suppose Zhenka's tucking into sturgeon in aspic,' mused Griaznov, as he chewed his bread and milk . . .

Two hours later four people emerged from the Peace restaurant: Troyan, Zhukov, and two newcomers. Zhenya was swaying and waving his arms about in a suspicious manner. I looked anxiously at Griaznov.

'Don't worry. He's putting it on . . .' He suddenly bawled: 'Step on it Vasya, get to Kutuzov 36 ahead of them!'

'How do you know?'

'What's signalling for, then? He made a sign meaning "We're going to Troyan's house".'

We were waiting again, this time on Kutuzov Prospect. It wasn't till half eleven that three people came out – and my heart sank. Troyan's two henchmen were dragging Zhukov.

'It's okay, Sashok. The show goes on . . .' said Griaznov quietly. 'Push on Vasya to Krizhanavosky . . . block 10.'

We pulled up on the odd-numbered side and observed the two drag Zhukov out of the car and sit him on a bench. Zhukov, judging by his movements was singing an operatic aria. The two got into the car, drove about a hundred yards then stopped. Zhukov had slipped off the bench and was attempting to get up. I couldn't believe he was sober, try as I might.

'Right. Vasya sits in the car and we go over to Zhenka. Not him, I mean his flat.'

We'd waited a good hour and a half on the landing before Zhukov finally appeared from the lift.

'I had a tough time getting rid of Troyan's heavies. Just sort a few things out and it's back to Kutuzov for us.'

We went into Zhukov's bachelor flat where he began changing into a black track-suit.

'This is the situation. Slava, fetch a bottle of Narzan from the fridge. I got car-sickness, terrible, I didn't have to pretend much. I'm handing over the whole transport column to Troyan. There's something really big afoot. Seven lorries are going to transport the explosives. I got Mr Edward drunk and he showed me a new type of automatic rifle, dismantled and assembled it in nine seconds – that's a record! Well, anyway, nuts to him . . . He got the rifle out of a concealed safe. We'll have to open it. Probably all the secrets are in there.'

Zhukov pulled out some mountaineering gear from a wall-mounted cupboard and checked over the crampons.

'What are you going to do?' Griaznov and I chorused in unison.

'You cover me on the roof, I'll lower myself to the window and try and get the safe open – all right? No cops required. Give me the camera.'

'Are you off your nut, Zhenya? There's a thunderstorm starting, its been brewing all day.'

'As they say in Bulgaria, at times like this there's nothing better than bad weather. And Edward Nikitich will be asleep for another two hours yet, not a cheep from him. I slipped him one of Shura's sleeping-pills. They strip-searched me worse than our customs. Didn't check my cigarettes though . . .'

Vasya stayed in the car, keeping an eye on Kutuzov Prospect while Griaznov and I stood in drenching rain in the courtyard of Block 36 watching Zhukov lowering himself on the rope from the dormer window under the roof. We could hardly make him out against the rain-dark wall. Down one storey, a second, third . . . Now he stopped, thrusting hard outwards with his legs, swung his supple body towards a narrow open window and disappeared into the dark interior; a few seconds later we again saw him at the window: he waved and threw a small bundle – the rope and the crampons – right in the middle of the children's sand-pit.

'Now it's upstairs and fast,' whispered Griaznov.

I took my Makarov out of its holster and pressed my ear to the door. Griaznov went over to the flat opposite, gun in hand, and crouched down, ready at any second to act on my signal and burst the door off its hinges. It was completely silent all around. I counted the seconds to myself, one . . . two . . . three . . . Would Zhenya be able to open the safe? . . . Forty-five, forty-six . . . What if Troyan did wake up, went to the toilet, for example? Two hundred and twenty . . . two hundred and twenty-one . . . I'd never taken sleeping-pills. All I knew about them came from text-books and novels . . . Eight hundred and fifty . . . eight hundred and fifty-one . . . 'Even if we perish, brothers in brotherhood . . .' One . . . two . . . three – I began the next thousand. 'And the great outcast gave this bowl his name . . .' Gudinas had certainly put a meaning into his ramblings . . . one hundred and thirty-four . . . I tensed and raised my pistol arm – I'd heard nothing, but I had seen the centre of the lock turning. And, as if it were the most natural thing in the world, Zhenya Zhukov walked out of Troyan's apartment.

'Pasha! Get your developers and fixers ready then carry on kipping. The investigator and I need to develop a film,' said Griaznov to the duty criminalist.

I had gone into the photo-labs with Griaznov to develop, fix and print the photographic material obtained by Zhukov that night. After a sleepy glance at us, the expert Pasha turned to the wall and went on with his 'duty'.

In an hour we had completed our photography and strode the echoing corridors of Moscow CID HQ towards Griaznov's office, where Zhukov was sleeping the sleep of the just.

I pushed the case-folders to one corner of the long desk and spread the pictures in front of me. On the first page of photographic paper, still not quite dry, was a written text, in a large clear hand with the heading: 'Memoranda: conferences with Marshal Stalin.' There was no doubting the authorship. After each note there were the letters E. T., Edward Troyan.

'Today, May 1st, Marshal Stalin decided to bring about a coup d'état in the immediate future – liquidating the Gensec and heading a newly constituted Politburo. Stalin will shortly announce the actual date. Marshal Stalin, the president of the Defence Committee, as well as taking the post of Party Gensec, will assume the duties of President of the Presidium of the Supreme Soviet and the Council of Ministers. The disgraceful period of weakness and flabby liberalism which began in 1953 is now at an end.

'I have been ordered to prepare empty camps for further use. No fewer than ten millions persons are earmarked for transfer to these. Stalin reckons this to be the number of enemies of the new Politburo.

'Stalin approved my suggestions – to reimpose an iron

curtain: discontinue all foreign tourism, all exchanges of scientists and students, stop all emigration. E.T.

'Today, May 9th, Marshal Stalin announced the time of the coup. The date is known to me, General Seri and his aide Gudinas, who is to be responsible for transport of explosives. Favourable factors: a) The Naval commander is in hospital for an operation – KGB frontier troops, easily neutralised b) Minister of Defence Sokolov and his deputies are away on manoeuvres in the GDR c) Politburo members Aliev, Vorotnikov, Shevardnadze and Zaikov will support the authority of the new Gensec in those places which they are visiting.

'The Minister of Internal Affairs, Fedorchuk in return for additional appointment as head of the KGB, has undertaken to bring the tanks of the Dzerzhinsky Division into Moscow at the appointed time.

'The pretext for seizing power is to be a disaster of unprecedented dimensions involving the death of 100,000 people. Those members of the Politburo left alive who have not declared for Marshal Stalin will be accused of organising the catastrophe and assasinating the Gensec. E.T.

'May 10th. Minimum programme laid down – institution of trials (on the lines of the Bukharin and Trotskyist trials) of ministers and department heads for aspiring to restore capitalism by way of their economic reforms;

'– increased severity of the criminal law with regard to the scientific, technical and artistic intelligentsia, servicemen, religious believers, industrial and agricultural workers who have supported the corrupt policies of the previous Politburo;

'– introduce privileges for Special Forces (increased pay, provisioning, living quarters) place Special Forces personnel in key posts.

'May 11th. Clash between Seri and Gudinas. Decision taken to liquidate Gudinas. E.T.

'May 14th. Gudinas arrested, accepted as irreplaceable; links with our group not established. Question of transport of explosives needs careful consideration. E. T.

'May 27th. Marshal Stalin announced to us his maximum programme.

'The essence may be summarised as a new course in international policy (total sovietisation of Afghanistan, an "iron curtain" . . .) and internal policy (marriage with foreigners forbidden, all socio-economic, religious and national movements eradicated, workers to be tied to their place of work for a minimum of five years – indisciplined to be drafted to public work projects). A harsh programme of ideological action is to be introduced with regard to the literary intelligentsia – neutralisation, bribery, liquidation; exposure of persons listening to foreign radio; introduction of criminal liability for such acts and persons guilty of infringement to be sent to camps . . . E.T.'

It amounted to a detailed variant of Gudinas' diary. Marshal Agarkin intended to bring about chaos in the country, and put himself forward as the man to deal with it, craftily employing the power vested in him by law. But what was this disaster the people were to suffer? Where did Agarkin's accomplices, the 'bitten' ones, intend to carry it out – and when?

'We've uncovered a massive conspiracy, Sashok. D'you think we're in line for a reward?'

I looked at Griaznov:

'Slava, give Zhenka a shove. We need more detail about where the explosives lorries have to be taken.'

'You needn't shove me,' Zhukov turned on the sofa. 'Read the rest.'

Griaznov and I read page after page with close attention – lists of personnel involved in the coup, names of commanders, immediate measures following the seizure of power, organisation of supplies to the populace, statement to foreign governments – all mixed together, apparently without system.

'These are copies of course.' said Slava, 'the Marshall himself has the originals, probably . . .'

'Of course they're copies,' mumbled Zhenka.

'You go to sleep, you've done your whack for today,' Griaznov told him. 'Aha – this is it! Look, Sasha . . .'

251

'Objective 1. Moscow State University (MGU)
Objective 2. Mosfilm Studios
Objective 3. Andreyevsky Bridge
Objective 4. Trubetskoy Park
Objective 5. Novedevichy Monastery
Each objective must have a guard for our people on the appointed day. All available reserves of E.M. are to be moved to main objective O.'

'What's it all mean, Sash . . . Do they want to blow them all up, or what?'

'I don't get it . . . Why blow up Trubetskoy Park?'

'You mean you do understand why MGU goes?'

'No irony Slava, please. MGU is a place with a lot of people, it would cause panic. No I don't think they want to blow up these five objectives. Let's have a look at a map of Moscow and see where they are. All that tomorrow. We'll have a meeting at the Prosecutor's Office . . .'

'What, you're going home? You've only got about four hours, have a lie down in any office here.'

'I feel a bit out of place here, Slava. I feel like going home. I would be most grateful if you could lay on a car. I think better behind a wheel . . .'

I drove through a deserted Moscow, clean and fresh after the violent storm. I had said to Slava – 'I think better behind a wheel'. What about? That everything had turned out well: we'd uncovered a conspiracy against the Party and the government, and we should get promotion: I'd be a Jurist, First Class, Griaznov would finally become a major, they'd take Zhukov back into the CID . . . something for everybody . . . Have to make Merkulov happy, now we'd really save Gevorkyan from the firing-squad . . . I passed Frunzenskaya metro where I'd first met Lana. What would happen to her? Her part in the plot couldn't remain a secret, she was a part of the Agarkin–Troyan alliance. What role would I play when everything was out in the open? I would be a prosecution witness against Svetlana Belova! But I'd been her unwitting accomplice! I hadn't wanted to listen to Kim, cowardly

252

ushered her out of the office and disconnected the phone at home. She had looked to me for protection and I'd rejected her like some useless, cumbersome thing . . . I'd blurted out a professional secret to a criminal person, informing Svetlana Belova that I had information of national importance as a result of which – my guilt in fact – Vanya Bunin had died . . . I'd carelessly given Klavdia some secret instructions which became known to Svetlana Belova – Morozov was murdered. I couldn't wash my hands of it, that was another death on my conscience. What court could condemn me? In the eyes of the law there was no reason to connect my actions with terrorist crimes. But how could I justify myself to myself? 'There we shall ignite our torch of death . . .' I couldn't get that Lithuanian's poem out of my head.

It was light by the time I arrived home. I cut the motor and lit a cigarette . . . A boy and girl, arms entwined, were walking along the embankment. In front of the Timur shop, a yard-sweeper was hard at it, sprinkling the forecourt for some reason, after hours and hours of teeming rain. My Makarov lay beside me on the seat. What if . . . I picked up the pistol and blew in the barrel for some reason. Just like that, one in the temple and it was all over in a flash. Not that I wanted to die. It was just that life seemed so loathsome that living had no meaning for me. I was like a rat, trained to find a way out of the labyrinth, and then put in a maze that had no way out so that it just lay down and chewed its paw off. I blew again into the black hole put the gun back in its holster and sighed with relief: no I certainly didn't want to die. What would be, would be. Tomorrow was Saturday. I hadn't had a day off in a month. Today there was lots to do but tomorrow I belonged to myself. I might go to Luzhniki Stadium with Irka. Lose myself among a hundred thousand others. I detest these colossal propaganda gatherings in a stadium designed for sporting competition. Applauding the patterns of trained bodies: 'Glory to the CPSU' or 'Peace to the World'. Then the kids would run up to the government box with their bouquets . . . and hundreds of doves would flutter upwards from the green bowl . . .

Amid mountains of rubbish, tares of slavery
There we shall ignite our torch of death.
And the great outcast gave this bowl
His name, dishonoured through the ages . . .

That was about the same green bowl I'd just been thinking
about? 'Slava, I think better behind a wheel.' The great
exile – yes, of course that was Lenin! The Lenin Central
Stadium! They want to blow up Luzhniki tomorrow!

I opened the glove-compartment and took out a map of
Moscow. Tomorrow they'd be bringing explosives to five
objectives round the stadium. Troyan would look after the
placing of the dynamite under the guise of checking the security of the Gensec. All the reserve explosive material would be
moved to the main objective O. O was not only the main
object but also a graphic representation of the stadium's
central arena. 'We will root out slavery in one second . . .' A
disaster of unprecedented dimensions – the destruction of
Luzhniki Stadium with more than 100,000 spectators. And
Irka, Lidochka and Lelya Merkulova, thousands of other
Irkas, Lidochkas and Lelyas, totally unconnected with any
struggle for power or any of that madness . . .

The police Volga revved up its powerful engine and in ten
minutes I was already cruising along Peace Prospect towards
Merkulov's house.

19

Merkulov was shaving in front of the mirror and I sat on the edge of the bath. I only needed ten minutes to cover the main points. The tip of Merkulov's nose was as white as the foam on his cheeks – it always goes white when he's excited.

He finished shaving, wiped his face and rubbed it with a towel:

'Sasha, we're going to Moiseyev's.'

'What's he got to do with this? We've got to inform the people most concerned about this plot . . .'

'But we're also against information leaks. Isn't that so?'

'But how does Moiseyev come in?'

'Semyon Semyonovich spent five years in the same group in the Law faculty of MGU with the present Gensec. In '52 he recommended him to the Party. He was his godfather for Party membership. Such things aren't forgotten, I think. Therefore in half an hour he'll give his godson a ring and fix a meeting. Even if only for five minutes. For all his colossal work-load, the Gensec can spare five minutes of his precious time to . . . to save his precious life.'

'Semyon Semyonovich, I'm sorry to come visiting so early,' said Merkulov as soon as Moiseyev opened the door.

'What d'you mean, early, Konstantin Dmitrievich! I've been up ages. I'm making some cheese straws for my sons. It's a holiday today, they're getting their diplomas at the tech college. So I've decided to pamper them with what "mother used to make". She always did cheese straws for the holidays.'

It was hard to breathe inside the flat. There was a smell of

255

sizzling oil and the smoke was hellish, it was about time to call the fire brigade. We didn't spend our time preparing Moiseyev for his call to the palace so much as getting his culinary efforts under control. While Semyon Semyonovich and I piled cheese straws into every possible container, suitable or not, Merkulov was talking on the phone to the republic prosecutor Yemelyanov. Merkulov was an exception in that the cautious, wily prosecutor trusted him unreservedly.

Moiseyev made me taste one of the crispy straws and to my surprise it was extremely good.

'My amendment to the recipe, Alexander Borisovich, has been a great success. I've increased the proportions in Anna's notes by four. I just thought it was a bit on the skimpy side.'

The RSFSR prosecutor's building is practically next door to Moiseyev's, five minutes normal walking, eight if you allow for Semyon Semyonovich's limp. We crossed Neglinka and walked up Kuznetsky Most.

One of the republic prosecutor's assistants conducted us into Yemelyanov's office and gave Merkulov a handbook with all the Party and government telephone numbers in it. There were several telephones in the room. The Kremlin one sat on a separate table, that red telephone could connect you with any leader on the national or republican level, even with the Gensec himself. Yemelyanov was in conference, but his assistant had instructions to be helpful; he explained the workings of the Kremlin line and departed.

Moiseyev spun the dial. He held a cigarette in his free hand and I could see the tip quivering.

'Allo, allo . . . Is this Mikhail Sergeyevich's apartment? Good morning, this is Moiseyev, Semyon Semyonovich . . . from the republic prosecutor's . . . Ask him, please, he does know me . . . Misha? . . . Mikhail Sergeyevich? Is it you?' began Moiseyev in a crowing voice – 'We must meet, urgently, and talk. It's extremely important . . .'

Semyon Semyonovich stubbed out his cigarette and removed the sweat which had moistened his upper lip.

'Who's calling? Semyon . . . Semyon Moiseyev . . . It's Semyon, you recognise me Misha?'

Semyon Semyonovich without covering the mouthpiece informed us joyfully:

'He recognised me – Misha!'

He spoke into the mouthpiece again.

'It's a very serious business, Mikhail Sergeyevich. Ten minutes would do . . . You personally . . . it concerns you personally . . . and the whole country. I wouldn't dare phone you otherwise would I? . . . Good, good, yes I've got it. I'm ready to come over at once, its only a step from Kuznetsky Most to the Kremlin!'

Moiseyev listened, grizzled eyebrows knitted.

'By 9.30, pass office, is that by the Spassky Gate? Yes, yes, right . . . I'll be there by 9.30. Till then, Mikhail Sergeyevich!'

Moiseyev put the phone down. Sweat was pouring down his forehead and cheeks. He leaned over the phone and solemnly declaimed over its gleaming surface:

'*Morituri te salutant!* Which signifies in Latin 'We who are about to die, salute you!'

Merkulov, without a word, poured a glass of water and produced a box of tablets.

'Now then Semyon Semyonovich, have a helenium tablet.'

'Right, Semyon Semyonovich, first of all it's the Agarkin plot and the planned blowing up of Luzhniki. Don't forget to show the documents. Secondly about the explosion in the metro and the freeing of Gevorkyan and the other innocents. Concentrate on the Afghan Brotherhood. If there's any time left, the Faust injections. Best if you note all this down.' Merkulov was issuing his last instructions to Moiseyev, while I removed the hairs from his shabby uniform and tied Merkulov's tie round his neck.

We parked the CID Volga near entrance 14 of the Russia Hotel and sat in the back to wait for Moiseyev's return from the Kremlin.

'It was obviously Agarkin's idea to create a secret terrorist organisation – the Afghan Brotherhood,' said Merkulov.

'Why would Agarkin need fanatics like that if he had the power of the Special Forces in his hands?'

'Remember, Sasha, Agarkin isn't just the head of Special Forces, he's the president of the Defence Council. He's the first military man to rise so high. From the time the Committee was created – October 64 – only our Party leaders have occupied that chair . . .'

'If he's got so much authority why does he have to mess about with a bunch of crazed terrorists?'

'So that Marshal Agarkin could have real power, not just nominal authority, like, say, the President of the Supreme Soviet. He created the Special Forces . . . He gathered units of well-trained troops, previously split up among the various service arms, into his iron fist . . . but to actually create his force he needed a reason. Agarkin announced: Special Forces are the shock detachments of the Party! That went down well and the Gensec took the bait. He needed independence from the KGB, MVD and the Defence Ministry.'

'You reckon Agarkin deceived the Gensec?'

Merkulov scowled.

'Precisely, the marshal deceived the Gensec. The Special Forces are not the shock detachments of the Party at all. They're the storm-troopers of Marshal Agarkin! And the Defence Council headed by him is only the tip of the iceberg. The base is – the Special Forces battalions, points of support in an ever-growing power, scattered around the whole country and even abroad . . .'

'I've seen that growing power in Afghanistan,' I muttered. 'But I still don't see why Agarkin needed the Afghan Brotherhood, with all his battalions.'

Merkulov spoke with his head bent, glancing up.

'In principle I've nothing against the army. In fact I sympathise with the servicemen. In our army at the present time there's a large percentage of the technical intelligentsia, graduates of various academies and institutes. They know the score. In the centre and wherever they are. If we are talking about them, if it was them getting closer to power, I don't know how I'd feel about that. I might even support it . . . But we're not talking about servicemen now, we're on about a seizure of power by one man. And his road to power . . . Let's keep in mind that if mass disorders break out nationwide, the Defence Committee has the right to use the new legislation and declare a state of emergency. And that means all the power of our triangle, Politburo–Presidium–Council of Ministers, passes to the Defence Committee! And the Council isn't the set of intelligent patriotically inclined technologist-servicemen I was talking about earlier, it's . . . Marshal Agarkin! All the power goes to him. Right, now, what has to happen before this state of emergency is declared. Disorders – massive disorders. How can they be brought about? Answer!'

I sat at attention:

'Explosions in the metro, explosions at stadiums, explosions in atomic power-stations . . . there's plenty of objectives . . .'

'Exactly! Now comes a rather important question: who can commit monstrous atrocities of the sort you listed?'

'A terrorist organisation.'

'That's why, Sasha, the specials were not enough for Agarkin by themselves, and why he needed the Afghan Brotherhood as well. They cause widespread disorders and the Special Forces put them down. The result of the combination is that Marshal Agarkin gets his hands on unrestricted power . . . Alley-Oop! A new dictator appears in the arena. The Special Forces and the Brotherhood are two sides of one medal, and the Luzhniki explosion planned for tomorrow is the best proof of that.'

Merkulov had got quite heated and had abandoned his usual image; he lit a cigarette nervously and the flame of the lighter lit up part of his high forehead and the stubborn, jutting chin. He offered the packet of Whiffs and went on:

'Agarkin made cunning use of Faust by removing the instinct of self-preservation from people. To get it accepted, he explained to the Politburo that a substance like that would be indispensable in a future atomic war – otherwise officers and men would desert their desks or rockets in an atomic attack.

During the last war, in the first months especially, our troops developed so-called "tank disease". As soon as German tanks made a frontal attack, they ran from their trenches. Mass psychosis caused by imminent atomic or hydrogen bomb attack would be far worse . . . Powerful drugs are needed to overcome "atomic fear". This was what Agarkin offered in Faust . . . Agarkin had hoodwinked the Politburo again. With the help of Faust, he'd not only got control of the people in Afghanistan but here in Moscow as well. Seen in that way the Afghan Brotherhood is a political phenomenon!'

'Good, Kostya. That is, not good at all. But suppose Agarkin seized power. He places his people in key positions. The Special Forces are on the leash. What would he want the Afghan Brotherhood for then?'

'Remember what Rogov told you about the reverse side of the medal in using narcotics: a tendency to criminality, excessive cruelty in civilian life. Agarkin reckoned on seizing power with the hands of madmen. After that he'd get rid of them, destroy them as criminals, they've got lists of all the soldiers who had injections. Besides, don't forget the troops had the injections without the so-called stabiliser, they're all headed for the madhouse or the camps. So Agarkin won't have too much trouble dealing with his assistants the day after he wins. I think Griaznov, Zhukov and you have uncovered a colossal crime. Now the main thing is for the Gensec to believe Semyon Semyonovich.'

Merkulov paused for a second only to go on at once with, for him, unusual intensity:

'I have no doubts about the integrity of the Gensec. Believe me, he'll liquidate the coup attempt and prevent the explosion, but he'll also set up an open enquiry and then a trial, true and honest. I'm certain he'll act in all respects according to the law. The guilty will be justly punished. The innocent will be released from prison with apologies!'

I didn't recognise Semyon Semyonovich. He had left us an old, sick man. Now he was the tribune of the people with fiery eyes and colour in his cheeks.

'How did it go?' I asked as soon as Moiseyev opened the door.

Merkulov was more specific:

'Did he believe us, Semyon Semyonovich?'

Moiseyev flopped into the seat. He was smiling with undisguished joy.

'Yes, yes and again yes! He believed me! Misha believed me! He thanked me, all of us – I told you, Misha is a person! A communist with a human face. He's so busy, yet he saw me. If you could have seen how he received me! Put off a meeting with some Shiv Pankar for an hour. He really made me welcome, asked me all sorts of questions. He remembered! Memory – what a memory, he remembered everything, how I lent him money from my grant to buy a suit . . . how we fell out over a girl. Me recommending him to the party! . . .'

Semyon Semyonovich was clearly in a state of euphoria. Euphoria is a heightened, joyful mood, a sense of well-being and contentment . . . not related to objective circumstances. That's what it says in the Russian dictionary.

'Excuse me, Semyon Semyonovich, but what did he say concretely about Gevorkyan's group?' asked Merkulov, 'When are they getting out?'

A silence.

'We didn't talk concretely about that. He said he'd look into it. Oh yes, Misha said that our information about the plot is – extraordinary. While I was there he arranged for a Politburo meeting at two o'clock. He said all the questions I had come with would be discussed at that meeting. Don't get excited, Konstantin Dmitrievich! I know Misha. He'll take the right decision. They'll let Gevorkyan and his lads out of Lefortovo tomorrow . . .'

I sat in my office doing nothing. I just sat in a corner thinking . . . about nothing . . . Several times I lifted the phone and set it down again. Finally I dialled Grechannik's number in Lefortovo Prison, where Lana was working that day.

* * *

261

'Why did you choose this cafe?' Lana smiled with her eyes only. 'A bit seedy.'

We were sitting in the open-air cafe in the Hermitage Gardens, where the two killers had sat the day after Kim's murder. I didn't have much time for talking, I had to be back at the Prosecutor's Office before the end of the working day. But I just couldn't bring myself to begin the final act of my inquiry. The waitress brought us coffee with liqueurs and I devoted considerable attention to the melting sugar lumps.

'If you want to propose to me, hurry up or it'll be too late,' Lana was laughing openly while I remained silent and carefully stirred the liqueur into the coffee with my spoon. Gudinas' incoherent poem kept whirling round in my head preventing me from concentrating. 'Amid mountains of rubbish, tares of slavery, There we shall ignite our torch of death . . .'

She would have to answer before the law as an accomplice in the murder of Kim, Vanya Bunin and young Morozov. But I wanted to see alarm in her green eyes, I wanted to tell her myself what I knew about her and sense the triumph of the victor.

A gust of wind blew the sugar wrappings off the table. Lana pressed her hands to her temples and her face became tense. The wind was her enemy. It might whip off her rich, beautiful curls and blow them away. I remembered how she'd tied her headscarf on when we'd been in the car and the wind had ripped in at the open windows. It was in that other life when Kim and Bunin had still been alive.

'I know who Kim opened the door to, Lana. Two young men in black jackets went up to the Lagin's floor. They didn't ring at once because one of them needed time. Why did he need those ten – fifteen seconds, Lana?'

She regarded me with interest as if I were telling her the plot of a detective film, but said nothing.

'So, why was it, Lana?'

'You seem to expect an answer. I'm sorry I didn't realise,' she let fall the words in her usual manner, 'I don't know, why was it?'

'To put that marvellous wig on, the one ordered by the doctor at the Botkin hospital.'

I reached out towards her head as if I intended to smooth down a wayward curl. And again, just as in the car, she struck my hand and her eyes blazed like two emeralds. Her face was calm and indifferent as if she had just rid herself of a troublesome fly.

'Don't be afraid,' I said, 'I'm not going to pull off your adornment or they'll recognise you here, this was the cafe you were in with Ivonin after Kim's murder. You moved the hands of the clock two hours ahead. That was a very good one – the investigator himself would confirm that at the time of the murder you were in his bed. A green headsquare and dark glasses make you unrecognisable on your trip to Ryazan. When the main puzzle is solved, the lesser mysteries all fall into place. But so much blood, so many lives, Lana, for what? Revenge for an unfaithful husband?'

At these words, something twitched in her face, her eyes clouded over. She looked at me with unconcealed hatred.

'You're sorry now that I wasn't in the car with Bunin? You really worked a neat trick there – Turetsky shoots his mouth off – he had information he wanted to pass on to Merkulov – so an excellent plan – blow him up along with his information in his own car . . .'

She rose from her chair, opened her bag, took out three roubles and placed them under her cup, then coolly turned on her high heels and walked to the exit.

I felt no kind of triumph at all . . .

Once more I sat in my office doing nothing. The back of my head ached and my ears were ringing. Like a cracked bell it foretold disaster. I didn't feel like talking to anyone. I didn't want to see anyone – all those masks, old and new, and you couldn't tell what they wanted who they were meant to be . . . I lusted for one thing – to get up, walk out and never come back.

At five Merkulov looked in. He said glumly that he, Moiseyev and I had to go over to Petrovka soon. I couldn't have cared less and didn't even ask who wanted us and why.

'Wait a minute, Kosty, don't go.'

Merkulov shut the door and sat down on the visitor's chair.

'Kostya, I'm going to have to put in an application . . . to resign.'

'I understand how you feel, Sasha. You're tired. Unwell. Disillusioned. All that will pass. Sorry for playing the philosopher, but investigation is your vocation.'

'It's something a lot different, Kostya. Take a look at that.'

I took out of my briefcase an identikit of one of Kim's murderers with hair and green bow added by a yellow flowmaster.

Merkulov looked stonily at the picture for a very long time.

'I did suspect something of the sort, but this . . .'

'That's not all. Svetlana Nikolayevna Belova is the wife of Marshal Agarkin. And the half-sister of Edward Troyan, on the mother's side. Troyan is the son of Nikita Kruschev, illegitimate of course.'

Merkulov's throat was giving him trouble. The wound he'd received three years before was acting up no doubt. He started coughing so badly I thought he would rupture his larynx. I rushed over to the decanter of water, but Merkulov started making signs towards his jacket and I pulled out a pile of medicaments from his inside pocket. Merkulov grabbed a phial of purple tablets and popped about five of them in his mouth.

When he'd recovered I told him everything – from the trip to Matveyevskoye with Lana until the last full-stop of my 'inquiry'. Having heard me out, Merkulov spoke, quietly but firmly:

'I agree with your conclusions . . . In your place I would also submit my resignation.'

I took a sheet of paper, wrote a report addressed to the City Prosecutor, Skaredov, handed it to Merkulov and said, barely audibly:

'Visa that for me, please.'

'I'll do that, Sasha. Only . . . indulge my request. You haven't used up your holiday for last year. Go away somewhere for a couple of months. You need a rest in any case. If you still want to go now, I'll put my visa on this paper and pass it to Skaredov.'

I looked at Kostya's downcast face.

'You're suggesting I think it over for two months?'

'No. I'm suggesting nothing. I'm simply asking. The rest is up to you. Any decision, yes or no, will be correct . . . in two months . . . By the way, Lelya's Auntie has a house empty on the Riga coast. In Yaundubulti . . .'

He looked at his watch:

'Time to go.'

All of our group had assembled in Romanova's office. Even Zhukov and Vasya were present. In Shura's chair sat a heavily-built man with a predatory nose and sparse gingerish hair. Bulging green eyes surveyed us in tense concentration from behind thick glasses. This was the KGB chief, Chebrikov.

'You're Merkulov? Moiseyev? And you're Turetsky?' he checked us one by one with a curt nod of the head.

When we were seated, he raised his eyes to Romanova and asked:

'Is everybody here?'

Shura raised her bottom slightly off her chair:

'Yes, Viktor Mikhailovich.'

'Then let's start operations,' said Chebrikov abruptly. 'Point by point. First. The Politburo has checked your statement and has decided to act upon it.'

'We have decided to liquidate the Afghan Brotherhood within twenty-four hours . . . And the head of Special Forces, those plotters too . . .'

I was looking hard at Chebrikov, but I could read nothing in that inscrutable face.

'Second. The Politburo has decided to take appropriate action to ensure that not a single person finds out there has been a conspiracy against the government. Not in this country, nor abroad . . .'

Here Chebrikov brandished a plump, menacing finger in

the direction of the Hermitage Gardens. Then he sighed and looked at us:

'. . . That is why I am here. Mikhail Sergeyevich requested me personally to bring together all concerned in the case and say . . . The Politburo have commissioned me to head the operations in eliminating the conspirators. All information concerning the plot, the conspirators and the explosions at the Vladimir Ilyich Lenin stadium must remain a secret. You will sign to that effect. If not . . . I'm not threatening, merely warning . . . you will be executed . . . But don't go home just now. In the first place we are concerned about your safety. In the second, I am requesting you to afford my men expert assistance – you know more about this affair than anyone else. After this operation is completed, you must forget about everything that has happened. Please let there be no misunderstanding. At a tense moment in our history when our country is at a turning-point we cannot . . . we have not the right to allow anyone, anywhere to find out about the conspiracy of Marshal . . . former Marshal Agarkin. He is a filthy traitor! That is all. If there are any questions I will answer them.'

'I have a question,' Kostya had raised his hand.

'Go ahead.'

'What decision has been taken with regard to Gevorkyan's group? I have checked through the case. They were not responsible for the sabotage in the metro, and the casualties there.'

'Is that all?' asked Chebrikov and tightened his thin lips.

'On that matter – yes.'

'My answer, comrade Merkulov, is this. The Politburo has decided to examine the cases of Gevorkyan and the others over the next two weeks. What decision the Supreme Court will come to, we do not know. We have no influence over the judicial power. However, I think the Soviet judges are unlikely to pat these terrorists on the head . . .'

'Excuse me, excuse me,' Moiseyev was incensed. 'A few hours ago Mikhail Sergeyevich told me personally that he would examine the case! Mikhail Sergeyevich is a lawyer. He understands the law! I know, we were in the law faculty together . . .'

Chebrikov had gone purple:

'Stop this nonsense! You studied together – good. And now don't blab about it. You think you won't see justice done? I repeat: The Supreme Court will decide! Is that all?!'

'No, it's not all!' I said. 'Surely there'll be inquiries followed by a trial of the conspirators from Special Forces and the terrorists of the Afghan Brotherhood?'

Chebrikov removed his spectacles and placed them in front of him. His eyes had gone narrow, mouse-like:

'Did you think at all before you asked? Don't you understand Russian, comrade Turetsky? Shall we send you to school again – first form? I have already said that you are to forget about this business once and for all. What we shall do and how we shall do it is not your worry!'

I tensed up as if I'd been hit in the solar plexus.

'Further questions dismissed!' said Chebrikov putting his glasses back on. 'This time it really is all . . .'

He got up clumsily from behind the desk stuck the papers we had signed in his pocket, sketched a smile on his wolfish features and departed.

20

Griaznov was the first to recover himself:

'Well there's nice! Not even a thank you! Sasha nearly a goner, Zhenka risking I don't know what. Upper echelons, is it? Bastards!'

'Alas . . .' Merkulov stated, got up and walked up and down the office. He paused behind my chair and touched my shoulder lightly . . .

'Ye-es, a mess-up . . .' drawled Zhukov pensively, then came to life suddenly, 'Alexandra Ivanovna! From this moment on I wouldn't give a wooden kopek for any of our lives! Well, if I have to go, I want music. What say I nip over to the Hermitage? Maybe we've still got time to finish off a bottle in this world.'

'Well I don't know, laddies,' said Romanova. Now she was looking a great deal older than her years. 'I am on call to Chebrikov's man . . . Well, you go on, why sit all night . . . as if you were in jail.'

We all fell asleep pretty soon, probably the nervous strain we'd all been under.

When I levered up my lids I saw Colonel Romanova with a glass of vodka in her hand. She swallowed, made a face sat down on a chair and . . . started crying. Griaznov asked quietly:

'What's up, Alexandra Ivanovna?'

'Well what's it all come to, laddies?' said Shura plaintively. 'Is this worth all your efforts? Is this the law? The Gee Bees have set up a Saint Bartholemew's Day Massacre . . .

They've told me from Lefortovo, confidentially, of course, that they've arrested nearly two hundred people and shot forty-four on the spot ... And another fifty killed resisting arrest. Here's the first official communication: 'An accident has occurred at 23.05, near the 23 km mark on the Simferopol highway: a government ZIL has crashed at high speed into a steam-roller left on the road. As a result of the accident Marshal Nikolai Arkhipovich Agarkin and his wife have been killed.'

I heard what Shura said, and I felt nothing – no pity, no pangs of conscience, no thoughts of triumphal revenge, nothing, apart from a cold emptiness in the chest. On Monday, Merkulov would stamp my application and I would work my official two weeks notice. No holidays, I'd find a job as a legal adviser, maybe I could squeeze into a college of barristers. Have to get ready to hand over the case ...

The assistance Chebrikov had spoken of had turned into hours of questioning carried on in the office of the CID chief by a commission of inquiry – two generals and three colonels from the KGB central apparatus ... I was called in first.

'Tell us Turetsky, do you believe in the unity of people and Party?' said a general, placing a hand on my shoulder.

'Yes, but what has that got to do with the case?'

The Gee Bees evinced no reaction to this.

'Would you agree with the opinion that there exist internal dissensions within our country?'

'I am not acquainted with such opinions, comrade general.'

At this, the Gee Bees exchanged fleeting glances then the next question, or rather, question-statement:

'When you've had the same thing drummed into you for years on end, teaching you to say not what you think but what people want to hear, it's hard to change in one evening, isn't that so?'

A feeble provocation, to which I responded with silence. I really didn't feel like replying but the questions came thick and fast, and now they were relevant:

'With whom have you shared your knowledge of the government plot?'

'To whom did you give information about the projected explosion at Luzhniki? About the Afghan Brotherhood? About the activities of the Special Forces?'

Then suddenly:

'Do you listen to the Voice of America? Radio Liberty? Do you read emigre journals?'

These questions put everything in context. These generals and colonels had tried out a 'lie detector' on me; they knew perfectly well I was lying – nobody's believed in the unity of people and Party for years. Including these high-ranking Gee Bees. But they were testing my reactions to the questions. The actual answer wasn't important; they already knew that.

Romanova called me over to her desk and held out a summary of events occurring in Moscow in the course of the 24-hour period still in progress: Lieutenant-Colonel Troyan, head of the General Secretary's personal bodyguard, had committed suicide, deputy commander of State Intelligence, Colonel-General Rogov had been found dead in his bath.

'I've got more information: nineteen service chiefs have died in puzzling circumstances, among them two army generals and an admiral . . . And a piece of info on the teletype from Kabul: General Seri fought off the Gee Bees till his last bullet. He kept that for himself . . .'

Towards morning the Gee Bee interviews drew to a close and they disappeared; before that we had to sign another official secrets form.

Romanova looked at our bloodless faces and said, faltering at every word:

'I have received information, strictly confidential. The General Secretary has ordered that we be spared . . . as a reward. He's fucking grateful.'

Despite my tiredness I decided to stroll along the Boulevard Ring as far as Kropotkinskaya. I wandered through morning Moscow with one idea in my head: go to bed and sleep for 48 hours. Till Monday. Till the minute when I officially left the Public Prosecutor's Office. I would receive money in lieu of leave, go along to the new president of the Collegium of Barristers, Voskresensky, or maybe the magazine *Citizen and Law* – they apparently wanted a roving correspondent.

A black Volga came hurtling towards me out of Sivtzev Vrazhek. I tried to jump out of the way as there came a squeal of brakes and my back was pinned against the iron railings of the boulevard. I didn't have the strength to get up as I waited for the black monster to turn and ... But a young man jumped out of the Volga and raced over to pick me up.

'I didn't do anything ... I didn't really hit you. Why did you fall down? Oh, you've ripped your pants ... Listen, no need for the police, eh? One blow in the breathalyser and my licence goes. Just write my name down and I'll pay for your trousers.'

And the young man proffered his driving licence.

'Oh, I don't need your name, push off, look there's people gathering round,' I said rubbing my bruised knee.

'I'm pushing off,' yelled the youth joyfully leaping into his car.

I stepped into a phone booth on Sivtsev Vrazhek and dialled Irka's number.

'Good morning, Ira. I have a serious question for you – can you mend trousers?'

Irka made some answer but I didn't listen to her because another question had occurred to me:

'When do your holidays start? Already? Right then, tomorrow you and I are going to the Riga coast, to ... Well, Yaundubulti say.'

THE END